ALSO BY DAVID PEACE

Tokyo Year Zero
The Damned Utd
GB84
Nineteen Eighty-Three
Nineteen Eighty
Nineteen Seventy-Seven
Nineteen Seventy-Four

OCCUPIED CITY

Occupied City

DAVID PEACE

Alfred A. Knopf   New York   2010

THIS IS A BORZOI BOOK
PUBLISHED BY ALFRED A. KNOPF

Copyright © 2009 by David Peace

All rights reserved. Published in the United States by Alfred A.
Knopf, a division of Random House, Inc., New York.
www.aaknopf.com

Originally published in Great Britain by Faber and Faber Ltd.,
London, in 2009.

Knopf, Borzoi Books, and the colophon are registered trademarks
of Random House, Inc.

Library of Congress Cataloging-in-Publication Data
Peace, David.
Occupied city / by David Peace. — 1st American ed.
p. cm.
First published: London : Faber and Faber, 2009.
ISBN 978-0-307-26375-9 (alk. paper)
1. Hirasawa, Sadamichi, 1982– —Fiction. 2. Criminals—Japan—
Tokyo—Fiction. 3. Serial murders—Japan—Tokyo—Fiction.
4. Bank robberies—Fiction. 5. Tokyo (Japan)—Fiction. I. Title.
PR6066.E116O25 2010
823'.914—dc22   2009043254

Manufactured in the United States of America
First United States Edition

For my mother

Tokyo

OCCUPIED CITY

— And what the writer found there . . .

The obedient and virtuous son kills his father.
The chaste man performs sodomy upon his neighbours.
The lecher becomes pure.
The miser throws his gold in handfuls out of the window.
The warrior hero sets fire to the city he once risked his life to save.

The Theatre & the Plague, Antonin Artaud, 1933

Preserving the Truth of WWII Japanese War, PO Box 366, Cupertino, CA 9505 (BA Min141R)

IN THE OCCUPIED CITY, you are a writer and you are running –

In the wintertime, papers in your arms, through this January night, down these Tokyo streets, you are running from the scene of the crime; from the snow and from the mud, from the bank and from the bodies; running from the scene of the crime and from the words of the book; words that first enticed and entranced you, then deceived and defeated you, and now have left you in-snared and in-prisoned –

Beneath a sky that threatens more than night, more than snow, now you huff and breath-puff, puff and breath-pant, pant and gasp –

For in your ears, you hear them coming, step by step, whispering and muttering. In your ears, you hear them gaining, step by step-step, drooling and growling, step by step-step by step –

A Night Parade of One Hundred Demons . . .

In the night-stagger, your spectacles fall from your nose. In the snow-stumble, your papers fall from your hand. In the night and in the snow, you scramble for your spectacles and for your papers, you search for your sight and for your work. But the ghost-laden wind is here now, again the be-specter-ed air is upon you. It steals your papers and it shatters your spectacles, it makes a sheaf-blizzard of the loose-leafs, a shard-storm of the slivered-lenses, as you claw through the laden wind, as you thrash through the haunted air –

But then the wind is dead and now the air is gone, the sheaves fall and the shards drop. You grab your spectacles, you grasp your papers, your manuscript; your manuscript of

the book-to-come;

this book that

will not

come –

This unfinished book of unsolved crime. This book of Winter, this book of Murder, book of Plague.

The blank sheets in your hands, the empty frames on your nose, now you see the Black Gate up ahead, and so you start to run again, through the January night, huffing and breath-puffing, down the Tokyo streets, puffing and breath –

Now you stop running.

Beneath the Black Gate, you seek shelter. In its damp shadows, you squat now. Under the eaves of the gate, here there is no one else, only the finger-night-tips, the foot-snow-steps. This gate once a treasure, this gate now a ruin, almost; but this gate still remains, this gate now a sanctuary, perhaps. No crows, no foxes, no thugs, no prostitutes tonight. Only night and only snow, their finger-cold-tips and their foot-dirty-steps. You breathe hard, your soaked-coat-through, you spit blood, your stained-papers-red. Your breath is bad and belly bloated, your eyes bloodshot and face swollen –

But here, under this Black Gate, in these damp shadows, here you will hide. Here inside, inside here –

Here you will hide –

Hide! Hide!

From this city, out of breath, from this city, out of time. This cursed city; city of riot and city of earthquake, city of assassination and city of coups, city of bombs and city of fire, city of disease and city of hunger, this city of defeat, defeat and surrender –

This damned city; city of robbery and

city of rape, city of murder,

of murder and plague –

These things you have witnessed, these things you have documented, in the ink you have spilt, on the papers you have spoiled. Inside here, here

inside –

'. . . a ghost-story-telling game popularized during the Edo period. By the mid-seventeenth century its form was established among samurai as a playful test of courage, but by the early nineteenth century it had become a widespread entertainment for commoners. The game begins with a group of people gathering at twilight in the pale-blue light of one hundred lit candles, each covered with a pale-blue paper shade. Each person in turn then tells a tale of supernatural horror and at the end of each tale one wick is extinguished. As the evening and the tales progress the room becomes dimmer and gloomier until, after the one hundredth tale has been told and the last candle blown out, the room is in complete darkness. At this moment it is believed that real ghouls or monsters will appear in the dark, conjured up by the terrifying tale-telling . . .'

The blood-blots, the tear-traces, the dead letters and the death sentences. You look up from your papers, you snatch sight of a stairway, a broad stairway to an upper storey, an upper storey away from the city. You rush to gather your papers, you run to climb the steps, finger-light-tips follow you up, foot-soft-steps echo your own –

One step, two steps, three steps, four –
Half-way up, you stop, stair-still,
stair-bent, you crouch,
breath-held –
In the chamber of the upper storey, high on the under-hide of
the roof, there is light above your head, here inside the Black Gate,
here you are not alone, here *in-presence-d* . . .
You climb again, you stop again, and now you see –
In the upstairs chamber, in an occult circle –
Twelve candles and twelve shadows –
In the Occupied City, beneath the Black Gate, in its upper
chamber, in this occult circle of these twelve candles,
now you are on your knees.
Suddenly, the ceiling of the chamber is illuminated by a flash
of lightning. You look, you listen. You hear a peal of thunder, the
fall of rain hard upon the roof of the gate. You listen, you look –
In the light of the candles, you see and now you hear a hand-
bell being shaken in the air; hear and see a bell and a hand –
The red bell and the white hand, the white arm and the red
sleeve, the red robe and the white face of a woman –
The woman, a medium, before you –
In the centre of the circle of the candles,
in their gutter-ring, she stands –
Her hair and her robes now flailing within a sudden tempest,
for the laden wind has found you here again, again the haunted air,
as the medium rattles the bell again and again, and again –
The bell, and now the sound of a drum beating slowly,
as the medium begins to dance, to spin and to turn –
Madly, the bell clattering and the wind howling,
the drum beating, on and on, over and over –
Feet moving through the splintered wood,
dancing, spinning and spinning, turning –
Suddenly she stops, suddenly still now,
frozen, the bell slips from her hand –
Abruptly, she faces you now, to say:
'Let the story-telling game begin . . .'
Then she tears towards you,
in this Possessed City –
The medium falls to the floor before you, now she sits upright,

3

taut and still, and now her mouth begins to open, to speak. In a disembodied drone, it speaks. It speaks the words of the dead –

'We are here because of you,' they whisper. 'Because of you, our dear sweet, sweet writer dear, because of you . . .

The First Candle –

The Testimony of the ~~Victims~~ Weeping

Because of you. The city is a coffin. In the snow. In the back of a truck. Parked outside the bank. In the sleet. Under the heavy damp tarpaulin. Driven through the streets. In the rain. To the hospital. To the morgue. In the sleet. To the mortuary. To the temple. In the snow. To the crematorium. To the earth and to the sky –

In our twelve cheap wooden coffins –

In these twelve cheap wooden coffins, we lie. But we do not lie still. In these twelve cheap wooden coffins, we are struggling. Not in the dark, not in the light; in the grey, we are struggling; for here is only grey, here we are only struggling –

In this grey place,

that is no place,

we are struggling all the time, always and already –

In this place, of no place, between two places. The places we once were, the places we will be –

The deathly living,

the living death –

Between these two places, between these two cities:

Between the Occupied City and the Dead City, here we dwell, between the Perplexed City and the Posthumous City –

Here we dwell, in the earth, with the worms,

in the sky, with the flies, we who are no longer in the houses of being. Beyond loss, flocks of birds fall from the sky and shower us with their bloody feathers and severed wings. *But we still hear you.* We who are now in the houses of non-being. Beyond loss, schools of fish leap from the sea and splatter us with their bloody guts and severed heads. *We still see you.* We want to breathe again, but we can never breathe again. Beyond loss, herds of cattle run from the fields and trample us with their bloody carcasses and severed limbs. *We listen to you.* We want to return again, but we can never return again. Beyond loss. *We watch you still.* Through our veils –

The veils which no longer hang before our eyes, these veils which now hang behind our eyes, their threads spun by our tears, their webs woven by our deaths, these veils which replaced our names, which replaced our lives –

Through these veils,

still we see –

Still we watch, we watch you . . .

Our mouths always open, our mouths already open. But we no longer talk, we can no longer talk, here we can only mouth, mouth:

Do we matter to you? Did we ever matter?

Our mouths always screams,

already screams, screams

that mouth:

Your apathy is our disease; your apathy, a plague . . .

We dwell beyond sorrow. *You close your mouths.* We dwell beyond pain. *You close your eyes.* Beyond grief, beyond despair. *You close your ears, for you do not hear us, for you do not listen to us . . .*

And we are tired, we are so tired, so very tired –

But still we dwell, between these two places –

Beyond dereliction, we lie. *Drunk, you harangue us.* Beyond oblivion, we wait. *Sober, you ignore us.* Forgotten and untended, buried or burnt, haunted and restless, under the earth and above the sky, without dreams and without sleep. *You are blind to our suffering.* We are so tired, so very tired. *You are deaf to our supplications.* We weep without tears, we scream without sound,

yet still we wait, and still

we watch –

Between the Occupied City and the Dead City, between the Perplexed City and the Posthumous City we wait, we watch and we struggle. Here in this grey place, here where we are waiting,

watching and struggling:

Cursed be you who cast us into this place! Cursed be you who keep us here! Fickle you are, so very fickle –

Fickle are you, fickle the living . . .

Forgotten are we, forgotten and denied –

Lives forgotten and deaths denied –

For you deny us our deaths . . .

Deny us and trap us . . .

In the Perplexed City, the Posthumous City, beyond the Occupied City, before the Dead City, here we are trapped, trapped in the greyness, trapped in this city. In this city that is no city,

this place that is no place –

Here we shuffle, we shuffle around, around in circles, with our boxes. *Did you hear our footsteps in your heart?* Our own ashes, around our necks, our own bones, in these boxes. *Did you feel our fingertips within your flesh?* We raise our shoulders, we raise our faces, we raise our eyes. *Have you come to lead us back, back towards the light?* Back towards the light, we begin to shuffle. *Back to the Occupied City?* In the Occupied City, we shuffle around, around these twelve candles, we gather around, around and around –

Back in the Occupied City, here we are the victims again –

Here, never the witnesses; always, already the victims –

So we are weeping. Always, already the weeping –

Here, we who were once the living –

Now weeping all the time, here –

Here tonight, weeping –

In the Occupied City, where the weeping seek the living. But the living are not here, not here tonight before these candles –

Here tonight, there are only the weeping –

Here tonight, only us:

And so again tonight we are Takeuchi Sutejiro, Watanabe Yoshiyasu, Nishimura Hidehiko, Shirai Shoichi, Akiyama Miyako, Uchida Hideko, Sawada Yoshio, Kato Teruko, Takizawa Tatsuo, Takizawa Ryu, Takizawa Takako and Takizawa Yoshihiro –

But we are still weeping. Always,

already the weeping,

always, already the weeping again in the Occupied City:

In the Occupied City it is 26 January 1948 again –

Here it is always, already 26 January 1948 –

This date always, already our wound –

Our wound which will never heal –

Here, here where it is always, already that date, that time; always, already, the last time:

For the last time. In the morning, we wake in our beds. *In our beds that are no longer our beds.* For the last time. In our homes, we dress. *In our homes that are no longer our homes, our clothes that*

7

are no longer our clothes. For the last time. We eat white rice. *Now we eat only the black rice, the black rice that empties our stomachs.* For the last time. We drink clear water. *Here we drink only the dark water, the dark water that empties our mouths.* For the last time. In our *genkans*, we say goodbye to our mothers and our fathers, our sisters and our brothers, our wives and our sons, our husbands and our daughters. *Our mothers and our fathers, our sisters and our brothers, our wives and our sons, our husbands and our daughters who are no longer our mothers and our fathers, no longer our sisters and our brothers, no longer our wives and our sons, no longer our husbands and our daughters.* For the last time. In the snow, we leave for work. *For our work that is no longer our work.* For the last time. Among the crowds, we catch our trains and our buses. *Our trains and our buses that are no longer our trains and our buses . . .*

For the last time. Through the Occupied City, we shuffle –

From the Shiinamachi Station, we shuffle. In the sleet. For the last time. Up the road, we shuffle. Through the mud. For the last time. To the Teikoku Bank. *The Teikoku Bank that is no longer a bank . . .*

For the last time. We slide open the door. *The door that is no longer a door.* For the last time. We take off our shoes. *Where are our shoes now?* For the last time. We put on our slippers. *Where are our slippers?* For the last time. We sit at our desks. *Our desks that are no longer, no longer our desks . . .*

For the last time –

Among the papers and among the ledgers, we wait for the bank to open. For the last time, on this last day, 26 January 1948 –

We watch the hands of the clock reach half past nine. For the last time. The bank opens and the day begins. For the last time. We serve the customers. For the last time. We write in ledgers.

For the last time –

In the glow of the lights, in the warmth of the heaters, we hear the snow turn to sleet, the sleet turn to rain, as it falls on the roof of the bank. And we wonder if today the bank will close early. We wonder if today we will be able to leave early, to go back to our homes, back to our families. Because of the weather,

because of the snow –

But the snow has turned to sleet, the sleet has turned to rain, and so the bank will not close early today and so we will not be able to leave early today, we will not be able to go back to our homes,

8

back to our families –

So we sit at our desks in the bank, in the glow of the lights, in the warmth of the heaters, and we watch the hands of the clock and we glance at the face of our manager, our manager sat at his desk at the back; we know Mr Ushiyama, our manager, is not so well. We can see it in his face. We can hear it in his voice. We know he has severe stomach pains. We know he has had these pains for almost a week. We all know what this could be; we know it could be dysentery, we know it could be typhoid. In the Occupied City,

we all know what this could mean –

In the Occupied City, we know

this could mean death, death –

But he will survive this,

he will live through

this . . .

For the last time. We watch the hands of the clock reach two o'clock and we see Mr Ushiyama rise from his desk at the back, his face is white and he holds his stomach. For the last time. We watch Mr Ushiyama bow and we listen to Mr Ushiyama apologize to us all. For the last time. We watch as Mr Ushiyama leaves early –

And we all know what this could mean –

We know this could mean death –

But he will survive, he will live. Back in his home that is still his home, back with his family that is still his family . . .

But we do not leave early today. We do not go back to our homes, back to our families. We sit at our desks, in the glow of the lights, in the warmth of the heaters, and we go back to our customers and back to our ledgers. And we listen to the sound of the rain –

And we watch the hands of the clock –

We watch the hands of the clock reach three o'clock and we watch as the bank closes its doors for the day. Among the stacks of receipts, we collate the day's transactions. For the last time. Among the piles of cash, we tally the day's money. For the last time. And then we hear the tap-tap upon the side door. For the last time –

We look up at the hands of the clock –

For the last time:

It is now twenty past three on Monday, 26 January 1948 –

Twenty past three, in the Occupied City –

The knock now upon the side door –

Twenty past three and he is here –
Our killer is here.

We watch as Miss Akuzawa gets up to open the side door for our killer. *You say he is forty-two years old.* Our killer presents his name-card: Yamaguchi Jirō MD; Technical Officer; Ministry of Health and Welfare. *You say he is fifty-four.* Our killer asks to see the manager. *You say he is forty-six years old.* Miss Akuzawa asks our killer to come round to the front door. *You say he is fifty-eight.* Our killer goes back outside. *You say he is five feet four inches tall.* Our killer opens the front door. *You say he is five feet three inches.* Miss Akuzawa has a pair of slippers waiting for him. *You say he is five feet five inches tall.* Our killer takes off his boots in the *genkan. You say he is five feet two.* We listen as Miss Akuzawa tells our killer that the manager has already left, but that the assistant manager will see him. *You say he has a thin build.* We watch as our killer nods and thanks Miss Akuzawa, as she leads our killer through the bank. *You say he has a medium build.* We watch our killer pass us in our rows of desks as we work. *You say he has an average build.* We listen as Miss Akuzawa introduces our killer to the assistant manager, Mr Yoshida. *You agree he is rather thin.* Our killer bows. *You say he has an oval face.* Our assistant manager offers our killer a seat. *You say he has a long face.* Our killer sits down, his face to the right. *You say he has a high nose.* Our assistant manager stares at the name-card: Yamaguchi Jirō MD; Technical Officer; Ministry of Health and Welfare. *You say he has a handsome face.* Our killer tells our assistant manager there has been an outbreak of dysentery in the neighbourhood. *You say he has a pale complexion.* Our assistant manager now presents his own name-card: Yoshida Takejiro; Assistant Manager; Teikoku Bank; Shiinamachi branch, Nagasaki-chō, Toshima Ward, Tokyo. *You say he has a jaundiced complexion.* Our killer tells Mr Yoshida that the source of the outbreak is the public well in front of the Aida residence in Nagasaki 2-chōme. *You say he has two brown spots on his left cheek.* Mr Yoshida nods and mentions that the bank's manager, Mr Ushiyama, has in fact left early due to severe stomach ache. *On his right cheek.* Our killer tells Mr Yoshida that one of Mr Aida's tenants has been diagnosed with dysentery and that this man made a deposit in our branch today. *You say he has a bruise on his left cheek.* Mr Yoshida is amazed that the Ministry of Health and Welfare has heard of the case so quickly. *A scar on his right.* Our killer tells Mr

10

Yoshida that the doctor who saw Mr Aida's tenant reported the case promptly. *You say he has close-cropped hair.* Mr Yoshida nods. *You say his hair is grey.* Our killer says he has been sent by Lieutenant Parker, who is in charge of the disinfecting team for this area. *You say his hair is rather long and grizzled.* Mr Yoshida nods again. *You say his hair is dark.* Our killer has been told to inoculate everyone against dysentery and to disinfect all items that may have been contaminated. *You say he wears a brown lounge suit.* Mr Yoshida nods for a third time. *You say he wears an old winter suit.* All members, all rooms, all cash and all money in this branch, says our killer. *You say he wears a uniform.* Mr Yoshida stares at the name-card again: Yamaguchi Jirō MD; Technical Officer; Ministry of Health & Welfare. *You are sure it was a uniform.* Our killer says that no one will be allowed to leave until his work has been completed. *You say he wears a brown overcoat.* Mr Yoshida glances at his watch. *You say he carries an overcoat.* Lieutenant Parker and his team will arrive soon to check the job has been done properly, says our killer. *You say he wears one coat but carries another.* Mr Yoshida nods. *You say he carries a spring coat.* Our killer now places his small olive-green bag on Mr Yoshida's desk. *You say he wears brown rubber shoes.* Mr Yoshida watches our killer open the bag. *You say he wears burnt orange rubber boots.* Our killer takes out a small metal box and two different-sized bottles marked in English. *You say there was mud on his shoes.* Mr Yoshida reads the words FIRST DRUG on the smaller 200cc bottle and SECOND DRUG on the 500cc bottle. *You say his boots were clean.* Our killer tells Mr Yoshida that this is an extremely potent oral antidote which the Americans have recently developed through experiments with palm tree oil. *You say he wears a white cloth band on his left arm.* Mr Yoshida nods. *You say it reads in red 'Leader of Disinfecting Team'.* It is so powerful that you will be completely immunized from dysentery, says our killer. *You say he wears a Tokyo Metropolitan Office armband.* Mr Yoshida nods again. *You say it reads in black 'Disease Preventative Doctor'.* Our killer warns Mr Yoshida that the administration procedure is complicated and unusual. *You say he wears a Toshima Ward armband.* Again, Mr Yoshida glances at the name-card on his desk: Yamaguchi Jirō MD; Technical Officer; Ministry of Health & Welfare. *You say it reads 'Epidemic Prevention Team'.* Our killer asks Mr Yoshida to gather his staff. *You say he carries a small olive-*

green shoulder bag over his right shoulder. Even the caretaker, his wife and two children? asks Mr Yoshida. *Or was it his left?* Our killer nods. *You say he carries a doctor's bag.* Mr Yoshida rises from his desk. *A black doctor's bag.* Mr Yoshida calls us over. *I am Takeuchi Sutejiro and I am forty-nine years old but here I am no longer Takeuchi Sutejiro and now I am no longer forty-nine years old; now I am always struggling, here I am only weeping.* We rise from our desks. *I am Watanabe Yoshiyasu and I am forty-three years old but here I am no longer Watanabe Yoshiyasu and now I am no longer forty-three years old; now I am always struggling, here I am only weeping.* We shuffle through the bank. *I am Nishimura Hidehiko and I am thirty-eight years old but here I am no longer Nishimura Hidehiko and now I am no longer thirty-eight years old; now I am always struggling, here I am only weeping.* We gather around Mr Yoshida's desk. *I am Shirai Shoichi and I am twenty-nine years old but here I am no longer Shirai Shoichi and now I am no longer twenty-nine years old; now I am always struggling, here I am only weeping.* We all watch as our killer turns to Miss Akuzawa, as our killer asks her to bring enough teacups for all the members of the branch. *I am Akiyama Miyako and I am twenty-three years old but here I am no longer Akiyama Miyako and now I am no longer twenty-three years old; now I am always struggling, here I am only weeping.* Miss Akuzawa fetches sixteen teacups on a tray. *I am Uchida Hideko and I am twenty-three years old but here I am no longer Uchida Hideko and now I am no longer twenty-three years old; now I am always struggling, here I am only weeping.* Our killer opens the smaller bottle marked FIRST DRUG. *I am Sawada Yoshio and I am twenty-two years old but here I am no longer Sawada Yoshio and now I am no longer twenty-two years old; now I am always struggling, here I am only weeping.* Our killer asks if everybody is here. *I am Kato Teruko and I am sixteen years old but here I am no longer Kato Teruko and now I am no longer sixteen years old; now I am always struggling, here I am only weeping.* Our assistant manager counts our heads and nods, everybody is here. *I am Takizawa Tatsuo and I am forty-six years old but here I am no longer Takizawa Tatsuo and now I am no longer forty-six years old; now I am always struggling, here I am only weeping.* Our killer holds a pipette as though it were a dagger in his hand. *I am Takizawa Ryu and I am forty-nine years old but here I am no longer Takizawa Ryu and now I* am no longer forty-nine years old; now I am always struggling, here I am only weeping. We all watch as our killer drips some clear liquid into each of our cups. I am Takizawa Takako and I am nineteen years old but here I am no longer Takizawa Takako and now I am no longer nineteen years old; now I am always struggling, here I am only weeping. We all listen as our killer tells each of us to pick up our own teacup. I am Takizawa Yoshihiro and I am eight years old but here I am no longer Takizawa Yoshihiro and now I am no longer eight years old; now I am always struggling, here I am only weeping. Each of us reaches for our own cup. We who are here now in the grey. Now our killer raises his hand in warning. We who are always, already struggling. We all listen as our killer warns us of the strength of the serum, the damage it can cause to our gums and tooth enamel if we do not watch our killer's demonstration carefully, if we do not follow our killer's instructions precisely. We who are always, already only weeping. We all watch as our killer now takes out a syringe. You define us as the victims. We all watch as our killer dips his syringe into the liquid. You damn us as the victims. We all watch as our killer draws up a measure of the liquid into the syringe. You are happy to remember us in the black and white of our deaths. We all watch as our killer opens his mouth. You are ignorant of us in the colour of our lives. We all watch as our killer places his tongue over his bottom front teeth and then tucks it under his lower lip. We are evidence at a crime scene. We all watch as our killer drips the liquid onto his tongue. We are bodies in a crime book; bodies, never characters. We all watch as our killer tilts his head back. In our lives you did not know us. We all watch as our killer stares at his wristwatch, his right hand in the air. Only by our deaths did you find us. We all watch as our killer's hand falls. At a crime scene. We all listen as our killer tells us that this medicine may damage our gums and our teeth, as our killer tells us we must all swallow quickly. In a crime book. We all nod. Our names, our faces. We all listen as our killer tells us that exactly one minute after we have taken the first medicine, he will administer the second medicine. In print and in photographs. We all stare at the 500cc bottle marked SECOND DRUG. Reduced to a number. We all listen as our killer promises us that after we have taken the second medicine, we will be able to drink water or rinse out our mouths. Twelve, you will always write 12. Now our killer tells each of us to lift up our cups. In this number, this number 12. We all

13

pick up our teacups. *In this number, we die again.* And now each of us drinks. *Again and again and again and again and again and again and again and again and again and again and again and again.* Our killer tells us to drip the liquid onto our tongues. *For we are not twelve.* And now we all taste the bitter liquid. *We are Takeuchi Sutejiro, Watanabe Yoshiyasu, Nishimura Hidehiko, Shirai Shoichi, Akiyama Miyako, Uchida Hideko, Sawada Yoshio, Kato Teruko, Takizawa Tatsuo, Takizawa Ryu, Takizawa Takako and Takizawa Yoshihiro.* We all swallow it down. *We who are here now in the grey.* And we hear our killer tell us he will administer the second drug in exactly sixty seconds. *We who are always, already struggling.* We see our killer looking at his wristwatch. *We who are always, already only weeping.* We see him staring at his wristwatch. *Weeping and waiting.* We all wait for the second drug. *Waiting and watching.* We all watch as our killer pours the second drug into each of our teacups. *Watching and reaching.* We all reach for our cups again. *Reaching and waiting, again.* Again we all wait as our killer checks his wristwatch, and again we all wait for the signal. *For the smile.* Now we all see our killer gesture for each of us to drink again. *With a smile.* And we all drink. *And you smile as we drink.* And we all see our killer waiting. *Still smiling.* And we all see our killer still watching us. *That smile on your face.* And now we all feel the second liquid in our mouths, now in our throats, now in our stomachs. *But you are smiling.* And now we all hear our killer telling us to rinse out our mouths. *Still smiling, still smiling, still . . .*

At twenty minutes past three on Monday, 26 January 1948, in Tokyo, and I am drinking and I am drinking and I am drinking and I am drinking and I am drinking and I am drinking and I am drinking and I am drinking and I am drinking and I am drinking and I am drinking and I am drinking and now, now we run and we retch, we stagger and we stumble, and we begin to fall, to fall and to fall –

Infected, we are falling and falling –

We are falling. We are falling –

We are falling in tears –

In tears, the tears –

We are weeping. We are weeping –

We are weeping all the time –

Always, already weeping,

here. But in the Occupied City, it is twenty minutes past three,

14

now it is twenty-one minutes past three,

now twenty-two minutes past,

twenty-three minutes –

In the Occupied City, the minutes and the hours, the days and the weeks, the months and the years will pass. But in the Perplexed City, the Posthumous City, between two places, the minutes and the hours, the days and the weeks, the months and the years will not pass.

Here where it is always, already January, but where January is not January; here where it is always, already 1948,

but where 1948 is not 1948;

here where we do not age –

In the Perplexed City, in the Posthumous City,

it will always, already be twenty past three –

But still we watch you age, watch

you age, and watch you forget . . .

Here, where it is always, already twenty past three –

Here, where it will always, already be grey –

Into the greyness, I am falling, I am falling, I am falling, I am falling, I am falling, I am falling, I am falling, I am falling –

I am falling, I am falling –

I am falling –

Falling –

Here, into the Perplexed City, the Posthumous City, this city that is no city, into the grey place, this place that is no place,

we all fall, away from the light,

from the Occupied City,

we all fall, into the earth and into the sky,

we all fall, fall, fall –

From your city, into our coffins . . .

Twelve cheap wooden coffins –

Your city, our coffin . . .

Here, here –

In the snow. In the back of a truck. Parked outside the bank. In the sleet. Under the heavy damp tarpaulin. Driven through the streets. In the rain. To the hospital. To the morgue. In the sleet. To the mortuary. To the temple. In the snow. To the crematorium. To the earth and to the sky. In our twelve cheap wooden coffins –

Ash for hair, soil for skin, among the flakes and the sod / We defy the fire and the rake, the spade and the grave / The grave in the

earth, the grave in the sky / In the abyss of the sky, in the abyss of the
earth / Your earth, your sky. Not our sky, not

>*our earth / not here, not now /*
>*Now into the heights, we*
>*fall, into the depths . . .*

These twelve cheap wooden coffins, in which we lie. But we do not lie still. In these twelve cheap wooden coffins, we are struggling. In the greyness, we are struggling. In this city, we are struggling. We are struggling and we are weeping, weeping the words:

>*Where is the law, we ask as we fall, from being into non-being,*
>*as we struggle, between one place and no place,*

>>*as we weep, where is the law?*

In the Ab-grund, in the Un-grund, the without ground, the non-ground / Here, other voices in this other-dom will speak this other-place with other-name –

In this un-place, in this un-city, between two places, in this other-dom / There are no swallows, no swallows fly here / Here, we shuffle across the carpet of their corpses, up and down, their bloated chests, their barren wings / Here, where their still eyes accuse us, yellow / Here, where their empty beaks stand open, yellow –

In this place of no place, we lie. It has a name
and it has none. So speak it,
now speak it: Caesura –
Between us –

In this place – no-place / un-place – this place called Caesura, named Caesura, this place that takes away our breath, this place that leaves us weeping. Always, weeping. Already, weeping –

>*You are deaf, you are dumb and you are blind,*
>*so you cannot and you will not hear us,*
>*cannot and will not help us,*
>*will you . . .*

In the Perplexed City, the Posthumous City, in Caesura, always, already –

>*You will not help us, will you, dear writer?*
>The first candle blown out –
>Always, already, out –
>*In-caesura, in-difference . . .*

Beneath the Black Gate, in its upper chamber, in the occult circle, her white face falling and her red robes flailing, the medium is flat upon the floor before you now. The wind, the bell and the drum all silent now, the medium mute and prostrate upon the floor,

the blood and tear-splin-taint-ed floor –

In-difference and in-caesura . . .

The first candle extinguished,

the medium exhausted –

Un-in-corpor-ated . . .

Possessed no more, you are alone here. Here in the Occupied City, alone and deaf, dumb and blind –

Yet still you try to write,

to pick up your pen,

to write again

here. Here in this place between the things you did and the things you did not do, between the things you felt and the things you did not feel, the things you said and the things you did not say,

here in this place between the done and the un-done, the felt and the un-felt, the said and the un-said –

Yet still you try to write,

to write again

here –

But here the done can never be un-done,

the un-done never done –

Here the felt can never be un-felt,

the un-felt never felt –

The said never be un-said,

the un-said never

said –

Here where you know the written can never be un-written,

and where you fear – fear, fear, fear – the un-written,

the un-written can never be written,

the un-written never written

here. Here where your see-ing is fading, now as your hear-ing is failing. Here and now where nightmares and headaches curse your days and nights. Here and now as you mistake the sun for the moon, moonlight for sunshine, sun-fall for rain-shine,

life for death, cough-cough,

death for birth. Here –

In this occult circle of the eleven candles, in this upper chamber of the Black Gate, you cough and you cough-cough, see-fading and hear-failing, you cough and you cough-cough, blood-blots and tear-traces here. Here among the blank tears and the falling papers, you are coughing, cough-cough, and now you are spinning, spinning and spinning, unable to write, unable to see,

still half-deaf to the foot-stair-steps,

to the sirens and the telephones –

'No more tears,' whispers a voice, the voice of an old man. 'No more tears, no more tears for him . . .'

You drop your pen, your ink-dry-pen. You open your eyes, your red-dry-eyes. The eleven candles have gone, the Black Gate has gone, the Occupied City has gone. You are standing in a shed, or a barn, with the earth-smell, the damp-smell. You are watching an elderly man opening up cardboard boxes, taking out files, dust-webbed and cob-covered, the elderly man leafing through papers and documents, documents and notebooks, notebooks upon notebooks –

'It was many years ago,' the old man is saying. 'Not so many people left now who remember what the Teigin case was really like.

'But I remember. Because I was in the Murder Room; Room #2 of the First Investigative Division of the Tokyo Metropolitan Police Board. And Room #2 was in charge of all murders.

'The head of our division was Suzuki and the head of our room was Minegishi . . .

'But you want to know what happened, yes?' repeats the old man. 'No? You want to know the truth? Make up your mind! Which do you want to know; what happened, or the truth? What do you mean they're the same? Of course they're not! I can believe something happened, but it doesn't make it true –

'Does it?

'For example, I once knew this detective. Married. Kid. The whole deal. Anyway, this detective, he starts to believe his wife is having an affair. A fling. With an American. A soldier. She wasn't. But that didn't stop him believing she was. He would tell me, last night my wife was off fucking this American soldier. She wasn't. But that didn't stop him believing it. Believing it happened. Believing it was real. Believing it was true. It was the truth for him. It was real for him, very real for her too, in the end. But that's another story. But you see my point, don't you? But, anyway, if you want to know what

18

happened, then I'll tell you what happened. It's all in here . . .

'Here in these boxes, here in these notebooks . . .

'But remember, no more tears –

'No more tears for him . . .

The Second Candle –

The ~~Testimony~~ Notebook of a Detective, H.

The city is a notebook. In pencil and on paper,
    in blunt pencil, on coarse paper –
    IN THE OCCUPIED CITY,
    I wrote these words:

1948/1/26; 16.00: Snow / Day-off / In the public bath / The call from Metro HQ / 'Ten dead in the jurisdiction of the Mejiro Police Station.' / 'Another Yakuza war?' / 'Much bigger. Mass poisoning. Report immediately!' / Trolley bus from Naka-Meguro to Ebisu / Taxi to the crime scene / The Shiinamachi branch of the Teikoku (Imperial) Bank, 39 Nagasaki 1-chōme, Toshima-ku, Tokyo / A one-storey building / Across from the Nagasaki Shrine / Hell / Ten bodies laid out in a line in one of the maintenance man's two rooms / Eyes open / Mouths open / Blood and vomit / Chalk marks where they were found / Behind the counter / In the washroom / In the hallway / In the maintenance man's living room / Six survivors taken to the Seibo Catholic Hospital / Doctors, neighbours, and journalists inside the bank / Crime scene contaminated / Evidence destroyed or misplaced / My room – Room #2 (Murder Room) of the First Investigative Division of the Tokyo Metropolitan Police Board – provisionally assigned the case.

The First Period (the first twenty days of the investigation; 26 January to 14 February, 1948) begins –

1948/1/26; 23.00: The second floor of Mejiro Police Station / Special Investigation HQ established / First meeting of the Special Investigation Team / Report based on evidence gathered at crime scene and statement taken from one of the survivors / Establishment of known facts / Two of the six survivors now dead / Victims now total twelve / Survivors four / Date and time of the crime: Fifteen minutes around 3.30 p.m., 26 January (Monday) 1948 / Place of the crime: Within Shiinamachi branch of Teikoku Bank, 39 Nagasaki 1-chōme, Toshima-ku, Tokyo. This establishment, formerly Fujita Pawnshop and consisting of one building with three entrances, is situated between the business and residential quarters in front of Nagasaki Shrine about sixty metres northeast of Shiinamachi Station on Seibu Agricultural Line (formerly called Musashino Line) / Victims: Yoshida Takejiro (43), now being under treatment, of 812 Oguchi-machi, Ota-ku; Watanabe Yoshiyasu (43), died, of 758 Oizumi-machi, Itabashi-ku; Nishimura Hidehiko (38), died, of 10 Shin Ogawa-machi 2-chōme, Ushigome, Shinjuku-ku; Shirai Shoichi (29), died, of 519 Asagaya 3-chōme, Suginami-ku; Sawada Yoshio (22), died, of 449 Fujisawa, Fujisawa-mura, Irima-gun, Saitama Prefecture; Tanaka Tokukazu, being under treatment, of 793 Kami-ochiai 2-chōme, Shinjuku-ku; Akiyama Miyako (23), died, c/o Akiyama Kunosuke, 18 Nagasaki 1-chōme, Toshima-ku; Uchida Hideko (23), died, of 5 Kita Toyotama, Nerima-ku; Akuzawa Yoshiko (19), being under treatment, c/o Akuzawa Shobei, of 14 Nagasaki 1-chōme, Toshima-ku; Kato Teruko (16), died, of 1–713 Ikebukuro 2-chōme, Toshima-ku; Takeuchi Sutejiro (49), died, of 170 Horikiri-chō, Katsushika-ku; Takizawa Tatsuo (46), servant, his wife Ryu (49), his daughter Takako (19) and son Yoshihiro (8), all of them died, all of them resident of Shiinamachi branch of Teikoku Bank / Offender: Name and address: unknown / He said he was a medical member of Sanitary Section, Tokyo Metropolitan Office and of Welfare Dept, Welfare Ministry, and had a title of Doctor of Medicine / Presented name-card: 'Yamaguchi Jirō MD; Technical Officer; Ministry of Health & Welfare.' / Description: Aged between forty-four and fifty, about five feet three inches in height, rather thin, with oval face, high nose, pale complexion, hair cut short or rather long and grizzled / Appearance: Dressed in a lounge suit (brown, figured weave, not new); with an overcoat or spring coat on arm; wearing brown rubber shoes (not certain); a white cloth band on left arm (which had on it the mark of Tokyo Metropolitan Office in red, and under the mark was written in black and good hand 'Leader of Disinfecting Team' or 'Disease Preventative Doctor' / Articles possessed by the offender: A metal box, about 3 cm × 15 cm in size, such as often carried by doctors (he took the poison out of this box); one small and one medium-sized glass medicine bottles (holding poison) / Characteristics: Two brown spots 1.5 cm long on left cheek (not scars of burns or boils, but such as often seen on the skin of an old man). A handsome man; well composed and looking like an intelligent man / Brief account of the case: The victims opened their business as usual at 0930 hrs, and after Ushiyama Senji, their manager, went home with stomachache about 1400 hrs, continued at their work till 1500 hrs, when they closed the front door and began winding up the remaining affairs for the day / At approximately 1530 hrs the offender made his sudden appearance at the side entrance and, showing his name-card (printed with false title, as described above) to Akuzawa Yoshiko, one of the victims, expressed his wish to see the chief. So the latter showed him into the office-room, and Yoshida Takejiro, the assistant chief, had a talk with him / According to the statement of the offender, there have cropped up a number of dysentery cases among those who drink the water of a public well in front of Aida's, and have been reported to Lieutenant Porton (or something sounding like that) as well as to the Japanese police. So a disinfecting team of the Allied Forces was coming, he said. He himself was dispatched by the lieutenant in advance of the said team to make an investigation, as a result of which he found that an inmate of the house of a dysentery sufferer had visited their office on the day. In accordance, everything in the office, including the books, papers, banknotes, etc., must receive a disinfecting process, for which nothing should be carried out till the arrival of the disinfecting team, he declared / When Yoshida said to him: 'How can you have got the knowledge so soon, I wonder?' the offender said in reply: 'In truth, the doctor who made an inspection of the sufferer has made a direct report to the Occupation authorities.' / 'The disinfecting team will soon be here,' continued the villain, 'and in the meanwhile you all must take this medicine given us by the Occupation authorities. This is a medicine so powerful and effective as to make you absolutely immune from the dysentery if you take it.' So saying, he took some phials, large and small, out of his medicine chest (a metal chest for a medical practitioner, as described above) / All the victims, wholly unsuspicious of the fiendish intention of the offender, whose perfect composure and plausible explanations as well as his armband of Tokyo Metropolitan Office having satisfied them to lay full credit in his words, formed a circle around him – a circle of poor victims sixteen in all / Then the devil opened his mouth and said: 'This medicine will injure the enamel of your teeth, and so I will show you how you must swallow it. Do as I am going to show you. There are two kinds of medicine. Take the second about a minute after you take the first. Be sure to drink it within a minute, or you will get a bad effect.' / After such explanations he poured into the victims' cups some liquid medicine, transparent and otherwise, out of the small phials with a fountain-pen filler, a filler for each / Then he took a cup of his own in his hand, and, saying, 'This is how to drink,' gulped its contents by dripping them drop by drop on to his tongue, which he had put out in the form of a shovel / So the poor victims, without exception, gulped the fatal water following the devil's example / The liquid in question had a burning taste, and the victims got a feeling as if they had taken some strong whisky / After about a minute, the tricky villain again showed them how to drink the second medicine, and again the poor innocents followed his example, not suspecting in the least that they were actually killing themselves / The devil had the audacity to advise them to rinse out their mouths so as not to injure their teeth, and they went to have some water at the tap several metres off in the passage / Just about this time they felt themselves suddenly overwhelmed with torpor, and fell one by one in the office-room, passage, matted-room etc., sinking into a complete comatose state / As a natural conclusion, nobody knows – but the devil and God – what the offender did after his victims fell senseless / SOME RULES FOR CI AGENTS TO ACT UPON: (1) Send warnings without delay to banks, post offices, and other places where large sums of money are handled, not to fall easy victims to some similar attempts. Institute at the same time a close investigation as to whether such attempts have been made in the past. (2) Make an immediate inquiry as to where the offender's name-card was printed, carrying your search into every corner of the Metropolis where some printer of name-cards may have printed some such items. (3) Make an immediate inquiry as to whether there lives some suspicious person at all similar to the description given of the fiendish offender, within the area you are assigned to cover. Pay a special attention to bank employees, disinfecting officials and their assistants, health officials and their men, physicians, druggists, and those who have some record of having been employed in the sanitary work of the Occupation authorities. (4) Examine any person, at all suspicious, more strictly

23

than ever, paying a special attention to his name-card, phials, and medicine chest, made of metal. (5) Try and catch some clue concerning those who may have some business or other connections with the bank in question. (6) Ransack your memory and memoranda for some person with criminal records (especially fraud), at all resembling the devilish offender described, either in his features or in his peculiar way of committing crimes. (7) Carry out a secret surveillance over the daily habits and characteristic features of the Metropolitan health officials and such others as are engaged in sanitary works in the Metropolis / **Insert:** *Memorandum from Director of Criminal Department, Metropolitan Police Board, to Chiefs of All Police Stations, Re: Instructions regarding Case of Killing Members of the Teikoku Bank: At approximately 15.30 today, the sixteen members of the Shiinamachi branch of the Teikoku Bank, located within the jurisdiction of the Mejiro Police Station, were asked by a man who called himself a member of the Sanitary Section of the Tokyo Metropolitan Office to swallow a liquid poison he brought which he said was a preventative against dysentery to be taken by them according to an order issued by the Occupation Forces, that ten of the victims were killed on the spot and two at the hospital, and the other four are being given medical aid but their fate is still to be seen. This crime, which was committed at the closing hour of the bank and in the assumed name of the Occupation Forces, killing many lives at one time and attempting to rob much money of the establishment, is one of the rarest and boldest crimes ever seen in the history of crimes. In view of the tremendous repercussion being shown by the public with regard to this case, we must, through cooperation of all police, take greatest possible efforts for apprehending the offender. For this reason you are asked to recognize the extraordinary importance of the case and, giving complete instructions to your subordinate officers in accordance with the following rules of investigation, make immediate report to the investigation headquarters whenever you get any data for furthering investigation and that with special care not to let the secret escape. Details of Place of the crime, Victims, Offender and Brief account of the case attached / N.B. Your speedy written report is impatiently expected at the Investigation Headquarters as soon as your task is completed* / Memorandum ends / One hundred detectives assigned to the case / My room – Room #2 (Murder Room) of the First

Investigative Division of the Tokyo Metropolitan Police Board –
confirmed in overall charge of the investigation under my boss,
Detective Inspector Minegishi / Minegishi to report to Chief
Inspector Suzuki, Head of the First Investigative Division, who in turn
will report directly to Tokyo Chief of Police Kita / Robbery Room
detectives to aid in investigation / Divided into three *ji-dōri*
questioning teams / Partnered with Detective Fukushi / Allotted
Nagasaki 2-chōme / Begin questioning the neighbourhood at first
light.

1948/1/27; 06.00: Fair, with northwesterly winds / Street by
street, house by house, door-to-door questioning of Nagasaki 2-
chōme neighbourhood with Fukushi-kun / Establish names and
occupations of all residents / Establish and verify whereabouts of
each resident at time of crime / Repeat description of suspect based
on statements of survivors / Note down any possible sightings of men
fitting description of suspect / Note down any suggestions as to
identity of suspect based on description given to residents / **18.00:**
Requested to return to Special Investigation HQ for emergency
meeting / Reports received of two similar cases / First case reported
to the Marunouchi Police Station at 15.30 this afternoon by Ogawa
Taizo (or Yasuzo), the manager of the Nakai branch of the
Mitsubishi Bank / Case occurred at approximately 15.20 on 19 January
this year at the Nakai branch of the Mitsubishi Bank at 4-chōme
Shimo-ochiai, Shinjuku-ku / According to the statement by Ogawa, a
man arrived at the bank as business was closing and presented the
name-card: 'Dr Yamaguchi Jirō, medical technician attached to the
Anti-Epidemic section of the Welfare Ministry' / The visitor told
Ogawa that he had been sent by a Lieutenant Porter or Parker to
disinfect the entire branch because money had been deposited that
day by a man named Ōtani from the Kinuhara Industrial Company of
4-chōme Shimo-ochiai / The visitor said that a mass dysentery
outbreak had occurred in the employee apartments of the Kinuhara
Industrial Company that day (19 January) with ten patients reported
so far / Ogawa asked the man if he knew the full name of this Ōtani
but the man did not answer clearly / Ogawa investigated the records
of the branch and found a deposit by a man named Ōtani of the
Kinuhara Industrial Company / However the deposit had been a
postal order for ¥65 and not cash / Ogawa presented the postal order

to the visitor / The visitor then took out a bottle of transparent, colourless liquid from his briefcase / The man sprinkled a small amount of the liquid over the postal order and the ledger / Ogawa asked the man if he wished to take the postal order away with him but again the man did not answer clearly / Ogawa then asked him if it was possible to be infected with typhoid from simply touching the postal order and again the man was unsure / Ogawa said, 'Surely we would have had to lick the postal order, or the customer's hand to become infected?' / The man agreed and stood up ready to leave / However, the man, looking around the room at the closed vaults, then asked whether or not the bank had already sent the day's cash deposits to the Central Bank / The man used the same technical terms used by the bank employees to talk about cash deposits and banking practices and procedures / However, before Ogawa could answer, the man bowed deeply, thanked the manager and left the branch / Ogawa described the man as being in his fifties, of medium build, round faced with a scar on his left cheek and close-cropped hair / He was wearing a uniform with an armband on which were painted the words: 'Tokyo Epidemic Prevention Centre' / Second case reported to Special Investigation HQ today by a Mr Kawasumi, acting manager of the Ebara branch of the Yasuda Bank / Kawasumi reported that on 14 October 1947, a man entered the Ebara branch of the Yasuda Bank at 722 Hiratsuka-machi 3-chōme, Shinagawa-ku and announced himself as a Dr Matsui Shigeru, an official from the Epidemic Prevention Unit of the Welfare Ministry / The man said, 'I came here with Lieutenant Parker in a jeep because a new typhus case has happened in the houses near the market located behind your bank and that because some of the residents of these houses are customers of the bank it is necessary for me to immunize the employees of the bank against infection.' / However, Kawasumi was suspicious of this Dr Matsui and so he sent an employee to the local Hiratsuka kōban to ask the officer on duty whether there had been an outbreak of typhoid in the neighbourhood / The officer was called Iida Ryuzo / Officer Iida said he hadn't heard of any outbreak but that he would check and then come to the bank / Meanwhile the manager agreed to cooperate with the disinfection / This Dr Matsui said he had to collect his equipment from his jeep and went outside / On his return, the man distributed some kind of medicine to all twenty-three employees of the bank / He told the employees it was a preventative

medicine for typhus control and directed them to drink it / The
medicine was given in two doses / The first dose was described as
being the colour of diluted soy sauce with an acrid aftertaste / The
second medicine was tasteless and is believed to have been water /
Each of the employees drank the doses down but suffered no ill
effects / At this point Officer Iida arrived and spoke directly with this
Dr Matsui / Officer Iida told this man Matsui that he had been out to
the neighbourhood to check and found there had been no outbreak of
typhoid / This Dr Matsui told Officer Iida that he must have checked
the wrong neighbourhood and suggested that he should go back out to
check the correct area / Officer Iida then left the bank to check the
area again / But the man did not wait for the officer to return and left
a few minutes later / However, Kawasumi has given Special
Investigation HQ the name-card the man left behind / 'Matsui
Shigeru; medical doctor; Gikan; Yobō Division; Health & Welfare
Ministry' / A doctor named Matsui Shigeru has already been located
in Sendai / Detective Tomitsuka (Bucho Keiji) of the First
Investigative Division, has been sent to Sendai to interview Dr
Matsui / Officer Iida has also been interviewed this afternoon by
Special Investigation HQ and has provided a detailed description of
the man / Iida described the man as being in his late forties to early
fifties, about 160 centimetres tall, with a mark on his left cheek / Mr
Kawasumi also stated that the man did not speak with the Tokyo
dialect but with the accent of another region (which he is unable to
name) / Because Officer Iida was unable to verify any reports of an
outbreak of dysentery in the vicinity, he reported the case to his
superior, Detective Meiga / Detective Meiga contacted the Ministry
of Health & Welfare and was told that a Dr Matsui Shigeru was
attached to their ministry but was posted in Sendai and did not fit the
description of the man who visited the Ebara branch of the Yasuda
Bank / Meiga and Iida wrote up a brief memo of the case and filed it
along with the name-card / No further action was taken at this point /
Iida seconded to Special Investigation HQ / Robbery Room
detectives removed from *ji-dōri* teams to form Name-card
Investigation Team under Chief Komatsu / **19.30**: Emergency
meeting ends / Officers told to report for second meeting of their *ji-
dōri* questioning teams / Each pair of detectives gives their report of
their day's work / No substantial leads reported / Officers told to
write up all statements given / Officers told to continue questioning

of their assigned neighbourhood tomorrow with emphasis on description of the suspect / Objections raised by Fukushi and me / Waste of time / Told to shut up and do our jobs.

1948/1/28; 06.00: Sleet / Back on the street, house by house, door to door through Nagasaki 2-chōme / Waste of time / **12.00:** Uniform from Mejiro tells us to report back to Special Investigation HQ immediately / Short handed / **12.30:** Meeting / Recap: Detective Tomitsuka of the First Investigative Division, sent to Sendai yesterday to interview Dr Matsui Shigeru / Dr Matsui Shigeru; the name on the card presented at the Ebara branch of the Yasuda Bank / Name verified as that of a person presently employed by the Health & Welfare Ministry in Sendai / But this Dr Matsui is now sitting in the interview room down the corridor here on the second floor of the Special Investigation HQ, Mejiro Police Station, Tokyo / Because this Dr Matsui reads the newspapers / This Dr Matsui listens to the radio / This Dr Matsui knows one of his name-cards was used in the incident at the Ebara branch of the Yasuda Bank / So this morning, Dr Matsui gets on a train to Tokyo for the funeral of a relative / Upon arrival in Tokyo, Dr Matsui comes straight here / Dr Matsui Shigeru now sitting in the interview room down the corridor on the second floor of the Special Investigation HQ, Mejiro Police Station, Tokyo / Investigation HQ short handed / Detailed to the interrogation team / **13.00:** Down the corridor to this Dr Matsui / This Dr Matsui sweating in his winter coat / *This man has secrets* / This Dr Matsui, face gaunt and pale, hands shaking and voice trembling / *All men have secrets* / Record of interview: 'Last year, the Emperor made a tour of the whole country. Last spring, the Emperor travelled to the six prefectures of the Tōhoku region. Prior to the Emperor's visit, I toured the six prefectures of the Tōhoku region, on behalf of the Health & Welfare Ministry, to determine whether these six prefectures were safe enough for the Emperor to visit. I checked for the risk of disease and epidemics in these six prefectures . . .' / 'Prior to my own tour, I had one hundred new name-cards printed . . .' / 'Where? Who by?' / 'In the basement of the Miyagi Prefectural Office.' / 'When?' / Dr Matsui Shigeru takes out a black-bound notebook / Dr Matsui opens the black-bound notebook / 'On 25 March 1947.' / This Dr Matsui is a very methodical and meticulous man / This Dr Matsui has kept a record in his diary of every person with whom he exchanged name-cards / This Dr Matsui has kept all the name-cards he received in exchange for his own name-card / This Dr Matsui stares again at the name-card which lies before him on the table in the interview room / 'Dr Matsui Shigeru, MD, an official of the Health & Welfare Ministry.' / This Dr Matsui acknowledges that the card used by the suspect at the Ebara branch of the Yasuda Bank last autumn appears to be his / This Dr Matsui admits that the suspect may very well be one of his acquaintances / Now this Dr Matsui opens his black-bound notebook again / Now this Dr Matsui gives us the names of all his acquaintances; the names of any acquaintances to whom he may have given a name-card; the names of fellow epidemic prevention officers / *All men have secrets, all men tell lies* / Dr Matsui keeps coming back to one name / A fellow epidemic prevention officer currently working in the Public Hygiene Section of Miyagi Prefecture / A Mr Hoshi Shōji / **15.00:** Interview suspended / Telephone calls to Tomitsuka in Sendai / Long wait / **18.00:** Meeting with Chief Kita / Kita relays Tomitsuka's report: *This morning Detective Tomitsuka visited the printer in the basement of the Miyagi Prefectural Office / The printer told the detective that the card used at the Yasuda Bank is definitely one from the same batch he made for Dr Matsui, judging by the uniqueness of the font / Typed in* Minchō *font on* Kentō *paper / Also, the kanji characters used to make the name Shigeru are so rare that the printer had to put two separate characters together to print the name correctly / To make the letter* 蔚 *, the printer put* 尗 *and* 尉 *together / Hence the character for Shigeru is a bit taller than the other characters / Hence there can be no doubt this card is from the batch given to Dr Matsui Shigeru on 25 March 1947 / Late this afternoon, following the call from Tokyo, Detective Tomitsuka tracked Mr Hoshi Shōji / Mr Hoshi Shōji is now in the interview room of the Sendai Police Headquarters / But Mr Hoshi does not match the description of the Teikoku Bank suspect / And Mr Hoshi cannot think of any acquaintance of his who might match the description of the killer / However, Mr Hoshi keeps coming back to one name / The name of a former medical sergeant major who was on Dr Matsui's staff during the war / Yet Mr Hoshi admits the man's description does not match that of the killer / But this man is now living in Tokyo /* **18.30:** Back to Dr Matsui in the interview room down the corridor / *This man has secrets* / This Dr Matsui, sweating in his winter coat / *All men have* *secrets* / Interview resumes / 'Do you know a former medical Sergeant Major Karajima?' / *All men tell lies* / This Dr Matsui, face gaunt and pale, hands shaking and voice trembling / 'Yes, I do . . .' / **19.00:** Special Investigative HQ puts out an APB for former medical Sergeant Major Karajima / Detectives told to report back to their *ji-dōri* questioning teams.

1948/1/29; 06.00: Cloudy, with northeasterly winds / Resume street-by-street, house-by-house, door-to-door questioning of Nagasaki 2-chōme neighbourhood with Fukushi-kun / Resident tells us of a man who always wore an armband and who repeatedly visited the house of a local widow / Rush to the house of the widow / As we knock on the front door, another pair of detectives are banging on the back door / Hot lead, obviously / Send Fukushi-kun back to HQ to report the lead immediately / Make sure we get the credit / The glory / Interview the widow / Boyfriend with the armband is a doctor with an insurance company / Good reputation / Alibi for Teigin incident / Her word / Back to HQ to use the phone / Ten calls later and the doctor turns out to be bogus / Ex-army medic, back from China, no licence / Lives in Shibusawa, down past Atsugi, on the Odakyū Line / Always carries a gun / Police Chief Kita gives the green light / Four-man arrest team / No sake, so we take a *mizu-sakazuki* each, a ceremonial shot of water before the battle / Pack a blanket for protection against gunshots / **12.00:** Train down to Shibusawa / Bogus doctor rents a room in a big house with a grass roof close to the station / Rest of the afternoon, most of the evening, crouched in a field of tea leaves / Bored, freezing and scared / **24.00:** Last train of the night and here comes the doctor / Suddenly he stops thirty metres from the house / Pisses on the bush where Detective Sudo and his partner are hiding / Rush him from the back, grab his neck / Sudo takes his legs / Few punches, handcuffs on / Haul him to the *kōban* in front of the station / Local uniform says, 'Doctor! What's going on?' / Uniform looks at four of us and says, 'This is an outrage! Do you know who this man is?' / 'Yeah! The Teigin killer!' / That shuts him up / Examine the good doctor's belongings / Find one Browning pistol loaded with four bullets / One for each of us / Hail the power of *mizu-sakazuki*! / Back up to Special Investigation HQ with suspect –

1948/1/30; 04.00: Interview with suspect / Alibi checks out / Charged with impersonation of a doctor and possession of illegal firearm / Waste of time / **06.00:** Street-by-street, house-to-house, door-to-door / Nothing / Had enough of this / **18.00:** Meeting of the entire Special Investigation Team / Chief of Police Kita present / All Tokyo Metropolitan Police leave cancelled / 20,000 officers mobilized nationwide / Kita predicts protracted inquiry / Prepare for long haul / Review of all significant leads to date / Repeated theories from some detectives of links to the wartime Tokumu Kikan (Special Operations Division) / Hunch based on military precision of Teikoku crime / Rumours of similar crimes in Occupied China / Further team to be formed from the Second Investigative Division to investigate links to Tokumu Kikan / Volunteer for 'Annex' / 'Why you?' / 'Old contacts.' / 'Use them.'

1948/1/31; 09.00: Rain / Ginza / Meeting with [NAME DELETED] / Old friend, ex-Tokumu Kikan, ex-big-shot in Occupied China / Post-war, new-life, new-office, still a big-shot; once a big-shot, always a big-shot / Deep bows and small talk / Tea and cigarettes / 'You're not here for old time's sake, are you?' / 'No.' / 'You're here because of that Teigin case, aren't you?' / 'Yes.' / 'You think it's someone who did the kind of work I did, don't you?' / 'Yes.' / 'Well, shall I tell you why you're wrong? Why you're wasting your time?' / 'Please . . .' / 'From what I hear, the man in the bank told the manager he was a doctor, yeah?' / 'Yes.' / 'And the manager obviously believed him?' / 'Yes.' / 'Because of the man's attitude, his behaviour and his character?' / 'Yes.' / 'Well, in my experience, all the men I know, all the men I worked with over there, they don't look good.' / 'No?' / 'No, they look rough, worn out by the lives they led over there.' / 'Yeah?' / 'Yeah, they are not the kind of men who could pass for doctors.' / 'Is that right?' / 'I know you don't believe me. I know you think I'm only telling you this so you won't go digging around in my past, in the pasts of my colleagues. But that's not the case.' / 'I believe you.' / 'Well, I hope you do.' / 'I do.' / 'Forget Tokumu Kikan. Stick with the doctors. Follow the name-cards.' / 'Thank you.' / Return to HQ / Tell the various chiefs to forget Tokumu Kikan / To stick with the doctors / To follow the name-cards / **18.00:** Re-assigned to *ji-dōri* questioning team / Shit.

1948/2/1; 06.00: No days off / Rain, sleet, snow / Printed notice handed to all detectives: *The Teikoku Bank has ascertained that the total money missing or stolen on 26 January from their Shiinamachi branch was ¥164,405. The Teikoku Bank have also ascertained that a cheque (number B09216) with a face value of ¥17,450, drawn in the name of a Gotō Toyoji, is also missing* / Out on the streets again / Endless *ji-dōri*; sometimes Shiinamachi area, sometimes around Nakai, sometimes to Ebara / Different neighbourhoods, same game / Street-by-street, house-by-house, door-to-door questioning of neighbourhood with Fukushi-kun / Establish names and occupations of all residents / Establish and verify whereabouts of each resident at time of various crimes / Repeat description of suspect based on statements of survivors / Note down any possible sightings of men fitting description of suspect / Note down any suggestions as to identity of suspect based on description given to residents / Waste of time, waste of time, waste of time.

1948/2/2; 06.00: Light snow, then rain / The second floor of Mejiro Police Station / Special Investigation HQ / Meeting of the Special Investigation Team / Chief of Police Kita present / New clue: cheque number B09216 for ¥17,450, listed as missing presumed stolen from the Shiinamachi branch of the Teikoku Bank on 26 January during the mass poisoning, was cashed at approximately 14.30 on 27 January at the Itabashi branch of the Yasuda Bank / Cheque endorsed by Gotō Toyoji, 2661 Itabashi 3-chōme, Itabashi-ku / Yasuda branch manager discovered cheque matched that listed missing or stolen during the Teigin incident yesterday / Notified police / Statements taken by detectives / Descriptions by bank staff of man who cashed the cheque do not match descriptions given by survivors of the Teigin incident / Man at Itabashi branch of Yasuda Bank described as being heavyset, wearing spectacles with tortoise-shell frame, and speaking coarsely / Officers sent to address written on back of cheque / No one named Gotō Toyoji lives at this address / Occupants have no knowledge of anyone of that name.
     [VARIOUS PAGES DAMAGED, DEFACED, OR MISSING FOR REASONS UNKNOWN]

1948/2/4; 06.00: Cold, rain / The second floor of Mejiro Police Station / Special Investigation HQ / Meeting of the Special

Investigation Team / Chief of Police Kita present / Composite drawing of suspect based on eye-witness description of suspect by Teigin survivors distributed to all detectives, all police stations and all newspapers nationwide / First time composite drawing of a suspect has been used in history of Japanese police / Anticipate large public response / Drawing to be used by all *ji-dōri* questioning teams / Ordered to re-interview households and individuals already interviewed, this time with composite drawing / Note to all detectives and police officers: Poison used in the murders now believed to be cyanic silver NOT potassium cyanide / Murderer believed therefore to be highly experienced in handling and use of drugs / **07.00:** Resume *ji-dōri* questioning with composite drawing / Same neighbourhoods, same streets, same houses, same doors, same faces, same waste of time.

[VARIOUS PAGES DAMAGED, DEFACED, OR MISSING FOR REASONS UNKNOWN]

The Second Period (the second twenty days of the investigation; 15 February to 5 March, 1948) –

1948/2/15; 06.00: Cloudy, then overcast / The second floor of Mejiro Police Station / Special Investigation HQ / Meeting of the Special Investigation Team / Chief of Police Kita present / Overview of Investigation to date / Over 500 suspects questioned / Innumerable leads followed up / All suspects eliminated and released / All leads investigated and exhausted / Back to *ji-dōri* / Back to meetings / Endless *ji-dōri*, endless meetings / Endless wastes of time / Endlessly taking us nowhere.

[VARIOUS PAGES DAMAGED, DEFACED, OR MISSING FOR REASONS UNKNOWN]

1948/2/23; 18.00: Cold / Meeting of entire First Investigative Division at Special Investigation HQ / SCAP–Justice Ministry Liaison Officer Miyakawa reports on results of meeting with Public Safety Division of Supreme Commander for the Allied Powers on 19 February 1948 / On behalf of the Investigation, Miyakawa requested the assistance of the SCAP Public Safety Division in locating a Lieutenant Hornet and a Lieutenant Parker / Both names associated with typhus disinfecting teams in the Tokyo area / Lieutenant Hornet believed to have been associated with the Toshima team in the Ōji and Katsushika Wards / Lieutenant Parker associated with the Ebara disinfecting team / Witnesses at the Ebara branch of the Yasuda Bank reported suspect as saying, 'I came here with Lieutenant Parker in a jeep because a new typhus case happened in the vicinity.' / At the Shiinamachi branch of the Teikoku Bank, the same individual is reported as saying, 'I came here because there have been many dysentery cases in the area. Lieutenant Hornet will be here soon.' / Miyakawa requested that the Public Safety Division of SCAP provide any information, names and addresses of Japanese individuals either connected with or having knowledge of the disinfecting work done by either of the above lieutenants, particularly interpreters or individuals who speak English / Miyakawa advised elimination of individuals below the age of thirty or above the age of sixty / Mr Eaton of the Public Safety Division informed Miyakawa that, having spoken with Mr Allen of the Tokyo MG Team Sanitation Control, ten low-ranking medical officers were used by the MG Team in typhus epidemic control activities in 1946 / However, at present, there are no military personnel employed by the MG Team in such work / All disinfecting work is now carried out by Japanese employees of the Tokyo Ward Offices / Furthermore, no such teams are employed by the Public Health & Welfare Department / Mr Eaton stated that some SCAP personnel are presently used in rodent control under HQ and Service Group, Repair and Utilities Division, but none by the name of Parker or Hornet / Finally, Mr Eaton stated that he would contact the AG Section of GHQ to ascertain the names and whereabouts of any lieutenants or captains by the name of Parker or Hornet who have been assigned to Japan / Meeting ends / Back to *ji-dōri* / Back to meetings / *Ji-dōri* and meetings / Endless, endless *ji-dōri* and endless, endless meetings / Endless, endless wastes of time / Endlessly, endlessly taking us nowhere.

[VARIOUS PAGES DAMAGED, DEFACED, OR MISSING FOR REASONS UNKNOWN]

1948/3/4; 18.00: Meeting of entire First Investigative Division at Special Investigation HQ / Police Chief Kita has requested that the Public Safety Division of SCAP assist in securing any information available pertaining to a group of former Japanese military personnel who were sent to Korea as poisoners during the

34

war / It is believed that these persons were highly trained in preparation of various poisons / It is also believed that SCAP is investigating these persons for possible war crimes / Meeting ends / Nothing now but more *ji-dōri*, more meetings / More *ji-dōri*, more meetings / More, more *ji-dōri*, and more, more meetings / More, more wastes of time / More, more, taking us nowhere.

[VARIOUS PAGES DAMAGED, DEFACED, OR MISSING FOR REASONS UNKNOWN]

The Third Period (the third twenty days of the investigation; 6 March to 25 March, 1948) –

1948/3/6; 06.00: Strong northeasterly winds / Meeting of entire First Investigative Division at Special Investigation HQ / Police Chief Kita gives overview of investigation to date and outlines direction of investigation for Third Period / Focus to be on new lead checking ex-personnel of the former Japanese Imperial Chemical Laboratory in Tsudanuma, Chiba-ken / Known that experiments were conducted with prussic acid as a poison / Corps sent to Manchuria during the war / Corps used poison on animals and humans successfully / Pamphlet on use of poison issued to Japanese army personnel / Modus operandi and use of prussic poison by the criminal very similar to the training developed by Tsudanuma Arsenal / Language used by the criminal indicative of training by this laboratory / Further evidence: use of 'First Drug' and 'Second Drug' in English; ability to drink from the same bottle as victims in knowledge that poison had been precipitated at bottom of solution; knowledge of precipitation of prussic acid using oil from palm trees / Furthermore, equipment used matches description of equipment used in Tsudanuma laboratory / Note: at end of war and closure of laboratory, employees took equipment home / Personnel information on former employees now been given by former Major Nonoyama and former Colonel Yokoyama / Request that all information be kept secret for fear of prosecution by War Crimes Tribunal / Police Chief Kita concludes meeting with statement that complaint about behaviour of press will be lodged with SCAP / Cheers / Meeting ends / **08.00:** Meeting of Room #2 for re-assignment / Retained with Fukushi on *ji-dōri* team / Argument with Suzuki (Head of the First Division) / Questioning is ineffective / Leading nowhere / Three crime scenes –

Ebara, Nakai and Shiinamachi – not helping / Suggest only follow hard evidence of Matsui and Yamaguchi name-cards / Track the cards, find the killer / Rebuked for insubordination / Transferred and demoted to Robbery Room with Fukushi / **09.00:** Report for re-assignment to Robbery Room / Small rented room next to Investigation HQ in Mejiro / Now under Inspector Iki-i / Eight men; four on Matsui, four on Yamaguchi / Assigned to Matsui card with Fukushi / All reports direct to Iki-i / Iki-i reports directly to Police Chief Kita / No information to be given to First Investigative Division (for fear of leaks to press) / Told to read through Robbery Room name-card files and notes to date / **09.30:** Begin with Detective Tomitsuka's report on interviews with Matsui and information and statements gathered in Sendai / Card one of 100 printed in the basement of Miyagi Prefectural Office on 25 March 1947 / Dr Matsui had exchanged 128 cards in total / Each person located, interviewed, asked to produce card received from Matsui / Persons unable to produce Matsui card allocated file / Told to work through each file / Re-check each file and mark for possible re-interview / Begin to re-check, re-check, re-check / No regrets.

1948/3/7; 06.00: Strong winds still / Re-check, re-check, re-check / One file, one name, stands out: *Hirasawa Daishō* / Hirasawa Daishō pen-name of Hirasawa Sadamichi, aged fifty-seven / Hirasawa resident in Otaru, Hokkaido with father and younger brother / Wife and three children resident in Tokyo / Request made to Otaru Police Station for information on Hirasawa / Report from Otaru: *Hirasawa famous artist of good character and reputation* / No further information or investigation received from Otaru Police / Detectives Tomitsuka and Iki-i travel to Otaru / Interview Hirasawa / Hirasawa states that he met Dr Matsui on the train ferry from Hokkaido to Honshū sometime in July last year / Hirasawa says he was travelling to Tokyo to deliver one of his watercolours to the Crown Prince / Hirasawa and Matsui exchange name-cards / Hirasawa states that he lost Matsui's name-card when his wallet was stolen by a pickpocket in Tokyo at Mikawashima Station on the Jōban Line in August 1947 / Hirasawa reported theft to the Mikawashima Station *kōban* / Detectives ask Hirasawa's whereabouts on 26 January / Hirasawa admits he was in Tokyo on the day of the crime / Hirasawa states he spent the morning and early afternoon with his daughter and son-in-law in the Marunouchi district / Hirasawa then took a train to his other daughter's house, where he spent the rest of the afternoon and evening playing cards with his daughter's boyfriend / Detectives conclude Hirasawa is not suspect / Innocent / Disagree; premature / Alibi not checked, statements not corroborated / Place file to one side / Continue to re-check, re-check, re-check other files.

[VARIOUS PAGES DAMAGED, DEFACED, OR MISSING FOR REASONS UNKNOWN]

The Fourth Period (the fourth twenty days of the investigation; 26 March to 14 April, 1948) –

1948/3/26; 06.00: Clear / Meeting of Robbery Room Name-card Team / Request permission to visit Mikawashima Station *kōban* to re-check Hirasawa pickpocket story / Other detectives sceptical / Waste of time, they say / But Inspector Iki-i grants permission / Make a telephone call / Ask about the officer who took down Hirasawa's statement about being pickpocketed in August last year / Find out when the officer will be on duty / **09.00:** Go to the Mikawashima Station *kōban* / Meet the officer / Nervous / File in hand / Apologizes for lack of detail and discrepancies in original report / Failure to note Hirasawa's date of birth / Age noted as forty-five years old etc. / Claims to have been mesmerized by the way Hirasawa spoke, his use of language, his reputation, connections to the Imperial Family etc. / Following the interview, admits he chased after Hirasawa to confirm age and date of birth / Hirasawa gone / Vanished / Officer and two colleagues agreed to write 'forty-five years old' in the report, based on their impressions / Tell officer that Hirasawa would have been fifty-six or fifty-seven years old in August 1947 / Note: survivors of the Teigin incident all stated that the perpetrator looked to be approximately 'fifty years old' / Note: Hirasawa appeared to be younger than he was to the Mikawashima Officers / Note: Hirasawa should not be eliminated on basis of age alone / Mikawashima officer then produces a fan from case file / Hirasawa had given the fan to the officer at the time of his statement / Hirasawa stated that the thief left the fan in his pocket when he stole his wallet / Fan is stamped with the name of an ice-vendor and his address / **10.00:** Leave Mikawashima Station *kōban* / Follow the fan / Address of ice-vendor in the same neighbourhood as one of Hirasawa's daughters / Speak with ice-vendor / Man sells coal and logs in the winter / Ice in the summer / Made fifty fans as a gift for regular customers last summer / Hirasawa's daughter is a regular customer / Ice-vendor remembers giving fan to Hirasawa's daughter / Story about pickpocket a lie / *Kuro-kuro* / Stand for a long time outside Hirasawa's daughter's house / *Blacker and blacker* / Do not enter / *Guiltier and guiltier* / **12.00:** Return to Robbery Room Name-card Team HQ / **13.00:** Meeting with Inspector Iki-i / Report on interviews with Mikawashima officer and ice-vendor / Told to write up report and attach to Hirasawa file / Told to move on to other files to re-check for re-interview / So re-check, re-check, re-check / To re-interview, re-interview, re-interview.

[VARIOUS PAGES DAMAGED, DEFACED, OR MISSING FOR REASONS UNKNOWN]

The Fifth Period (the fifth twenty days of the investigation; 15 April to 4 May, 1948) –

[VARIOUS PAGES DAMAGED, DEFACED, OR MISSING FOR REASONS UNKNOWN]

The Sixth Period (the sixth twenty days of the investigation; 5 May to 24 May, 1948) –

[VARIOUS PAGES DAMAGED, DEFACED, OR MISSING FOR REASONS UNKNOWN]

The Seventh Period (the seventh twenty days of the investigation; 25 May to 13 June, 1948) –

1948/5/25; 06.00: Warm / Meeting of Robbery Room Name-card Team / Inspector Iki-i gives us the news we've all been waiting to hear / Permission granted and budget approved for travel to Tōhoku and Hokkaido to interview each individual with whom Matsui had exchanged name-cards / Ordered to confirm and detail situation in which each name-card was exchanged / Ordered to retrieve each Matsui name-card from each individual / 128 cards in total / Detectives Iiga and Fukushi assigned the seventy-seven cards exchanged in the Tōhoku area / Assigned with Inspector Iki-i to investigate the fifty-one cards exchanged in Hokkaido / Top of the list: Hirasawa Sadamichi / Told to expect to be away for one month / Return home to pack.

1948/5/26; 06.00: Warm / Leave Ueno Station for Hokkaido.

1948/5/27; 06.00: Cool, slight breeze / Sapporo, Hokkaido / Begin investigation.
[VARIOUS PAGES DAMAGED, DEFACED, OR MISSING FOR REASONS UNKNOWN]
Every day a different bus or a different train to a different town and a different interview / Every interview, a different high-ranking local government official / Every official produces the card Dr Matsui gave them in exchange for their own / Every day, another name crossed off the list / Another report to write up, another call back to Tokyo / Every night, a different inn or the floor of a different police station or kōban / *Every night, the same dream, the same name* / Kuro-kuro / *Hirasawa Sadamichi* / *Blacker and blacker* / *Every day, nearer and nearer / Guiltier and guiltier . . .*
[VARIOUS PAGES DAMAGED, DEFACED, OR MISSING FOR REASONS UNKNOWN]

1948/6/6; 08.00: Humid / Shikinai-chō, Otaru, Hokkaido / Residence of Hirasawa Sadamichi's father / The second floor of the house / Hirasawa's father sat before the unlit stove in the first room, smoking a pipe / Hirasawa sat in a kimono in the next room, before a canvas of poppies / 'You start painting very early . . .' / 'It is my habit to start early every day. Today is no exception.' / Note: paint on the canvas is dry and hard / 'Do you only paint flowers?' / 'I went to an exhibition at the Mitsukoshi department store in Tokyo on the day of the Teigin incident. I am not the killer.' / 'We didn't say you were. We are only here to ask you about Dr Matsui's name-card.' / 'I am not the man you are looking for.' / 'Well then, that day on the ferry, did you exchange cards with anyone else other than Dr Matsui?' / 'I do not remember.' / 'Can you tell us why you stay here, even though your wife and children live in Tokyo?' / 'My father could pass away soon. So this is my last obligation as a good son to his aged father.' / Note: Hirasawa's father is a former colonel in the Kempeitai and appears in good health / Conversation continues in circles / Hirasawa claims forgetfulness, pleads ignorance / Evasive / Ask Hirasawa for a photograph to take back to Tokyo to show eye-witnesses for purposes of elimination / 'I do not have any photographs.' / Conclude interview / In the *genkan*, canvas shoulder bag hanging from a peg / Note: Teigin killer reported to have carried a canvas shoulder bag / 'Is that your bag?' / 'No.' / **09.00:** Leave Hirasawa residence / Stand for a long time outside Hirasawa's house / *Kuro-kuro* / Inspector Iki-i agrees Hirasawa's behaviour and statements suspicious / *Blacker and blacker* / Iki-i agrees Hirasawa strongly resembles composite drawing of Teigin suspect / *Guiltier and guiltier.*

[VARIOUS PAGES DAMAGED, DEFACED, OR MISSING FOR REASONS UNKNOWN]

1948/6/12; 18.00: Hot, rainy / Investigation of fifty-one name-cards complete / Return to Tokyo via Otaru / Hatch plan to take photograph of Hirasawa / Re-visit Hirasawa residence / Invite Hirasawa to local restaurant for dinner / Hirasawa readily accepts invitation / 'But please remember, I am not the killer. I am not the man you are looking for.' / Casual conversation in local restaurant / Again Hirasawa suddenly says, 'On January 26th, I spent the morning and the early afternoon with my daughter and son-in-law in the Marunouchi district of Tokyo. There we visited the shipping firm of my nephew. His name is Yamaguchi. Then, at a little after 2 p.m., I took a train to Nippori to see my nephew's daughter, Hanako. I also bought some charcoal briquettes. At about 5 p.m. I returned to my house in Nakano. My other daughter had invited a guest, an American GI named Wayne Ely, I think. I spent the evening speaking English and playing cards with her guest.' / Steer conversation on to casual topics; food, weather etc. / Hirasawa repeatedly mentions his connections to the Imperial Family, his good reputation as a painter and as a man / Restaurant photographer asks if we are ready for traditional dinner-table portrait / Hirasawa reluctant / Puts on his spectacles, sticks out his chin / Portrait taken / Then, without prompting, Hirasawa suddenly says again, 'I regret having lost Dr Matsui's card. I enjoyed meeting him and talking with him. I would like to see him again. Unfortunately, a thief picked my pocket last August. He stole my wallet which contained ¥10,000 and all the name-cards I had received, including the card Dr Matsui gave me.' / Meal finishes / Inspector Iki-i pays for dinner-table portrait / Bid farewell to Hirasawa / Iki-i places portrait in Hirasawa file / Return to Otaru Police Station / No sleep.

1948/6/13; 06.00: Take train back to Tokyo.

The Eighth Period (the eighth twenty days of the investigation; 14 June to 3 July, 1948) –

1948/6/14; 06.00: Rain, humid / The second floor of Mejiro Police Station / Full meeting of the Special Investigation Team, including Robbery Room Name-card Team / Police Chief Kita present / Inspector Iki-i details interviews conducted in Tōhoku and Hokkaido / Photograph of Hirasawa and report of interview distributed to all members / Chief Inspector Suzuki (Head of the First Division) and other members of First Investigative Division sceptical / Hirasawa's alibi checked months ago / Alibi solid, reputation good / Photograph does not match composite drawing etc. / Age and appearance do not match witness descriptions of Teigin killer / Iki-i restates that Hirasawa is a strong suspect, behaviour suspicious / Strong hunch, good lead / Suzuki not interested / Waste of time / Other leads, better leads / Move on.
      [VARIOUS PAGES DAMAGED, DEFACED, OR MISSING FOR REASONS UNKNOWN]

1948/6/25; 08.00: Hot / Meeting of Robbery Room Name-card Team / Directive issued: *Detectives should pay particular attention to the following persons who have i) experience in handling medicines or hygiene, ii) experience in medical research, experiments or study, iii) experience in China with the above, and iv) former members of the Tokumu Kikan or Kempei because the suspect had experience and knowledge of i) the quantities of poison needed, of ii) the timing needed, of iii) the control of the victims, of iv) the amount he himself could take and of v) the equipment and tools needed* / Emphasis again taken off the name-card teams / Information ignored / Sidelined again / Despondent.
      [VARIOUS PAGES DAMAGED, DEFACED, OR MISSING FOR REASONS UNKNOWN]

The Ninth Period (the ninth twenty days of the investigation; 4 July to 23 July, 1948) –

[VARIOUS PAGES DAMAGED, DEFACED, OR MISSING FOR REASONS UNKNOWN]

The Tenth Period (the tenth twenty days of the investigation; 24 July to 12 August, 1948) –

[VARIOUS PAGES DAMAGED, DEFACED, OR MISSING FOR REASONS UNKNOWN]

The Eleventh Period (the eleventh twenty days of the investigation; 13 August to 1 September, 1948) –

[VARIOUS PAGES DAMAGED, DEFACED, OR MISSING FOR REASONS UNKNOWN]

1948/8/13; 08.00: Hot, humid / Meeting of Robbery Room Name-card Team / Police Chief Kita present / Chief Kita states all other leads exhausted / Kita orders direct investigation of Hirasawa Sadamichi / Begin with Hirasawa's family in Tokyo / Report results of investigation directly to him at his residence in Meguro / Do not disclose direction of investigation or share information with First Investigative Division / All information classified SECRET.

1948/8/14; 10.00: Hot / Visit the father of Hirasawa's daughter-in-law, wife of Hirasawa's eldest son / Father of Hirasawa's daughter-in-law addicted to gambling / Heavy debts, minor charges / Lean on him for information / Provides us with list of guests at wedding of his daughter to Hirasawa's son / Suggests we speak directly to Hirasawa's eldest daughter / Claims daughter has voiced suspicions about her father and Teigin incident / **14.00:** Visit Hirasawa's daughter's place of work; Marufuku coffee shop / Nervous and intimidated / Request to talk to her in private / Outside workplace, daughter suddenly says, 'This is about the Teigin incident and my father, isn't it?' / 'Why do you say that?' / 'Because you've already interviewed him and because he looks so much like the composite drawing.' / 'You think he resembles the drawing?' / 'Not only me. The manager of the coffee shop – he was a police chief in Kanagawa before the war – and he said the resemblance was enough to make the police suspicious.' / Tell her this questioning is just routine / Make small talk to relax her / Begin to ask about her father and his relations with rest of the family / She says they have not seen him since the end of January / Ask if this is usual / 'No.' / 'How do you all manage with your father in Hokkaido and you in Tokyo?' / 'Before he left for Hokkaido, he gave my mother ¥80,000.' / '¥80,000 is a lot of money.' / 'Yes, but he told her it was to last for eight months. He told her if she was to spend only ¥10,000 a month, it would be enough.' / 'And your father gave your mother this ¥80,000 at the end of January?' / 'Yes.' / *Kuro-kuro* / 'Not before?' / 'No.' / *Blacker and blacker* / 'You're certain?' / 'Yes. Why? Have I said something I shouldn't have?' / *Guiltier and guiltier* / 'No.' / Now says she must return home to her two children / Escort her home to her residence in Nakano Ward / Buy her box of peaches as a thank-you present for taking up her time / **18.00:** Report back to Robbery Room Name-card Team / *Blacker and blacker, guiltier and guiltier.*

1948/8/16; 06.00: Very hot, very humid / Meeting of Robbery Room Name-card Team / Divide into *ji-dōri* teams to question Nakano neighbourhood about Hirasawa family / **08.00:** Begin questioning of Nakano area / Street by street, house by house, door to door / All day / **22.00:** Meeting of Robbery Room Name-card Team / Chief Kita present / Each *ji-dōri* team reports day's questioning / Inspector Iki-i then details information gathered about Hirasawa's finances / In December last year, Hirasawa was in considerable debt; for example, he did not have the cash to purchase a small wardrobe priced at ¥2,500 / *Kuro-kuro* / Hirasawa and his wife forced to borrow variously ¥500 and ¥1,000 from friends and relatives / *Blacker and blacker* / However, following the Teigin incident, the Higashi Nakano branch of the Mitsubishi Bank shows ¥20,000 in his wife's account and ¥44,500 in Hirasawa's own account / *Guiltier and guiltier* / Sudden deposits unexplained / Re-state statement by Hirasawa's eldest daughter concerning ¥80,000 given to his wife at the end of January / Chief Kita states he will present all evidence and information to the Tokyo Prosecutor's Office tomorrow morning / Kita confident arrest warrant will be granted / Told to prepare to travel to Hokkaido to arrest Hirasawa and bring him back to Tokyo for formal interrogation / Elation.

1948/8/17; 08.00: Hot / Gather at Inspector Iki-i's residence in Ōmori / Collate all evidence and information on Hirasawa / Prepare request for arrest warrant for Hirasawa Sadamichi / Prepare requests for search warrants for houses of Hirasawa's family and relatives in Tokyo / No sleep.

1948/8/18; 13.00: Hot / Robbery Room Name-card Team HQ / Receive telephone call from Hirasawa's eldest daughter / Frantic, desperate / Asks for meeting / Claim to be too busy / Desperate, persists / Daughter says family worried / Her mother's younger brother, her uncle, accusing her of selling her own father to the cops for a box of fruit / Speak to Inspector Iki-i / Agree to meeting / **16.00:** Meet Hirasawa's eldest daughter with Iki-i on second floor of Marufuku coffee shop / Daughter requests we visit her mother at family home to ease her fears and worries / Promise to visit in next few days / Daughter persists / Asks exactly which day at exactly what time / Promise to visit her mother in three days / **17.00:** Meeting with daughter ends / Return to Iki-i residence in Ōmori / Detective [NAME DELETED] of First Investigative Division waiting / States that imminent arrest of Hirasawa now common knowledge / Newspapers already sniffing around / Requests that he arrest Hirasawa on our behalf / Argument, fight / Table upturned, punches thrown / Detective [NAME DELETED] says, 'You Name-card guys are all crazy.' / Detective [NAME DELETED] leaves / **20.00:** Telephone call from Investigation HQ / All expenses and funding for Name-card Team suspended until further notice / Obvious attempt to stop Name-card Team travelling to Hokkaido to arrest Hirasawa / **21.00:** Inspector Iki-i calls his bank manager at home / Arranges mortgage of Ōmori house and telephone line to cover cost of travel to Hokkaido if arrest warrant granted / All anxious, all nervous / No sleep.

1948/8/19; 17.00: Very hot, very humid / Meeting of Robbery Room Name-card Team at HQ / Police Chief Kita present / Arrest warrant for Hirasawa Sadamichi granted / Elation / Chief Kita cautions that news of arrest warrant has already been leaked to newspapers / Suspects detectives from First Investigative Division / Anger / Kita states that Chief Inspector Suzuki has requested presence of First Investigative Division Detective Tomitsuka at arrest

44

of Hirasawa / Fury / Kita notes Detective Tomitsuka has already left Tokyo for Otaru / Resignation / No sleep.

1948/8/20; 06.00: Hot / Leave Tokyo for Otaru, Hokkaido via Niigata and Akita / Travelling with Inspector Iki-i, and Detectives Iiga and Fukushi / Very slow train, very hot train / No conversation, no sleep / Very anxious, very nervous.

1948/8/21; 10.00: Arrive in Otaru, Hokkaido / Meet First Investigative Division Detective Tomitsuka / Go to Hirasawa's father's residence / Hirasawa's father and younger brother greet us formally / Shown upstairs / Hirasawa dressed and waiting, seated before same canvas / Arrest Hirasawa on suspicion of the murder by poison of the twelve employees of the Shiinamachi branch of the Teikoku Bank on 26 January this year, and the attempted murder of four other employees at the same place on the same day / **11.00:** Take Hirasawa to Otaru Police Station / Telephone calls to Tokyo HQ / Warned of press reports / Make necessary travel arrangements / Spend rest of day and night at Otaru Police Station / No sleep.

1948/8/22; 06.00: Hot / Return to Tokyo on Tōhoku Honsen Line / News of arrest leaked to press / Crowds at every station en route to see Hirasawa / Newspapermen and cameramen board the train at Morioka, Sendai and Taira / Train repeatedly delayed by crowds / Spend journey keeping press at bay / Hirasawa crouched on floor / Blanket over his head / Does not speak, sleep, eat or drink.

1948/8/23; 05.45: Hot, humid / Arrive Ueno Station / Chaos, crowds / Time of arrival leaked to press / Members of First Investigative Division and Officials of Tokyo Prosecutor's Office waiting / Hand Hirasawa over to members of First Investigative Division and officials of Tokyo Prosecutor's Office / Lose sight of Hirasawa Sadamichi in the chaos and the crowds –
     [THE NOTEBOOK ENDS HERE]

Beneath the Black Gate, in its upper chamber, in the occult circle, the detective now says, 'That was me finished. And the rest you know. The interrogation and the confession. The recantation and the trial. The conviction and the sentence. The appeals and the campaigns.

'But I cannot die,' the detective continues. 'I cannot die until I see Hirasawa executed. For I know he did that crime. I know he killed those people. So no more tears. No more tears for him.

'For this city is a notebook. In blunt pencil and on coarse paper. A notebook now closed. A case now closed . . .'

A second candle now out.

But in his city of conviction, you say, you laugh, you scream, 'I will give you tears, you dog! You deceitful, lying dog!'

Because you hate detectives, and you hate dogs, and all detectives are dogs, all dogs detectives, and so you push this detective, this dog, to the ground and you kick him in his gut and you kick him in his head, in his deceits and in his lies, and then you tip open his boxes and you rip up his notebooks, and now you take out your matches and you start a fire, a fire of his boxes and his notebooks, shouting, 'Liar! Liar! Liar-Dog! Dog-Liar! You lie! Lie!'

But the detective is laughing at you, laughing and barking, 'He did it! He did it! And you, you should thank me!'

Among the smoke and among the flames, his fingers and his paws, still laughing and still barking, as you shout –

'It wasn't him! I know it wasn't him!'

But now the pasts and the futures, their memories and their dreams, their deceits and their lies, their voices and their words, are all gone again; the Black Gate, the occult circle spinning again, spinning and spinning, and you are spinning, spinning and spinning,

through the laden wind, through the haunted air,

spinning and spinning, the detective gone –

Only his notes, his words remain –

Taunting you, mocking you –

You and your book, your book that is no book, as you pick up your pen and then drop your pen, drop and pick up, start and then stop, stop and then –

Here beneath the Black Gate, in the occult circle of its ten candles, a voice whispers, whispers from the shadows, 'I am a Survivor. And I have the same dream, night after night . . .'

And from out of those shadows, a woman crawls towards you, on her hands and on her knees, and she says again, 'The same dream. 'Night after night, the same dream . . .

The Third Candle –

The Testimony of a Survivor

The city is a purgatory. Night after night, the same dream, IN THE OCCUPIED CITY, night after night, the same dream:

I AM THE SURVIVOR

But of course I know: only through luck

Have I survived so many friends.

But night after night

In dream after

Dream

I hear these friends saying of me: 'Those who survive are stronger.' And I hate myself

I hate myself

IN THE OCCUPIED CITY, I wake up. It is cold, in the Occupied City. It is Monday and I do not want to get up. I do not want to get dressed. I do not want to go to work. *Something is wrong.* I want to lie all day beneath this quilt. To sleep and to dream, of food and warmth, of the man who will come and take me away from the cold and the hunger, of the man on a white horse who will save me from the Occupied City. But I must get up. I must get dressed. I must eat breakfast and leave for work. For it is Monday.

Monday 26 January 1948.

In the Occupied City, I walk through the mud and the sleet, the mud on my shoes and the sleet in my hair. *Something is wrong.* Maybe today the bank will close early. Maybe today we can leave early. Maybe today I can go back home early. Maybe I can lie again beneath my quilt. *Because something is wrong.* But I walk through the mud and the sleet, past the shrine and up the hill.

The road is busy and crowded, people coming to Shiinamachi to work, people leaving Shiinamachi to work. An American jeep sounds its horn and makes us all jump to the side. The wheels of the American jeep turn and splatter us with mud.

I know something is wrong.

I slide open the wooden door. I step inside the *genkan* to the bank. I take off my dirty shoes. I put on my freezing slippers. I go down the corridor into the bank. I say good morning to Miss Akuzawa and Miss Akiyama. We talk about the weekend and we talk about the weather as we change into our blue uniforms. We wonder if today the bank will close early. We wonder if today we will be able to leave early. To go back to our homes, back to our quilts. Then we go down the corridor into the main room of the bank.

In the warmth of the heater, in the light from the lamps, I take my seat at the counter and I wait for the bank to open, for the working day to begin, the working week.

Just before half past nine, Mr Ushiyama makes his usual speech which starts every week and we all bow and the clock chimes half past nine and the bank opens and the working day begins, another working week.

The customers come, from out of the mud and out of the sleet, and I greet them and I serve them and I think about my lunch and I listen to the sleet turn to rain as it falls on the roof of the bank. And just after half past twelve, Mr Yoshida tells me I can take my lunch. I change places with Miss Akiyama. I go down the corridor. I sit in the changing room. I take out my *bento*. I open the lunch box. I eat my cold rice and sour pickle. I drink hot tea from my teacup. I listen to the rain as it falls on the roof of the bank and I know I won't be able to leave early today. And just before one, I go back to my seat at the counter and I greet the customers and I serve the customers.

Then, just before two, Mr Ushiyama tells us that he is not feeling well, not feeling well at all. He tells us he must leave early. He apologizes to us and he bows and he leaves.

'Poor Mr Ushiyama,' whispers Miss Akiyama. 'He's been sick since last week. It must be serious. He should go to the doctor. It could be, it could be . . .'

I stare at the counter and I nod my head. *Something is wrong.*

'And then what if it's contagious?' says Miss Akiyama. 'We might all have caught it. We might all become sick. We might all . . .'

I stare at the counter and I nod my head. *Very wrong.*

But I go back to my work. I go back to my thoughts:

Will no one save me from the Occupied City?

Just before quarter past three and the bank has closed for the day, and now I have only thirty deposits left to check. I will be able to do them in ten minutes. In ten minutes, I will be able to leave.

In ten minutes, I will be able to go back to my home, back to my quilt and back to my dreams. *But something is wrong, very wrong. Something is not right today . . .*

And then I hear the knock upon the side door. I have only twenty-five deposits left to check. I see Miss Akuzawa get up to open the side door. I have only twenty deposits left to check. I see Miss Akuzawa go into the back of the bank. Fifteen deposits. I see Miss Akuzawa go to the front door of the bank. Fourteen deposits. I see the front door open and a man step inside. *Is this the man?* Thirteen deposits. I see the man take off his boots and put on the pair of slippers Miss Akuzawa offers him. *The man who will save me?* The man is in his forties but he has a handsome, oval face. *Save me from the Occupied City?* I hear Miss Akuzawa tell the man that the manager has already left, but that our assistant manager will see him.

I hope this does not mean extra work. I hope this does not mean I cannot leave soon. I see Miss Akuzawa lead the man past my counter and into the back of the bank. Now Miss Akiyama gets up from her seat next to mine and I turn back to the deposits:

Twelve, eleven, ten, nine, eight, seven, six deposits. Five, four, three, two, one deposit, none. I have finished now.

But something is wrong, very wrong . . .

Miss Akiyama comes back to her seat at the counter. She nudges me and she whispers, 'Did you see that man? That man is a doctor from the Ministry of Health and Welfare. I just heard him tell Mr Yoshida that the Ministry of Health and Welfare have discovered an outbreak of dysentery in Shiinamachi. The Ministry of Health and Welfare have traced the outbreak to that well in front of Mr Aida's house. You know Mr Aida?'

I look up from my pile of deposits. I nod my head.

'That doctor from the Ministry of Health and Welfare just told Mr Yoshida that one of Mr Aida's tenants has been diagnosed with dysentery. That doctor said that this tenant came into the bank today and he made a deposit . . .'

'What was his name?' I ask her.

Miss Akiyama is shaking her head, flicking through her pile of deposits on the counter. 'I didn't catch it but if it's that well, this will be why Mr Ushiyama's been so sick. This will mean we could all be infected. This could mean . . .'

I look back down at my pile of deposits, all checked and all finished. I start to flick through them, looking for the Aida address.

'The doctor will have to inoculate everyone against dysentery,' whispers Miss Akiyama. 'And he'll have to disinfect everything that may have been infected. All the rooms, all the money. No one will be allowed to leave until he's finished . . .'

I stare at the deposits and I nod again. Now I know I won't be able to leave soon. *Now I know something is very wrong.* Now I know I won't be able to go back to my home, not back to my quilt, not back to my dreams, for now I know those dreams are all gone.

Mr Takeuchi comes over to the counter. Mr Takeuchi sighs and he says, 'We all have to assemble at Mr Yoshida's desk. We all have to take some medicine . . .'

'I told you, I told you,' whispers Miss Akiyama as we get up from our seats at the counter and go over to Mr Yoshida's desk at the back of the bank.

Miss Akuzawa has brought all our teacups on a tray to Mr Yoshida's desk. The doctor from the Health and Welfare Ministry is opening a small bottle. This doctor is in his forties.

And now I look him in his face.

It is round, very round.

Like an egg. And I know, I know I will never forget this face.

Now I look at the bottle in his hand. I read FIRST DRUG written in English on its label.

'Is everybody here?' asks the doctor.

Mr Yoshida quickly looks at each of us, counting our heads. Even Mr Takizawa's two children are here. Mr Yoshida nods.

'Good,' says the doctor and picks up a pipette. The doctor drips some clear liquid into each of our cups. The doctor tells us to each pick up our own teacup. I reach for my teacup.

I lift it up to my mouth but I stop.

The doctor has his hand raised in warning. The doctor says, 'This serum is very strong and if it touches your teeth or gums it can cause great damage. So please listen and watch carefully as I demonstrate how to swallow the serum safely.'

Now the doctor takes out a syringe. The doctor dips the syringe into the liquid. The doctor draws up a measure of the liquid

51

into the syrinhe. The doctor opens his mouth. The doctor places his tongue over his bottom front teeth and tucks it under his lower lip. The doctor drips the liquid onto his tongue. The doctor tilts back his head and lets the medicine roll back into his throat.

Now the doctor looks at his wristwatch, his right hand raised, poised in the air. Suddenly, the doctor's hand falls and he says, 'Because this medicine may damage your gums and your teeth, you must all be sure to swallow it quickly. Exactly one minute after you have taken the first medicine, I will administer a second medicine . . .'

I look down at Mr Yoshida's desk again. I see another bottle, a bottle marked SECOND DRUG in English letters.

'After you have taken the second medicine, you will be able to drink water and rinse out your mouths.'

We all nod. I nod.

'Now lift up your cups,' says the doctor.

I pick up my teacup.

'Now drip the liquid onto your tongues.'

I put my teacup to my lips and I drink the liquid. It is horrible. It tastes so bitter, so very, very bitter.

'Tilt back your heads.'

I tilt back my head.

'Now swallow.'

I swallow.

'I will administer the second drug in precisely sixty seconds, so please put your teacups back on the table.'

I put my teacup back down on Mr Yoshida's desk. I look up at the doctor. The doctor is staring at his wristwatch. I can still taste the liquid in my mouth.

'It tastes a bit like gin,' laughs Mr Yoshida.

'I don't think I've swallowed any,' says Mr Tanaka. 'Perhaps I should have another measure. Just to be sure . . .

'Just to be safe.'

But the doctor shakes his head, still staring at his wristwatch.

'It tastes disgusting,' says Miss Akiyama. 'May I please gargle with some water?'

But again the doctor shakes his head, still staring at his wristwatch.

'But it's so very vile,' says Miss Akiyama again.

Now the doctor begins to pour the second drug into each of our teacups. Then the doctor looks up at us all. And the doctor says, 'Please pick up your teacups again.'

I pick up my teacup again.

Now the doctor checks his wristwatch again. Now the doctor gestures for us each to drink.

And now I put my teacup to my lips again and now I drink the second liquid and now I can taste the second liquid in my mouth, in my throat, and it is horrible too, and now I need to drink some water, some water, some water, and now I can hear people complaining and people coughing, and now I hear the doctor saying –

'You can rinse out your mouths now . . .'

– and now I see everyone rushing for the sink, for the tap, for the water, and now I am rushing for the sink, for the tap, for the water, and now I see people falling to the floor, and now I see Miss Akiyama lying on the floor, and now I am trying to reach her but I need the sink, the tap, the water, and now I am thinking I'll get to the sink, to the tap, to the water, then I'll come back to Miss Akiyama, people coughing, people retching, people vomiting, and now I can feel people pushing past me, people clambering over me to get to the sink, to the tap, to the water and now I am drinking and drinking and drinking, but now the light is fading and fading and fading, now the light is leaving us, leaving us here, here in the Occupied City, and now I feel a grey-ness coming and into the grey-ness,

I am falling, I am falling, I am falling,

I am falling, I am falling,

I am falling,

into the grey-ness, I am falling,

falling and falling away,

away from the light,

from the Occupied City, towards a grey place,

a place that is no place. But then the light

grips me, it holds me tight, tight,

tight, it pulls me back

Down the bank's corridors, into the bank's genkan. Help me! *Through the doors, into the street.* On my hands and on my knees, I crawl through the Occupied City. *Into the light, into the sleet.* Help me, I say. *She is drunk, she is mad.* In the mud and in the sleet, on my hands and on my knees, in the Occupied City. *Help me . . .*

'Please help me!'

IN THE OCCUPIED CITY, I hear boots in the mud, I hear sirens in the sky. But I am falling again. In the Occupied City, people are asking me my name. I am still falling. In the Occupied City, I do not know my name. For I am falling. In the Occupied City, I am moving. I am falling. In the Occupied City, I am in a white room. But I am still falling. In the Occupied City, people keep asking me my name. In the Occupied City, I do not know my name. For I am falling. In the Occupied City, people are asking me what happened. I am still falling. In the Occupied City, I do not know what happened.

And then I stop. I stop falling

IN THE OCCUPIED CITY, a young woman. Help me. On her hands and on her knees, she crawls through the Occupied City. Help me, she says. In the mud and in the sleet, on her hands and on her knees, in the Occupied City.

Please help me

IN THE OCCUPIED CITY, nuns are sticking a hose down my throat, doctors are pumping my stomach, and I am coughing and I am retching, fluid and bile, rambling and ranting. But I can speak again. And I am talking now. Men sat beside my bed. Men stood beside my bed. Men holding my hand. Men whispering in my ear.

And I am talking, talking to the men beside my bed. The men who are holding my hand, holding it tight, tight, tight.

'The drink,' I whisper. 'The drink . . .'

'But what did you eat?' they ask.

'It was the drink. The drink . . .'

'What did you drink?'

'It was medicine . . .'

'A medicine?'

'A doctor . . .'

'What doctor?'

'Dysentery . . .'

The men beside my bed let go of my hand. The men beside my bed stand up now. The men beside my bed say, 'This is not a case of food poisoning, Detectives.'

And now the men beside my bed leave, shouting, 'This is a case of murder! Of robbery . . .'

And then the men are gone and I am alone, in the white room, I am alone again, in the Occupied City.

And I am afraid.

I am scared.

That night, that dream, IN THE OCCUPIED CITY, that night, for the first time, that dream: I AM THE SURVIVOR

But of course I know: only through luck

Have I survived so many friends.

But night after night

In dream after

Dream

I hear these friends saying of me: 'Those who survive are stronger.' And I wake and I hate myself

I hate myself

In a white room, I wake again. It is a hospital. There are nuns and there are nurses and there are doctors. They are giving me drugs. They are giving me medicines. But I am afraid.

I am afraid in this place, of this place, this hospital. I am afraid of the nuns. I am afraid of the nurses.

I am afraid of the doctors.

I am afraid of their drugs. I am afraid of their medicines.

But in this place, in this hospital, I close my eyes and, for the second time, I dream the same dream: I AM THE SURVIVOR

But of course I know: only through luck

Have I survived so many friends.

But night after night

In dream after

Dream

I hear these friends saying of me: 'Those who survive are stronger.' And I hate myself

I hate myself

IN THE OCCUPIED CITY, I open my eyes. I am awake again in the white room. In the hospital. But a man in a white coat is holding my hand, a man whispering in my ear, a man sat beside my bed. And I am afraid and so I pull away from this man in a white coat beside my bed, this man who is whispering in my ear and holding my hand, and I say, 'Get away! Get away! Get away from me!'

And now this man lets go of my hand and now I am alone again in this white room, in this place

IN THE OCCUPIED CITY, a young woman. Help me. On her hands and on her knees, she crawls through the Occupied City. Help

me, she says. In the mud and in the sleet, on her hands and on her knees, in the Occupied City.

Please help me

'I can help you. Please believe me. I can help you . . .'

IN THE OCCUPIED CITY, I am awake again, my hand in another hand again, the whispers in my ear again:

'I can help you. You can trust me . . .'

'Who are you? Are you a doctor?'

'No, this white coat is just so I could talk to you. That's all. I just want to talk to you. I just want to help you.'

'But why? Who are you?'

'My name is Takeuchi Riichi. I am a journalist.'

In this place, in this white room, in this hospital, I want to cry, but I am laughing, 'You're a journalist?'

'Yes, with the *Yomiuri.*'

I want to laugh, but I am crying, 'Get away from me!'

And again, the hand is gone, and again the whispers are gone, and again I am alone in this place, in this white room, in this hospital, and again I am afraid in this place, and again

IN THE OCCUPIED CITY, a young woman. Help me. On her hands and on her knees, she crawls through the Occupied City. Help me, she says. In the mud and in the sleet, on her hands and on her knees, in the Occupied City.

Please help me

'I can help you. Please believe me. I can help you. I can make that dream go away . . .'

In this place, I open my eyes. In this white room, I squeeze his hand. In this hospital, I whisper, 'How can you help me?'

'I can save you from this place, these dreams.'

'Until yesterday,' I say. 'I thought a cup was a cup. Until then, a table was a table. I thought the war was over. I knew we had lost. I knew we had surrendered. I knew we were now occupied.

'But I thought the war was over. I thought a cup was still a cup. That medicine was medicine. I thought my friend was my friend, a colleague was a colleague. A doctor, a doctor.

'But the war is not over. A cup is not a cup. Medicine is not medicine. A friend not a friend, a colleague not a colleague. For a colleague here yesterday, sat in the seat at the counter beside me, that colleague is not here today. Because a doctor is not a doctor.

56

'A doctor is a murderer. A killer.

'Because the war is not over.

'The war is never over.'

'I know,' says the man in the white coat beside my bed, the man who is not a doctor, the man who is a journalist, this man called Takeuchi Riichi, this Takeuchi Riichi who now squeezes my hand tight, tight, tight, and who says again and again and again, 'I know.'

'I was still going through that day's thirty deposits when the killer arrived. I didn't see what time it was when he entered, but business had closed as usual at 3 p.m., and I had then immediately begun to count up the deposits. The thirty deposits would have taken me no longer than ten minutes, which means the killer must have arrived sometime between 3 p.m. and 3.10 p.m.

'When the killer began to distribute the poison, I looked him in his face. I will never forget that face. I would know it anywhere.'

'I know,' he says. 'I know.'

'I am a survivor,' I tell him. 'But of course I know only through luck have I survived so many friends. But night after night, in dream after dream, I hear these friends saying of me: "Those who survive are stronger." And I hate myself.

'I hate myself.'

'I know,' he says again, 'But I will help you . . .'

IN THE OCCUPIED CITY, it is 4 February 1948.

There are flowers and there are presents, photographers and well-wishers. The nuns, the nurses, and the doctors stand in a line to bow and wish me well. And I bow back and I thank them and then I leave this place, this hospital, and I step outside.

But something is still wrong . . .

IN THE OCCUPIED CITY, it is cold and it is grey, and there are more flowers and there are more presents, more photographers and more well-wishers. Mr Yoshida, Mr Tanaka and Miss Akuzawa are here too, and we greet each other for the first time since that day, trying to smile as the cameras flash and the reporters shout, thinking of our colleagues who are not here, who will never be here to receive these flowers and these presents as the smiles slip from our lips and fall to the floor of this cold, grey Occupied City.

And now we are led through the crowds to the cars, the cars which are waiting to take us back, back to the bank, the bank and the scene of the crime. And so we sit in the backs of these cars and we stare out at the cold, grey Occupied City, the cold, grey Occupied City which stares back into these cars at us and whispers through the windows, '*In due time, in due time . . .*'

The cars turn up past the Nagasaki Shrine and now the cars pull up outside the Shiinamachi branch of the Teikoku Bank and I don't want to get out of the car, I don't want to get out of the car, but a policeman has the door open and my hand in his as I step out of the car and into the mud and into the sleet and I want to drop to the ground and crawl on my hands and on my knees away from this place, away from this city, but where would I crawl, where would I go, for there are no white horses here, no one here to save me from the Occupied City, and now I am standing in the *genkan* of the bank, taking off my hospital shoes, putting on my freezing slippers and going down the corridor into the bank with my eyes closed tight, tight, tight; tight, tight, tight for I AM THE SURVIVOR

But of course I know: only through luck

Have I survived so many friends.

But night after night

In dream after

Dream

I hear these friends saying of me: 'Those who survive are stronger.' And I hate myself

I hate myself

IN THE OCCUPIED CITY, I wake up. It is cold, in the Occupied City. I do not know what day it is and I do not want to get up. I do not want to get dressed. *For something is wrong.* But I do not want to lie all day beneath this quilt. I do not want to sleep because I do not want to dream. So I get up and I think, *something is wrong.* The room is cold and I know, *something is very wrong.* I walk through the house but no one is here. I open cupboards and I open drawers. Among the rubbish I find the newspaper and I open the newspaper and I look for his name, for *Takeuchi Riichi.* And I find his name and I see the story he has written, a story about a letter, a letter his paper has received and I read the story, I read his words:

Dear Teikoku Bank, Shiinamachi, Toshima Ward.

I am sorry I caused quite a disturbance the other day. At first I had an unpleasant feeling watching so many people writhe and

squirm in agony but later I didn't mind at all. I let Miss Murata Masako live because I have some use for her later.

In due time, I shall pay her a second visit.

Signed, Yamaguchi Jirō.

And now I hear the tapping on the front door and I am walking through the house and I am opening the door, hoping and praying that he will be here, here to take me away, to save me from the Occupied City, but it is only another policeman, only another car, another car come to take me back to the police station, back for another interview and another look through another book of photographs, and so I sit in the back of another car and I stare again at the cold, grey Occupied City, the cold, grey Occupied City which stares back into the car at me and whispers again and again and again through the window, *'In due time, in due time . . .'*

IN THE OCCUPIED CITY, in the Mejiro Police Station, the detectives say, 'The man's name is Hibi Shosuke. He was arrested two days ago by the Toyohashi Municipal Police on a shoplifting charge. When Hibi was taken into custody, the Toyohashi Police found on his person newspaper clippings relating to the Teigin incident as well as a map of Itabashi Ward, ¥10,000 in cash and ¥1,000-worth of lottery tickets. Subsequent inquiries have revealed that Hibi applied for a four-day vacation from the Electro Communications Engineering Bureau where he works, from 24 to 28 January. Hibi also bought ¥10,000-worth of savings bonds on 31 January. According to his company, Hibi has easy access to potassium cyanide through his work. Finally, Toyohashi Police believe Hibi's features exactly match those of our Teigin suspect.'

Now the detectives place a piece of paper on the table before me and say, 'So we would like you to carefully study this telephoto of the suspect from Kyodo's Nagoya office . . .'

I stare down at the piece of paper on the table before me, hoping and praying that he will be here, here to take me away, but I shake my head and I say again, 'When the killer began to distribute the poison, I looked him in his face. I will never forget that face.

'I would know it anywhere.'

'We know,' they say.

'But this is not that face. This is not his face. I am sorry.'

The detectives take away the piece of paper from the table and say, 'Thank you for your time. A car will take you home.'

And again the police are gone, and again the questions are gone, and again I am alone in my room, alone in this city, and again I am afraid in this city, afraid in this place

IN THE OCCUPIED CITY, a young woman. Help me. On her hands and on her knees, she crawls through the Occupied City. Help me, she says. In the mud and in the sleet, on her hands and on her knees, in the Occupied City.

Please help me

IN THE OCCUPIED CITY, I wake up. It is warm now, springtime in the Occupied City. But it is Monday and I do not want to get up. I do not want to get dressed. *For something is still wrong.* But today I cannot lie all day beneath this quilt. Today I must get up. I must get dressed. But I do not want to eat breakfast. Today I cannot eat breakfast. For today is my first day back at work.

Work. Work. Work.

In the Occupied City, I walk through the mud and the drizzle, the mud on my shoes and the drizzle in my hair. *Something still wrong.* But I walk through the mud and the drizzle, past the shrine and up the hill, the road busy and crowded, people coming to Shiinamachi to work, people leaving Shiinamachi to work. An American jeep sounds its horn and we all jump to the side. The wheels of the American jeep turn and splatter us with mud.

Something always wrong.

I slide open the wooden door. I step inside the *genkan* to the bank. I take off my dirty shoes. I put on my cold slippers. I go down the corridor into the bank. I say good morning to Miss Akuzawa. But we do not talk about the weekend and we do not talk about the weather as we change into our blue uniforms. We do not talk at all. Then we go down the corridor into the main room of the bank.

In the warmth of the heater, in the light from the lamps, I take my seat at the counter and I wait for the bank to open, for the working day to begin, the working week.

Just before half past nine, Mr Ushiyama makes his usual speech which starts every week and we all bow and the clock chimes half past nine and the bank opens and the working day begins, another working week, but I know *something is wrong . . .*

For the police come every week, every day, to take me away from the bank, back to Mejiro, for more interviews and more books of photographs. And then the press come and the photographers. And I spend more time with the police and with the press than at work in the bank. And sometimes he comes, Takeuchi Riichi of the *Yomiuri*. And sometimes he takes me for coffee. And sometimes he brings me flowers. And sometimes he invites me for dinner. But every night I go back to my room, back to my quilt, and every night I close my eyes tight, tight, tight and I remember I AM THE SURVIVOR

But of course I know: only through luck

Have I survived so many friends.

But night after night

In dream after

Dream

I hear these friends saying of me: 'Those who survive are stronger.' And I hate myself

I hate myself

IN THE OCCUPIED CITY, I wake up. It is hot now, summertime in the Occupied City. And there is banging on the door and I am walking through the house and I am opening the door, hoping and praying that he will be here, here to take me away, to save me from the Occupied City, but it is only Takeuchi Riichi with another car, another car come to take me to Ueno Station, and so I sit in the back of another car and I stare again at the hot, humid Occupied City, the hot, humid Occupied City which stares back into the car at me and whispers, *'In due time, in due time . . .'*

IN THE OCCUPIED CITY, in Ueno Station, Mr Takeuchi leads me through the crowds, through the crowds that have come to see a man, a man who everyone believes is the man who murdered my colleagues and my friends, the man who tried to kill me, a man called Hirasawa Sadamichi. But I cannot see this Hirasawa Sadamichi. For this Hirasawa Sadamichi is hiding his face beneath heavy blankets. And then this Hirasawa Sadamichi is gone, lost in the crowds, and I am holding on tight, tight, tight to Takeuchi Riichi, my eyes closed tight, tight, tight because

IN THE OCCUPIED CITY, a young woman. Help me. On her hands and on her knees, she crawls through the Occupied City. Help me, she says. In the mud and in the sleet, on her hands and on her knees, in the Occupied City.

Please help me

IN THE OCCUPIED CITY, at the Sakuradamon Police Station, the detectives lead me into the interrogation room, and Hirasawa Sadamichi looks up from the table at me and now I stare back at him. I look him in his face and now Hirasawa Sadamichi looks away, back down at the table, and then the detectives take me away, away down the corridor, away to another interrogation room, another interrogation room where I say, 'When the killer began to distribute the poison, I looked him in his face.

'I will never forget that face.'

'We know,' they say.

'I would know it anywhere.'

'We know,' they say again. 'And this is that face . . .'

But now I shake my head and I say, 'This man is not the killer. The killer had a round face. Very round, like an egg. That man in that room has a square face. Very square, like a box. He is also too old. He is not that man. I am sorry. He is not the killer. I am sorry.'

'But your colleague, Mr Tanaka, is convinced that man in that room, that man Hirasawa, is the killer . . .'

'I am sorry. He is not the killer.'

'But Mr Tanaka swears he is.'

'I am sorry.'

IN THE OCCUPIED CITY, at the Sakuradamon Police Station, three times the detectives lead me into the interrogation room, and three times Hirasawa Sadamichi looks up from the table at me and three times I stare back at him. Three times I look him in his face and three times Hirasawa Sadamichi looks away, back down at the table, and three times the detectives take me away, away down the corridor, away to another interrogation room, another interrogation room where three times I say, 'When the killer began to distribute the poison, I looked him in his face. I will never forget that face.'

And three times they say, 'We know. We know. We know.'

'I would know it anywhere.'

Three times they say, 'And this is that face . . .'

But three times I shake my head and three times I say, 'This man is not the killer. The killer had a round face. Very round, like an egg. That man in that room has a square face. Very square, like a box. He is also too old. He is not that man. I am sorry.

'He is not the killer. I am sorry.'

'But your colleague, Mr Tanaka, is convinced that man in that room, that man Hirasawa, is the killer . . .'

'I am sorry. He is not the killer.'

'But Mr Tanaka swears he is.'

'I am sorry. I am sorry . . .'

IN THE OCCUPIED CITY, a young woman. Help me. On her hands and on her knees, she crawls through the Occupied City. Help me, she says. In the mud and in the sleet, on her hands and on her knees, in the Occupied City.

Please help me

IN THE OCCUPIED CITY, I wake up. It is still hot, September now in the Occupied City. And again there is banging on the door and again I am walking through the house and again I am opening the door, and again I am hoping and again I am praying that he will be here, here to take me away, to save me from the Occupied City, but it is only Takeuchi Riichi, Takeuchi Riichi come to tell me, 'He's confessed! Hirasawa has confessed!'

IN THE OCCUPIED CITY, in early November, I marry Takeuchi Riichi. The wedding ceremony is coordinated by Riichi's closest friend, one of Police Chief Kita's principal deputies.

And I know something is wrong, very, very wrong . . .

But I close my eyes tight, tight, tight, and try to forget. But every night I close my eyes tight, tight, tight and I remember:

I AM THE SURVIVOR

But of course I know: only through luck

Have I survived so many friends.

But night after night

In dream after

Dream

I hear these friends saying of me: 'Those who survive are stronger.' And I hate myself

I hate myself

IN THE OCCUPIED CITY, and later in the Liberated City, I wake up. I wake up tired all the time. For they never leave me alone. I have given them interview after interview. And now I am tired all the time. I had hoped they would go away, but still they come and ask their questions. Once a year, every year, every January, they come again with their questions. Every 26 January, on my second birthday; the day I pray for my three fellow survivors. The day I pray for my twelve murdered colleagues. The day I pray for someone to come and take me away, to save me from the Occupied City, but no one comes.

For there are no white horses, no white horses any more . . .

IN THE OCCUPIED CITY, I wake again. And I look again for him; in the doorway, at the window, at the table, by my bed, opening a small bottle, dripping its liquid into a teacup

And now I am reaching for that cup

Lifting it to my mouth

But then I stop. For he is not here. He is never here. Never

In due time, in due time . . .

And so I crawl on, I crawl on, through this city

This place, this purgatory, I crawl on

Beneath the Black Gate, in its upper chamber, on her hands and on her knees, she crawls towards the ten candles, in their occult circle, on her hands and on her knees, she crawls towards the third candle,

the third candle which gutters, gutters and then dies,

and she is gone, back into the shadows.

But in this occult circle, you are crawling now, among its nine candles, you are crawling, in the upper chamber of the Black Gate, on your hands and on your knees, crawling around, among the ruins,

the ruins of this city, the ruins of this book,

your book, your ruined

book; here where you fluctuate between despair and elation, despair at the death and destruction, elation at the death and destruction, here among the rivers of ink and the mountains of paper, the bonfires of words and the pits in the ground, the pits to be filled in with the ashes, the ashes from those bonfires,

the ashes of meaning.

But among these ashes and ruins, among this death and destruction, you do not crawl for long –

For now beneath the Black Gate, in this occult circle, a pair of trousers, a suit of clothes, are swinging from a beam, and now you look up and now you see, you see a white clay mask where a face should be, the white clay mask of a mouse, swinging back and forth, swinging forth and back, among strange balloons, among green crosses, and beneath the cuffs of its trousers, there sits the medium,

the medium who sits and who speaks,

speaks now and says:

'I was a medical doctor. I was a bacteriologist. And I was a colonel. I served at Camp Detrick, the secret headquarters of the US Chemical Warfare Service in Maryland. My job was to develop BW defensive measures and devise means for offensive retaliation in case of a biological attack against the United States or its combat forces. From 1943 to 1945 I was responsible for research into bacteriology, virology, medicine, pharmacology, physiology and chemistry. My job was to find out how diseases were passed from person to person, especially those diseases which can be transferred to man by rats, by fleas, by ticks, by lice or by mosquitoes. That was my job.

'And it was a dangerous job.

'During our exploration of brucellosis, my entire team

succumbed to it. The same with tularemia. There were casualties in the workshop. Many of my fellow scientists succumbed.

'Many of my fellow scientists died.

'And many, many went mad.

'But it was a race against time because we knew the Germans, the Soviets and the Japanese were already ahead of us in the game.

'Especially the Japs. For we knew, even then, we knew –

'For in 1944, I was called into the office of the Scientific Director, Dr Oram C. Woolpert; Intelligence had received news of Jap germ warfare attacks on the Chinese in Manchuria –

'Tommy, we think they've killed a lot of people,' he told me. 'We think they've been poisoning reservoirs, poisoning wells . . .'

'So we knew, even then, we all knew.

'Then, in the Summer of 1945, General MacArthur personally requested that I join him in Manila to await the coming assault on the Japanese mainland. So I flew to Manila. I went straight to MacArthur's headquarters. I met with General MacArthur, General Charles Willoughby and Karl T. Compton. I had met Compton before. I knew he was the former president of the Massachusetts Institute of Technology, that he was a civilian who wore the three stars of a lieutenant general, the chief of Scientific Intelligence. I had not met Willoughby before. But I knew he was the head of G-2, US Military Intelligence. And I had not met General MacArthur before. But I immediately liked him. I immediately respected him. He knew the weight of the responsibility he was carrying. He also knew the dangers of BW. The General asked me what I thought. He asked me what I feared. He listened to me and then the General said –

'We need you very badly here, Tommy.'

'Then they told me about Operations Olympia and Coronet, the planned land, sea and air assaults on the Japanese home islands. They told me I would go ashore at H plus 6; H plus 6 meant six hours after the first bombardment; H plus 6 meant the very first wave of assault troops –

'Be careful not to break your test tubes, Tommy,' laughed the General. And so I waited. And I waited.

'But H plus 6 never came.

'The first bomb was dropped on August 6, the second bomb on August 9, and the Japs surrendered on August 15. But I was already on my way to Japan aboard the USS *Sturgis*. For I had been given a new mission. This time I had been well briefed.

'This time they had knocked. This time they had introduced themselves. They told me they were from G-2. They told me they were from Scientific Intelligence. They said I was the top man in biological warfare. They said I was needed in Japan. My mission was to find out as much as I could, and as quickly as I could, about the Jap biological warfare programme. About Unit 731. About Unit 100.

'About Shirō Ishii; they told me to find Ishii.

'But the Japs had been told about me.

'The Japs were waiting for me . . .'

And now a bundle of envelopes, a heavy, heavy wad of envelopes bound and tied with another length of rope, a thick, thick cord, falls from a dead pocket of the swinging suit and now you crawl, on your hands and on your knees, into the centre of the occult circle and you tear open these heavy, heavy envelopes and pull out a thick, thick wad of papers, and by the light of the nine candles, in the upper chamber of the Black Gate, you read through these papers, these papers that are half-letters / half-documents, sometimes hand-scrawled / sometimes type-written, but always tear-stained and already blood-blotted, you read, always tear-stained and already blood-blotted, among strange balloons, among green crosses,

you read, stained and blotted, you are
among strange balloons, among
green crosses, always stained,
already blotted . . .

The Fourth Candle –

The (Dead) Letters of an American

Marked PERSONAL

Dai-Ichi Hotel, Tokyo, Japan
September 18, 1945

My dearest Peggy,

I hope this letter finds you & the children all well.

I am well, so please do not worry about me (even though I know you do). I am only sorry that I have not been able to write to you sooner, but work has been very busy since I left Manila.

I doubt I will ever forget my first sight of Japan's coastline. It stretched before us like a long thin line of green earth with a thin line of white surf. It looked peaceful & un-peopled – no smoking chimneys, or trains, or traffic. Of course, it was an illusion!

We finally docked in Japan at Yokohama on August 21st & from day one I have found this to be a very strange place & the Japs to be a very strange people. Of course, their country is completely hurt & ruined in a way that is unimaginable to people back home. Our bombing of Tokyo, & I suppose of most other cities, certainly hit the Japanese home, right where the average man would feel it most. One can hardly believe the reports in American papers that the Japs do not know they lost the war. The evidence of it is everywhere, inescapable, & in many respects permanent. There are places here where, as far as one can see, lies only miles of rubble. Some temples & museums are gone for good, & the rest will take decades to restore. The ordinary people look ragged & distraught. They remind me of timid mice (but there are others among them who are as sharp as rats). The children are the friendliest.

As you know, my mission is to find out as much as I can about the Japanese biological warfare program. However, it seems the Japs already know more about me than I know about them!

My interpreter is called Dr Naitō & he was waiting for me on the quayside at Yokohama. He actually had a photograph of me taken back at Camp Detrick (& heaven only knows how he got hold of that). He walked up the gangway to meet me & his first words were, 'Dr Thompson, I presume?'

Naitō is very friendly but is not to be trusted and I'll give you an example of what it is like here with some of them. The first night I was in Tokyo, Naitō took me out for dinner to one of the big hotels (there is still the good life here for some of them). The hotel restaurant was in the traditional Japanese style, very Spartan with mats & sliding doors. Naitō even unlaced my shoes for me! He then introduced me to this very old, tiny Jap who said, 'Welcome to Japan, Dr Thompson. I hope you like tempura?'

Naitō told me that the man was a senior vice-president of a major Japanese company, the equivalent of our General Electric. Then dozens of waitresses appeared in kimonos with trays of Japanese food & alcohol. Naitō & the old man proposed lots of toasts to new friendships & they were most impressed I could use their chopsticks. But at the end of the evening the old man suddenly said, 'How would Dr Thompson like to earn $5,000 a week for the rest of his life?'

I imagined your reaction & I laughed & I said who wouldn't want to earn $5,000 a week for the rest of their life! But then the old man said, 'Well, it's very easy. By doing nothing!'

I then realized they were being very serious & so I became very angry. I turned to Naitō & told him in no uncertain terms that I wanted to leave immediately. Of course, they were very embarrassed. All the way back to the hotel, Naitō apologized again & again because he was sure I would sack him or report him. I must admit I was sorely tempted but I need him if I am to complete my mission quickly (& get out of here). So, as I say, they are not to be trusted.

By the way, tell George that General MacArthur arrived in Tokyo on August 30th & that I was waiting for him at the US embassy. The General had assembled a huge motorcade of men & equipment & had even arranged for air cover from fighters & bombers. The General meant to teach the Japs a lesson & so he thundered through the city, in his motorcade, with his air-cover, the short distance from the embassy, past the Imperial Palace, to the Dai-Ichi Building, his new headquarters. Tell George that I was in the third jeep behind the

69

General. The streets were deserted, the lights all out, but we knew they were watching & the hairs rose on the back of my neck. You can also tell George that I have a personally signed portrait of the General for him (& let's all hope it will one day be <u>President</u> MacArthur because he is a great man & an inspiration. It is true he can often be brusque, but I guess you have to be something of an egotist if you get to that position of authority. You are very aware though that he feels very heavily the weight of the responsibility he is carrying. He has talked to me for hours about BW & what I think & what I fear).

Finally, another interesting thing happened the other day when Naitō & I were walking along the Ginza (their main shopping street). I saw this old Jap tumble off his bicycle in the middle of the traffic & so I automatically ran forward to help him up from under the wheels of the passing cars & dusted him down. But then this old Jap turned to me & spat in my face & rode away! I asked Naitō why; was it because I was an American, because we had won the war? But Naitō said it was because I had saved the old Jap's life & so now he would feel he owed me his life. He would also know he could never repay me. So he spat in my face! Well, that's gratitude for you!

As I say, it's certainly a very strange place & the Japs are a very, very strange people.

Please kiss the children for me. Tell George that the Japs are still crazy about baseball & so I get all the latest news & tell Emily I'll bring back one of those Jap dolls for her (as I promised).

All my love, Murray.

*

Stamped RESTRICTED

APO 500-Advanced Echelon
September 27, 1945

To: Colonel Harlan Worthley, Office of the Chief Chemical Warfare
Service, Special Project Division,
Gravelly Point, Washington, D.C.

Dear Colonel Worthley,

Sufficient time has now elapsed since my arrival in Japan to permit a preliminary analysis of Japanese BW activities. While this is a purely informal statement sent to you with Colonel Copthorne's permission, it will give you an idea of what may generally be expected in the near future. Detailed reports will of course be available through channels.

To begin with, I was very fortunate to be assigned to the scientific section under Drs K. T. Compton and E. L. Moreland. This was entirely due to the energetic and timely action of Colonel Copthorne. I feel quite strongly that this temporary attachment has permitted a type of investigation that would not have been possible under other circumstances. I should also like to emphasize that the chief chemical officer has demonstrated an unusual appreciation of technical problems. As a result of being associated with this committee my work has had an impetus which will, I think, permit evaluation of the problem (for whatever it is worth).

So progress is being made at this end and I think the pace will soon be greatly accelerated. So far as my mission is concerned, it has been necessary to follow GHQ policy in dealing with the Japs. However, efforts have been made to place me in an advantageous position. Up to this time, I have been permitted to contact only civilians and have spent a good deal of time at the Ministry of Public Health and the Government Institute for Infectious Diseases. Most fortunately one of my number one targets in the person of Prof. Miyagawa has been in the latter institution. He is a virus man, is familiar with all my work, and is apparently most anxious to stay in good graces (I trust none of them). I have approached Miyagawa as the Theatre Surgeon's representative. It is fortunate that this is true and that I am investigating recent advances in infectious diseases for the Surgeon. It provides an excellent means of entry and to date I have not mentioned our subject for fear that the target will vanish.

However, I am amassing a prodigious file and will have material for reports soon. I do think it will be desirable to write a very detailed report for Special Projects Division when I return, more detailed than the Chemical Theatre Officer or Surgeon would wish.

Thanks to Miyagawa I have had extensive conferences with senior scientists and I have several things to report:

1. A great deal of work has been done in infectious diseases. If half of the Jap claims are true – and I am going to have chance to check – then there is a tremendous amount of investigation to do.

2. For the past two or three years, Miyagawa himself (he seems to be top dog in the field) has worked on a method for large-scale preservation of biological materials at room temperature. He claims to have perfected this method and has tested the following substances after one year of preservation (with no loss of potency):

a) Bacillus coli
b) B. prodigiosus
c) Rickettsia
d) Lymphogranuloma
e) Drugs
f) Blood constituents
g) Colloidal suspensions of certain metals which he claims have marvelous therapeutic qualities.

Next week I am taking a trip with him to investigate the apparatus and to meet his colleague, a physicist. Naturally, as a medical officer representing the Surgeon, I am interested in blood components and in drugs which may be of therapeutic value.

I also have appointments at the Army Medical College and certain other installations. On the whole I am impressed with potentialities here and elsewhere and feel that I can say a definite start has been made.

No mention of several vaccines and certain epidemiological observations have been made because I wish to check protocols and laboratory findings.

However, as a result of my status with the committee it is also apparent that the present and the immediate future will be the productive periods. Dr Moreland plans to leave Japan in five or six weeks and it will be necessary for me to carry out my principal investigations during this time. Colonel Copthorne is in agreement with me that my mission will probably be completed shortly after this committee is dissolved.

I plan to return to the United States when my work is brought to an end, which should be sometime in November.

Sincerely, Lt. Col. Murray Thompson.

*

Marked PERSONAL

Dai-Ichi Hotel, Tokyo, Japan
October 27, 1945

My dearest Peggy,
I hope this letter finds you & the children all well. Thank you so very much for your last letters and parcel. I cannot tell you how much it meant to me to read all your news of home and the children.
I am well, so do not worry about me. I have been working hard since my last letter & I hope now my work here is almost done.

72

Initially, however, I was worried that I would not be able to complete my report as I was receiving little or no cooperation from the Japs. They connived & they lied to keep me in the dark. They gave me nothing & they told me nothing. I could not help blaming Naitō for this state of affairs. To be very honest, Peggy, I felt despondent.

However, the General summoned me to his office & advised me to call their bluff. As always, it was good advice. I returned to my own office & I told Naitō that I had lost face with the General & that he was sending me home as I was a total failure as an inquirer. I told Naitō that the General had ordered a much tougher investigator to be sent here to replace me as the General felt I had been too kind to him (Naitō) because I had given rations to him & his family. I also told Naitō that the General said it was now time for the Soviets to be involved. Well, you should have seen Naitō's face drop!

The next morning Naitō was waiting for me with a handwritten document marked, PRIVATE (SECRET) INFORMATION FOR COLONEL THOMPSON'S EYES ONLY. Naitō said he now felt it was his duty to tell me all he knew about BW to help my 'sincere investigation as a fellow scientist'.

I was elated as I knew the General's advice & my bluff had paid off but, naturally, I still played it cool with Naitō (you have to, with all of them). I severely rebuked him for not giving me this information sooner. But Naitō claimed he had wanted to tell me all this from Day One but felt he could not do so without the permission of the higher officers of Jap HQ.

I must say, Naitō did seem very scared & he repeatedly begged me to burn the pages he had given me after I had read them & never to use his name when speaking to the men he had listed. He claimed he would be killed if anyone discovered he had given me this information. I believed him but, then again, he may well have been acting (they are _all_ very, very good actors).

I still had one question for Naitō (the _only_ question that really matters to me) & so I asked him then & there, 'Were Allied prisoners ever used as experimental guinea pigs?'

Naitō vowed to me, 'on the lives of his children, on the souls of his parents', that no Allied prisoners were ever used as experimental guinea pigs. Again, I believed him & so I wrote in my own hand at the end of his document, 'I have asked Dr Naitō whether prisoners were ever used as experimental guinea pigs. He *vows that this has not been the case' and I signed it, Dr M. Thompson, Lt. Col.*

I then took the document directly to the General himself. I must admit it was one of the most exciting moments of my life because this document was the breakthrough we needed. It was dynamite. The General & all his top men (Willoughby & Compton) were equally delighted with the document & my bluff. Of course, I knew now the hard work would really begin &, even though we had the names we needed (thanks to Naitō), there was still no guarantee that if we found these men they would talk to me. We were also worried about the Soviets scaring them all away. But I had a plan & I suggested to the General that we tell Naitō that no one involved in BW would be prosecuted as a war criminal, as long as they told us everything we needed to know. I felt this was the only way to make them all come out of hiding & start talking. The General & all the other guys agreed with me that this was the best way & the General himself said (& I quote), 'Well, Tommy, you're the man in charge of the scientific aspects of this investigation. If you feel you cannot get all the information, we're not given to torture, then offer him (Naitō) that promise as coming from General MacArthur himself – and get that data!' I must admit I felt very proud of myself!

So I immediately put the deal on the table to Naitō & I swear the Jap had tears of gratitude in his eyes as he thanked me.

Well, after all that, it has been plain sailing. I have been able to speak to all their top men & to get all their information.

As I write to you today, my report is being typed up. Once it has been checked & submitted, I believe I will be able to return home to you all, via Manila. Of course, I will wire you with my exact arrival as soon as it is confirmed through channels.

So, until that happy day, kiss George & Emily for me, and start dusting down the bunting as I will see you all <u>soon</u>!!!

With all my love, Murray.

*

Stamped SECRET

APO 500-Advanced Echelon
November 1, 1945

To: Colonel Harlan Worthley, Office of the Chief Chemical Warfare
                Service, Special Project Division,
                Gravelly Point, Washington, D.C.

Dear Colonel Worthley,

I am enclosing my finished report and I would like to take this opportunity to supply further background details about my investigation and how much of the information was gained.

On October 4, I received handwritten information from Lt. Col. Naitō, a Japanese medical officer. It was written in very poor English, difficult to understand, but I immediately realized these twelve pages were dynamite because the document lays out the organization of the Bōeki Kyūsuibū (Water Purification Unit) and admits that it had been engaged in BW. It also ties Ishii with the Unit and with BW and it even seems to tie in the Emperor (though Naitō denies it, of course).

Colonel Naitō stated that he was divulging this information, which was considered by the Japs as secret, only because he felt that the information would be developed later and that by an effort on their part to be truthful we would be more lenient with them. My request for the military to supply us with information on BW, according to Naitō, created consternation among the higher officials of the General Headquarters of the Japanese army. After much discussion and debate, it was decided by the General Staff to furnish us with the information requested. Naitō indicated that the chief of the Bureau of Medicine of the Japanese army and the chief of the Section of Sanitation and other technical personnel were in favor of furnishing us with all details. On the other hand, the members of the General Staff, comparable to our own OPD, were opposed to giving the information.

To summarize, Naitō stated that the Japanese army had an organization for BW, both defensive <u>and</u> offensive. The offensive operations were under 'Second Section of War Operation' under the General Staff. The research and defensive work was under the Bureau of Medical Affairs and known as 'Section of Sanitation'. Three organizations figured prominently in the actual work. Foremost of these was the installation at Harbin, Manchuria, under the jurisdiction of the Kwantung Army. The other two were under the China Army in Nanking and at the Army Medical College here in Tokyo.

The main research work at Harbin was under the direction of Lt. Gen. Shirō Ishii and apparently was conducted between the years 1936 and 1945 (there is some likelihood that Ishii will be apprehended shortly).

Colonel Naitō stated that the reason for planning offensive research was because the Japs expected that Soviet Russia might attack Japan with

BW, especially in Manchuria. He states that there was some BW sabotage (inoculating horses with anthrax) in the northern part of Manchuria during 1944 or 1945 while the Japs were building the Peiangcheng–Heiho railroad. Further, he stated that Japan should be prepared for revenge in case the enemy used illegal warfare.

Naitō advised that the Emperor did not like the preparation for chemical warfare by the Japanese army or navy. Because of this the scale of research for chemical warfare was not permitted to be large. Since the General Staff was cognizant of the Emperor's feeling on chemical warfare they insisted that the work on biological warfare should not refer to offensive preparations. They therefore referred to all work on BW as being purely defensive.

Naitō stated that General Headquarters made no attempt to begin active BW and did not plan to unless the enemy initiated this type of warfare. As an afterthought he stated that the circumstances during the last period of the war became such that the Japs were unable to start BW.

The following agents were listed by Naitō as having been studied: Plague, cholera, dysentery, salmonellas and anthrax. He stated that none of the filterable viruses were studied because of, 'the difficulty to get them in mass'!

Colonel Naitō fears that all the experimental records at Harbin may have been burnt at the beginning of Russia's sudden invasion. He stated, however, that if we succeed in securing one of the key personnel of the Harbin installation, it should be possible to obtain information concerning the work carried on there.

The following studies were made by the Army Medical College in Tokyo:

- a) Studies on cheopis flea, zoological studies for the purpose of defense and tests of insecticides.
- b) Studies on mass production of bacteria, in connection with possible sudden large-scale demands for immunizing agents to combat large cholera or plague epidemics.
- c) Studies on some poisons which are hard to detect, for instance 'fugu' toxin.
- d) Studies on keeping bacteria in a living state by the lyophile process.

Comment: I asked Naitō whether prisoners were ever used as experimental 'guinea pigs'. Naitō 'vows' that this was never done.

Finally, it is gratifying to note, as you will see in my report, that our intelligence on Jap BW activities collected during the war was accurate insofar as the defensive organization was concerned.

I now plan to return to the United States and I look forward to seeing you again on your next visit to Camp Detrick.

Sincerely, Lt. Col. Murray Thompson.

DOCUMENT INSERT, ATTACHED TO LETTER:

SECRET

REPORT
OF
SCIENTIFIC INTELLIGENCE SURVEY IN JAPAN

September and October 1945

VOLUME V

BIOLOGICAL WARFARE (BW)

TABLE OF CONTENTS

SUMMARY: BIOLOGICAL WARFARE (BW)

1.   Responsible officers of both the army and navy have freely admitted to an interest in defensive BW.
2.   Naval officers maintain that offensive BW was not investigated.
3.   Information has been obtained that from 1936 to 1945 the Japanese army fostered offensive BW, probably on a large scale. This was apparently done without the knowledge (and possibly contrary to the wishes) of the Emperor. If this was the case, reluctance to give information relative to offensive BW is partially explained.
4.   BW seems to have been largely a military activity, with civilian talent excluded in all but minor roles.
5.   The initial stimulus for Japanese participation in BW seems to have been twofold:
     a)   The influence of Lt. Gen. Shirō Ishii.
     b)   The conviction that the Russians had practiced BW in Manchuria in 1935, and that they might use it again (the Chinese were similarly accused).

6. The principal BW center was situated in Pingfan, near Harbin, Manchuria. This was a large self-sufficient installation with a garrison of 3,000 by 1939–40 (reduced to 1,500 in 1945).

7. Intensive efforts were extended to develop BW into a practical weapon, at least eight types of special bombs being tested for large-scale dissemination of bacteria.

8. The most thoroughly investigated munition was the Uji type-50 bomb. More than 2,000 of these bombs were used in field trials. The Ha bomb, too, was exploded experimentally. Note that whereas the Uji bomb was an all-purpose munition, the Ha bomb was constructed and produced with only one purpose in mind – the dispersion of anthrax spores. The immediate effect was gained by shrapnel bursts with secondary considerations given to ground contamination. The statement has been made that a scratch wound from a single piece of shrapnel was sufficient to produce illness and death in 50–90% of the horses, and in 90–100% of the sheep exposed in experiments. More than 500 sheep were used in such field trials and estimates of horses similarly expended vary from 100 to 200.

9. Employing static techniques and drop tests from planes, approximately 4,000 bombs were used in field trials at Pingfan.

10. By 1939, definite progress had been made, but the Japanese at no time were in a position to use BW as a weapon. However, their advances in certain bomb types was such as to warrant the closest scrutiny of the Japanese work.

11. <u>Japanese offensive BW was characterized by a curious mixture of foresight, energy, ingenuity and at the same time, lack of imagination with surprisingly amateurish approaches to some aspects of the work.</u>

12. Organisms which were considered as possible candidates for BW, and which were tested in the laboratory or in the field included: all types of gastrointestinal bacterial pathogens, P. pestis (plague), B. anthracis (anthrax) and M. malleomyces (glanders).

13. Japanese defensive BW stresses:
    a) Organizations of fixed and mobile preventive medicine units (with emphasis on water purification).
    b) An accelerated vaccine-production program.
    c) A system of BW education of medical officers in all echelons (BW Defensive Intelligence Institute).

14. The principal reasons for the Japanese failure were:
    a) Limited or improper selection of BW agents.
    b) Denial (even prohibition) of cooperated scientific effort.

c) Lack of cooperation of the various elements of the army (e.g. ordnance).
d) Exclusion of civilian scientists, thus denying the project the best technical talent in the Empire.
e) A policy of retrenchment at a crucial point in the development of the project.

CONCLUSIONS:

It is the opinion of the investigating officer that:
a) If a policy had been followed in 1939 which would have permitted the reasonably generous budget to be strengthened by an organization with some power in the Japanese military system, and which would have stressed integration of services and cooperation among the workers, the Japanese BW project might well have produced a practical weapon.
b) However, since the Japanese dreaded the United States' capacity for retaliating in kind (i.e. BW) or with chemical warfare agents, it is most unlikely that they would have used a BW attack against American troops even if the weapon had been at hand.
c) The Japanese are fully aware of the reasons for the failure in their development of BW. It is extremely unlikely that they would repeat their mistakes.

SUPPLEMENT 1a, ATTACHED TO DOCUMENT:

Map indicating that the Japanese army had 'water purification units' attached to their 18th, 31st, 33rd, 49th, 53rd, 54th, 55th, and 56th Divisions stationed in Burma, with larger fixed field 'water purification units' at Rangoon and Mandalay.

DISTRIBUTION

Report on Scientific Intelligence Survey

Agency	Vol. V
C/S, GHQ, AFPAC	1
Chief Surgeon, GHQ, AFPAC	2
Chief Chemical Officer, GHQ, AFPAC	2
Nav. Tech. Jap.	2

A C of S, G-2
          Att: War Department Intelligence   3
                      Target Section.
War Department, G-2
          Att: Scientific Branch   39
Air Technical Intl. Group, FEAF   2
Lt. Col. M. Thompson   1

Stencils have been sent to G-2, War Department, where additional copies may be made available upon request.

– Report ends –

*

Marked PERSONAL

Dai-Ichi Hotel, Tokyo, Japan
November 18, 1945

My dearest Peggy,
I hope, with all my heart, that you and the children are all well. As you know, I had hoped (& prayed) to be home with you all by now or, at the very latest, for Thanksgiving.
Unfortunately, things have taken a turn for the worse here. I know now that they have lied to me (these Japs) & my work here is far from done. I realize that they flattered me in order to distract me, faking respect for my reputation & my work at the College of Physicians & Surgeons. I realize, too, that I have been blinded by their titles & ranks, their own reputations & work.
There is something, however, I should have told you before but I suppose I was ashamed even then because I already knew (in my heart of hearts) that I had made a mistake. I suppose, also, that I was worried you would think less of me as a husband & as a father (& as a man) had you known (& I worry you may yet think so).
Back in October, before I had even completed my report, I received a strange visit at my room here at the Dai-Ichi Hotel. I was lying on my bed, tired as usual, but unable to sleep when I heard a curious scratching outside my window. Imagine my surprise when I opened the curtains & saw a Jap, clinging for dear life to the water pipe, & staring back through the window at me. I ran back to my bed & grabbed my revolver from under my pillow. I

80

then opened the window & grabbed the Jap by the hairs on his neck & hauled him into the room. He was wearing a beret, a sweatshirt & trousers & he was cowering & shaking before me. But he then pulled a document from the belt of his trousers & held it out to me. I took it from him with my left hand but all the time I kept my finger on the trigger of my revolver. I asked him who he was & what this document was. He told me he was a former BW engineer & that this document was the blueprint of a bomb known as the Uji bomb. He told me that this bomb was loaded with plague germs, that over one hundred were produced but that they did not work very well. He also told me experiments were carried out using Chinese prisoners.

I asked him for more details & he told me that the prisoners were chained to stakes at varying distances from the bomb, that the bomb was then detonated & records were taken as to the differing impact of the bomb & its germs on the prisoners at their various distances. He told me many prisoners died. He then told me that the prisoners were both Chinese <u>AND</u> American.

Of course, I was shocked & asked him where these experiments took place. He told me the experiments were conducted in a place called Pingfan, a suburb of Harbin, & and also at Mukden. He told me they also <u>inoculated</u> Chinese <u>&</u> American prisoners of war with bubonic plague.

As you know, my dearest Peggy, first and foremost, above all else, I am a medical doctor. I took the Hippocratic Oath & I believe in the words of that oath. I believe in the sanctity of human life.

So I knew then that I had made a mistake, a huge & terrible mistake, a mistake that would haunt me from then on if I did not take immediate steps to correct it. I knew I had to rectify my mistake.

I went straight to the General's office. I told the General (& Willoughby & Compton) that Naitō had lied to me, lied to us all. I told them that we had no choice now but to scotch their immunity deal, that we had no choice now but to <u>prosecute them all</u>.

Well, the General raised his eyebrows & lit his pipe & then he said (& I quote), 'Well, first we need more evidence. We can't simply act on this. So keep going, keep going . . .'

Willoughby & Compton agreed with him (as usual) & Willoughby even added that I should 'keep quiet.'

I admit I was surprised by their reaction. Most of all, I was surprised they were <u>not</u> surprised by this new information.

Of course, I went straight back to Naitō & I gave him a piece of my mind. As usual, he was most apologetic but it cut no ice with me.

I demanded he give me all the information he had on this place called Pingfan & that if he did not, I would have him arrested as a war criminal on General MacArthur's orders (this was a lie but two can play at that game, I thought).

Anyway, lie or not, it had the desired effect on Naitō. He told me he didn't really know much about the place, just what he'd heard from conversations he'd had with scientists who had worked there. But he thought that Unit 731 (the name they use) chose Pingfan because it was 'the perfect place'; the temperature was ideal, with an average wind speed of ten to twelve miles per hour, the optimal conditions for disseminating bacteria. The perfect place, he kept saying. He also said (& I quote again), 'But, I promise you, no human beings were involved in the experiments there.' Liar, I thought to myself & I knew then that Pingfan was a place I must see with my own eyes.

Well, the plane (a B29) was ready & waiting for me at Tokyo airport to fly me to China and Pingfan. I was aboard, the propellers turning, when the engine suddenly stopped & the pilot came back down the plane. He said he had just received orders from General MacArthur himself & that I was recalled & was not to go to Pingfan. I could not believe it & so I headed straight back to GHQ.

The General was waiting for me with Willoughby & Compton. He said it was simply too risky for me to go to Pingfan because relations with the Soviets were deteriorating daily & the General could not risk a B29 falling into their hands.

Willoughby also now claimed that all our intelligence in mainland China indicated that Pingfan had been razed on the day of surrender & that it was nothing but a ruin now, that there was nothing to see. Nothing to see indeed, I thought to myself. That is the story of my time here.

So to my regret & to my shame (but on their orders), nowhere in my report, neither with regard to the Uji bomb nor the Ha bomb, did I make reference to any human experiments, nor is there reference to the blueprint I had received from the BW engineer & his allegation that prisoners of war had been killed in experiments.

Things then took a further bad turn within hours of me filing the report. I was back at the hotel, already packing & dreaming of seeing you all, when there was a knock on my door. It was a reporter from the wire services. He was holding a copy of my report & said it looked 'very interesting' & that he wanted to know more. Of course, I asked him how on earth he got hold of it & he said that there was a heap of them on a desk at GHQ, that they were only marked RESTRICTED & that the press were allowed to read anything marked RESTRICTED. I immediately commandeered a jeep from the desk clerk & drove back to Dai-Ichi HQ. I ran up the stairs to the General's outer office. It was dark and unlocked & there, on the desk, was a pile of my reports all marked RESTRICTED. I counted them up. There were twenty-eight, twenty-nine including the one in my hand. However, if the General's secretary had done as I had asked & made thirty copies, then one copy was still missing.

There is no doubt in my mind that Naitō had taken the missing copy (though, of course, he denies it) & that my report was already being read out in the suburbs by the senior members of Unit 731. No doubt too, they were celebrating my incompetence.

I hope you will also understand, from all I have told you, why I cannot return home to you & the children until I have corrected my mistake. I beg your understanding, patience & forgiveness.

Think of me this Thanksgiving, as I will be thinking of you all that day, as I think of you and miss you all each and every day.

With all my love, your husband, Murray.

*

Stamped TOP SECRET

APO 500-Advanced Echelon
December 9, 1945

To: Colonel Harlan Worthley, Office of the Chief Chemical Warfare
            Service, Special Project Division,
            Gravelly Point, Washington, D.C.

Dear Colonel Worthley,

It is with great regret, and heavy heart, that I write this letter to you. However, I am duty- and honor-bound to tell you that I sincerely regret writing the report dated November 1, 1945.

Almost immediately upon completion of the above-mentioned report, I was confronted with new information which contradicted statements included in my report. I realize now that my report includes statements that are not only contradictory but also <u>false</u>.

Many of these contradictions & falsehoods are the result of my (misplaced) trust in Lt. Col. Naitō. I thought Naitō was quick, helpful, efficient and very humble. I thought he worked a long day, every day, and then went home dutifully to his wife. I now know (though he does not know I know) that he does nothing of the sort. Every night, he leaves my office here at Supreme Allied HQ in the Dai-Ichi Building and makes immediately for a rendezvous with senior members of Unit 731 and Unit 100 who are hiding here in the suburbs of Tokyo. He goes to brief them on what I am finding out which – thanks to him – is precious little. I know now he has been controlling me and it is his job to make sure I don't find out too much. He has been very good at his job (up to now).

It is true that thanks to Naitō I was able to interview Yoshijirō Umezu, the chief of the Army General Staff and commander-in-chief of the former Kwantung Army. I also interviewed Tadakazu Wakamatsu, the Vice-Minister of War; Lt. Gen. Torashirō Kawabe, vice-chief of the Army General Staff; Hiroshi Kambayashi and Nobuaki Hori, the army and navy Surgeon Generals; Colonel Saburo Idezuki, chief, Division of Preventative Medicine, Tokyo Army Medical College; Colonel Takamoto Inoue, chief, Bacteriological Section, Tokyo Army Medical College; Colonel Tomosada Masuda, Ishii's deputy; Major Junichi Kaneko, the BW bomb expert; Lt. Col. Seiichi Niizuma, a senior army technical expert.

I asked them about fuses, detonations and scattering devices. I asked them about their 'bacillus bomb'. I showed them the *Red Book* – the book with the details of Special Bomb Mark 7 – which we had captured in the South Pacific in May 1944.

Of course, they must have known that this was all I knew, that this was all we had. They also knew all I really wanted to know was where Ishii was. But, repeatedly, they all told me they presumed the commander of Unit 731 was still in Manchuria, or even dead. But I now know they were lying (all of them).

However, based on these interviews and the information that Naitō gave me, and which at that time I believed (wrongly) to be true, it was my recommendation to SCAP that no one involved in the Jap BW program be prosecuted as a war criminal. I made this recommendation in the sincere (but false) belief that no prisoners were ever used as experimental 'guinea pigs', as Naitō had 'vowed' that this was never the case. This I know now was a complete and utter lie (among many, many others).

Now I have a new and secret informant – whose identity, at this stage, I cannot reveal. But I will say that my new informant was an engineer with Unit 731 in China and has supplied me with the documentation and information which details the extent of the offensive Jap BW program. Furthermore, this informant is willing to testify that prisoners were used as 'guinea pigs'. It is my belief that this informant of mine has provided the documentation and testimony needed to prosecute members of Unit 731 and Unit 100 as war criminals.

As protocol dictates, I have furnished SCAP with this new intelligence but, for reasons that remain unclear, I have yet to receive any direction or instruction as to how to proceed. I fear, however, that time is of the essence and that we cannot afford to procrastinate any longer.

As you know, President Truman has appointed Joseph B. Keenan as our chief prosecutor at the IMTFE and Keenan is expected here in Tokyo any day now with his team of lawyers. I believe a meeting with the prosecution should be arranged as soon as possible, but await confirmation of your consent and further instructions in all these matters.

Sincerely, Lt. Col. Murray Thompson.

*

Marked PERSONAL

Dai-Ichi Hotel, Tokyo, Japan
January 27, 1946

My dearest Peggy,

I hope you & the children are all well & that you were able to enjoy a merry Christmas & a happy New Year. I am only sorry, with all my heart, that I was not there to enjoy the holidays with you. However, I fear I would have been poor company as I have had a bad cough (though worry not, I am certain I am over the worst of it now).

To be honest, these past few weeks have not been easy ones & I have now been forced to take matters into my own hands in regard to my work. I did so only after much thought & soul searching but in the sincere hope that I would be able to bring matters here to a head & a swift conclusion would follow. I am still hopeful that this will prove to be the case & that sooner-than-you-think I'll be walking up the driveway to our house (never to leave again!).

To my consternation, & in spite of many interviews with the General & letters to Washington, I have still received no response to my urgent requests to follow up on the allegations of human experiments &, in particular, to locate & question Lt. Gen. Ishii (the top man in charge of the offensive Jap BW program in China).

But, as my father used to say, you have to beat the ground to startle the snakes & so I have been beating the ground very hard here in Tokyo. Very hard, indeed!

Earlier this month, I received a copy of George Merck's personal report to Secretary of War Patterson on Allied BW activities during the war.

Merck included in his report the following sentence: 'There is no evidence that the enemy ever resorted to this (BW) means of warfare.' But, in his conclusion, Merck stressed that continued efforts in BW research were vital to America's security.

Having read this report, I realized I needed help. I called the one Jap journalist who has been helpful to me & I gave him everything I knew about Ishii & Unit 731. I told him he could run the story, but not to use my name. I then asked him for a favor in return. I asked him to call The Pacific Stars & Stripes newspaper & to give them everything I had given him. Of course, I asked him to leave out my name & to attribute all quotes to 'Japanese Communist leaders'.

Two days later the article ran, quoting Japanese Communist leaders accusing 'members of the Japanese Medical Corps' of inoculating American & Chinese prisoners of war with bubonic plague virus. It went on (& I quote): 'Dr Shirō Ishii, former lieutenant general in the Japanese Surgeons' Corps and former head of the Ishii Institute in Harbin, directed "human guinea pig" tests both at Mukden and Harbin.'

The article claimed that experiments at Canton had backfired & that plague had broken out in the city. It further stated that Ishii, despite having had a mock funeral staged, was alive & well & living in Japan. Well, as you can imagine, all hell broke loose & before I knew it I was back in the General's office (though no one suspects it was me who so well & truly let the cat out of the bag)!

Anyway, Willoughby (who I do not trust) told me that Masaji Kitano, the commander of Unit 731 from 1942 to 1944, was already on a plane from China & I was to question him upon his arrival in Tokyo. But they saved the best for last – Ishii had also miraculously turned up in Chiba Prefecture & I was to interview him too.

So I am finally to meet the devil & talk with him.

Wish me luck & pray that I'll be back home with you all very soon now. I cannot tell you how much I miss you all & am looking forward to seeing you, so kiss the children from me.

All my love, Murray.

*

APO 500-Advanced Echelon
February 25, 1946

To: Colonel Harlan Worthley, Office of the Chief Chemical Warfare
        Service, Special Project Division,
        Gravelly Point, Washington, D.C.

Dear Colonel Worthley,

I would like to take this opportunity to thank you for your timely and continued support of my request to remain in charge of the Jap BW investigation. I am only too aware that not every one (particularly in G-2) felt I, or anyone from Camp Detrick, should even remain involved.

As you are no doubt aware, the International Prosecution Section for the Tokyo War Crimes Trial is now here in Tokyo and in full swing. I have a meeting scheduled (for March 8) with Lt. Col. Thomas H. Morrow of the IPS, whose brief is to prepare the prosecution's case in relation to Japanese military aggression and war crimes in China. From my initial conversations with Lt. Col. Morrow it is clear that he wishes to bring BW matters before the Tokyo trial.

As you are also aware, I have just completed a series of interrogations with Lt. Gen. Ishii and Lt. Gen. Kitano and much of what was said will be of interest and relevance to Lt. Col. Morrow. However, before sharing any of our information with the IPS, I feel it is only proper to fully brief yourself and the Chemical Warfare Section. To that end, I will be sending – through proper channels – the stenographic transcripts of my interrogations with Lt. Gen. Ishii and Lt. Gen. Kitano. However, I feel it is my duty to bring some matters raised by the interrogations to your immediate attention.

The interrogations were conducted over the best part of the last seven weeks, commencing January 18, after Ishii was finally located (thanks to my 'informant') and brought to Tokyo from his home village in Chiba (where he had been residing all along). During this period, we have also interviewed a further twenty-five intimates of Ishii about him and his work.

I would like to note for the record, however, that it was a great pity that Ishii was not arrested and interned in Sugamo, instead of being merely asked to reside in his Tokyo house while charges against him were being investigated. I do strongly feel that had Ishii been interned in Sugamo with the rest of them, then we would have been able to gain more substantial (and damning) testimony from him. I am aware that Ishii's health is not good (he has chronic chole-cystitis and dysentery), but I feel that should have in no way dictated the location of the interviews (his Tokyo home).

I would also like to note for the record that it was a further source of regret that all interview sessions were conducted in the presence of Ishii's daughter (Harumi). At the request of Lt. Col. D. S. Tait of Technical Intelligence and Lt. E. M. Ellis of the War Department Intelligence Section (who were also both present throughout each interview), and with the approval of GHQ (but against my own wishes), Ishii's daughter also recorded each interview and then typed out the transcriptions which she then delivered on a daily basis to the GHQ building at the Ichigaya garrison in Tokyo (where the War Crimes Trials are to take place). Lt. Ellis also acted as interpreter and it was my personal impression that the answers to many of my questions had already been 'rehearsed' (and the same, in fact, can be said of all the Japs I have interviewed).

It is my opinion that Ishii therefore had ample opportunity to consult his former associates – several of whom we know to be present in Tokyo and the vicinity – since the interrogations were intermittent and much of his information was presented to me by charts and written in answer to our questionnaires.

Furthermore, many of the 'interrogations' were conducted in a far too casual and relaxed environment for my liking (particularly given the severity of the crimes I believe Ishii and Kitano to be guilty of). We were, for example, frequently served meals and invited to attend dinner parties in the company of geisha and hostesses etc. I, of course, refused such offers of hospitality as being inappropriate (but I know others did accept).

I would ask you to bear in mind that the transcripts (to follow) have been reported in the first and third person for purposes of simplification and so I would emphasize that, while the context has been accurately recorded, they are not a verbatim literal record as the interpreter (Lt. Ellis) acted as a channel in the interviews.

The particular points I would like to bring to your attention are as follows:

From the outset, I found Ishii's answers to be guarded, concise and often evasive. Furthermore, I believe that Ishii's repeated claim that all BW records were destroyed to be a pretense, not least because the technical information we did obtain from him (in response to our questionnaires) indicates an amazing familiarity with technical data. Such familiarity naturally leads one to question his contention that all records pertaining to BW research and development were destroyed. As stated above, it is my belief that, in all probability, much of the information Ishii did present was compiled with reference to documentation and with the assistance of his former associates at Pingfan and, no doubt, following much discussion as to what – and what not – to share with us.

Ishii also continues to maintain that no official directive existed for the prosecution of an offensive BW program and that it was conducted purely as a phase of military preventive medicine. He seeks to portray his BW research as being a local, small-scale, almost renegade operation, confined exclusively to Pingfan, and tested on only small animals ('monkeys, rats, squirrels, and other small animals'). He denies any field tests whatsoever were ever conducted, and categorically denies that any experiments were conducted using human 'guinea pigs' ('no humans at all were used in the tests').

Ishii maintains that such allegations and rumors (of human experimentation) have been falsely and maliciously spread about himself and his unit ('A lot of men in my unit, and others who know nothing about it, have been spreading rumors to the effect that some secret work has been carried on in BW . . . I want you to have a clear understanding that this is false') and he claims to be the victim of an orchestrated campaign of blackmail and extortion by disaffected and destitute former subordinates. Tait and Ellis seem to believe him and claim to have seen the proof (in letters and telegrams), though they have yet to share this evidence with me (despite my repeated requests).

Ishii continually stated that all work done in BW was purely defensive and in anticipation of a Soviet BW attack. He claims to know that the Soviets have 'tularemia, typhus fever, cholera, anthrax, and plague bacteria' and that the Soviets had 'completed their BW preparations' and that such knowledge 'frightened' him.

While political analysis is not within the province of the present mission, I feel I would be negligent in my duty as an investigating officer if I did not point out that such diatribes against Russian intrigue stem from poorly informed as well as from thoughtful and responsible sources. The colossal effrontery against common sense is thoroughly demonstrated by such a statement as 'Originally we had no intention of waging war against the United States. The Soviet Union has always been our future possible enemy.' It has been my experience that confused thought and conflicting statements have permeated all my discussions with the highest Jap officers and Lt. Gen. Ishii is no exception. Of course, on the other hand, I do believe that claims about Russian BW activity can hardly be discounted without further evaluation, but it is also my belief that the Japs are also well aware that by making such claims they are telling us (or some of us) <u>what we want to hear</u> while, at the same time, skilfully exonerating themselves.

In regard to plague – of particular interest to me, as you are aware – Ishii made the following statements:

'Due to the danger of it [plague], there were no field experiments with it. There were a great many field mice in Manchuria and it would have been dangerous to conduct field experiments with plague because the field mice would very easily carry the organisms and start an epidemic. We conducted experiments with plague only in the laboratory.'

I asked what kind of experiments.

Ishii stated: 'We put rats in cages inside the room and sprayed the whole room with plague bacteria. This was to determine how the rats became infected, whether through the eyes, nose, mouth or through the skin. But the results were not too effective as we usually got only a 10 percent infection.'

'By which route?'

'Through the nose and also through an open wound; animals were shaved and it was found that they would become infected through the microscopic abrasions caused by the shaving. We found that the lymph nodes became inflamed and that was how we then knew if the animal had become infected.'

In response to further questioning, Ishii then went on to say: 'The spray test was not conducted in a special chamber. However, the windows in the room were double-plated and paper was put all over the walls. The room was made as air-tight as possible and human beings did not enter the room. They conducted the test from an outside corridor. After the experiment, we sprayed formalin in the room and did not enter it for one day. We also wore protective clothing, masks, and rubber shoes. Before we touched the animals, we put the cages, the animals, and all, into a solution of creosol.'

I asked had there been any accidents.

'Yes. One person who handled the animals after the experiment got infected and died.'

'How about outside?'

Ishii said, 'No.'

I then stated: 'We have heard from Chinese sources that plague was started in Changteh, in 1941, by airplanes flying over and dropping plague material and a plague resulted. Do you know anything about this?'

Ishii said, 'No, and anyway, it is impossible from a scientific point of view, as I thought you would have known, to drop plague organisms from airplanes.'

'But what if rats, rags, and bits of cotton infected with plague were dropped and later picked up by the Chinese and that is then how it was to have started?'

'If you drop rats from airplanes they will die,' laughed Ishii. 'There is no chance of a human being catching plague as a result of dropping organisms from an airplane.'

'How about balloons?'

'I would imagine balloons might be rather hard to control and navigate, wouldn't you, Dr Thompson?'

As you can see from the above exchange, Lt. Gen. Ishii is an extremely confident man. However, Ishii – in my impression of the man – is also prone to boast about his achievements (for example, about his invention of a porcelain bomb for plague dissemination, about his water filters for field use, and an anti-dysentery pill he claims to have developed) and I believe this egotism and vanity will be his undoing.

In conclusion, and regardless of Ishii's contention, it is evident to me from the progress that was made that BW research and development in all its phases was conducted on a large scale, and was officially sanctioned and supported by the highest military authority.

It is also evident that BW research was not confined to Pingfan and mainland China, as we have been led to believe. It is my belief that work in this field was also carried on in the Army Medical College in Tokyo. Therefore, it is impossible that the military leadership here in Tokyo was unaware of the program and that it was almost certainly conducted with the support and sanction of the highest military authority.

This leads, of course, to the inevitable (and political) question of exactly how high that sanction extended and I am aware that this is also the question uppermost in the minds (and worries) of both SCAP and Washington. In response to my direct questioning as to whether the Emperor himself was informed of BW research, Ishii replied that the Emperor was 'a lover of humanity and never would have consented to such a thing.'

However, I strongly believe we have only scratched the surface of Ishii and his work. I am convinced that sometime soon, if we continue to question Ishii and his associates, we will be able to break him. Ishii is a proud, determined, almost ruthless individual and no one, in my experience, with such personal characteristics can fail to have made enemies. As you are aware, GHQ has received, and continues to receive, literally thousands of correspondences from disaffected Japs containing allegations of war crimes. Among these many telegrams and letters there are sure to be some which will refer to BW experiments in China and also in Japan. However, it is a slow and time-consuming process verifying each individual allegation and we simply do not have the necessary manpower at our disposal.

Finally, there are also some additional, highly important and extremely CONFIDENTIAL remarks I would like to make to you.

I took the liberty of showing the notes I had made of my interviews with Ishii and Kitano to my tame informant (the former BW engineer). As you know, it has been my experience that these Japs are simply not to be trusted (they are all good actors and accomplished liars). It was my intention therefore to verify the information I had received from Ishii and Kitano with my informant.

However, my informant gave me a startling and unexpected piece of information. He claims to have recently met with one of his acquaintances, who himself was a member of Unit 731. This acquaintance told my informant that he had personally met with Lt. Gen. Kitano, who told him that 'just prior to the American Army inquiry [that is to say, my own interrogation of Kitano and Ishii], GHQ gave Ishii and myself [Kitano] a hearing and granted us permission to consult with each other in order that we could arrange not to contradict each other over items which were to be kept secret.'

My informant also claims that 'the Americans knew all along that Ishii, Kitano, etc., had secretly fled back to Japan after the end of the war and they planned to make secret contact with them. Between the end of last year and the early months of this year, the Americans held secret meetings with Ishii and other ranking officers [a total of five persons] in a restaurant in Kamakura [just south of Tokyo]. During these meetings, which are known as the "Kamakura Conference", Ishii revealed all about the experimentation and the bacteriological weapons. In return for providing the data that he had brought back from Manchuria, he asked that none of the unit members would be indicted for war crimes. The Americans accepted this condition and a secret contract was made between them.'

My informant refuses to name the 'acquaintance' who gave him this information but states that the acquaintance is a 'former military physician, a Lt. Col (born in 1902), in Osaka, who had been a member of Unit 731.' This former Lt. Col. also stated that he had recently met with Lt. Gen. Ishii, who boasted, 'It is I who helped all you guys out and saved your skin!'

Of course, I have (for now) no way of knowing whether or not this information is true. However, if it is true, and I am aware it is a 'big if', it would certainly explain a lot.

To be very candid, sir, the politics of all this is beginning to weigh on me and I would be most grateful if you would tell me frankly and honestly (and in the utmost confidence) whether another section – G-2 or Scientific Intelligence, for example – are, to your knowledge, also engaged in any Jap BW investigation of their own and, if that is the case, whether they might have cut some kind of deal with the top Jap BW men (to the exclusion of the rest of us).

However, and whatever the truth of the matter, I remain very hopeful that my second report on Jap BW activities will be much more comprehensive than my first and that it will be completed and with you by the end of May, at the latest, as previously discussed.

Sincerely, Lt. Col. Murray Thompson.

*

St Luke's International Hospital, Tokyo, Japan
September 9, 1946

My dearest Peggy,

I am sorry I have worried you by my silence & lack of communication. However, I truly hope this letter finds you & the children all well (despite the worry I have no doubt put you through).

As (I hope) you were informed, I collapsed with a severe hemorrhage on March 10 & was diagnosed with TB. Since then I have been hospitalized here at St Luke's International Hospital, Tokyo. It is embarrassing for a doctor to admit, but I realize now that I had ignored the warning signs as for some time I had been feeling very weak. However, I put this down to the stress of the job. I should not, however, have been so reckless in ignoring the fevers & coughs that had plagued me on & off since last September.

I do now feel that I am on the mend (& the doctors agree), so please do not worry. I am resting & taking things easy (I have little choice in the matter as the nurses are very strict!).

I must admit, though, that I have been following the progress of the War Crimes Trial & it has done nothing for my mood!

A couple of days before my collapse I actually met with Morrow (who is one of our investigators in our prosecution) & I gave him all I had. I also told him in no uncertain terms that I believed that Ishii & his gang were guilty of serious war crimes (Ishii's rank of lieutenant general also means he could be prosecuted as a Class 'A' war criminal). For starters, BW is outlawed by every civilized nation & furthermore Ishii carried out human experiments on both prisoners of war & civilians. The rest of his gang also committed enough crimes to be considered as 'B' & 'C' class war criminals. In our meeting, Morrow seemed very keen to go after Ishii & his subordinates & promised he would.

Imagine my surprise & disappointment then to find that nowhere in the lists of the accused is there any mention of Ishii or any of his subordinates. As far as I am aware, the sole mention of BW to date occurred last week during the prosecution's case about what the Japs did in Nanking. One of the assistant prosecutors (Sutton, I think his name was) suddenly stated in court that the Tama Detachment (which was the name for Ishii's unit at Nanking) had taken Chinese civilians & American prisoners of war & used them for experiments (which we all know to be true). He said that the Japs had injected them with *toxic bacteria to see how their bodies reacted. Of course, this caused uproar in court & he was asked by the judges for more evidence, at which point Sutton said he did not anticipate introducing any additional evidence on the matter!*

I refuse to believe that this will be all that is said on the matter, so I keep reading the newspapers every day in hope.

Anyway, as you can imagine, I have had plenty of time to think & reflect on my many shortcomings, both professionally & personally, as a doctor & a soldier, & as a husband & a father. I realize now that I have failed every one & it is my sole aim now to put things right as soon as I am discharged from here.

I can only apologize for all the anxiety & worry I have caused you but, hopefully, I am now on the road to recovery & will soon be well enough to travel & finally return home to you all.

Until then, with all my love, Murray.

*

Stamped TOP SECRET

St Luke's International Hospital, Tokyo, Japan
January 9, 1947

To: Colonel Harlan Worthley, Office of the Chief Chemical Warfare
           Service, Special Project Division,
           Gravelly Point, Washington, D.C.

Dear Colonel Worthley,

Sir, as you are no doubt aware, soon after my last letter to you (of February 25, 1946) I suffered a severe hemorrhage and was diagnosed with tuberculosis. As a result, I have been forced to remain here in Tokyo, hospitalized under doctor's orders (and only doctor's orders?) for the past year. My health has somewhat recovered now, but I am still unable to leave hospital and return either to my work or home to my family.

To the best of my ability, and it has not been easy, I have tried to keep abreast of developments in the BW investigation, through the occasional report in newspapers and the (even more) occasional visit from colleagues. However, and I hope you will forgive the abrupt and rude comments of a sick man, I cannot help but feel a strong sense of disappointment and frustration.

It would seem to me (from here, at least) that none of the information I gathered and passed on to you in my last letter, nor any of the information I gave to Lt. Col. Thomas H. Morrow and the IPS, has been acted upon, particularly in regard to Lt. Gen. Ishii. I would go so far as to say that (from Day One) no one seems to have taken me seriously (or anyone from Camp Detrick, for that matter). I know we are the new kids on the block, so to speak, but they have no respect for us or our work. I cannot help but feel that this is because we are essentially civilians and are in no way connected with the old-line Chemical Corps (and its old-boy network).

If one was prone to paranoia – and this city and this Occupation, these Japs and our own men, certainly do nothing to discourage such feelings – then one might even think that my sudden illness and enforced removal from the investigation are viewed in the Dai-Ichi Building as providential intervention. There are days when, I admit, I feel very much like a pawn that has simply been swept off the board when the game was not going the way some people upstairs might have desired it to go.

However, the IMTFE is still in session and so there is still time to act upon the information I gathered and passed on to you (and to the IPS) and to bring Ishii and his subordinates to justice. My only regret is that my health problems (and the doctors) prevent me from personally ensuring that this is done. Hence this rather rude and abrupt letter, which I hope you will forgive but understand and, more importantly, <u>act upon</u>.

Finally, I would like to state for the record that as soon as my health permits I am most eager to resume my work in what I hope is the ongoing investigation into the Jap BW program, in whatever capacity you deem fit.

Sincerely, Lt. Col. Murray Thompson.

*

Marked PERSONAL

St Luke's International Hospital, Tokyo, Japan
July 9, 1947

Dear Peggy,

As you can see from the above address, & as you probably already know through other channels, I am still confined on doctor's orders (& quite possibly on MacArthur's orders, too) to this hospital. They say my illness has taken a turn for the worse, but I do not believe them. I now believe they may even be experimenting on me, for they seem incapable of curing my illness, only prolonging it.

So the days turn into weeks, the weeks into months, the months into years, & I cannot tell you how much I miss you, Peggy, & how much I miss the children (who doubtless do not even remember me). I also cannot tell you how much I want to leave this bed, this hospital, this city, & this country! But I know that even if I can leave this bed & this hospital, I will not be able to leave this city & this country until I have corrected all the mistakes I know I have made, until I have righted all those wrongs.

For as I lie here, hour after hour, day after day, with nothing but time on my hands, I cannot help but go over & over, again & again, all the events that have left me here, that have STRANDED me here so very far from you & all I hold dear. Particularly, I cannot help but go over & over all the choices & mistakes I have made. Peggy, I go back, again & again, over & over so many things.

Do you remember the balloons, Peggy? I see now that was where it all started for me, with those balloons, for that was when they first came for me, those men who never knock, who never introduce themselves, those men who came that day in November 1944, who told me of Jap germ warfare attacks on the Chinese in Manchuria. They've killed a lot of people, they said, they've poisoned wells, poisoned reservoirs. So <u>we knew</u>. Even then, back in 1944, we knew, <u>I knew</u>. Then they told me of the strange balloon that had been found in Butte, Montana, thirty feet in diameter, ninety-one feet round, & made of rice paper, told me of ten other strange balloons that had been found, & told me to come to Washington.

Do you remember how excited I was, Peggy? How I stood in that circle around those balloons, that circle of military & scientific experts, how I told them these strange balloons had obviously come from Japan, that prevailing winds could easily carry balloons from Japan to the US mainland? How I warned them that if any of these balloons contained Japanese B-encephalitis, then we were in real trouble because mosquitoes are the best vectors of Japanese B-encephalitis & we have plenty of mosquitoes here in the States? How I warned them that our population had no defenses against B-encephalitis, that we had no experience of the disease so we were totally vulnerable, that four out of every five people who contracted B-encephalitis would die? Of course, I didn't stop there, did I? I told them it was equally possible that the Japs could have contaminated the balloons with anthrax, that anthrax is a tough bug, sturdy & cheap to produce, that <u>we knew</u> the Japs had already used it in China. I warned them back then that the Japs could splatter the west & southwest of Canada & the United States, that they could contaminate the pastures & the forests, kill all the cows & sheep, all the horses & pigs, plus a considerable number of human beings. I also told them there would be widespread panic & hysteria, so they placed rigid censorship on all radio & press reports of the finding of any balloons.

But the balloons kept coming, didn't they, Peggy? By the end of March 1945, over two hundred balloons had been found from Hawaii to Alaska & down to Michigan & I pored over each one of them, inch by inch, but I found no hint of bacteria, no trace of disease. Nothing except incendiary devices, only two of which actually detonated – do you remember those, Peggy? The one in Helena, Montana, that exploded & killed a woman, the other in Oregon which killed six men out fishing, do you remember?

But I refused to believe that the Japs had not infected the balloons. I could not believe there were no bacteria, no disease, that these were the only balloons. So I spent hour after hour in the glass belly of a B19, tracking up & down the west coast of the United States, hour after hour looking for thirty feet of rice paper hanging in a tree or lying punctured in a field, & still I found nothing.

But I refused to give up, even then. I gathered up every field report I could find. I asked for meetings at the headquarters of the 7th Service Command in Omaha, Nebraska & the headquarters of the US Western Defense Command in San Francisco. I spoke for hours, I spoke for days, telling them <u>what we knew</u>, <u>what I knew</u>, even then, in March 1945. I told them about biological warfare & about strange balloons. I told them about the Jap germ attacks on the Chinese & about the Jap use of anthrax, the Jap use of plague –

PLAGUE, even then, PLAGUE.

I told them about the man who headed the Jap BW project, though I could not yet name him. I told them about the Jap BW headquarters (which I then believed to be in Nanking). I told them about the prisoner-of-war statements which mentioned a bacillus bomb (the Mark VII, Type 13, Experimental Bacillus Bomb). I warned them of possible targets, possible means of dispersal, possible biological agents & diseases. I told them about Jap attempts to get a strain of yellow fever virus from the Rockefeller Institute in New York & about a similar attempt in Rio de Janeiro. I told them it was quite possible that the Japs now had the virus through Germany. I warned them of the threat to our cattle & livestock from rinderpest, that rinderpest kills & spreads rapidly, that we were 100 percent vulnerable to rinderpest. I warned them that one single balloon could be crossing the Pacific that very minute, carrying enough cholera to start an epidemic, that we were 100 percent vulnerable to cholera.

97

I told them & I warned them because I KNEW, Peggy, I KNEW, even then, I KNEW.

But then, of course, the call came from MacArthur & that was the last time I saw you, the last time I saw the children, that last time before I ended up here in THIS PLAGUED CITY.

I know now for sure, Peggy, that they'd already been told about me before I even set foot in this place, that was why they were waiting for me, why they had my photograph!

That photograph of me in Camp Detrick is another thing I keep coming back to, over & over, again & again. How had the Japs got hold of that photograph? I know that our own guys, our own G-2, must have given it to the Japs, that G-2 must have already made contact with Naitō & the top men in the Jap BW program & that was why he was waiting for me, why he had my photograph in his paws, why he knew I wasn't up to the job because THEY HAD TOLD HIM, because THEY HAD ALREADY MADE THEIR DEAL.

Of course, I knew even then that I could not & should not trust them but I see now that I personally was far too ready to believe all that I was told. So I believed that the Kwantung Army operated on the mainland with a high degree of independence from the military leadership back in Tokyo & I believed that, within the KA, Ishii was a law unto himself, that the Army Medical Department exercised no control over Ishii & his operations.

I realize that I became obsessed with Ishii, believing Ishii, & Ishii alone, to be the one who should bear sole burden for their BW program. I realize now that this was what I wanted to believe.

Now I believe more than ever that the deal (deals? Who knows how many deals were made?) was a mistake. But I swear to you, Peggy, that I did not know that human guinea pigs had been used when I suggested the arrangement to MacArthur, Willoughby & Compton. And now we know about the bacillus & anthrax bombs & their use on American prisoners of war & Chinese civilians, now we have the evidence, there is still time to prosecute Ishii & all the other guilty Japs at the Tokyo Trial. But no one here or in Washington takes my claims about the human experiments seriously or, should I say, no one wants to take them seriously because it does not suit them & what they (wrongly) believe to be 'our best interests'.

But in years to come future generations will ask, who knew? Who knew and who made the deal? And the answer is, they all knew. They all knew, myself included. We all knew and so we are all guilty, guilty of the things we did, and guilty of the things we did NOT do.

I cannot bear the thought that George or Emily might one day read of all this & know that their own father knew, know that their own father was guilty (which I am), & that he did nothing.

All that I now plan to do, I do for our children.

Perhaps I should not tell you this, Peggy, but there are days here when I wake, my eyes still closed, & I can hear the voices of the children & I believe, for just one moment, I am home again, home with you & the children, & that I am finally & forever home, out of this bed & this hospital, away from this city & this country, from this <u>hell</u>. But then, of course, I open my eyes & I know I am not home, that I am still here, here in this bed in this hospital in this city in this country, <u>in this hell</u>, that those voices were not the voices of our children but the voices of vermin, of mice & of rats, in the walls & under the floor, muttering & whispering, & then I fear I will never leave this bed & this hospital, never leave this city & this country, <u>that I will never leave this hell</u>, that I will never hear the voices of our children again, will never see their lips move again, never even see their faces again. But I swear to you, Peggy, I WILL NOT LET THIS HAPPEN, I will not let their experiments succeed, I will not let them get away with this.

So, as soon as I am able, I plan to discharge myself & check back into the Dai-Ichi Hotel. I plan to finish the task at hand, to correct all my mistakes, as quickly as I can, so I can then finally, finally put all this behind me & return to you all a new & better man, a better husband to you & a better father to the children.

With all my love, always, Murray.

*

Stamped TOP SECRET

From the Diseased, Infected & Plagued City,
In the Place & Hour of No God,
January 26, 1948

<u>To whom it may concern, but not for the eyes or the knowledge of my wife or my children, or any who have felt or shown affection toward me. A second letter is for their eyes, and only their eyes.</u>

I write this letter here and now, in this laboratory, at the end, not as explanation or vindication of my actions or inactions, but to document, and to warn. For I know now for certain that they have been experimenting on me and that they have been successful, that they are the ones who are

99

behind the mutterings and the whisperings, in the walls and under the floors, that it is their voices that every day mutter and whisper, 'Get up, Tommy! You still have work to do. Get up!'

They are the ones behind that voice on the telephone this evening – that thick and heavy-accented voice – that voice which said, 'On your head are these dead.'

These men who never knock, who never introduce themselves, these men who sit and who stare, who watch me and who follow me, on the corners and in the doorways, in their protective masks and rubber shoes. ALWAYS FRIENDLY, VERY FRIENDLY. But I know I will never see their faces, never know their names, for they all wear masks – monkey masks, squirrel masks, but mainly the masks of mice, the masks of rats – white clay masks. THEY ARE THE RATS BOARDING THE SINKING SHIP, testing me, experimenting on me, in this city that has become their laboratory, with its double-plated windows and its paper-covered walls, THIS PLAGUED CITY that is their laboratory of the Apocalypse.

In this laboratory, IN THIS PLAGUED CITY, here at the end, I see the Angel of History and the Angel of Pestilence, and I feel the breath of their wings upon me now, and I close my eyes.

In the history of the world, there have been as many plagues as there have been wars. They rise and they triumph, then they decline and they disappear. But they always return, plagues and wars. They always return, these plagues and wars, to take men equally by surprise. Until now, now men have married plague and war in an unholy, godless matrimony.

And I see visions, visions of plagues, my eyes open / my eyes closed, the same visions. The dead rat on the stair, gray and yellow, the cat convulsing in the kitchen, a bloody red flower blossoming in its mouth. That is how it will start. The rats in the daylight, from out of the walls, from under the floors, they will first come in files, and then die in piles, six thousand dead in one day, burnt in bonfires through the night, and then the rats will be gone and the fevers will start, the swellings and the vomiting, the yellow and the gray, before the asphyxiation and then the death, the red and black death, the red and black death of the people, death of this city, this gray and yellow city of gray and yellow eyes, then red and black eyes, of yellow blossoms and red flowers here and there, on the corners and in the doorways, this gray and yellow, red and black city wherein men will take to their beds and leave them on stretchers, in coffins, in hearses, until there are no more stretchers, no more coffins and no more hearses.

ON YOUR HEAD ARE THESE DEAD!

Just the swellings and vomiting, the asphyxiation and death, the death of this city, death of this country, this (w)hole world.

ON YOUR HEAD!

For it is coming! It is coming! It is coming!

And I know I am to blame, too.

For I know it is my fault.

ON MY HEAD!

My mistake IN THE PLAGUED CITY, this city of public records and private erasures, of half-truths and whole-lies –

LIES! LIES! LIES!

Again and again, I come back to that incident, over and over, that incident on the Ginza with the old mouse on his bicycle.

For I can still feel his spit upon my face.

Still taste his spit in my mouth.

His spit in my blood.

In my blood.

My blood, infected and signed, *Dr M. Thompson, Tokyo, 1948.*

   – Stamped, MISSION TERMINATED, 2/27/48 –

Beneath the Black Gate, in its upper chamber, you are crawling, crawling again, crawling beneath the swinging shoes of a dead American, round and around, in the occult circle, in the light of its candles, round and around you crawl, beneath the swinging shoes of all the dead, the swinging shoes of all the dead upon your head, the dirty soles of their swinging shoes upon your head,

round and around, on your head,

round and around,

you crawl –

And now the ropes snap, and the shoes fall, and the bodies fall, on your head, another candle, on your head, extinguished,

on your head. Out –

Out. Out –

But in this occult circle, in the light of its now-eight candles, still you crawl on, in circles, on you crawl still,

in circles, circles of conspiracies, circles of agendas, conspiracies and agendas that form narratives and give meanings, narratives and meanings, fictions and lies –

For on your hands, you are still clothed in your despair, on your knees, still digging your own grave, still-born in your own tomb, this airless, artless tomb of ink and words, still enticed and entranced, still deceived and defeated,

in-snared and in-

prisoned –

In the flicker-light of these eight candles, where there are no keys and there are no doors, where there are only locks and only walls, but still you turn the yellow-pages of your notebooks, your ink and their words, still searching for clues and searching for maps, in their clippings and in your copies, in the ghosts of their stories,

your stories of their ghosts:

NEIGHBOURHOOD INVESTIGATIVE HQ

A local organization named Mejiro Chian Kyōkai Nagasaki Shibu *has founded a 'Civil Investigative Headquarters' because 'the locals will be upset unless the [Teigin] case is solved quickly,' said the Chief of the HQ, Mr Shimizu.*

The HQ is located in the office of the Nagasaki Shrine, and their investigation is mostly focused on the killer's tracks. They summon those who had been in the vicinity of the crime scene, and who had hurried to rescue the victims, as well as local children who may have also witnessed the crime. Shimizu and his team plan to gather up all these testimonies and give their reports to Mejiro Police Station.

Each member of the team runs a separate district of the neighbourhood and witnesses are summoned to the Nagasaki Shrine HQ, even in the night, to be questioned by these amateur cops. For now, Chief Shimizu ignores his own business and devotes himself entirely to the investigation, twenty-four hours a day. 'I take 5 or 6 Hiropon injections per day but, what-the-heck, I'll do beyond my best till we get him,' said Mr Shimizu, and he will not disband the HQ until the killer is caught.

However, one local housewife complained, 'I really wish the killer would be caught very soon, or he [Mr Shimizu] will be back to ask us for another donation to his association!'

In the flakes and in the flurries, in the night and in the snow, the medium stands before you now, in a cape and in a hat, and she says, 'I am Shimizu Kogorō. I am the Occult-*Tantei* . . .'
Before you now, in his cape and his hat,
with his curses and his spells, stain-
tear-ed and stain-blood-ed, nailed
to the back of a door, IN THE oCcULT CITY

The Fifth Candle –

The Curses & the Spells of the Man in the Shrine

The city is a curse, this city is a spell;
webs of curses, weaves of spells.
For this is the oCcULT CITY.
But I am its nemesis –
Here to break its spells, to exorcize the curses,
IN THE oCcULT CITY . . .

✡

IN THE oCcULT CITY, in the shadows of my private shrine, beneath the branches of its winter trees, they are unloading the trucks outside the bank. *One, two, three, four.* They are stacking the coffins along the side of the bank. *Five, six, seven, eight.* They are waiting to take them away again. *Nine, ten.* I tear open the box of Hiropon. I take out a syringe. And another. I take off my hat. And my cape. My jacket. I unbutton the left cuff of my shirt. I roll up the left sleeve of my shirt. I shake the bottle. I twist off the cap. I break the seal. I attach the bottle to the needle, the needle to my arm, to my vein, my blood. And I press down. Down, down. Now I remove the needle from my blood, from my vein, my arm. I throw away the needle. The bottle. I roll down the left sleeve of my shirt. I button up the left cuff of my shirt. I put my jacket back on. And my cape. My hat. Now I lean back against the trunk of a winter tree. I light a cigarette. In the shadows of my private shrine, I cough. They are loading the ten coffins into the trucks. *One, two, three, four.* They are stacking the coffins in the backs of the trucks. *Five, six, seven, eight.* They are taking them away, again. *Nine, ten . . .*

✡

Under a blood-red moon, low in a dirty-yellow sky,
sirens across my city, sirens through my night.
Here among these branches, here among these limbs,
I am lost in a forest of broken bones and dead skin,
in my defeated city, now occupied,
I shuffle through this forest,
the broken bones and the dead skin.
I stain the trees,
the branches and the limbs.

✡

IN THE oCcULT CITY, in the shadow of the scene of the crime, across the road from the Shiinamachi branch of the Teikoku Bank, I have formed a local organization. I have named it the *Mejiro Security Association – Nagasaki Shrine Branch*. I have established a *Civil Investigative Headquarters*. I have opened an office for business in the back of the Nagasaki Shrine, Shiinamachi. I have cut out the articles, the reports. I have stuck them onto paper, into notebooks. I have pinned a map of the oCcULT CITY to the wall of the office in the shrine. I have plotted the points on the map; the Ebara branch of the Yasuda Bank, the Nakai branch of the Mitsubishi Bank, and the Shiinamachi branch of the Teikoku Bank. The three points to date. *To date*, for there will be six points; Six Points to His Evil Star. For I will map the Six Points of His Evil Star in the oCcULT City and I will stalk the steps of the Killer through this oCcULT CITY. I will track His trail through this oCcULT CITY. I will talk to the witnesses, the women and the children who were here, the women and the children who saw the aftermath of the crime. I will record their testimonies. I will take their testimonies to Mejiro Police Station. For I am here to help, twenty-four hours a day, seven days a week, for I will not sleep. I will take six Hiropon injections every day. I will do my very best, I will go beyond my best, until the Killer is caught, until His curse is lifted. For I will lift the curse of His crime from this neighbourhood, the curse of all the crimes from this city, for I have come to solve all crimes, I have come to MURDER all curses and spells.

I am here to assassinate MAGICK –

To break its seal.

He is here, He is here, He is here,
and He smiles and He says,
'Leave this place! Leave this city,
this oCcULT CITY,
for this is not your city,
this is my city!'
But I am not afraid, not afraid of Him,
and so I smile and I say,
'Be gone from this place! Be gone from this city,
this oCcULT CITY,
for this is not your city,
this is my city!'

✡

IN THE oCcULT CITY, across the road from the Nagasaki Shrine, there are workmen, inside and outside the Teikoku Bank. Through the doors of the bank, I hear the sound of hammers, the hammers and nails to hide the stains. Down the corridors of the bank, through its doors, the smell of new tatami mats, the new tatami mats to cover the stains. Out in the streets, I see policemen, their hats soaked black and their boots stained white, trampling over our neighbourhood; our neighbourhood cursed and stained by His crime; His crime that poisoned and murdered our neighbourhood. North to South, they are tearing apart the entire city. East to West, twenty thousand detectives searching for the Killer. For clues. Top to bottom. Following up every lead, following up every report. Banging on doors. Every hint, every rumour. Inside and out. Every shadow, every whisper. Upstairs and down. Interviewing and talking. Street after street. Bullying and shouting. House after house. But they do not know. For they cannot know. So I put on my cape. I put on my hat. I go out into the streets. To the houses. To bang on doors. To interview. To help. For I know. I know the face of the Killer. For I have seen His face. In my dreams.

✡

He is here, He is here, He is here again –
He shuffles through the forest, He shuffles through the trees,
for He has brought their carcasses to this place,
here to parade their meat,
their flesh to hang from the branches,
their blood to drip from the leaves,
IN THE oCcULT CITY.
But I am here, I am here, I am also here –
For I am stalking His steps. I am on His trail,
through the forest, through the trees,
for I will bring His carcass to this place,
I will parade His meat,
hang His flesh from the branches,
drip His blood from the leaves,
IN THE oCcULT CITY

✡

IN THE oCcULT CITY, they will burn the dead today. So I walk up Shinobazu-dōri. I come to the Gokokuji Temple. The mass funeral begins at three. These temples are their sanctuaries, their last sanctuaries from Him. For here they are safe, here I am safe. In these temples He cannot see through the smoke, in here He cannot smile His evil smile. Not like in the shrines, the shrines He likes. For the shrines of Tokyo are now evil shrines. Magnets for evil, repositories of evil. The Evil Magick now victorious, the Holy War now lost –

The Holy War which began in 1873 when the Ministry of Religion forbade the practices of all exorcists, faith-healers, fortune-tellers and shamans. The War which continued with the 1880 Meiji Criminal Code and its prohibition against our talismanic prayers, and then the Revised Criminal Code of 1908 which further criminalized and imprisoned, *'Those who spread gossip and wild rumours or false alarms which deceive people. Those who without authority tell fortunes; or who conduct exorcisms and incantations; or who otherwise mislead people by conferring on them things resembling talismans. Those who conduct spells, exorcisms, and incantations for the sick; or who impede medical care by giving amulets and holy water . . .'* Those like me; Shimizu Kogorō, the Occult-Detective –

But their Holy War, their Crusade against the likes of me, found its bloodiest battlefield in the shrines of Japan. For their War, their Crusade sought to control all the shrines of Japan and destroy any that would resist their Crusade, their control and their codes –

For in their Holy War, in their Crusade, there could only be one winner, only one victor; the unbroken Imperial line, descended from Amaterasu, and enshrined at Ise –

And so began the shrine mergers of 1906 to 1912, and the destruction of the People's Shrines, the rule of just one shrine per administrative area, and the birth of Yasukuni; Yasukuni –

The centre of the Six Points of His Evil Star . . .

From 1905 to 1910, the spirits of 88,243 War Dead were forcibly enshrined in the Yasukuni Shrine in Tokyo –

88,243 spirits who were thus denied a final repose with their ancestors, forbidden the memorial rites of the Buddhist dead, and robbed of their last return to their homes –

Denying, forbidding and robbing their families of the care and the company of their spirits –

Their spirits imprisoned at Yasukuni in Tokyo, hundreds and thousands of miles from their homes and their families, at Yasukuni, in the oCcULT CITY –

The oCcULT CITY which trembles with the spirits of these restless Dead, the oCcULT CITY which shook with the cries of these imprisoned Dead in 1923, and which trembles now, with so many more dead from so many more wars, and which will shake again –

Shake and fall again, unless I can free the Dead and fetter the Evil, the Evil that now runs amok in the oCcULT CITY.

For all their new codes and all their official shrines have given free rein to Evil Magick and its practitioners, outlawing the old Folk Magick and its old believers, the ordinary and the good –

Those like me; Shimizu Kogorō, the Occult-*Tantei*, with my pockets full of coins, coins full of holes, holes and only holes; my pockets full of holes, holes and only holes. For I am here to cleanse this city of all its shrines and all their evils, their curses and their spells, their magick and their murder. For I am here –

Here to liberate these restless Dead –

To free them from their chains –

The Dead, Dead, Dead.

IN THE oCcULT CITY, they have burnt the dead. The mass funeral has ended. They are safe now, safe from Him. But not me, never me. I leave the Gokokuji Temple. I leave this sanctuary. I walk back up Shinobazu-dōri. Here there is no sanctuary, no sanctuary from Him. Here I am not safe, not safe from Him. In His city –

In His city of shrines, the shrines He likes –
The Evil Magick victorious for now –
The Holy War lost, lost for now –
IN THE oCcULT CITY.

✡

The oCcULT CITY is a séance,
a city of cries, a city of pleas,
of prayers and of whispers.
In this forest of broken bones and dead skin,
among these branches, among these limbs,
I listen for their voices.
I touch the branches, I touch the leaves,
I taste their stains,
their bones and their skin.
They are here, they are here, they are here now –
IN THE oCcULT CITY,
and they are crying, and they are pleading.
But now they are gone, they are gone, they are gone again,
for now He is here, He is here, He is here again,
here again to parade their meat.
And I say, 'If I die, I die . . .'
And He smiles, and He says, 'You will die, you will die . . .
'I promise you.'

✡

IN THE oCcULT CITY, in the shadows of the shrine, the sound of their feet in the snow, the sound of their fists on my door. In their black hats and their white boots, they knock me from my chair and they drag me from my office. They push me down the steps of the shrine, they bundle me into the back of their car. They drive me to their police station, they carry me into their interview room. They sit me on a chair, they shine a light on me. They talk about conspiracies, they talk about coincidences. But they do not know there are no conspiracies, they do not know there are no coincidences. They do

109

not know there is only Magick; Good Magick and Evil Magick; Evil Magick & Evil Plague. For they have forgotten and so they no longer understand. But I have not forgotten, so I still understand. For I know my destiny, I know my future. For I have seen my future, all our futures, from a fortune-teller, at a makeshift stall, in an ancient alley, a fortune-teller who smiled at me, and who told me, 'You will save this city, Shimizu Kogorō. You will cure this city . . .'

'Ha, ha, ha, ha, ha, ha, ha, ha, ha, ha, ha, ha . . .'

And so I tell them I am Shimizu Kogorō, I am the Occult-Detective. I tell them I am only here to help them, I am only here to save them. Here to catch their Killer, here to close their case –

'Ha, ha, ha, ha, ha, ha, ha, ha, ha . . .'

But they laugh at my words, and they slap my face. They knock me from their chair, they kick me down their stairs. They throw me through their doors, they leave me in His streets. In the snow and in the sleet, the echoes and the whispers –

IN THE oCcULT CITY –

'Ha, ha, ha, ha, ha, ha . . .

✡

'Ha, ha, ha, ha, ha, ha, ha, ha, ha, ha, ha, ha . . .'
I can hear Him laughing at me, I can hear Him mocking me,
but I have a new plan, so I will set a new trap,
and then I'll have the Last Laugh!
Ha, ha, ha, ha, ha, ha, ha, ha, ha . . .
For to catch a demon, I must become a demon.
So I will dress as a demon dresses, and I will do as a demon does,
and I will become His doppelgänger,
His double-goer.
Ha, ha, ha, ha, ha, ha . . .
So I cut my hair short. I dye my hair grey.
I tattoo two brown spots to the left side of my face.
I buy a brown lounge suit. I buy a spring rain coat.
I buy burnt-orange rubber boots.
I buy a white cloth band to put upon my left arm –
'LEADER OF THE DISINFECTING TEAM'
Now I stand before the mirror. Now I laugh before the mirror –
Ha, ha, ha . . .

110

Now my plan is laid, now my trap is set;
now who'll have the Last Laugh,
Ha . . .?

✡

IN THE oCcULT CITY, it is Wednesday 4 February 1948, and it is almost light, and the moon and the stars have all gone to sleep now. But I do not sleep, for I cannot sleep. In the oCcULT CITY, in my *Civil Investigative Headquarters*, in the back of the Nagasaki Shrine, I stare at the map I have pinned to the wall of my office. I stare at the points I have plotted on the map; the three points to date – the Ebara branch of the Yasuda Bank, the Nakai branch of the Mitsubishi Bank, and the Shiinamachi branch of the Teikoku Bank – and I trace the three points to come. *To come*, for there will be three more points to complete the Six Points of His Evil Star. And I have mapped these three points to come. And so today I will stalk the steps of the Killer through the oCcULT CITY. Today I will track His trail through this oCcULT CITY. And today I will catch the Killer in the oCcULT CITY. For today is Wednesday 4 February, 1948 –

And today is the day of Setsubun –

The festival marking the end of winter and the beginning of spring, according to the old lunar calendar, the cleansing away of all the evil spirits of the former year, the driving away of all disease-bringing spirits for the year to come . . .

In my brown lounge suit, in my spring rain coat, in my burnt-orange rubber boots, with my white cloth band upon my left arm –

'LEADER OF THE DISINFECTING TEAM'

With my hair cut short, with my hair dyed grey, and with the two brown spots tattooed to the left side of my face, I leave the office of my *Civil Investigative Headquarters*, I leave the Nagasaski Shrine, and I leave Shiinamachi. For I have stared at the map, I have plotted the points, and now I know where He will be today.

Today I take the long roads through the oCcULT CITY, the long roads of the oCcULT CITY which were once its rivers and its canals, but the rivers and the canals of the oCcULT CITY have all been filled in with the ashes of the Dead, so where once there was water, once there was life, now there is only ash, now only death –

Death and the Dead, the Dead under the ground –

The Dead, the Tokyo Dead –

The Tokyo Living Dead –

For I can hear them scream, scream from under the ground, the Tokyo Living Dead, who scream this day, every day and every night, from under the ground. And I can see them now on every street, on every corner, at every junction, at every station, the Tokyo Living Dead, the war-wounded in their white-wear, on every street, on every corner, at every junction, at every station, with their blind-eyes and their deaf-ears, their burnt-skins and lost-limbs, they come up from under the ground, up from out of the ground, to lean on their sticks, to squat on their mats, their caps on the floor and their hands outstretched, on every street, on every corner, at every junction, at every station, I hear them and I see them as I take the long roads –

The long roads, in my brown lounge suit, down Yamate-dōri, in my spring rain coat, along Mejiro-dōri, in my burnt-orange boots, up Shinobazu-dōri, with my white cloth band upon my arm, right on to Kasuga-dōri, with my hair cut short and my hair dyed grey, on the long roads through the oCcULT CITY, with my two brown spots tattooed to the left side of my face, till I come to Kanda –

For I have stared at the map and I have plotted the points. And so I know where He'll be today, today He'll be here –

'Demons be outside! Fortune be inside!'

At the Kanda Myōjin Shrine –

'Oni wa soto!'

Here among the crowds, the crowds who have come, come in their thousands, in their thousands to exorcize the evil spirits of the old year, to ward against the evil diseases of the new year, in their thousands and in their masks, their masks of demons –

'Oni wa soto! Fuku wa uchi!'

Demons with their pictures of Him –

'Oni wa soto!'

And now the crowd sees me, in my brown lounge suit, in their thousands, in my spring rain coat, in their masks of demons, in my burnt-orange boots, with their pictures of Him, with my white cloth band upon my left arm, now they see me, *LEADER OF THE DISINFECTING TEAM*, and they grab handfuls of roasted beans, with my short hair, in their thousands, my grey hair, in their masks of demons, my two brown spots on the left side of my face, and now they throw their handfuls of beans at me, handful after handful –

'*Oni wa soto! Fuku wa uchi!*'

In their thousands, in their masks –

'*Oni wa soto!*'

Handful after handful, my face stung, swarm after swarm, my face bleeding, in their thousands, they are putting their arms through the arms of my brown lounge suit, in their masks, they are lifting my burnt-orange boots off the ground –

'*Oni wa soto!*'

IN THE oCcULT CITY, I am flying now, past the mid-night, through the blue-sky, the moon and the stars all out tonight and they look good, so good tonight, and now they put me down, down where the tall grass grows, down among the branches and the leaves, the sky a dirty yellow now, the moon a bloody red, in this forest of broken bones and dead skin, He is coming now, shuffling through the forest, He is here, shuffling through the trees, He is here, He who has brought my carcass to this place, to this defeated city, here to parade my meat, in the occupied city, my flesh to hang from its branches, my blood to drip from its leaves, to stain the trees, the branches and the limbs of the oCcULT CITY, in this place where the flies begin to gather now, this place where death will come as a wasp, a wasp in the Wintertime, in its light that sheds no light, with its sunfall and rainshine, where I will be but shadow, shadow at the side of the road.

And now He lays me down, and He stretches me out, and He smiles and He says, 'This city is no séance. This city is a mirror.'

And He holds the mirror up to my face, the nails to my hands, my hands to His door, and now He laughs,

the Last Laugh, 'Ha!'

Beneath the Black Gate, in its upper chamber, the door falls, the medium falls, and now the fifth candle is extinguished,

another candle, another life, out, out, out,

and once again you are alone,

alone in the occult circle,

alone in the light

of its seven

candles,

with no new words and no new book, among the rivers of ink and the mountains of paper, the bonfires and the ashes,

you crawl, in circles, on your hands

and on your knees, you crawl, through old words and old books, and you pick up the books and then you drop the books, drop the books and then pick up your pen, pick up your pen and now you write, write more and more insincerities, again and again, more and more lies, day after day, the same insincerities, the same lies, over and over, day after day, again and again,

until now you drop your pen,

drop your pen again, here –

Alone by the rivers of ink, alone on the mountains of paper, on your hands and on your knees, in the smoke and in the ash –

IN THE OCCUPIED CITY, beneath the Black Gate, in its upper chamber, in the occult circle of its seven candles,

among the flurries and the flakes, the paper flurries of paper flakes, these now-black and white flurries

of news-paper flakes,

spinning, spinning

and spinning, deaf again to the steps on the stairs, the sirens and the telephones, startled anew by the hand on your shoulder, you look up from your ink, up from your papers, and you see a smile, a smile that says, that says, 'My dear, sweet writer –

'I know this river, I know this mountain. The smell of these fires, the taste of these ashes. I know all about insincerities, I know all about lies. For I am a Master of Insincerities, a Master of Lies. For I trade in insincerities, I trade in lies. For I am a journalist and these are my stories . . .

The Sixth Candle –

The Stories of a Journalist

The city is a story, so many tales for her to tell, so many chronicles for me to chronicle. For the city is a chronicle, a journal, in black and white, and I am its chronicler, its journalist, in hat and coat. A thousand stories for every day, every night; never one city, but a thousand cities – heaven for some, hell for others. And for every story there are two sides, two sides at least, for the city is always, already a fiction, this city made of paper, this city made of print –

IN THE FICTIONAL CITY, I am Takeuchi Riichi, Homicide Reporter for the *Yomiuri Shimbun*. Every day, every night, I walk the city and I hear the city, her streets and her stories. I catch her stories and I collect her stories, to pin and mount them, on paper and in print, to display and exhibit, in black and white –

Monday 26 January 1948 . . .

In the Fictional City, this story starts like every story, with a siren, and then another, and another, another ambulance siren.

In the late winter afternoon, I am standing around a stove in the press office of the Tokyo Metropolitan Police Board with all the other homicide reporters, my rivals from the *Mainichi*, the *Asahi*, and all the other newspapers, and we are listening to the sirens, waiting for a statement. But no one comes down from upstairs, no detective with a statement from the MPB, and so we ignore the sirens, warming our hands as we wait for a story –

A sniff of a story . . .

In the Fictional City, the tap on my shoulder, the word in my ear; 'A moment of your time,' whispers Shiratō Sakari. Shiratō is the Public Health reporter for the *Yomiuri*. Shiratō doesn't often come down to Police HQ. Shiratō leads me out into the corridor.

'You heard all those sirens, the ambulances?' he asks. 'Well, they're all heading up to the Shiinamachi branch of the Teikoku Bank in Toshima-ku. Biggest case of food poisoning in years.'

'Food poisoning? When? How many?'

'The whole bank, at least ten people, about an hour ago. Loads of police up there, all saying nothing for now, but it's a big, big story. And we can get the scoop . . .'

The face out of the door, the shout down the corridor; 'Takeuchi, telephone!'

'Wait here,' I tell Shiratō, and I go back into the press office, the rival eyes of all the other reporters watching me as I shrug and I sigh, pick up the telephone and say, 'Hello, Takeuchi here.'

'I know everyone in the room is watching you,' says Ono, my editor at the *Yomiuri*. 'So just answer yes or no.'

'OK,' I say.

'Did you hear those ambulances about an hour ago?'

'Yes.'

'Has there been any statement from the MPB about where they were going, about what's happening?'

'No.'

'Have you spoken with anyone about them?'

'Yes.'

'Shiratō?'

'Yes.'

'He told you it was a big case of food poisoning at the Teikoku Bank in Shiinamachi?'

'Yes.'

'He still with you?'

'Yes.'

'Good, keep him there. I've sent Tomizawa up to Shiinamachi and he's going to phone back all the details to you because I want you to write this. So you stay put because this is not food poisoning. This is mass murder and robbery, ten dead at least, and the bank's takings stolen, so get writing the story now. Fill in the details with Tomizawa later. You understand what I've said?'

'Yes . . . Er no.'

'Quickly,' says Ono. 'Which is it?'

'Yes. Maybe,' I start to say, but Ono's gone, the line dead. I replace the receiver gently. I turn around as casually as I can but I know I will have fooled no one; the rival eyes of all the other reporters still watching me. I fake a yawn but they are shaking their heads. I walk as slowly as I can towards the door but still they are

116

shaking their heads and now, as I open the door, as I step outside, back into the corridor, the rival hands of all the other reporters are reaching for the telephones, their rival fingers dialling their editors –

'What was all that about?' asks Shiratō.

'It was the boss. He says it's not food poisoning. He says it's mass murder. Robbery. Ten dead, at least. The takings gone.'

'How does he know? Who's he been talking to?'

'Well, it'll be one of his usual hunches, won't it?' I wink. 'And, as usual, he'll be right, won't he? So he wants us to stay here and to start work.'

'Work?'

'Yeah,' I laugh. 'Work . . .'

In the Fictional City, at my desk in the press office, I begin to write the story:

MASS MURDER IN SHIINAMACHI –

Ten Workers of Teikoku Bank Slain In Broad Daylight – Robbery Behind Killing?

TOKYO, Jan. 26 – Ten were killed and (XX) others are in critical condition as a result of the attempted robbery and poisoning of the entire staff of the Shiinamachi branch of the Teikoku Bank at Nagasaki-chō, Toshima-ku, Tokyo by a (gang of) cold-blooded criminal(s) who apparently tried to snatch away heaps of bank notes in broad daylight on the afternoon of January 26.

The sensational 'poison bank holdup' case was perpetrated about X o'clock Monday afternoon shortly after the bank had closed for business for the day when a man (men) entered the building.

In no time the bank turned into a veritable death chamber with all the victims writhing in agony. When the relief party arrived at the scene, 10 of the victims had already died. XX others were rushed to the XX hospital and remain in a critical condition.

According to the police, who are strictly keeping away outsiders in an effort to find a clue, XXXXXXXXX.

An intensive police search is being conducted across the city for the bank robber(s).

A telephone rings. A voice shouts, 'Takeuchi, telephone!'
I stop writing. I go over to the phone. I say, 'Takeuchi.'

'Takeuchi? It's Tomizawa.'

'Where are you?'

'Shiinamachi.'

'What's going on? What have you got?'

'There's still been no statement from the MPB?'

'No,' I say, turning the pages of my notebook, licking the tip of my pencil. 'So give me everything you've got.'

'Well, it's not food poisoning. It's murder. Murder by poisoning. Ten dead for now. Six taken to the Seibo Hospital.'

'Have you got a chronology for me?'

'Locals found a young woman who works in the bank crawling around in the street outside at about 4 o'clock . . .'

'Name? Age?'

'No name yet, but early twenties.'

'OK. Go on . . .'

'Apparently she was trying to get to the local liquor store to telephone for ambulances and the police, so one local woman ran to the liquor store to call for the ambulances and police while another local stayed with the young woman who was losing consciousness, meanwhile other locals rushed up the road and into the bank . . .'

'Great,' I say. 'What did they find? What did they see?'

'A death chamber,' says Tomizawa. 'Bodies lying everywhere. In the corridors, on the floor, in the bathroom. A line of corpses by the sink. All of them with their eyes still open. Their mouths running with blood and vomit . . .'

'Fantastic,' I say. 'Go on . . .'

'Some of them were still alive . . .'

'Any of them talking?'

'No,' says Tomizawa. 'Coughing, spitting, losing consciousness. And then the police and the ambulances arrived.'

'The locals say how many were alive?'

'Six, but two were very bad.'

'Have you been inside?'

'Yes. When I got there it was still chaos, so I flashed my wallet, making out I was a detective, and I was in there for about ten minutes before they realized and threw me out.'

'So go on, what did you see?'

'Well, the bodies were still there, and there were loads of police, but there was a strange calmness, yeah calmness. All the

118

desks were just as you'd imagine them, with ledgers and papers spread out. Stacks of cash on the desks as well . . .'

'Stacks of cash?'

'Yeah, just sitting there, untouched. A tray of cups as well. It was just as if it was a normal working day in a normal bank. Apart from the bodies and all the police, the police drawing chalk marks around the bodies, their photographers taking their pictures. There were even some of the locals in there, trying to tidy up . . .'

'And the police? What were they saying?'

'Well, you know the police. Not much. Muttering about it being food poisoning, not murder. And then of course they twigged who I was and they threw me out . . .'

'So the cops, they don't think it's murder? Is that what you're saying? They still think it's food poisoning?'

'Not any more,' says Tomizawa. 'Back outside, I was stood among the crowd – massive crowd by now – finding out what I could, when the Big Boys from the MPB arrived. Minute they got inside the bank, they threw out all the locals. But some of those locals had heard the detectives saying it was mass murder and that the bank was a crime scene and it had to be protected . . .'

'You know what made them change their minds?'

'Well, one of the uniforms who'd been inside the bank and was then sent outside to keep people away, I asked him what was going on, and he said one of the victims up at the hospital, she was talking and had told them some kind of doctor had come to the bank and given them some kind of medicine for dysentery, that they'd all drunk this medicine and that was when they'd all collapsed. No mention of food, only a doctor and some medicine.'

'Just the one man, not a gang?'

'Far as I know, just the one.'

'Description?'

'Not yet.'

'Right then,' I tell Tomizawa. 'You stay where you are. I'm going to finish off the piece for the Boss and then head up to the hospital. Call us in a couple of hours . . .'

I replace the receiver. I turn around. The rival eyes of all the other reporters are no longer watching me, their rival ears already at the other phones, their rival fingers already writing in their notebooks, every other reporter either listening or writing –

In the Fictional City, I go back to my desk in the press office. I re-write the story:

MASS MURDER IN SHIINAMACHI –

Ten Workers of Teikoku Bank Slain In Broad Daylight – Robbery Behind Killing?

TOKYO, Jan. 26 – Ten were killed and 6 others are in critical condition as a result of the attempted robbery and poisoning of the entire staff of the Shiinamachi branch of the Teikoku Bank at Nagasaki-chō, Toshima-ku, Tokyo by a cold-blooded criminal who apparently tried to snatch away heaps of bank notes in broad daylight on the afternoon of January 26.

The sensational 'poison bank holdup' case was perpetrated about 4 o'clock Monday afternoon shortly after the bank had closed for business for the day when a man entered the building posing as a health official. The fiendish doctor told the entire staff to drink a dysentery preventative medicine.

In no time the bank turned into a veritable death chamber with all the victims writhing in agony. When the relief party arrived at the scene, 10 of the victims had already died. 6 others were rushed to the Seibo Hospital in the neighbourhood and remain in a critical condition.

According to the police, who are strictly keeping away outsiders in an effort to find a clue, an intensive search is now being conducted across the city for the bank robber.

I stop writing. I file the story. I get my hat and my coat. I tell Shiratō to wait where he is, that I'm going to the Seibo Hospital, and I'll be back in a couple of hours.

IN THE FICTIONAL CITY, in the Seibo Hospital, I am wearing a stolen white coat, I am pretending to be a doctor –

Pretending, impersonating, deceiving . . .

I smile at the policeman. I open the door. I step inside the room. She is alone in the room, lying in the only bed, her eyes closed. I walk to the end of the bed. I read the name above her head –

I write it down in my notebook:

Murata Masako . . .

I sit down in a chair beside the bed. I see her hand on top of the blankets. I sit forward in the chair beside the bed. I reach for her hand on the blankets. I hold her hand. I lean towards her face. I whisper in her ear, 'Miss Murata, Miss Murata . . .'

I see her swallow in her sleep –
'Can you hear me, Miss Murata . . .?'
I see her eyelids flicker –
'Can you tell me what happened to you, Miss Murata?'
I see her eyes opening. I see her looking at me now –
'Can you tell me what happened to you in the bank?'
Now her body starts to tremble. Her mouth begins to open –
'Get away!' she shouts. 'Get away from me!'
I let go of her hand. I stand up. I want to apologize. I want to explain. But I turn away. And I walk away –
'Get away! Get away from me!'
Out of the room. The hospital.

IN THE FICTIONAL CITY, I walk her streets and I hear her stories, telephones ringing and voices whispering, along the wires and down the cables, a telephone and a voice with a time and with a place –

An hour later, I turn a corner off the main street, and I walk down an alley of pawnshops and mahjong parlours. Half-way down the alleyway, I push open a frosted-glass door. A bell above the door rings and five pairs of eyes glance up from the shadows of the dark and narrow room. I walk through these shadows, past their glances that are now stares, and I sit down on a sofa at the back of the room. Across a large porcelain brazier, a man is sitting opposite me, reading a newspaper, my newspaper –

The *Yomiuri* . . .

The man slowly folds up the newspaper. He takes off his glasses. He puts the glasses in the breast pocket of his jacket. He sits forward in his chair. He stretches out his hands over the edge of the brazier. He looks up at me and he says, 'I hope you brought your wallet with you?'

IN THE FICTIONAL CITY, the MPB have made a statement, and then another, and another, and so I write a story, and then another, and another:

WIDE MANHUNT ON FOR POISON KILLER;
INVESTIGATORS WORK ON DESCRIPTION GIVEN BY
4 MASS MURDER SURVIVORS

Slayer Believed Familiar With Medicines;
Assisted By Several Accomplices?

WANTED!

Description of culprit in Teikoku Bank Shiinamachi branch
mass poison murder case:

Sex: Male. Age: From 45 to 56. Height: 5 ft. 2 or 3 in.

Thin, long-faced, pale, high-nose,

crop-haired with a sprinkling of grey hair.

Brown blemish on left cheek.

Was wearing brown overcoat at time of crime.

TOKYO, Jan. 28 – With the above description of the culprit given by the four survivors as the chief clue, the Metropolitan Police Board, mobilizing its most experienced criminal investigators, is on the search for the perpetrators of one of the coldest-blooded crimes of modern times.

The search is on for the man who, as reported yesterday, posed as a health inspector and induced 16 persons at the Shiinamachi branch of the Teikoku Bank to take poison, killing 12 of them.

The police base their belief (a) that the culprit was familiar with medicine and epidemic prevention and (b) that he was someone who knew the district and the bank well on the following two factors:

1. Dysentery cases had been reported in the district recently.

2. The criminal wore the armband of the Tokyo Metropolitan sanitation bureau and did not arouse any suspicion among the 16 who drank the poison.

Investigation headquarters have been established at the Mejiro police station.

The names of the victims of the mass poison slaughter have been ascertained as follows:

Dead: – Watanabe Yoshiyasu, 43, chief treasurer; Shirai Shoichi, 28; Kato Teruko, 16; Uchida Yuko, 22; Takeuchi Sutejiro, 48, messenger; Nishimura Hidehiko, 38; Akiyama Miyako, 22; Takizawa Tatsuo, 46, messenger; his wife, Takizawa Ryuko, 51; Takizawa's son, Yoshihiro, 7; Takizawa's daughter, Takako, 18; and Sawada Yoshio, 21.

Those in critical condi-tion: – Yoshida Takejiro, 42, assistant manager; Akusawa Yoshiko, 18; Murata Masako, 21; and Tanaka Norikazu, 28.

The first of the two bottles that the culprit induced his victims to drink is ascertained to have contained potassium cyanide.

The armband he wore is believed to have been one issued at the time of the recent flood disaster to students, hospitals, ward offices, and volunteer workers.

The crime is believed to have been planned by several persons in conjunction with the culprit who appeared at the bank.

Four persons who figured in a similar attempt made previously at the Nakai branch of the Mitsubishi Bank are believed to have some connection with the Teikoku Bank case.

The latest check shows that from ¥110,000 to ¥120,000 of the bank's money are missing.

Doctor Suspected

TOKYO, Jan. 28 – Police suspicion in the Teikoku Bank mass murder case has fallen on a certain middle-aged doctor living within the jurisdiction of the Mejiro police station who fits the description given by Miss Murata Masako, one of the survivors, it is learned.

Linked With Case?

TOKYO, Jan. 28 – A man committed suicide with potassium cyanide at a hotel not far from the Shiinamachi branch of the Teikoku Bank early this morning.

As the poison taken by the suicide is the same as that which killed the bank employees, the Mejiro police station is investigating whether he is connected with the mass murder case.

The suicide, who registered as Yokobe Kunio, a company official at Komagawa-mura, Iruma-gun, Saitama prefecture, put up at the Kiraku Inn at 2156 Shiina-machi 5-chōme, Toshima-ku, yesterday at about 9.30 p.m. and took the potassium cyanide today at about 6 a.m.

He was wearing a grey sweater, khaki coat, black serge trousers and black overcoat. In his wallet was only about ¥100.

His hair was not cropped.

In the Fictional City, this city of millions, millions will buy my newspaper, millions will buy my stories.

IN THE FICTIONAL CITY, I am back in the Seibo Hospital, back wearing a stolen white coat, back pretending to be a doctor –

Pretending, impersonating, deceiving . . .

Back beside her bed, her eyes closed, her hand in mine, I am whispering, 'Can you hear me, Miss Murata. . . ?'

There is sweat on her brow, in her hair, shadows on her cheeks, round her eyes. Her mouth opens and then closes, her fingers tighten and then loosen. She is dreaming, dreaming bad dreams –

'Miss Murata, I can help you. Please believe me . . .'

Her eyes are open now but still not close, she is struggling to get back, back to this room, this white room in this hospital –

'I can help you,' I tell her. 'You can trust me . . .'

Her fingers turn in my hand, tighten around my own, as she looks at me now and asks, 'Who are you? Are you a doctor?'

'No, this white coat is just so I could talk to you. That's all. I just want to talk to you. I just want to help you . . .'

'But why?' she says. 'Who are you?'

In the Fictional City, in the Seibo Hospital, in my stolen coat, I say, 'My name is Takeuchi Riichi. I'm a journalist.'

'You're a journalist?' she laughs. 'Not a doctor?'

'No,' I smile. 'A journalist, with the *Yomiuri*.'

She turns her face away from me now, not laughing any more. I let go of her hand. *I want to apologize.* She stares at the white wall, tears on her pillow. I stand up. *I want to explain . . .*

'Get away from me!' she cries.

IN THE FICTIONAL CITY, a telephone rings, a voice whispers, along wires, down cables, with another time, another place –

Down another alley, in another room, through the shadows, past the stares, in another chair, another man –

A man with an envelope.

I open the envelope. I read the letter. I take out my wallet. I hand him the cash and I say, 'I hope you didn't write it yourself.'

The man counts the cash. The man puts it in his jacket pocket. The man smiles and says, 'What difference would it make?'

IN THE FICTIONAL CITY, with an envelope and a letter on my desk, an editor and a deadline on my back, I write another story:

SINISTER NOTE RECEIVED IN PUZZLING BANK CASE

Reward for Capture Now ¥80,000;
Police Still Baffled

Painfully slow progress was being made in the Teikoku Bank 'Poison Holdup' case as police officers continued to be enmeshed in difficulties because of the lack of tangible evidence.

Rewards for the capture of the diabolical killer of 12 bank employees rose to ¥80,000 and one silver cup.

A sinister letter was received on January 29 by the manager of the Shiina branch of the Teikoku Bank. Signed 'Yamaguchi Jiro', the alias used on the day of the diabolical crime, the letter said in part: 'I am sorry I caused quite a disturbance the other day. I let Murata Masako (the girl who crawled into the streets to seek help) live because I have some use for her later. In due time, I shall pay her a visit. . . . At first I had an unpleasant feeling watching so many people writhe and squirm in agony but later I didn't mind at all . . .'

Police are investigating to see whether it really came from the poisoner or from some callous citizen with a dubious sense of humour.

Meanwhile, the description of the man who claimed the cheque stolen from the scene of the crime failed to tally with that of the poisoner.

Police officials, however, expressed gratification for public cooperation in the manhunt and said that scores of letters and phone calls are being received daily at the search headquarters.

In the Fictional City, so many letters and so many calls, so many stories and so many tales, so many doubts and so many, many questions.

IN THE FICTIONAL CITY, in the Seibo Hospital, there is sweat on her brow, in her hair again, shadows on her cheeks, round her eyes again. Her mouth opening and then closing, her fingers tightening and then loosening. She is dreaming, dreaming bad dreams again –

'Help me,' she says in her dreams. 'Please help me . . .'

In this white room, her hand in mine, I say, 'I can help you. Please believe me. I can make that dream go away . . .'

Pretending, impersonating, deceiving . . .

She opens her eyes. She stares into me. She squeezes my hand. She whispers, 'How can you help me?'

'I can save you,' I tell her –

Pretending, not pretending . . .

'Until yesterday,' she says, 'I thought a cup was a cup. Until then, a table was a table. I thought the war was over. I knew we had lost. I knew we had surrendered. I knew we were now occupied.

'But I thought the war was over. I thought a cup was still a cup. That medicine was medicine. I thought my friend was my friend, a colleague was a colleague. A doctor, a doctor.

'But the war is not over. A cup is not a cup. Medicine is not medicine. A friend not a friend, a colleague not a colleague. For a colleague here yesterday, sat in the seat at the counter beside me, that colleague is not here today. Because a doctor is not a doctor.

'A doctor is a murderer. A killer.

'Because the war is not over.

'The war is never over.'

'I know,' I say, pretending to pretend, in my stolen white coat, not pretending to pretend, beside her hospital bed, squeezing her hand and telling her again, 'I know, I know.'

'I was still going through that day's thirty deposits when the killer arrived,' she says. 'I didn't see what time it was when he entered, but business had closed as usual at 3 p.m., and I had then immediately begun to count up the deposits. The thirty deposits would have taken me no longer than ten minutes which means the killer must have arrived sometime between 3 p.m. and 3.10 p.m.

'When the killer began to distribute the poison, I looked him in his face. I will never forget that face. I would know it anywhere.'

'I know,' I say again, and again, 'I know, I know.'

'I am a survivor,' she says, still staring into me, deeper and deeper, still squeezing my hand, tighter and tighter. 'But of course I know only through luck have I survived so many friends. But night after night, in dream after dream, I hear these friends saying of me: "Those who survive are stronger." And I hate myself . . .'

Again and again, she says, 'I hate myself.'

And again, again I say, 'I know . . .'

Pretending, not pretending . . .

'But I will help you.'

IN THE FICTIONAL CITY, I walk down the long, long table to my editor's desk at the head of the long, long table and I stand before him and I say, 'I'm very sorry to disturb you, Boss : . .'

'Ah, Takeuchi,' smiles Ono. 'Just the man I wanted to see. Liked that piece on the "Sinister Note" very much. Very much.'

'Well, actually, that was what I wanted to talk to you about. I'm not sure it's entirely legitimate. So I was thinking maybe you could hold it back for now while I checked into it a bit more . . .?'

'Too late for doubts,' laughs Ono, tapping his watch. 'It's already been set and the presses are rolling.'

'I see,' I say.

'I've told you before,' he tells me again. 'You worry too much. In our business, there's no time for doubts, no time for procrastination. Don't get me wrong, I admire your integrity. But in our business we've got to go with our guts, run with our hunches, and your gut, your hunch, was to run with this. So forget it now, and get after the next one. After all, not like you made it up yourself, is it?'

IN THE FICTIONAL CITY, it is Wednesday 4 February, and I am standing outside the Seibo Hospital with all the other reporters and all the photographers. In the Fictional City, we are watching the survivors leave the hospital, watching them bow and thank the nurses and the doctors, their arms full of presents, full of flowers. In the Fictional City, all the other reporters are shouting out –

'Mr Yoshida! Mr Tanaka! Miss Akuzawa . . .

'Miss Murata! Over here, Miss Murata . . .'

Her eyes searching through the shouts of all the reporters, searching through the flashes of all the photographers –

'Miss Murata! Over here, Miss Murata . . .'

Her lips smiling through the shouts and through the flashes, her eyes searching, lost and not smiling –

'She's beautiful, isn't she?' says Matsuda, the photographer from the *Yomiuri*. 'She'll be on every front page tomorrow . . .'

And now the police are leading her away through the crowds, taking her away to their car, with her arms full of presents, full of flowers, and I am walking away among all the other reporters and the photographers, with our heads full of stories, full of fictions –

'Lucky she's so good-looking,' laughs Matsuda, tapping his camera, winking at me. 'Sell more papers for us . . .'

In the Fictional City, back at my desk in the *Yomiuri* building, I stare at Matsuda's photographs and I write another story:

Happy over their narrow escape with death, the four lucky survivors of the Teikoku Bank 'Poison Holdup' case were discharged as fully recovered from the Seibo Hospital, Wednesday. Shown as they received presents from congratulating friends are: (Left to right) Acting Manager Yoshida Takejiro, 44, Miss Murata Masako, 22, and Tanaka Norikazu, 20. They revisited the scene of the crime to reconstruct what had taken place for the police investigators. The first inkling of the tragedy was made known when the attention of passers-by was attracted by the beautiful Miss Murata who, despite her rapidly failing consciousness, had bravely managed to drag her agonized body into the street.

I stop writing. I start reading. I stop reading—

'*I know only through luck have I survived so many friends . . . But night after night, in dream after dream, I hear these friends saying of me: "Those who survive are stronger."*

'*And I hate myself. I hate myself . . .*'

I stand up. I put on my coat.

IN THE FICTIONAL CITY, it is night again, night again as I walk her streets, as I hear her stories, from Nihonbashi up to Hongō, from Hongō and onto Kasuga-dōri, along Kasuga-dōri then down Shinobazu-dōri, down Shinobazu-dōri and onto Mejiro-dōri, along Mejiro-dōri onto Yamate-dōri, Yamate-dōri to Shiinamachi –

But I do not go to the scene of the crime, I go to her house, Murata Masako's house. In this Fictional City, in its long, long night, I stand across the street from her house. *Is she awake?* Her house is dark. *Or is she sleeping?* The lights off. *Dreaming?* The curtains closed. *Dreaming that dream again?*

'*And I hate myself. I hate . . .*'

The footsteps in the shadows, the grip on my shoulder, the voice at my back, 'Who are you? What are you doing here?'

I try to turn, the grip too tight –

'Don't move, just talk!'

'I'm a journalist,' I say. 'From the *Yomiuri*.'

The hand inside my coat, inside my jacket, my pocket now my wallet. The grip relaxed, a torchlight on –

I spin round, shove him in his chest, snatch back my wallet and now say, 'Who are *you*?'

The man smiles, the man before me, in his hat and in his cape, and he bellows, 'I am Shimizu Kogorō, Occult-*Tantei*. Head of the Nagasaki branch of the Mejiro Security Association . . .'

Across the street, her house is no longer dark, the lights on and the curtains open, a face at the window –

Her face at the window, afraid.

IN THE FICTIONAL CITY, in a dancehall on the Ginza, with its heavy drapes and broken ventilation, its bad perfume and cheap pomade, through the cigarette smoke on the sticky floor, young men in zoot suits and aloha shirts are cheek-to-cheek with the hostesses and their cracked faces, their acne-scars, dancing to a swing band in the reflecting lights, in this dancehall on the Ginza, in this Fictional City, I am waiting for a character, waiting for their story, looking at the door and fiddling with my watch, but tonight he does not show, tonight he stands me up, no character, no story, not tonight, but here in the cigarette smoke, tonight in the reflecting lights, I open my notebook and I read through my pencil-marks, for there is always a character, always a story somewhere in the Fictional City.

IN THE FICTIONAL CITY, a new day, a new story, another story for another day; there is always another day, there is always another story in the Fictional City:

NEIGHBOURHOOD INVESTIGATIVE HQ

A local organization named Mejiro Chian Kyōkai Nagasaki Shibu *has founded a 'Civil Investigative Headquarters' because 'the locals will be upset unless the [Teigin] case is solved quickly,' said the Chief of the HQ, Mr Shimizu.*

The HQ is located in the office of the Nagasaki Shrine, and their investigation is mostly focused on the killer's tracks. They summon those who had been in the vicinity of the crime scene, and who had hurried to rescue the victims, as well as local children who may have also witnessed the crime. Shimizu and his team plan to gather up all these testimonies and give their reports to Mejiro Police Station.

Each member of the Interview Team runs a separate district of the neighbourhood and witnesses are summoned to the Nagasaki Shrine HQ, even in the night, to be questioned by these amateur cops. For now, Chief Shimizu ignores his own business and devotes himself entirely to the investigation, twenty four hours a day. 'I take 5 or 6 Hiropon injections per day but, what-the-heck, I'll do beyond my best till we get him,' said Mr Shimizu, and he will not disband the HQ until the killer is caught.

However, one local housewife complained, 'I really wish the killer would be caught very soon, or he [Mr Shimizu] will be back to ask us for another donation to his association!'

In the Fictional City, I put my head down on my desk, I close my eyes, and I pretend to sleep.

IN THE FICTIONAL CITY, I knock on her door and I try to open it, but her door is locked and so I knock again, and I wait –

'Who is it?' she says from behind the door.

'It's Takeuchi,' I say. 'From the *Yomiuri*.'

'What do you want?'

'Well, I just wondered if you'd come for a coffee with me.'

'Why?' she asks.

'Well, actually I don't know,' I say. 'I suppose I just wanted to see you, to see how you are, not for a story. Just . . .'

The lock turns now. The door opens –

Miss Murata Masako stares at me –

I ask, 'Do you remember me?'

'Yes,' she says. 'I remember you, Takeuchi Riichi of the *Yomiuri*, in your white coat, pretending to be a doctor.'

I bow and I say, 'I'm sorry about that.'

'So you want to take me for coffee as an apology, is that it?'

I smile and I say, 'Well, maybe. Yes . . .'

'OK, then,' she says and, in the *genkan* to her house, she reaches for her coat and puts it on, then steps out of a pair of sandals and into a pair of shoes, and finally she ties a scarf around her face, over her hair, and says, 'Come on, then.'

In the Fictional City, we walk in silence through the streets of Shiinamachi, in silence through the mud and the sleet, in silence to a coffee shop by the station. We open the door to the coffee shop and we step inside, the coffee shop filled with customers and conversation, and we sit down at a table and she takes off her scarf. Now the conversations stop and the customers stare, and she looks down at the table, at the sugar bowl and the ashtray, and she says, 'I'm sorry. I want to go home.'

IN THE FICTIONAL CITY, he walks through the cigarette smoke, across the sticky floor, and he sits down and he says, 'Sorry about the other night. I tried to call you, but you'd already left the office.'

'It doesn't matter,' I say. 'Forget it. You're here now. So what have you got for me, Detective?'

'Well, it's not something you can probably print, not for now, but I think it's something you should know. What they're not saying in their statements is that there's a growing feeling among many of the detectives that this case is connected with the Tokumu Kikan and their operations in Occupied China during the war. There are rumours of similar cases to the Teigin case that occurred in Shanghai during the war, that the culprit is ex-Tokumu Kikan, with experience handling medicines and civilians, and that's who we should be looking for. On the other hand, there are some detectives, particularly the older guys, who think all these rumours are just a distraction, that it's nothing to do with Tokumu Kikan and Occupied China. So there are almost two rival lines of inquiry now. But, as I say, what I'm telling you is nothing you can print, but there's also nothing to stop you looking into the China connection, is there?'

IN THE FICTIONAL CITY, I have walked her streets, I have heard her stories, her stories of old soldiers, her stories of new poisons –

In the Fictional City, her stories in my notebook.

Now I take these stories from my notebook and I write them out. I write them out in letters. In letters, on grids –

TEIGIN POLICE CHASE POISON SCHOOL LEAD

SCAP Assistance Sought In Hunt For Mass Murderer

TOKYO – Police investigating the Teikoku Bank 'Poison Holdup' case are now actively pursuing two new lines of inquiry in their frantic efforts to catch the cold-blooded fiend responsible for the diabolical poison-murders.

Senior detectives have requested the assistance of the SCAP Public Safety Division in locating a Lieutenant Hornet and a Lieutenant Parker, both names being used by the mass killer and associated with typhus disinfecting teams in the Tokyo area.

Witnesses at the Ebara branch of the Yasuda Bank reported the suspect as saying, 'I came here with Lieutenant Parker in a jeep because a new typhus case happened in the vicinity.' While at the Shiinamachi branch of the Teikoku Bank, the same individual is reported as saying, 'I came here because there have been many dysentery cases in the area. Lieutenant Hornet will be here soon.'

Police believe Lieutenant Hornet to have been associated with the Toshima Team in the Ōji and Katsushika Wards, while Lieutenant Parker was associated with the Ebara Disinfecting Team.

Investigators have requested that the Public Safety Division of SCAP provide any information, names and addresses of Japanese individuals either connected with or having knowledge of the disinfecting work done by either of the above lieutenants, particularly interpreters or individuals who speak English.

Meanwhile, police are also checking a new lead concerning ex-personnel of the former Japanese Imperial Chemical Laboratory in Tsudanuma, Chiba-ken.

It is known that experiments were conducted at the Tsudanuma Laboratory with prussic acid as a poison. Police believe that the modus operandi of the Teikoku Bank 'Poison Holdup' case and the use of prussic poison by the criminal are very similar to the training developed by Tsudanuma Arsenal.

In the Fictional City, I stop writing and I read what I have written. These letters in their grids. I stop reading. Now I get up from my desk, and I walk down the long, long table to my editor's desk –

'Ah, Takeuchi,' smiles Ono. 'What have you got for me today? Something meaty, I hope, something juicy . . .'

I hand him the paper. I say, 'I think so.'

Ono sits back in his chair. He adjusts his glasses. He starts to read, nodding, nodding, nodding and now smiling, he says, 'Great!'

'Thanks,' I say. 'They're denying it, of course . . .'

'Of course,' says Ono. 'But that's their problem. Not yours.'

IN THE FICTIONAL CITY, in the *genkan* to her house, she looks at the bunch of flowers in my hand, and she asks, 'Why?'

'The other day,' I say. 'It was a mistake. The coffee shop. I didn't think. All those people. It was a bad idea . . .'

'It wasn't your fault,' she says.

I hold out the flowers. I say, 'Please. They are for you . . .'

She bows. She takes the flowers. She says, 'Thank you.'

The door to her house closes now, locked again.

IN THE FICTIONAL CITY, among the stained-suits and the bad-skins, beneath the swing band and the reflecting lights, he hisses, 'I was taking a big risk telling you the things I did, showing the documents I did. A big, big risk. And what for? For nothing. I read your so-called newspaper every day and every day I see nothing. Nothing about the SCAP connection, nothing about the Tsudanuma Arsenal. So it seems to me I took a big, big risk for nothing . . .'

'Not exactly nothing,' I tell him. 'Yes, you took a risk, but you also took my cash. I paid you . . .'

'Not enough. Not enough for the risk I took. So I want to know what's happening, why I took a risk for nothing . . .'

'I wrote the story,' I tell him. 'I gave it to my boss, he read it in front of me and he liked it, liked it very much . . .'

'So where is it then, this story of yours, this story your editor says he liked, liked so very much?'

'I don't know,' I say.

He stands up. He says, 'Well, find out. Or you can forget about any more help, any more stories from me.'

IN THE FICTIONAL CITY, I stand before my editor's desk at the head of the long, long table and I say, 'Excuse me, Boss . . .'

'Takeuchi,' mutters Ono, not smiling. 'What is it?'

'Well, I'm sorry to disturb you,' I say. 'But I was wondering what had happened to that piece I wrote on the Poison School? You'd seemed very happy with it, you'd said you liked it, but . . .'

'Yes,' nods Ono. 'I did like it. Very much . . .'

'Thank you,' I say. 'But it hasn't run yet . . .'

'Not yet,' says Ono. 'Not been the time, not yet. Thought we'd wait and see if there was any statement from the MPB first. Maybe then get some quotes from them, flesh it out.'

'I see,' I say.

'I've told you before,' he tells me again. 'In our business, you have to choose your time, pick your moment carefully. Don't get me wrong, I like the story, like it very much and I'll run it, I will. But in our business, there's always a right time, always a wrong time to run a story. But that's my job, my worry, not yours. So you just leave it with me, forget about it now, now you've done your bit, and you just get after the next one. Because there's always a next one, isn't there? Always another story, out there somewhere . . .'

IN THE FICTIONAL CITY, in a restaurant far from Shiinamachi, far from the scene of the crime, I ask her, 'How is work? It must feel strange being back there at the bank now, after everything . . .'

'Are you asking me as a reporter,' she whispers, 'or as a . . . As a what? What are you? Who are you, Mr Takeuchi?'

I look down at the table, the glass jar of toothpicks, the white bottle of soy sauce, and I say, 'A friend, I hope . . .'

'Then thank you,' says Murata Masako. 'I hope so, too.'

IN THE FICTIONAL CITY, a telephone rings, a voice whispers, along the wires, down the cables, with a time and with a place –

Down an alley, in a room, another room of shadows, another room of stares, another man hands me another envelope –

I open the envelope. I read its contents:

GENERAL HEADQUARTERS
SUPREME COMMANDER FOR THE ALLIED POWERS
Civil Intelligence Section, G-2
PUBLIC SAFETY DIVISION

APO 500
11 March 1948

Memorandum

SUBJECT: Teikoku Bank Robbery Case

To: Mr H. S. Eaton, Chief Administrator, Police Branch

1. Interference by Japanese newspaper reporters with the police investigation of the Teikoku Bank Robbery case, as reported by Jiro Fujita, Chief of Detectives, Tokyo Metropolitan Police earlier on 11 March 1948 was discussed informally by Bryon Engle, Administrator in Charge, Police Branch, and this investigator; at 1100 hours this date with Major D. C. Imboden, OIC, Press and Publications Section.

2. In response to suggestions of PSD representatives, Major Imboden approved Mr Fujita's projected press conference for the purpose of discussing the Teikoku case with Japanese newspaper executives in order that the problems created by interference of news reporters might be fully explained to the newsmen and for the purpose of soliciting the cooperation

---

of the newspapers in halting such reported practices as reporters following suspects in the case and shadowing police investigators working on the case as well as reporters representing themselves to be detectives in order to secure news matter. Major Imboden advised Mr Engle at 1300 hours this date that telegraphic advice had been dispatched to all Japanese newspapers not to interfere with the police investigation in the Teikoku case or indulge in such practices as have been ascribed to the Tokyo reporters by Mr Fujita.

   3. Major Imboden also stated that he would communicate personally with the publisher of the Yomiuri Shimbun in Tokyo and advise him to have his reporters removed immediately from their reported watch on the homes of persons working or secretly assisting in the investigation. He also said he would discuss the matter with Allied censorship authorities exercising control of Japanese publications and request the censors cooperate in stopping publication of any article containing any reference to the police investigation of a Japanese Army Poison School being connected with the Teikoku case; further he will request the censors screen all articles pertaining to the Teikoku case on the basis of whether publication of the article will hinder apprehension of the culprit.

JOHNSON F. MUNROE
Police Investigator

   I stop reading. I put the document back in its envelope. I hand him back the envelope. I take out my wallet. I hand him the cash.
   The man counts the cash. The man puts it in his jacket pocket. The man smiles and says, 'Didn't think you'd like it, but thought you should see it. Explains a lot doesn't it ?'

IN THE FICTIONAL CITY, days pass and stories pass; days of snow, days of wind, days of rain and days of sun, stories of food poisoning, stories of strikes, stories of cabinets resigning and stories of cabinets forming, the end of Katayama and the beginning of Ashida, as winter turns to spring, spring to summer, the sky falling and the temperature rising, as censorship turns to coercion, coercion to complicity in the Fictional City, where days pass and stories pass, days and stories passing in complicity and in columns until Sunday 22 August 1948, and a story, a story not in my paper, not in the *Yomiuri* –
   A story in our rival paper, in the *Mainichi*:

Teikoku Bank Poison Robbery Suspect Arrested in Otaru

OTARU, Aug. 22 – A well-known water-colour artist residing at Shinkinaimachi, Otaru City, Hokkaido, yesterday morning was arrested by detectives of the Metropolitan Police Board as a highly important suspect in the Teikoku Bank 'mass poison murder' case.

The arrival of the Tokyo detectives specifically for the purpose of arresting Hirasawa Sadamichi, 57, and taking him to Tokyo for questioning has given strong reason for believing that the police may finally have nabbed the long-sought-for Teikoku Bank criminal.

It is understood that Hirasawa previously had been listed by the manhunt headquarters in Tokyo as a likely suspect.

The arrested man was reported closely to fit the description of the diabolic Teikoku Bank murderer.

On April 16, last year, Hirasawa is said to have secured a name-card from Dr Matsui Shigeru, Welfare Ministry employee, when he met the doctor aboard an Aomori–Hokkaido ferryboat.

He is suspected of having used the name-card in holding-up the Teikoku Bank on January 26, this year. It is known that Hirasawa left Yokohama for Otaru aboard the Hikawa Maru on February 10, this year, shortly after the Teikoku Bank case.

Furthermore, suspicion has been heightened against the suspect by information obtained by the police that he transmitted a sum of ¥80,000 to his wife Masako, 55. Besides, the letter once sent to him by his wife said: 'Please don't do such a bad thing again.'

Hirasawa is well known in Tokyo art circles as a member of a water-colour artists' association. He is said to have presented his paintings to the Bunten Art Exhibition numerous times.

In the Fictional City, I run down the long, long, long, long table to my editor's desk, the *Mainichi* in my hand –

'Just the man I wanted to see,' says Ono. 'Though that's not the story I wanted to see, least not in that paper!'

I say, 'We've been scooped . . .'

'No time for tears now,' sighs Ono, tapping his watch. 'This suspect, this Hirasawa, he'll be arriving at Ueno Station first thing tomorrow morning and I want you there with your girlfriend . . .'

I start to say, 'She's not my girlfriend . . .'

'No time for denials now,' laughs Ono. 'You've got a busy day and night ahead of you, a lot of ground to make up. Before that train pulls into Ueno Station, I want an interview with this Hirasawa's wife. Here's her address . . .'

I take the address from him and I ask, 'How did they get all that information, the *Mainichi*? Who are they talking to and why are they not talking to us? We've sat back, done what we've been told, played the game, been good little boys. It's not fair . . .'

'I've told you before,' he tells me again. 'You think too much. In our business, there's no time for thoughts, no time for theories. In our business, we've just got to get on and get after the next story. And your next story is Hirasawa Masako . . .'

The next story, the next story . . .

In the Fictional City, I'm expecting the worst; expecting crowds of reporters and their photographers outside Number 32, 2-chōme, Miyazono-dōri, Nakano-ku, the wife and children of Hirasawa Sadamichi already in hiding or already waiting at the Mejiro Police Station, waiting for the arrival of Hirasawa Sadamichi. But in the Fictional City, there are no reporters and their photographers outside Number 32, 2-chōme, Miyazono-dōri, Nakano-ku, just a woman tending to some flowers, some poppies –

'Excuse me,' I say. 'Are you Hirasawa Masako?'

The woman looks up from the flowers, the poppies, and wipes her face on a towel and says, 'Yes. Can I help you?'

'My name is Takeuchi Riichi,' I tell her. 'I'm a journalist for the *Yomiuri* newspaper. I was wondering if I could talk to you about your husband, Hirasawa Sadamichi? Please?'

'My husband?' she says. 'Why?'

'Well, I'm very sorry to tell you that he's been arrested . . .'

'Arrested?' she says. 'What's he been arrested for?'

'The Teikoku Bank murder case.'

'What?' she laughs. 'Don't be ridiculous . . .'

But now another car is pulling up outside Number 32, 2-chōme, Miyazono-dōri, Nakano-ku, another journalist jumping out of the car, another journalist shouting 'Mrs Hirasawa? Please . . .'

I say, 'I'm afraid it's true. But I think we should go inside, if you don't mind. Then I'll tell you everything I know . . .'

The wife of Hirasawa Sadamichi is still laughing, but she is nodding now, ushering me up her path and into her house, calling her daughter out of their kitchen as I turn back now, closing their front door in the face of the other journalist with an, 'Excuse me . . .'

'They've arrested Father,' Mrs Hirasawa is telling her daughter. 'For the Teikoku Bank murders!'

'What? Father?' says her daughter, looking at me, then at her mother, and now she is laughing, too –

'It must be a joke . . .'

Laughing but looking at the front door to their house, listening to the banging on the door, the tapping on the window –

'A joke . . .'

In the Fictional City, back in my office, back at my desk, I am writing another story:

Wife Refutes Charge

Tokyo, Aug. 23 – Mrs Hirasawa Masako, wife of the latest Teikoku Bank 'poison holdup case' suspect, yesterday denied as 'ridiculous' reports that her husband was the long-sought diabolic criminal on being interviewed at her residence in Nakano here.

Mrs Hirasawa said that her husband left Tokyo for Otaru, Hokkaido, on February 10 for the purpose of paying a visit to his ailing brother.

She said that whereas her husband's age and greying hair may fit the description of the wanted man, it was unbelievable that he committed such a diabolic crime.

Mrs Hirasawa added that there was no reason for her husband to commit such a crime to obtain money, as her three daughters were earning a total of ¥15,000 monthly, which is quite enough to support them.

She hoped that the survivors of the Teikoku Bank murder case swiftly would be given an opportunity to see her husband, as she was confident that their judgment would clear her husband of all suspicion.

IN THE FICTIONAL CITY, it is not yet dawn but it is already hot as I knock on her door. Again and again I knock on her door, banging and banging, until she says from behind the door, 'Who is it?'

'It's me,' I say. 'Takeuchi.'

'What do you want?'

'The police have arrested a man in Otaru,' I tell her. 'The police believe this is the man. The train bringing him to Tokyo will arrive at Ueno at 5 a.m. I've got a car to take you to Ueno.'

'Why?' she asks.

'Well, I thought you'd want to see him,' I say. 'To see if it really is him, really is the man you saw that day . . .'

'Wait then,' she says now and I wait, I wait in the street outside her house. *Is she afraid?* Her house still dark. *Or is she excited?* The lights still off. *Hoping?* The curtains still closed—
Praying it is that man, that man again?

The door opens now. Miss Murata Masako stares at me. Murata Masako says, 'Are you here as a reporter or as a friend?'

'Both,' I say. 'But mainly as a friend, I hope.'

'I hope so, too,' says Murata Masako. 'Come on, then.'

In the Fictional City, we sit in silence in the back of the *Yomiuri* car, in silence as she stares out of the window at the city, the city rising, in silence as we are driven through the heat, the heat rising, in silence until we arrive at Ueno Station, at Ueno Station where she turns to me and whispers, 'In due time, in due time . . .'

'Pardon?' I ask. 'What did you say?'

'Nothing,' she says and now she gets out of the car in front of the station, out of the car and into the crowds, the crowds that have come in their thousands, in their thousands to see this man, this man who the crowds believe murdered her co-workers and her friends –

This man who tried to murder her, to kill her –

Now she grabs my hand suddenly and she holds my hand tightly as I push and I shove through the crowds, the crowds in their thousands who are pushing and shoving to catch a glimpse, a glimpse of this man, this man called Hirasawa Sadamichi –

This man who tried to murder her –

But the train is late, the train delayed, and the crowd is growing and growing, pushing and shoving, and now the train has arrived, the train is here, and the crowd are pushing and shoving, harder and harder, and I am holding her in front of me, my hands on her waist, tighter and tighter, pushing her forward, raising her up, higher and higher, hoping and praying she'll see him, hoping and praying she'll see him and say that this is the man, this is the man who murdered her co-workers –

This man who –

'I can't see,' she whispers. 'I can't see him . . .'

IN THE FICTIONAL CITY, in the dancehall on the Ginza, with its sticky suits and sweaty faces, its jungle rhythms and deafening shoes, in this Fictional City, I am shouting, shouting over the drums and the feet, 'I thought you were my man-on-the-inside, my man-in-the-know, but I'm the last-man-to-know, I've been scooped . . .'

He shrugs. He says, 'Everyone's in the dark. Not just me, not just you. They kept the rest of us chasing suspects with military backgrounds, with medical backgrounds, telling us to forget about the name-cards, giving it to Robbery, moving Robbery out of HQ . . .'

'But they told us not to write about the military men, the medical men; told us to keep it out of our papers,' I say. 'And look where that's got us? Duped and scooped . . .'

He laughs, 'You think you guys, your paper, are the only ones who get censored? Wake up! This is an Occupied Country. They can do what they want. It's a set-up . . .'

'He's innocent?'

He sighs, 'Course he is. But they're desperate. They followed the name-cards and this is where it's led them. But there are seventeen name-cards which have not been traced, that are unaccounted for. This guy is just one of seventeen and the moment the survivors set eyes on him, that'll be that . . .'

'That'll be what?'

He laughs again, 'The end of their case. The survivors won't be able to identify him and then they'll have to let him go . . .'

'You think so?'

He winks at me now and says, 'I know so. All of us do, all of us except Ikki and his name-card team. It's all circumstantial . . .'

'But off-the-record, they're telling us they're 100 per cent certain. That's why they've gone so public with his arrest . . .'

'And, of course, you believe everything you hear,' he laughs. 'Everything they tell you. Well, you just watch . . .'

IN THE FICTIONAL CITY, I write a story, half-a-story:

Well-Known Artist Held As Poison Holdup Suspect

The latest Teikoku Bank 'mass murder' suspect arrested in Otaru, Hokkaido, arrived at Ueno Station yesterday morning under the custody of seven policemen.

The suspect, Hirasawa Sadamichi, 57, spent most of the trip from Hokkaido hiding under a blanket as crowds gathered at every major railway station along the route

140

to get a glimpse of the man suspected of the 'poison holdup' which resulted in the death of 12 bank employees.

Metropolitan police authorities, however, warned that it was too early to jump to premature conclusions and said that Hirasawa's connection with the case would most likely be cleared up within 48 hours.

Hirasawa is a well-known water-colour artist and left for Hokkaido soon after the Teigin mass murder.

Police said there was only circumstantial evidence against him. He was slated to be interviewed by the survivors of the mass murder.

Bearing a close resemblance to the murderer, Hirasawa had been under suspicion before but was released for lack of evidence. His testimony concerning the name-card he admitted receiving from Dr Matsui Shigeru differed from that given by the latter.

Mrs Hirasawa Masako, wife of the suspect, yesterday denied as 'ridiculous' the reports that her husband was the long-sought mass murderer. While the general description may fit that of the wanted man, she said that it was unbelievable that he should commit such a diabolic crime.

In the Fictional City, this city of millions, millions will read my newspaper, millions will half-read my half-a-story, and then some of these people will form mobs and these mobs will attack the house of Mrs Hirasawa and her daughters, with sticks and with stones, Mrs Hirasawa and her daughters in hiding now, now and for ever in the Fictional City.

IN THE FICTIONAL CITY, in a restaurant far from Shiinamachi, far from the scene of the crime, I look up from the table, the glass jar of toothpicks, the white bottle of soy sauce, and I ask her, 'So what happened? Did you see Hirasawa? Was Hirasawa the man who . . .'

'They took me to the Sakuradamon Police Station,' she says. 'And they took me into an interrogation room, and this man, this Hirasawa Sadamichi looked up from the table at me and I stared back at him, looked him in his face, hoping and praying that I had seen his face before, that this was the man who had murdered my colleagues and my friends, the man who had tried to kill me . . .'

'And was it?' I ask her. 'Was it him?'

'When the killer began to distribute the poison,' she whispers, 'I looked him in his face. I will never forget that face.'

'I know,' I say.

'I would know it anywhere.'

'I know,' I say again. 'And was his face that face?'

'No,' she says, shaking her head. 'It was not the face I saw that day. The face I saw that day was round. Very round, like an egg. This man Hirasawa has a square face. Very square, like a box. He's also too old. He's not that man. Hirasawa is not the killer.'

I look back down at the table, the glass jar of toothpicks, the white bottle of soy sauce, and I say, 'I'm sorry.'

'Me too,' she says. 'Me too.'

IN THE FICTIONAL CITY, a telephone rings again, a voice speaks, along the wires again, down the cables, with a time and with a place –

Down an alley, in a room, another room of shadows, another room of stares, a man I know is sitting with a man I don't –

The man I know gestures at the man I don't and he says, 'This gentleman here works for the Free People's Rights League and this gentleman has something for you, don't you?'

The man hands me an envelope.

I open it. I start to read –

The man I know says, 'You don't need to read it all now. It's for you. You can keep it. But, as you can see, the document details the many ways in which the arrest of Hirasawa violated his civil rights under our new constitution . . .'

I put the document back in its envelope. I take out my wallet. I take out my cash. The man I know points to the man I don't –

He smiles and he says, 'Give it to him. Not me.'

The man I don't know, this man from the Free People's Rights League, counts my cash. The man puts it in his jacket pocket. This man smiles now and says, 'Thank you.'

In this Fictional City, this city of inclement weather, this city of demonstrations, the man I know says, 'But don't forget, everything's a set-up . . .'

IN THE FICTIONAL CITY, I write a new story for a new day:

Mass Murder Suspect Cleared; Police Baffled;
Suspect's Arrest Raises Civil Rights Issue

Horizaki Shigeki of the First Criminal Investigative Section of the Metropolitan Police Board yesterday expressed the hope of releasing Hirasawa Sadamichi from custody sometime the same evening. Officials of the Tokyo Procurators Office said after cross-examining Hirasawa that two major points still need to be cleared up relative to Hirasawa's action at the time of the crime and subsequently. The first was said to be Hirasawa's alibi as to what he was doing on January 26, the date of the crime. The other puzzling point, they said, was the suspect's construction of a new home and the fact that he possessed ¥45,000 in cash at home, which he alleges to have borrowed from a friend.

—

The seven-month-old question as to who perpetrated the diabolic Teikoku Bank 'poison holdup case' remained a baffling mystery today following the clearance of Hirasawa Sadamichi from suspicion as being the long-sought criminal.

Hopes entertained by police authorities, especially Inspector Ikki, who made the arrest and went so far as saying that Hirasawa's guilt was '100 per cent certain', fell dismally flat Monday evening when 11 persons who saw the Teigin criminal could find no resemblance

in the much-publicized latest suspect.

Although the 'screening' was conducted under a tense atmosphere and all who saw Hirasawa were given ample time to make up their minds, not a single person charged the water-colour artist as being the Teikoku Bank criminal.

Six of them, in fact, were certain that he was not the man who committed the diabolic crime.

Hirasawa was the fourth important suspect directly questioned by the Metropolitan Police Board in connection with the Teikoku Bank 'poison holdup case'.

—

Meanwhile, Government and police authorities appear destined to face sharp criticism from numerous public organizations on the charge of failing to safeguard basic civil rights in the event investigations should clear latest Teigin suspect Hirasawa Sadamichi of all association with the Teikoku Bank 'poison holdup case'.

Lessening of suspicion against Hirasawa has switched public attention to the issue of basic civil rights concerning police action and the indignities to which the latest suspect was subjected.

Already, two civic organizations – the Tokyo Bar Association and the Free People's Rights League – are reported to be preparing a campaign of protest against Government authorities for their action against Hirasawa in the event the latter should be freed of all suspicion.

Both of these bodies favour the institution of legal action against the Government on behalf of Hirasawa to obtain payment of damages or a formal apology from authorities for their failure to uphold basic civil rights in the latest case.

In this connection, Attorney General Suzuki Yoshio admitted that the incident involving Hirasawa's arrest may enmesh the Government in a suit for payment of damages on the charge of failure to safeguard basic civil rights.

The Attorney General said he personally felt that officials associated in the manhunt possessed ample suspicion for carrying out the arrest but it had been 'imprudent' for them to have prematurely disclosed their action.

He said, moreover, that there appeared justification in criticism levelled against the remark by Police Inspector Ikki that he was '100 per cent certain' that Hirasawa was the criminal who perpetrated the Teikoku Bank case. Authorities of the Metropolitan Police Board, on the other hand, defended their action relative to Hirasawa. They stressed that they had secured enough incriminating information to arrest Hirasawa, although they felt that Police Inspector Ikki had gone 'a bit too far' in making a flat personal statement of his view. But Tanaka Eiichi, Inspector-General of the Police, also pointed out that police had done no wrong in handcuffing Hirasawa in the course of bringing him to Tokyo from Otaru. He said that such a measure was duly provided in police regulations in such instances.

I look up from the paper. I turn around from my desk, my editor standing over my shoulder, and I say, 'What's wrong?'

'Hirasawa's just tried to kill himself . . .'

IN THE FICTIONAL CITY, in the *genkan* to her house, she takes her hand from her mouth and she asks, 'Why? What happened?'

'Apparently Hirasawa had a piece of glass on him,' I tell her. 'And sometime this afternoon he tried to sever the artery of his left wrist with the piece of glass and with the point of a pen . . .'

'Is he all right?' she asks. 'Will he survive?'

'Yes,' I tell her. 'Luckily, Hirasawa wasn't alone at the time. There were other prisoners in the cell with him and so they raised the alarm. Doctors were quickly in the cell and they were able to bandage his artery before there was any great loss of blood. So he'll live.'

'Why?' she asks again. 'It's not him. He's innocent?'

'I don't know,' I say. 'But I'm going to find out . . .'

IN THE FICTIONAL CITY, down an alley off the main street, on the sofa at the back of the room, I say, 'I thought Hirasawa was in the clear. I thought they were going to release him . . .'

'I told you it was a set-up.'

'And so this is all part of the set-up, is it?' I ask. 'The suicide attempt, keeping him locked up like this?'

'They won't give up,' he says. 'Especially not now, not now there's all this talk of his civil rights, of suits and of damages. They'll find other crimes, other crimes to investigate, other crimes to detain him on. They'll never give up . . .'

IN THE FICTIONAL CITY, they don't give up, they never give up:

4 FRAUD VICTIMS IDENTIFY ARTIST

Police to Indict Suspect in Teikoku Bank Case on Four Charges

TOKYO, Sept. 2 – Hirasawa Sadamichi, 56, well-known water-colour artist, who is now held at the Metropolitan Police Board as a suspect in the Teikoku Bank mass poisoning murders, is expected to be indicted in a few days on charges of absconding with a deposit book issued by the Marunouchi branch of the Mitsubishi Bank and committing three abortive attempts fraudulently to secure money with it.

The discovery that the latest Teigin suspect had been engaged in such unlawful practices was bared by Prosecutor Takagi of the Tokyo district prosecutor's office as a sequel to further intensive police investigations into Hirasawa's past activities.

The four persons said to be victims of his acts have identified him and this has brought hope to the long-harassed police that these cases may lead to the murder case. For it appears that there was some extremely pressing need for Hirasawa to obtain at least ¥100,000 and thus might have made him desperate enough not to stop at murder. Another point about these charges is that they invariably have to do with banks.

The police still cannot say as yet whether they believe Hirasawa to be the Teikoku Bank murderer but the attempted swindles, with one connected with a branch of the

Teikoku Bank, place him under heavy suspicion. Investigation on the case will be continued with Hirasawa held on the four charges.

HIRASAWA HELD ON FRAUD CHARGE

Authorities Still Pinning High Hopes of Linking Artist with Bank Case

TOKYO, Sept. 5 – The Tokyo District Public Procurator's Office Friday prosecuted Hirasawa Sadamichi, water-colour artist and the latest suspect in the Teikoku Bank holdup-murder case, for falsification of private documents and fraud to which he has confessed, as the period for its investigation of the man as a Teigin murder suspect expired.

The procuratorial authorities, who are said to be 80 per cent confident that Hirasawa is the Teigin murderer, will continue to investigate his suspected crime after his prosecution for other crimes, it was learned.

The Yomiuri has also learned that the procuratorial authorities have decided to have the handwriting endorsing a cheque, the only clue to the bank murderer, studied by experts to determine whether the handwriting is not that of Hirasawa.

A number of people who saw the bank murderer have had a look at Hirasawa but most of them are not sure that he is the murderer.

On Friday Hirasawa had his hair cropped before a photograph was taken of him. Three officers in charge of the case were dumb-struck at the sight of Hirasawa with his hair cut. They said that the man now answered the description of the murderer.

Is Hirasawa Culprit In Teigin Murder Case?

Is Hirasawa Sadamichi the actual culprit who perpetrated the diabolic Teikoku Bank mass poisoning murder?

On the left is the hypothetical drawing of the murderer made immediately after the murders on the basis of the description given by the eye-witness survivors.

On the right is a photo just taken at the special investigation room of the Metropolitan Police Board of Hirasawa with his hair cropped close.

PAST ACTIVITIES OF ARTIST BARED

Teigin Suspect Found to Have Made Big Deposits Under Assumed Names

TOKYO, Sept. 9 – Police efforts to trace the source of a large amount of questionable money acquired by Hirasawa Sadamichi have led to a fresh exposure that the latest Teigin suspect deposited a sum of ¥80,000 with the Hongoku-cho branch of the Bank of Tokyo three days after the Teikoku Bank 'poison holdup case'.

The latest discovery showed thereby that the water-colour artist, who is known to have had no steady income about that time, opened two deposits under assumed names shortly following the Teigin crime.

Meanwhile, handwriting experts studying Hirasawa's handwriting with that on a money order which is believed to have been used by the Teigin criminal, said that there was some likeness between them but declined to give a decisive answer pending a further check-up.

A fresh slant relative to Hirasawa's suspected use of potassium cyanide in the Teikoku Bank case was also offered to the police on Monday when a conference of scientific experts clarified that the Teigin criminal did not have to possess expert knowledge in the use of the poison. This has stirred police to make a renewed effort to trace how and where Hirasawa may have possibly obtained the poison.

POISON SEEN USED IN MIXING COLOURS

Presence of Cyanide in Tempera May Pin Teigin Suspect

TOKYO, Sept. 14 – Police who have been trying hard to establish whether latest Teigin suspect Hirasawa Sadamichi ever possessed or knew anything about potassium cyanide are now believed to have unearthed positive evidence that the 57-year-old artist had frequently used the lethal poison in mixing colour for his tempera paintings.

Investigators working on the case are said to have found that Hirasawa frequently used potassium cyanide with copper materials and coins to produce light green colour for his tempera paintings. He is said to have neutralized green colour obtained from such a mixing with the white of eggs.

Furthermore, in producing light green colour, Hirasawa is reported to have used a small syringe similar to the one which the Teigin criminal is said to have used in perpetrating the diabolic crime.

Police efforts to ferret out conclusive evidence that Hirasawa committed the diabolic 'poison holdup case' have now entered the fourth week of investigation with the question of Hirasawa's guilt still unsolved.

However, in the course of these past investigations, investigators have uncovered a wealth of other circumstantial and puzzling information, strengthening suspicion against Hirasawa in the Teigin case and proving that Hirasawa, at any rate, has been guilty of numerous cases of fraud.

HIRASAWA FACES ABORTION CHARGE

Teikoku Bank Suspect Is Alleged to Have Used Drugs in Treatment

TOKYO, Sept. 15 – Police authorities investigating latest Teikoku Bank suspect Hirasawa Sadamichi have come across information that the latter personally administered illegal abortion to more than 10 women, the Yomiuri learned.

This information is said to have been tendered to the police by a certain artist and another unnamed person, both of whom are well-acquainted with Hirasawa. The artist friend is alleged to have revealed that Hirasawa personally brought about more than 10 cases of abortion in Hokkaido by claiming knowledge of a method for inducing abortion through physical pressure. The other person is reported to have told the police that Hirasawa induced abortion by the use of drugs.

Should these allegations prove true, Hirasawa is liable to further indictment on the charge of violating medical practice.

Furthermore, it is said Hirasawa's alleged use of drugs may lead to shedding important light on his believed employment of potassium cyanide in the Teigin case.

TEIGIN MURDER CASE

New Poison Angle Found; Will It Finally Lead To Hirasawa?

TOKYO, Sept. 20 – Police authorities who have been striving for some time without success to definitely link latest Teigin suspect Hirasawa Sadamichi with the Teikoku Bank case are reported to have turned up a new poison angle involving the daughter of his mistress.

It has become known that Hirasawa obtained some potassium cyanide from Miss Kamata Michiko, 25-year-old daughter of his mistress, shortly after the end of the war.

Miss Kamata is said to have told the police that this came about through her acquisition of some potassium cyanide while working as a typist for a firm in Tokyo during the war and shortly thereafter.

About this time, she said that Hirasawa frequently came to see her mother and is believed to have walked off with her potassium cyanide after she had shown it to him.

Meanwhile, authorities were said to be investigating other phases of the poisoning case, such as Hirasawa's possible acquisition of potassium cyanide while working as a member of the special painting material research centre of the Kisarazu airfield during the war.

POLICE CLARIFY HIRASAWA CASE

Declare Teigin Suspect Is On The Point Of Making Vital Confession

TOKYO, Sept. 26 – Teigin suspect Hirasawa Sadamichi is believed to have been driven to the verge of making a vital confession at any time as a sequel to renewed, detailed police questioning relative to fresh incriminating evidence that has turned up concerning his possession of a large amount of questionable money shortly following the Teikoku Bank 'poison holdup case'.

Chief Fujita of the Detective Section, Metropolitan Police Board, commenting on the progress of the latest investigation, said that it may lead the 57-year-old artist finally to come forth with a vital confession.

'At any rate, the investigation has reached a highly important stage,' he said, adding that if such a confession should be made the press would speedily be informed.

MURDERER OF 12 CONFESSES CRIME

Hirasawa Admits He Administered Poison to Bank Workers; 'I Confessed My Guilt On Own Free Will,' Says Hirasawa; Family Stands By Him

IN THE FICTIONAL CITY, again and again I knock on her door, until she says from behind the door, 'Who is it?'

'It's me,' I say. 'It's Takeuchi.'

'What do you want?'

'He's confessed,' I tell her. 'Hirasawa has confessed!'

The lock turns. The door opens. Murata Masako stares at me. Murata Masako says, 'But it wasn't him. I know it wasn't him.'

'But it was him,' I tell her. 'He's confessed everything, says he made the unsuccessful attempts to poison and rob the employees at Ebara and Nakai, that he did what he did at the Teikoku Bank for money, that he needed the money for his tempera paintings and for family reasons, and that it was him and him alone . . .'

'I don't believe it,' she says. 'I can't.'

'Well, you should and you must . . .'

'Why?' she asks. 'Why must I?'

I step forward into her *genkan*. I take her hand in mine. I say, 'Because it means it's over, it's finished now. You don't have to be afraid any more, you can forget it, forget him. You can move on now, you can start a new life. We can start . . .'

'*We?*' she laughs. 'We? Us?'

'Yes,' I say. 'Together . . .'

'Are you asking me to marry you?' she whispers.

'Yes,' I say. 'I'm asking you to marry me.'

'As a reporter,' she says. 'Or as a . . .'

'As a man,' I say. 'I'm going to quit my job . . .'

'You're going to quit your job? Really?'

'You don't believe me?' I ask her.

In the Fictional City, in the *genkan* to her house, Miss Murata Masako stares at me, Miss Murata Masako stares at me and says, 'I don't know what to believe any more . . .'

'Believe me,' I say. 'Please . . .'

'I'm not sure I can . . .'

'Then pretend,' I say. 'Let's both pretend . . .'

IN THE FICTIONAL CITY, I walk her streets and I hear her stories, but I've had enough of her streets and enough of her stories, her telephones and her voices, her wires and her cables, her alleyways and her back rooms, all her times and all her places –

'I just want to know who did it . . .'

The man slowly folds up the newspaper. He takes off his glasses. He puts the glasses in the breast pocket of his jacket. He sits forward in his chair. He looks up at me and he says, 'But why?'

'For me,' I say. 'Not for a story, not for the paper.'

The man smiles and says, 'What difference would it make? They've got their man and you've got your story . . .'

'I don't want any more stories,' I tell him.

The man laughs, 'No more stories? Bit late for that, isn't it?'

'Yes,' I say. 'But no more stories, please . . .'

IN THE FICTIONAL CITY, I stand before my editor's desk –

'Ah, Takeuchi,' says Ono. 'You still here?'

'Well, not for much longer,' I say. 'But I just wanted to say goodbye and also to thank you for all you have done for me.'

'So you've not changed your mind, then?' asks Ono. 'Never too late to change your mind, you know . . .'

'No,' I say.

'Well then, I'm sorry to lose you,' says Ono. 'I had high hopes for you, very high hopes for you.'

'Thank you,' I say.

'No, don't thank me,' says Ono. 'It's probably all for the best. I always told you, in this business there's no room for doubters, no room for quitters. Don't get me wrong, I thought you had potential, thought you had a future. But if this business is not for you, it's not for you. So what is for you? What now, what next, Takeuchi?'

'The Japan Advertising and Telegraph Service.'

'Advertising?' laughs Ono now.

'Yes,' I say. 'Copywriting.'

'Well, I hope you've got a good imagination . . .'

IN THE FICTIONAL CITY, it is November 1948, and the headlines on today's newspaper, my old newspaper, all the newspapers read:

TOJO AND 6 OTHERS ARE SENTENCED TO HANG; 16 DRAW LIFE; SHIGEMITSU GIVEN 7 YEARS; ACCUSED GUILTY ON 1 TO 8 COUNTS

In a hotel room full of journalists and policemen, of survivors and witnesses, we are sitting side by side on a stage in our wedding costumes, Masako with her eyes closed, tight –

In the Fictional City, I whisper –

'Let's pretend . . .'

IN THE FICTIONAL CITY, let's pretend that an innocent man is guilty, that he deserves to be convicted and sentenced to death, and that the police conducted a proper and thorough investigation, let's

151

pretend that the Government and GHQ did not conspire to pervert the course of justice, that the newspapers and their reporters were not complicit in their stories, and that everything we read is true –

In this city made of paper, this city made of print –

In this Fictional City, let's pretend . . .

Beneath the Black Gate, in its upper chamber, among the flurries and the flakes, the paper flurries of paper flakes, these black and white flurries of news-paper flakes, this former Master of Insincerities, former Master of Lies, he looks up from the damp floor of the occult circle and now he whispers, 'Let's pretend that this city is not a story, not a fiction, not made of paper, not made of print . . .

'Let's pretend that we are not just your stories, not just your fictions, that we are not made of paper, not made of print . . .

'Let's pretend all your papers are now a finished manuscript, that your manuscript is now a book, a book called –

'Teigin Monogatari . . .

'Let's pretend that this book has come, this book not a fiction, and that this book absolves the innocent and accuses the guilty . . .

'Let's pretend that this book ends the whole mystery, that this book solves the whole case, that this book solves the crime . . .

'This crime and all crimes, all mysteries . . .

'All stories, all fictions now ended . . .

'Let's pretend, sweet writer . . .

'Let's pretend . . .'

Now he closes his eyes and begins to count, to count out loud, 'I say one, I say two, I say three, I say four, I say five, and I say six.'

And now the journalist opens his eyes and stares at the candle before him, the sixth candle. But now the journalist shakes his head.

He leans forward on his knees, on the damp floor, in the occult circle, leans forward towards the sixth candle.

Now the journalist blows out the candle –

The sixth candle.

In the half-light, you are alone again, in the upper chamber of the Black Gate, in the occult circle of now-six candles,

and in their half-light, alone again,

you half-whisper, you half-beg,

'Let's pretend, please . . .'

That all these words are not just the sum of their absences, that you, you are not the sum of your absences;

that a man is not what he lacks,

this city, this country,

not what they lack,

this world –

'Lacks?' laughs a voice now, the Black Gate spinning,

spinning and spinning. 'Lacks what? Look outside this window, Mister Writer. Look at the height of those buildings, those skyscrapers. Look at those people down below, in their suits and in their cars. Not on their hands, not on their knees –

'They lack for nothing. Nothing!

'Because of me! Me! Me!'

The six candles gone, the occult circle gone, the upper chamber gone, the Black Gate gone, and now you are standing in an enormous room, on thick carpet, high above the city,

THE FUTURE CITY rising, here, now –

'But I am everything you hate,' laughs the man beside you, his hand on your shoulder, fingers in your flesh and nails in your bones. 'For I am the future, your future! Now . . .

The Seventh Candle –

The Exhortations of a
~~Soldier, Gangster,~~ Businessman and Politician

The city is a market, a black market, a stock market, a free market. And I run this city. I rule this city. For I built this city. From ash, through wood, to concrete, steel and glass –

Rise up Tokyo! Rise up Nippon!

You are not ash. You are not wood. You are concrete, steel and glass. I have dragged you out of the ash, through the wood to be here now, in concrete, steel and glass –

Fight! Fight! Fight!

Beneath skies crossed and matted grey with your tangled strings, across grounds crawling and stained with your severed strings, you are all puppets. But I am no puppet –

I have cut my strings!

From Defeated and Ruined City, Surrendered and Occupied City, to Olympic and Future City, in less than twenty years –

THIS IS MY CITY . . .

MY CITY!

¥

IN THE OCCUPIED CITY, in Mejiro town, in a wooden building, in an upstairs office, tap-tap, knock-knock, bang-bang, 'Who's there?'

'Boss, boss!' pants my best puppet. 'They've robbed the Teikoku Bank up by the Nagasaki Shrine. They've killed all the staff. Police everywhere, all over the place, all over the town . . .'

I look up from the cards. I look up from the die. I say, 'This is my town. No one robs a bank in my town. No one murders its staff. Not in my town. So you find out who did this . . .

'And you bring them to me . . .

'And you do it now!'

Tap-tap, knock-knock, bang-bang, 'Who's there?'

In a bunk in China, I am a soldier. I wake. I rise. Step by step. I rob. I rape. I kill. For Dai Nippon, for the Emperor –

Fight! Fight! Fight!

For you, for me –

Fight! Fight!

Spring, summer, autumn, winter, morning, afternoon, evening, and night – in all these times – Dust, mud, desert, jungle, field, forest, mountain, valley, river, stream, farm, village, town, city, house, street, shop, factory, hospital, school, government building and railway station – in all these places – Soldier, civilian, man, woman, child and baby, I kill them all and I get money and I get medals –

But these fields of slaughter, these forests of skeletons, they trade not in bravery, trade not in honour, they deal in luck, they deal in death; lucky soldiers and dead soldiers –

For the War Machine rolls on, never stopping, never resting, never sleeping, on and on, always rising, always consuming, always devouring. On and on, the War Machine rolls on, across the fields and through the forests, on and on, over looted house and over stripped corpse, on and on, and from severed hand into bloody hands, forever-bloody hands, money passes, money changes, money grows –

Lesson #1: dog kills dog.

¥

IN THE OCCUPIED CITY, in Mejiro town, in a wooden building, in an upstairs office, tap-tap, knock-knock, bang-bang, 'Who's there?'

'It was a doctor,' says the puppet in the uniform. 'Or at least a man pretending to be a doctor. A public health official.'

I look up from the flowers on the cards, the spots on the die, and I say, 'Describe this doctor to me . . .'

'Aged between forty-four and fifty. About five feet three inches tall. Thin build with an oval face. A high nose and a pale complexion. Hair cut short and flecked with grey. He was dressed in a brown lounge suit, wearing brown rubber boots. He had a white armband on his left arm on which was written "LEADER OF THE

DISINFECTING TEAM". He had a raincoat over one arm and he was carrying a doctor's bag . . .'

'Anything else?'

'Yes, he had two distinctive brown spots on his left cheek. The survivors also said he was a distinguished and intelligent-looking man with the air of an educated doctor.'

'Do you have any suspects?'

'No,' he says. 'Not as yet.'

'Well then,' I say, 'let's see if me and my men can't jog a few memories, get you a few names, shall we?'

'Thank you,' he says with a low bow, my pills in his wooden hand, his paper money in mine.

¥

Tap-tap, knock-knock, bang-bang, 'Who's there?'

In a courtroom, in a dock, I am a criminal, a war criminal. I wake. I rise. Step by step. But I do not cry. I do not apologize. I do not speak. For Dai Nippon, for the Emperor–

Fight! Fight! Fight!

For you, for me –

Fight! Fight!

Spring, summer, autumn, winter, morning, afternoon, evening, and night – in all these times – Dust, mud, desert, jungle, field, forest, mountain, valley, river, stream, farm, village, town, city, house, street, shop, factory, hospital, school, government building and railway station – in all these places – Soldier, civilian, man, woman, child and baby, I appal them all and I get shunned and I get accused –

And they may hang me, they may jail me, they may pardon me, or they may release me, for their courts trade not in justice, trade not in truth, they deal in retribution, they deal in vengeance –

For the War Machine rolls on, never stopping, never resting, never sleeping, on and on, always rising, always consuming, always devouring. On and on, the War Machine rolls on, across the victors and across the losers, on and on, over justice and over injustice, on and on, and from innocent hand to guilty hands, forever-guilty hands, money passes, money changes, money grows –

Lesson #2: dog eats dog.

IN THE OCCUPIED CITY, in Mejiro town, in a deserted factory, in a dark space, tap-tap, knock-knock, bang-bang, 'Who's there?'

'But I don't know anything!' screams the beaten, bruised and naked puppet on the concrete floor. 'I know nothing!'

'That's a great pity,' I tell him, 'because no one needs an ignorant man, do they? They are simply surplus to requirements. Human garbage, in fact. Waste . . .'

'Please, please, please . . .'

'And you know what we do with garbage and waste, don't you? No you don't, do you? Because you don't know anything, you know nothing. Well then, I'll tell you. We drive the garbage and the waste out of the city and we dump it in holes . . .'

'Please, please . . .'

'Deep holes,' I tell him. 'Because no one likes the sight or the smell of garbage and waste . . .'

'Please . . .'

'Next!'

¥

Tap-tap, knock-knock, bang-bang, 'Who's there?'

In a market, a black market, I am a gangster, a racketeer. I wake. I rise. Step by step. I steal. I sell. I steal things. I sell things. I make money. For Dai Nippon, for the Emperor –

Fight! Fight! Fight!

For you, for me –

Fight! Fight!

Spring, summer, autumn, winter, morning, afternoon, evening, and night – in all these times – Dust, mud, desert, jungle, field, forest, mountain, valley, river, stream, farm, village, town, city, house, street, shop, factory, hospital, school, government building and railway station – in all these places – Soldier, civilian, man, woman, child and baby, I exploit them all and I get money and I get respect –

I license the market stalls. I take money and I make money. I burn down rival markets. I take money and I make money. I set up gambling dens. I take money and I make money. I set up whore-houses. I take money and I make money. I get money –

For the War Machine rolls on, never stopping, never resting, never sleeping, on and on, always rising, always consuming, always devouring. On and on, the War Machine rolls on, across the strong and across the weak, on and on, over the satiated and over the starving, on and on, and from scared hand to scarred hands, scarred hands into top-pockets and back-pockets, fat back-pockets, money passes, money changes, money grows –

Lesson #3: dog steals another dog.

¥

IN THE OCCUPIED CITY, in Mejiro town, in the police station, in an upstairs office, tap-tap, knock-knock, bang-bang, 'Who's there?'

'Thank you for coming,' says the local chief puppet. 'I know you are a busy man. Thank you for making the time to see me.'

'You're welcome,' I say. 'It's my pleasure. Thank you for inviting me and taking the time yourself.'

'Well, I wanted to thank you personally for all your efforts in helping us in our investigation . . .'

'You're welcome,' I say again. 'It's not only my pleasure but also my duty as a local citizen . . .'

'Thank you,' says the chief puppet again. 'Unfortunately, as you are aware, our investigation has yet to reach a conclusion.'

'It's a great pity,' I say. 'But I know you and your men are working tirelessly to catch this fiend. And I am certain, in the end, that you will be successful in your investigation.'

'I appreciate your encouragement and support,' says the chief puppet. 'Thank you. As you are also aware, the Metro Detectives no longer believe the culprit to be a local man. They believe him to be a man with a military and medical background, who quite possibly served on the mainland during the war . . .'

'Is that right?' I say.

'That's their thinking, yes,' he says. 'That the culprit possibly even served with the Tokumu Kikan in China . . .'

'Really?' I say.

'Yes,' he says. 'And so the Metro Detectives are planning to question all the former members of the Tokumu Kikan they can find.'

'That's very interesting,' I say.

'Yes,' nods the chief again. 'I thought you'd be interested to

159

know their present thinking, the current course of the investigation, as a concerned local citizen . . .'

'Thank you.'

'You're very welcome,' says the local chief puppet, being pulled to his feet. 'It's my pleasure. Please keep in touch . . .'

'Thank you,' I say again, bowing and leaving, a fresh fish and a bottle of sake on his desk.

¥

Tap-tap, knock-knock, bang-bang, 'Who's there?'

In the upstairs room of a police station, I am a strike-breaker. I wake. I rise. Step by step. I provide men, big men. I provide sticks, big sticks. I crack heads, red heads. I break bones, red bones. In newspaper plants and in film studios, in factories and in universities. For Dai Nippon, for the Emperor –

Fight! Fight! Fight!

For you, for me –

Fight! Fight!

Spring, summer, autumn, winter, morning, afternoon, evening, and night – in all these times – Dust, mud, desert, jungle, field, forest, mountain, valley, river, stream, farm, village, town, city, house, street, shop, factory, hospital, school, government building and railway station – in all these places – Soldier, civilian, man, woman, child and baby, I intimidate them all and I get money and I get more work –

I beat up strikers on their picket lines. I take money and I make money. I burn down the houses of union officials. I take money and I make money. I threaten and I bully, bully, bully –

For the War Machine rolls on, never stopping, never resting, never sleeping, on and on, always rising, always consuming, always devouring. On and on, the War Machine rolls on, across the workers and across their unions, on and on, over their rights and over their jobs, on and on, and from dirty hand into dirtier hands, under the table and into back-pockets, back-pockets into wallets, big fat wallets, money passes, money changes, money grows –

Lesson #4: dog sells stolen dog to another dog.

160

IN THE OCCUPIED CITY, on the Ginza, in a concrete building, in a brand-new office, tap-tap, knock-knock, bang-bang, 'Who's there?'

'Thank you for seeing me, Boss,' I say. 'I know you are a very busy man so, really, thank you very much.'

'We're all busy men,' laughs the Big Boss. 'Times may be tough, but there are still lots of opportunities for the man who is prepared to be busy. Still money to be made, always money to be made. Lots of money for the busy man . . .'

'That's the truth, all right.'

'Yes,' says the Big Boss, 'and that's why none of us likes anything to stand in the way of opportunity. Anything like a police investigation, a city-wide manhunt; obstructing our opportunities, impeding our businesses; asking questions none of us want asked, turning over stones that should be left as they are . . .'

'So you've heard about the change in the course of the investigation, the Tokumu Kikan theory, then?'

'They've already been here.'

'Is it a problem?'

'Don't worry,' he says. 'I'll deal with the Metro Detectives. But I'd like you to deal with the newspapers . . .'

'The newspapers?'

'Yes,' he smiles. 'The newspapers. It's a promotion. A step up for you. A fresh opportunity . . .'

'Thank you very much.'

'Congratulations,' laughs the Big Boss, pulling my strings and making me rise and making me bow, making me walk backwards.

'Thank you,' I say again, rising and bowing, walking backwards out of the brand-new office. 'Thank you, Boss.'

Tap-tap, knock-knock, bang-bang, 'Who's there?'

In a brand-new factory, I am its brand-new owner. I wake. I rise. Floor by floor. I take old parts. I turn old parts into new parts. I sell new parts. I make money. For Dai Nippon, for the Emperor –

Fight! Fight! Fight!

For you, for me –

Fight! Fight!

Spring, summer, autumn, winter, morning, afternoon, evening, and night – in all these times – Dust, mud, desert, jungle, field, forest, mountain, valley, river, stream, farm, village, town, city, house, street, shop, factory, hospital, school, government building and railway station – in all these places – Soldier, civilian, man, woman, child and baby, I take from them all and I sell to the rich and I get money –

I take from the Japanese, his goods and his labour. And I sell to the Americans, his people and his military –

For the War Machine rolls on, never stopping, never resting, never sleeping, always rising, always consuming, always devouring. On and on, the War Machine rolls on, over the Korean War and over the Cold War, on and on, across the Vietnam War and across the Gulf War, on and on, from hand into wallet, wallet into banks, big banks / little banks, money passes, money changes, money grows –

Lesson #5: dog buys two dogs.

¥

IN THE OCCUPIED CITY, in a suburb, down a lane, outside a two-storey house, tap-tap, knock-knock, bang-bang, 'Who's there?'

'Are you Mr XXXX of the XXXX newspaper?'

'Yes, I am,' says the puppet in the doorway.

I step back into the shadows. My best puppet steps out of the shadows. My puppet strikes Mr XXXX of the XXXX newspaper.

Mr XXXX of the XXXX newspaper is stunned. He touches his plaster forehead. He stares at his wooden hand. At the blood.

I step back out of the shadows. I pull a string to lift up the chin of Mr XXXX of the XXXX newspaper, to look into his eyes –

His blinking and his bloody eyes –

I say, 'No more stories.'

¥

Tap-tap, knock-knock, bang-bang, 'Who's there?'

In a firm, I am its managing director. I wake. I rise. Floor by floor. I buy. I sell. I make companies. I buy companies. I sell companies. I make money. For Dai Nippon, for the Emperor –

Fight! Fight! Fight!

For you, for me –
Fight! Fight!

Spring, summer, autumn, winter, morning, afternoon, evening, and night – in all these times – Dust, mud, desert, jungle, field, forest, mountain, valley, river, stream, farm, village, town, city, house, street, shop, factory, hospital, school, government building and railway station – in all these places – Soldier, civilian, man, woman, child and baby, I recruit from them all and I pick their brains and I use them –

The graduates of the Tokyo and Kyoto Imperial Universities. The alumni of Ping Fan. I buy blood. I manufacture blood. I process blood. I sell blood. *Black Blood and White Genes* . . .

For the War Machine rolls on, never stopping, never resting, never sleeping, always rising, always consuming, always devouring. On and on, the War Machine rolls on, across the little company and across the big company, on and on, over the successful company and over the unsuccessful company, on and on, and from hand into wallet, wallet into bank, bank into loans, cheap, cheap loans at low, low interest, money passes, money changes, money grows –

Lesson #6: dog breeds dogs.

¥

IN THE OCCUPIED CITY, in Mejiro town, in a wooden building, in an upstairs office, tap-tap, knock-knock, bang-bang, 'Who's there?'

'Boss, boss! At the Kanda Myōjin Shrine, there's a man there, looks exactly like the drawing of the Teikoku killer, wearing the same clothes and everything. It's him! It's got to be him!'

I look up from the flowers. I look up from the spots. I ask, 'Where is he now, this man? Is he still at the shrine?'

'Yes,' says my puppet. 'He's still there.'

'Then let's go . . .'

¥

Tap-tap, knock-knock, bang-bang, 'Who's there?'

In the boardroom of a company, I am its president. I wake. I rise. To the top floor. I buy. I sell. I make shares. I buy shares. I sell shares. I make money. For Dai Nippon, for the Emperor –

Fight! Fight! Fight!

163

For you, for me –
Fight! Fight!

Spring, summer, autumn, winter, morning, afternoon, evening, and night – in all these times – Dust, mud, desert, jungle, field, forest, mountain, valley, river, stream, farm, village, town, city, house, street, shop, factory, hospital, school, government building and railway station – in all these places – Soldier, civilian, man, woman, child and baby, I have sold to them all and they thank me and they admire me –

For I have given them nice houses to live in and nice offices to work in, nice cars to drive and nice clothes to wear, I have given them the healthiest economy and the most stable government, the best technology and the safest streets in the world, I have given them comfort and security, good food and sound sleep –

But the War Machine rolls on, never stopping, never resting, never sleeping, always rising, always consuming, always devouring. On and on, the War Machine rolls on, across empires and across democracies, on and on, over the well-fed and over the ill-fed, on and on, and, all the while, from hand to hand, hand into wallet, wallet into bank, bank into loan, loan to stocks and shares, my stocks and my shares, money passes, money changes, money grows –

Lesson #7: dog sells more dogs.

¥

IN THE OCCUPIED CITY, to Kanda, to the Myōjin Shrine, to the Setsubun crowds, tap-tap, knock-knock, bang-bang, 'Who's there?'

'*Oni wa soto! Fuku wa uchi! Oni wa soto . . .*'

'Him!' points my puppet. 'Over there. That's him!'

Aged between forty-four and fifty. About five feet three inches tall. Thin build with an oval face. A high nose and a pale complexion. Two distinctive brown spots on his left cheek. Hair cut short and flecked with grey. He is dressed in a brown lounge suit, wearing brown rubber boots. He has a white armband on his left arm on which is written 'LEADER OF THE DISINFECTING TEAM'. He has a raincoat over one arm and is carrying a doctor's bag –

'It's him, Boss!' say all my puppets. 'It's him!'

I nod. I say. 'Yes, it's him. Take him . . .'

'*Oni wa soto! Fuku wa uchi!*'

Tap-tap, knock-knock, bang-bang, 'Who's there?'

In a backroom, I am a politician. I wake. I rise. Floor by floor. I buy. I sell. I buy people and I sell people. I buy votes and I sell votes. I make deals and I sell deals. For Dai Nippon, for the Emperor –

Fight! Fight! Fight!

For you. For me –

Fight! Fight!

Spring, summer, autumn, winter, morning, afternoon, evening, and night – in all these times – Dust, mud, desert, jungle, field, forest, mountain, valley, river, stream, farm, village, town, city, house, street, shop, factory, hospital, school, government building and railway station – in all these places – Soldier, civilian, man, woman, child and baby, I smile at you all and I laugh at you all, ha, ha, ha, ha, ha, ha –

In my department stores and in my advertisements, in my newspaper columns and in my television shows, in my education acts and in my sound-trucks, in the history I teach you and the news I give you, in every piece of legislation, from every loudspeaker, I lie to you and I laugh at you, ha, ha, ha, ha, ha, ha, ha, ha, ha –

For my War Machine rolls on, never stopping, never resting, never sleeping, always rising, always consuming, always devouring. On and on, my War Machine rolls on, across the rich and across the poor, on and on, over the bad and over the good, on and on, from hand to hand, hand into wallet, wallet into bank, bank into loan, loan into stocks and shares, stocks and shares into budgets, budgets and power, power, power, money passes, money changes, money grows –

Spring, summer, autumn, winter, morning, afternoon, evening, and night, money grows, money blossoms and money blooms –

Lesson #8: dog is always hungry for more dog.

¥

IN THE OCCUPIED CITY, in Mejiro town, in a deserted factory, in a dark space, tap-tap, knock-knock, bang-bang, 'Who's there?'

'It's you!' screams the beaten, bruised and naked puppet on the concrete floor. 'You are the killer! Not me . . .'

'Just confess,' I say again, 'and then the fear will stop, the pain will stop, and we'll tend to your wounds, we'll deliver you to the police, and everything will be all right. If you just confess . . .'

'Be gone from this place!' he screams. 'Be gone from this city, this Occult City, for this is not your city, this is my city!'

'Leave this place?' I laugh. 'This city? This Occult City? This is not your city! This is my city!'

'This is not your city,' the puppet mumbles now, through his broken teeth and bloody lips. 'This city, this city is a séance . . .'

'A séance?' I laugh. 'This city is no séance.'

Now two of my good puppets lay this bad puppet down and they stretch it out upon a door which lies upon the concrete floor.

I take a mirror from my pocket. I crouch down beside it. I hold the mirror to its plaster face. I say, 'This city is a mirror. Look!'

But the puppet upon the door upon the floor does not look. The puppet does not move. The puppet does not breathe.

'It's dead, Boss,' say my own puppets.

I look up from the mirror. I say, 'That's a great pity.'

'What if it really was him?' ask my puppets. 'What if it really was the Teikoku killer? What are we going to do, Boss?'

'There's always another puppet,' I say. 'Next!'

Beneath the Black Gate, in its upper chamber, spinning and spinning, in this now-enormous room, on this now-thick carpet, spinning and spinning, high above the city, the man still-beside you shouting, 'Look outside this window, Mister Writer! Look at the breadth of this city, the height of its buildings, the speed of its trains, and the wealth of its people. This city that was once ash, that was then wood, fields of ash and forests of wood, that is now concrete, steel and glass, mile upon mile of concrete, steel and glass.

'In less than twenty years, this city rose from ash to become an Olympic City. Did you know that, Mister Writer? Mister Puppet?

'Of course not! How could you? You'll never know it, you'll never see it. Because it's too late, too late for you, Mister Writer –

'But not for me! Not me! This is my time! This is my city!

'I run this city. I rule this city. I walk where I want. I sit where I want. I eat what I want. I buy what I want. Who I want. I build what I want, where I want and when I want. I take what I want. I say what I want. I do what I want. Because this is my city. My city! And in my city, everything is mine. Everybody mine! Mine! Mine! Mine!

'Soldier, war criminal, gangster, strike-breaker, factory-owner, managing director, company president and politician, they are all me and this is all mine! Mine! Mine! Mine! In my city! My city!'

And now beneath the Black Gate, in its upper chamber, in the occult circle of the six candles, he blows out one more candle –

'But it's too late, too late for you, Mister Writer . . .

'For you are out of time, Mister Puppet . . .

'Out of time, little puppet . . .'

In the light of now-five candles, in their occult circle, in the upper chamber, beneath the Black Gate, you thrash and you shout –

'I am not a puppet! I am not a puppet!'

Hands above your head, you dance in the light of the circle, chopping and cutting at the strings and at the webs –

'I will cut all strings. I will cut all ties –

'I will smash all clocks, all time!'

But now you stop. You lower your head. You close your eyes. For you want to rest. You want to sleep. To never –

'Wake up, decadent!' now shouts a thick and heavy-accented voice and so you try to open your eyes, to open your eyes to the gloom of the five candles, still in the upper chamber,

still beneath this Black, Black Gate –

'Wake up, degenerate!'

The medium upright, taut and still, her mouth opening, opening and speaking, speaking and saying, 'I am *Homo Sovieticus* –

'I am Comrade Andrei Kaidanovsky –

'And this is my journal –

'My martyr-log . . .

The Eighth Candle –

The Martyr-log of a *Homo Sovieticus*

Tokyo, January 9, 1947

This city, this country, is a wilderness to me and so these words, these pages, will document my temptations, my trials. Hence there are words for reports, for the tops of desks, the desks of others, ~~and then there are words for diaries, the drawers of memories~~.

I finally arrived here in Tokyo from Khabarovsk two days ago. Yesterday I met with Comrade Maj. Gen. A. N. Vasiliev, one of our Associate Prosecutors at the International Military Tribunal for the Far East. I had been told in Khabarovsk that it was Comrade Vasiliev who had personally requested my presence in Tokyo. ~~However, it was clear from our first meeting that Comrade Vasiliev had made no such request.~~ Comrade Vasiliev was aware, though, that it had been I who had conducted the interrogations of Major Karasawa Tomio and Maj. Gen. Kawashima Kiyoshi in Khabarovsk last year. Comrade Vasiliev had read the transcripts of my interrogations of the prisoners and my report and its conclusions on the Japanese Bacteriological Warfare programme as it pertained to possible prosecutions for war crimes, both in Tokyo at the IMTFE, and in Khabarovsk at our own proposed trials of former servicemen of the Japanese army.

I had been told in Khabarovsk that an informal approach had been made to the Americans to interview Ishii, Ōta and Kikuchi. Hence, my presence in Tokyo would be required to conduct the interviews. Comrade Vasiliev confirmed that a low-key approach had been made through the backroom staff of the American IPS. However, the G-2 (Intelligence) Section of the American GHQ had informed Comrade Vasiliev that any such request must be submitted in writing, detailing the reasons for the interrogations.

On my arrival, Comrade Vasiliev was therefore in the process of submitting a formal request to Maj. Gen. Willoughby, chief of G-2, to interrogate Ishii, Ōta and Kikuchi and I was able to assist in the preparation of the request:

'At the disposal of the Soviet Division of the International Prosecution Section,' we wrote, 'there are materials showing the preparation of the Kwantung Army for bacteriological warfare. To present these materials as evidence to the Military Tribunal it is necessary to conduct a number of supplementary interrogations of persons who worked previously in the Anti-epidemic group (Manabu) N731 of the Kwantung Army. These persons are:

1. Lt. Gen. of Medical Corps Ishii, commander of the Anti-epidemic group N731.
2. Colonel Kikuchi, Chief of the 1st Section of the Anti-epidemic group N731.
3. Colonel Ōta, Chief of the 4th Section (and prior to that, chief of the 2nd Section) of the Anti-epidemic group N731.

'These persons', we continued, 'are to testify about research work on bacteria carried out by them for the purpose of using bacteria in warfare and also about cases of mass murders of people as the result of those experiments. I believe that it would be expedient to take preliminary measures preventing the spreading of information concerning this investigation before the investigation is completed and the materials are presented to the Tribunal, i.e., to take from these witnesses certificates to the effect that they promise not to tell anybody about the investigation of these matters and to conduct the preliminary interrogations not in the premises of the War Ministry building.

'In connection with the above-said, I ask you to render us assistance through the IPS in conducting the interrogations of the said persons on January 13, in premises specially assigned for this purpose, and after taking from them certificates containing promises not to speak about the investigation.

'Besides that,' we concluded, 'I request you to provide the Soviet Division of the IPS with certificates of the whereabouts of Lt. Col. Murakami Takashi, former chief of the 2nd Section of the Anti-epidemic group N731, and Nakatome Kinzo, former chief of the General Affairs Section of the same group. These certificates are needed for the purpose of submitting them to the Tribunal.'

Both Comrade Vasiliev and I felt the letter carried just the right amounts of deference and contempt, promise and threat. Still, I could not help but feel – given all we know that they know and all they know that we know – that our knees were bent, our caps in hands. Then again, if the child does not cry, the mother cannot know it is hungry. ~~And as long as I get my hour with Ishii, I do not care if I have to beg.~~

January 12, 1947

Early this morning, before the light, I walked down to Tokyo Bay and I stood on the docks and waited for the dawn. As I watched the faint winter sun struggle up the heavy winter sky, I thought of the thousands of dawns I had seen, the thousands of miles I had walked, over these past ten years, to stand there on those docks, in this city, in that dawn, on this day.

And maybe it was the water and the light, maybe the hour and the season, but I was suddenly beset with childhood memories of post-revolutionary Petrograd in that eerie winter of 1917–18, when the city and its people seemed to have broken free of their moorings, when the city and its people seemed to be floating off somewhere unknown.

Roads are never straight for long; they twist and they turn, they rise and fall, fork and diverge. With or without maps, there are always choices to be made; always choices and always consequences, whether you stay or whether you go, choices and consequences, consequences and farewells.

All those farewells, some said and some unsaid, but all those people still gone, floating off somewhere, somewhere unknown, somewhere down the river, somewhere behind me.

For behind me this morning, on those grey docks, were the ruins of Tokyo, the ruins of Japan, of Asia, North Africa, and the Middle East, of our Russian Motherland and our Soviet Republics, of Germany and of Europe, all lain flat out behind me, everywhere and everyone collapsed, the cities and the people, the people still suffering.

But in front of me, across that bay, across the ocean, I knew there was America; an America not in ruins, for America has no ruins. America does not know invasion. America does not know siege.

America does not know surrender. America does not know defeat. America does not know suffering as the rest of the world knows suffering.

Between their West and our East, there is not only a curtain, there is a vastness – across plains and over mountains, from the sea to the sky – a vastness and a sorrow. Two worlds now divided, as Comrade Andrei Alexandrovich Zhadanov observed, into the Imperialistic and the Democratic.

And this city and these people would seem to have made their choice, to have chosen their side. And once again, they seem to have chosen the wrong side of the river; once again, the wrong moorings. And though I have been here only three days, this Occupied City is a hard place to like, and its people – both the Occupiers and the Occupied – arouse in me no sense of either fraternity or sympathy.

~~But as the great Nikolai Vassilyevich Gogol once wrote, 'It is no use to blame the looking-glass if your face is awry.'~~

January 15, 1947

The Americans have been stalling but, finally, early this morning I went to the War Ministry with Comrade Colonel Lev Nicholaevich Smirnov and our interpreter. Comrade Smirnov, along with Comrade Colonel Mark Raginsky, has only recently arrived in Tokyo to assist our prosecution team at the IMTFE, now that the Nuremberg trial has concluded. And though this was the first time I had met Comrade Smirnov, I had of course read in newspapers and other reports of his heroic words as one of our prosecutors at Nuremberg.

The Americans were represented by Lt. Col. McQuail of G-2, Major Keller of the Chemical Warfare Service, a D. L. Waldorf from the International Prosecution Section, and their own interpreter who was very obviously also from G-2.

Of course, the meeting went entirely the way we had predicted it would; Lt. Col. McQuail asked us to explain what information we had which led the USSR to want to interrogate the subjects Ishii, Kikuchi and Ōta. So it was time for us to show our hand, so to speak, as we knew would happen.

Comrade Smirnov began by giving brief details of the capture, ranks and responsibilities of our prisoners Karasawa and Kawashima (during which the Americans feigned disinterest). Comrade Smirnov then began to detail the information obtained from our interrogations of the prisoners, mainly being the extensive experiments in BW at the Pingfan Laboratory and its associated field experiments, using Manchurian and Chinese bandits as materials, of whom approximately 2,000 are believed to have died as results of these experiments at Pingfan.

It was most interesting and very telling to note the reaction of the Americans to the evil catalogue of horrific murders and gruesome torture through perverted experimentation that Comrade Smirnov detailed for them: <u>NOTHING.</u> This proved to us that 'our friends' were either already familiar with these details from their own interrogations and sources, or completely devoid of all moral feeling. The only question that Lt. Col. McQuail remembered to ask Comrade Smirnov was in regard to Pingfan; to what extent had it been destroyed and by whom?

To this question, Comrade Smirnov replied that Pingfan had been completely destroyed by the Japanese themselves in their retreat and in an obvious attempt to cover up all evidence. All documents were also destroyed. So thorough was the damage, that our own experts did not even bother to photograph the ruins.

It was hard not to laugh at them, ~~and also ourselves,~~ but then Comrade Smirnov let them know we were not there to joke around, to play the fool for them.

'The Japanese', he said, 'have committed a horrible crime, killing 2,000 Manchurians and Chinese, and Ishii, Kikuchi and Ōta were involved. Furthermore, the mass production of fleas and bacteria is very important. At the Nuremberg trials, an expert German witness testified that the spreading of typhus by fleas was considered the best method of BW and it would now seem that the Japanese have this technique. So it would be of value to the USA as well as the USSR to get the information. So it is our request that the Japanese be interrogated without being told they are liable to be charged and prosecuted as war criminals, and that they be made to swear not to tell anyone about the interrogations.'

With these remarks, the meeting concluded with the usual false promises and outright lies of quick replies and further meetings, of consultation and cooperation.

~~At the door, while the Colonels were trading boasts, this man Waldorf from the IPS suddenly whispered, 'Tell me honestly Comrade, how long have you really known?'~~

~~'Since the summer of 1938,' I told him.~~

~~'So long?' asked Waldorf. 'But how?'~~

~~'*Chyornye voronki*,' I said, knowing then that tonight I'll dream again of the *chyornye voronki*.~~

~~But tonight I will not dream of the *black ravens* of Harbin, driven by the Japanese, to kidnap the Chinese. No, tonight I will dream of other black vans, driven by me. Tonight, I will be driving again down the streets in my second-hand leather jacket, streets that lead to forests, forests that lead to graves, and these streets will not be Chinese streets, these forests not Chinese forests, these graves not Chinese graves, the streets will be Russian streets, the forests Russian forests, and my cargo will be Russian cargo, Russian citizens for Russian graves.~~

January 18, 1947

Was at the cinema in the ballroom below the Foreign Press Club. I went with Comrade B.G. and Comrade B.A. to see *Rhapsody in Blue*. Afterwards, we were joined by two of the American correspondents and we drank and argued once again about who won the war, and who will win the next one.

At the end of the evening, when we had all drunk too much, one of the Americans said to me, 'So, Comrade, did you enjoy the movie? Do you like Gershwin?'

'No,' I said~~, but it was a lie for, although I did not like the film, I do like Gershwin.~~

February 9, 1947

Inquiring daily for decision. Told via IPS channels that our request is still being considered. Of course, from our intercepts of their communications we are fully aware as to the truth of the situation: Uncle Sugar Sugar Roger is being given the good old American-style runaround.

Comrade Vasiliev had a 'full and frank exchange' of opinions with their Colonel Bethune in regard to our request to interrogate former Lt. Gen. Ishii, et al. First of all, Comrade Vasiliev demanded to know whether or not the interrogations would be permitted. Colonel Bethune stated – through his G-2 interpreter – that no decision had been made as to whether or not the interrogations would take place. Comrade Vasiliev then asked if the location of the subjects – Ishii, et al. – were known. Colonel Bethune stated that if they were in Japan they could be found 'presumably'. ~~At this point in this ludicrous charade, I very much wanted to take out my pen and a piece of paper and write down Ishii's address for him.~~ Finally, Comrade Vasiliev insisted that the USSR merely wanted information pertaining to war crimes and agreed to make available to American interrogators the documents and the witnesses which we have, if desired. But Colonel Bethune merely reiterated that when the interrogations had been authorized by 'a higher authority', then the IPS would be notified. Comrade Vasiliev was not placated and demanded to see Gen. Willoughby in person to resolve the issue. Of course, this demand was denied.

March 7, 1947

Increasingly unpleasant exchanges between ourselves and 'Our American Friends' at GHQ. Comrade Lt. Gen. Kusma Derevyanko, our member of the Allied Council for Japan, submitted a memorandum in regard to the 'stalemate'; there are five Japanese prisoners of ours who 'our friends' would like turned over to them for war crimes. Similarly, we request that 'our friends' turn over Ishii, et al., for war crimes. As usual, we have been told to wait 'while Washington is consulted'.

April 12, 1947

Comrade Lt. Gen. Derevyanko finally received a written reply from Willoughby: *Despite no clear-cut war crimes interest by the USSR in acts allegedly committed by the Japanese against the Chinese, permission is granted for SCAP-controlled Soviet interrogations of*

Gen. Ishii and Cols. Kikuchi and Ōta as an amiable gesture toward a friendly government. It should be noted, however, that the permission granted in this instance does not create a precedent for future requests, which shall continue to be assessed on their individual merits.

No doubt now the real waiting will begin while 'Our Amiable Friends' in GHQ debrief Ishii and his gang.

May 9, 1947

Today was a day of the greatest jubilation for today was Victory Day in the Soviet Union, marking the end of the Great Patriotic War. But has the Great Patriotic War ended? I remember when the tide turned at the Front, how our newspapers blared forth fanfares, and how our evening skies were lit up by ever more extravagant displays of fireworks. And I also remember looking up at that sky, at those fireworks one night – where? Was I still in Moscow? – and, feeling only sorrow, ~~only anger, I heard from somewhere someone whispering, 'Be careful, this victory is not what you think it is at all, you will have to answer for it and pay the due retribution . . .'~~ And then, of course, I silenced myself; my duty, of course, is to rejoice. Rejoice! Rejoice!

June 6, 1947

The clock showed midnight, then one o'clock, two o'clock. Still there was no answer. The calendar showed Monday, then Tuesday, Wednesday. April, then May, now June. Still there was no answer. So days and weeks have passed~~, but thoughts and memories have not. For external time and internal time never correspond and so they remain unchanged, these thoughts and these memories~~. And then yesterday the answer finally came; we are to be allowed to interview the criminal Ishii, but only in the presence of the Americans, and only at the criminal Ishii's residence, and only tomorrow, that is, today.

So an American jeep picked up our own interpreter, our own stenographer and me this morning. Of course, I had not slept, but had spent the entire night preparing for this encounter, not knowing if further interviews would be granted.

We were seated in the back of the jeep, the windows obscured, and driven around the city in various directions for well over two hours until, finally, we arrived at our destination; 77 Wakamatsu-chō, Shinjuku-ku, Tokyo.

At the Ishii residence, the atmosphere rather resembled a luncheon party than a criminal interrogation. As well as their own interpreter and stenographer, there were two uniformed officers whom I did not recognize and two men who were quite obviously from Camp Detrick, as well as Lt. Col. McQuail and Mr Waldorf. Ishii's wife and daughter were also present as well as Ishii's pet monkey (who, from its friendly disposition towards certain nationalities present, had obviously already met these particular Americans, or else it had been specifically trained to display antagonism only towards citizens of the Soviet Union). And then, of course, there was the General himself.

The criminal Ishii was bedridden and feigning ill health. However, he could not disguise his own inherent arrogance and also his contempt and disdain for the Soviet Union. The man, though, had been well coached by his American friends and so, for example, while admitting that he had authorized and overseen experiments on Chinese and Manchurian captives, Ishii repeatedly denied that any such experiments had been conducted upon Allied or Soviet prisoners.

This diary is not the place to record or repeat the full extent of either my questions or his answers. But, suffice to say, Ishii answered my specific questions only with generalities, denying he could remember, or presently had access to, any specific technical data. To quote him, 'I cannot give detailed technical data. All the records were destroyed. I never did know many details, and I have forgotten what I knew. I can give you only general results.'

And in an obvious attempt to curtail any further investigation on our part, Ishii was also keen to portray himself as the person who should take full responsibility for Pingfan and N731 –

'I am responsible for all that went on at Pingfan. I am willing to shoulder all responsibility. Neither my superiors nor my subordinates had anything to do with issuing instructions for experiments. I do not want to see any of my superiors or subordinates get in trouble for what occurred as a result of my instructions.'

However, in regard to his research into plague as a BW agent and the mass production of fleas, Ishii was categorical in his denial, stating that no such work had taken place. Of course, we know this to be an outright lie and it only confirms that an arrangement has already been made with the US in regard to this information.

And so it went on for almost two hours; vague generalities and professions of guilt, followed by categorical denials and outright lies.

However, a second and final interview with the criminal Ishii has been granted and is scheduled to take place in the criminal Ishii's residence, again in the presence of the Americans, in one week's time. At the conclusion of my interview today, I asked Ishii if he would agree to hold the second interview at a different location. To this Ishii replied, 'I prefer to be interviewed at my house because of my health and also because I am afraid to leave my house.'

~~But at least now I have one full week in which to consider what action I should take at our next and final meeting.~~

June 13, 1947

I doubt I have slept more than one or two hours each night of this past week. ~~My head and my thoughts have been filled with numbers; the numbers of the dead and the numbers of the hurt, the number of my temptations and the number of my sins (all of which I know now to be countless). Repeatedly, I have found myself forsaking the documents, the reports and the transcripts, and returning instead to the Ten Commandments, the thirty steps of the Divine Ladder of Ascent, and the forty days and forty nights Christ spent in the wilderness. How many days and nights have I spent in the wilderness, how far have I fallen from the steps of the Divine Ladder, how many of the Commandments have I broken?~~

As before, we were picked up and driven around for an hour in an American jeep. Again, as before, at the Ishii residence, the criminal was bedridden. And again, as before, he spoke only in generalities or lies. This was as I had expected.

~~But the meeting was not entirely pointless for, as I bid him farewell, I handed Ishii a letter. And, for the first time, the man looked frightened and worried. I have no doubt he will show the letter to his American friends. But still, tonight I shall pray he will reply or seek to make contact, if only to be rid of me and the threat of further interrogation.~~

There is the death and then the mourning, and after the mourning there is the forgetting. That was how it was with our father and our mother; the death, the mourning, and then the forgetting. That is how it should be, how it must be.

But if someone said to me: You should forget your brother now. You must move on. Then I would strike that person down. I would strike that man down!

For his is a death imagined. There was no body. There is no grave. No damp mound of fresh earth on which to fall, to lie, prostrate in the soil with my tears.

Imagine if we could never forget the dead, imagine if we were always mourning, imagine then a world of tears, everything flooded, everyone drowned. That is my world, this city, all flooded, all drowned.

The Year 2000 43rd of April

An extraordinary incident occurred last night. I had fallen asleep rather early, fully clothed upon my hotel bed, when I suddenly awoke again. I looked at my watch and I saw that it was a quarter to three in the morning and, at that precise moment, a man stepped out of my wardrobe.

The man was Japanese, dressed in black and wearing a beret. He had a pistol tucked into the belt of his trousers. I immediately jumped up from my bed and grabbed the pistol from out of his belt, knocking the beret off his head. I switched on the light and I pointed the pistol at the man.

The man fell to his knees, cowering and shaking. He claimed to be a former BW engineer. He told me he had important information to share with me. He told me he had evidence of war crimes by detachments 100 and 731. He told me he had documentary proof of experiments conducted on Chinese, Manchurian, American AND Soviet prisoners of war. He told me that all of this was in addition to the information and evidence that he knew we already possessed.

Of course, I wanted to believe him and was more than curious to hear his information and to see his evidence. However, equally, I could not help but have my doubts and suspicions about his words and about the man himself. For though he claimed to be a former BW

179

engineer, he seemed to me to have the air more of a medical man than of a technician.

And though he had fallen to his knees, cowering and shaking before me, though he had offered no resistance when I had disarmed him, I did not believe the man was afraid of me. His actions, it seemed to me, were rather those of a highly trained actor, well versed in the dissemination of lies. And above all else, beneath this façade, it was difficult for me to determine the motivations of the man, what had led him to my room, to my wardrobe, the reasons he had for telling me the things he was telling me, and what reward he sought.

All was a mystery to me.

But still I listened to him. And still I agreed to investigate his claims. But in return, I had something to ask of him. And so I wrote a name on a piece of paper torn from this very martyr log. And I gave him the name on the paper, telling him it was a test.

And I kept his pistol.

<del>Martober the 86th, between day and night</del>

<del>Terrible dreams, every night, these dreams of Moscow, of the War College. First, of the fleas. Next, of the rats. Then, of the cells. The floorboards ripped up. Replaced with wire nets. And finally, the men. Barefoot men, naked men. The men thrown into the cells. The men thrown onto the wire. The rats beneath the wire floor. The rats hungry, the rats biting. Up through the wire. Deep into the skin. Infected, plagued. Every night, these dreams. But in the dream last night, on the far wall was written, with blood for ink, in my brother's hand, the words, 'Avenge me.'</del>

<del>No date at all. The day was dateless.</del>

The man from the wardrobe visited me again last night. And, as he had promised he would, he returned the page from this martyr-log on which I had written a name. And, as I had feared he would, beneath the name he had written an address – the address I have been searching for this last year. I know now I have no more excuses, only decisions to make.

<del>Don't remember the date. There was no month, either. Devil only knows what there was.</del>

180

Recently, I often think of those rotting, stinking old saints, their fossilized remains dug up from their graves and displayed in the Museum of Godlessness in the former Saint Basil's Cathedral in Red Square opposite the un-rotting, un-stinking body of the Great Vladimir Il'ich Ulyanov.

~~Recently, I often think of the decay of the saints and, particularly, the temptations of Jesus in the wilderness. I often think those forty days and forty nights were not so long, those temptations not so great, not compared to these years in this city, this wilderness and its temptations.~~

~~Every night before I sleep I say my brother's name three times. Then I say the Jesus Prayer three times. Finally, I spin the gun's barrel three times and I pull the trigger, once.~~

~~The Great Lev Nikolayevich Tolstoy once wrote that God sees the truth, but waits. But this poor citizen now knows, Man also sees the truth, but then he runs.~~

~~**The 1st date.**~~

The man from the wardrobe was here again. This time he was not shaking with fear, but shaking with anger.

'You are the same as the Americans, Comrade,' he spat. 'I give you information, I give you evidence, but you do not use it for justice, you use it only for your own ends. You are just the same. All the same!'

~~The man then took out a piece of paper, a document and he read, 'In 1941, in Ulan Bator and other areas of Mongolia, a Professor Klimeshinski carried out BW experiments on human beings using plague, anthrax and glanders. The subjects of these experiments were political prisoners and Japanese prisoners of war. The prisoners in chains were brought into an 8-man tent, on the floor of which were kept, under wire nets, a number of rats infected with pest fleas; the latter transmitted the infection to the subject of the experiment. The experiments were positive in most cases and infection ended in bubonic plague. Beside the rats, ground squirrels and other rodents also proved efficient intermediary hosts. It is known that the escape of one prisoner infected with bubonic plague started a great plague epidemic among the Mongols in the summer of 1941. To check the further spread of the epidemic, a chase was unleashed with the~~

~~participation of many air units, during which some 3 to 5,000 Mongols met their death.~~

~~'Glanders,' he continued to read, 'may be spread by guerillas, secret agents, or airplanes in regions in the possession or under the occupation of the enemy.~~

~~'It is also known that in Moscow, from 1939 to 1940, a group of investigators, with the code name WAR COLLEGE, used infected food to try anthrax on political prisoners and prisoners of war who had been isolated in experimental cells.~~

~~'It is believed that the Russians favour the infection of herds or pastures, or letting loose infected animals in enemy territory as dissemination by aircraft has proven unsatisfactory.~~

~~'However, in conclusion, it is our belief that Stalin will not initiate BW until it is an absolute necessity and only as a last resort should German troops penetrate deep into Russian territory and an anti-Soviet revolution breaks out in the country. In that instance, Stalin will order the use of BW agents, alleging that it was first started by the Germans.'~~

The man from the wardrobe stopped reading and he put away the piece of paper. And then he smiled and he said again, 'Just the same. All the same. But not me! I will show you, show you all – Japanese, American, Chinese and Soviet – I will show you all. I will teach you all. I will infect you all!

'First, I will infect Tokyo. Then, the whole of Japan. Finally, the world itself.

'How you ask – never why, only how; always the first question and always the last – too late, always much too late – is the question why. Perhaps it is because, hidden in your hearts, you already know why. So you only, always ask how –

'Well simply, I will poison the water supply. I will release fleas. I will release rats. And they will drop like flies – occupiers and collaborators alike – writhing in intestinal pain. There will not be enough ambulances, enough stretchers or beds. They will lie where they fall, one on top of the other, or side by side, their faces up and faces down, their hands raised, frozen and petrified, at their throats, dying in agony, fear and silence. And on your head will be these dead . . .'

The man is obviously mad and so I have nailed the wardrobe door shut.

Each night I sleep, I dream of Russia, I dream of Moscow. In last night's dream, in my second-hand leather jacket, I was pursuing a man when I saw that this man, this Japanese man who was running away from me, in his turn, was pursuing a third man who, not sensing our chase behind him, was simply walking at a brisk pace along the pavement. Then this third man heard the sound of our running boots and he turned to look behind him and I saw that the third man was my brother. Of course, when I awoke, I was still in Tokyo but my toes felt cold, my socks were damp and the bed muddy.

Maybe he is alive and it is I who am dead. My hands injected, frozen and black, and then hacked off like the handles on a clay pot before my own eyes. Maybe it is I who am screaming, 'Avenge me! Avenge me! Avenge me!'

And so maybe it is I who am stood on the banks of the river among the silent legions of the murdered dead, the countless legions of the war dead, my threadbare overcoat rotting into the stagnant water and its tangled weeds, maybe it is I who am waiting for him to avenge me –

~~Stop! Stop! Lord Jesus Christ, son of God, have mercy on me, a sinner. Spin! Spin!~~

~~Click! Click!~~

I could no longer put off this day. I woke early again from a fitful sleep and I took the train out to Chiba. I got off the train at Funabashi Station. With the piece of paper in my hand – the piece of paper originally torn from this martyr-log, on which the man from the wardrobe had written an address below the name I had given him – I walked through the snow and the mud. Finally, I came to the house, *his* house, his big house by a shrine where he lives with his wife and his children. And I stood across the road from his house, in the sleet and the declining light, and I waited, with the pistol in my belt and the rain in my face, the encroaching night at my back. I watched the lights go on in his house. I heard children's voices. I thought I could smell food cooking. And then the lights in the house went out and I thought I could see a figure at a window watching me, watching him.

But frozen and soaked, incapable of either action or thought, I simply stood there.

~~The Date 25th~~

I dreamt of Pieter Brueghel the Elder's 'Winter Landscape with a Bird Trap' and, in the same dream, I heard the music of Bach. And when I awoke, clouds of snow hung low over the city, but it was ash that fell from the sky. And in that sky were written three words, three Russian words in our Cyrillic alphabet:

мстите за менЯ

Avenge me . . .

And again I hated this city, this trap, and again I hated its people, these insects.

But I dressed quickly and I took the train back out to Chiba. I tried to keep my eyes on my boots, on the floor. But at every station, each time I glanced up, I saw that same sky out of the stained windows and I saw those same words, those three stained words, following me, watching me, suspended on strings, carried by swallows, flocks of swallows, in their beaks, three stained words:

мстите за менЯ

I got off the train and I walked through the sleet and the mud up the long road to his house by the shrine, my eyes on my boots, my eyes on the ground. But all the time, with every heavy step, I felt the sky above me, those words above me, swallows flying blind, leading me, pointing:

There he is, before you now –

And then, sure enough, when I looked up, there he was before me, walking towards me and I knew: This man is murder, this man is death; this man is my brother's murderer, his killer; and there he was before me–

~~Lord Jesus Christ, son of God, have mercy on me, a sinner.~~

And then the man, this murderer, he said in broken, halting English, 'I know who you are and I know why you are here. I knew you would come and so I have been expecting you, waiting for this day. Now the day is here and the wait is over.'

I unbuttoned my coat and I took out the pistol.

~~Lord Jesus Christ, son of God, have mercy on me, a sinner.~~

The man glanced at the gun and said, 'I am ready, for I think you know, Comrade, as well as I do, that war is within all men, regardless of their politics, regardless of their religion, regardless of their nationality, regardless of their race. It is the abyss beneath all our skins, the abyss within all our skulls. And once we have looked as we have looked, into that abyss, once we have stared as we have stared, into that void, then we cannot look away, for the abyss stares back at us, turning our hearts black and our hair grey. And with our black hearts and our grey hair we are no longer human, we are only war, are only murder, only death.

'And so shoot me, and then shoot yourself. Or arrest me, then hang me, and then yourself.'

~~Lord Jesus Christ, son of God, have mercy on me, a sinner.~~

I stepped towards him, tears on my cheeks. I grasped his head with my left hand, the pistol in my right hand. I brought his face towards mine, tears on his cheeks. I dropped the pistol. I kissed him on his lips. And then, then I walked away.

~~Lord Jesus Christ, son of God,~~
~~have mercy on me,~~
~~a sinner.~~

~~Da 26 te Mth yrae January 48~~

~~'Only then do we set ourselves free from external oppression, when we have set ourselves free from internal slavery,' wrote Nikolai Berdyaev. How right he was then, how right he is now.~~

This evening outside the hotel, they were waiting for me. I have no more strength to endure. I hear a chair fall in the room next door. I put on a clean, white shirt. That's it now—

$$1 + 1 = 1;$$
$$2 + 2 = 5;$$
$$3 + 3 = 7;$$
$$4 + 4 = 9$$

Signed, Comrade / Saint Kaka / Akakos,
Comrade Yurodivy or St Shit,
Ward No. 6

Beneath the Black Gate, in its upper chamber, the medium closes this journal, this martyr-log, and now she holds this journal, this martyr-log over one of the five candles until the pale flame catches its pages and now this journal, this martyr-log begins to burn –

'See,' the medium laughs, 'manuscripts do burn . . .'

Burning the journal, the martyr-log in the flame of the candle, the journal, the martyr-log now only ash, the candle,

the eighth candle now out –

'I was and remain the best and brightest of all that is Soviet. Indifference to my memory and rumours about my death will be a crime. My body will be transported back to Moscow and my ashes placed alongside Gogol and Mayakovsky in the Novo-Devenchy Cemetery, under a red and black monument and an iron wreath of flywheels, hammers and screws. An iron wreath for an iron man –

'So now, farewell Tokyo, murderous city . . .'

Beneath the Black Gate, in its upper chamber, eight candles gone, another ghost gone, there are no red and black monuments here, no iron wreaths, for you are a tarnished, rusted and corroded man –

Tarnished, rusted and corroded by the tears-that-will-not-come, the book-that-will-not-come, in this place-of-no-tears, this place-of-no-book, only these words, *on your head are these dead*,

these words you have heard before, *on your head are these dead*, words you have heard twice now, *on your head*

are these dead, on your head

are these dead . . .

But beneath the Black Gate, in its upper chamber, in this now-occult square, the light of its now-four candles, there are sirens again,

two sirens, an ambulance siren and a police siren –

And now the medium lies before you, crumpled and flattened inside the circle, hands raised and stiff in the candlelight, a detective's identification wallet in her black and broken fingers,

the medium a detective; a dead detective –

And now you crawl towards her, on your hands and on your knees, towards her prone body, and you put your fingers on her face to close her eyes, her two pitch-black eyes staring up at the ceiling of the upper chamber, the roof of the Black Gate, and in these two pitch-black eyes, in the eyes of this dead detective, you spy a crow, and in her eyes, you follow the flight of this crow,

in these two pitch-black eyes,

through the city, across its rooftops, down its streets, into its alleyways, in her eyes, her pitch-black eyes, and now these eyes, these two pitch-black eyes, these eyes they blink, alive again –

The medium, her left hand behind your head, pulls your face towards her own, and now her lips open your lips, her tongue touches your tongue, moving up and down, her tongue inside your mouth, up and down, in and out, up and down, in and now out –

For now, in the light of the candles, these four candles in their occult square, now the medium pushes you away and she whispers, she whispers the words of the dead detective –

'You are not him. You are not the man I seek, the man I failed *the man I failed* THE MAN I FAILED

The Ninth Candle –

The Thirty-six Wounds of a Second Detective, N.

Act I

1. The city is a wound *the city is a wound* THIS CITY IS A WOUND In the half-burnt pages of my half-destroyed notebooks *in the half-said whispers of the half-heard voices* IN THESE HALF-REMEMBERED MEMORIES OF THIS HALF-FORGOTTEN DETECTIVE In the Occupied City *in the Occupied City* IN THE OCCUPIED CITY We uncover the murders of 169 new-born babies in a maternity home in Shinjuku *they parade the guilt of 28 soon-dead men in a court house in Ichigaya* THEY WILL FIND YOU GUILTY AND THEY WILL HANG YOU, UNTIL YOUR BLADDER EMPTIES AND YOUR NECK BREAKS My father is dead and my mother has remarried *your wife was once a whore, and she is a whore again* IN THE FAMILY ALBUMS, IN THE HISTORY BOOKS Even the Emperor has married again, in his top hat and tails, an American General, with a pipe in his mouth *your child is not your child* WE ARE ALL WHORES I hate all Americans *your family is cursed, your house is cursed* IN THE RUINS OF THE CITY, IN THE EYES OF THE DEAD I took their job, I take their money *the ground beneath is hollow ground* THROUGH THE LOOKING-GLASS I sharpen pencils, I write reports *under your chair, under your desk* WHAT WILL YOU FIND In my unstable chair, at my untidy desk *something is moving, moving behind you, moving beneath you* THROUGH THE LOOKING-GLASS The telephone rings *from a music box, what is that tune* WHO WILL YOU FIND The clock strikes *that familiar, scratched tune* GOOD DETECTIVE, BAD DETECTIVE And the case begins, this last case begins *a light glowing above the city, a fire*

raging across the town DON'T LOOK BEHIND YOU On January 26, 1948 *it's coming your way, don't look behind you* IN THE SILENCE, NOTHING BUT SILENCE The telephone, the clock, and this last case *it makes you hold your breath* AS THOUGH THE WORLD WAS DEAD

2. Across the Occupied City, in our borrowed cars *you follow a tune, the sound of scratching* IN HEAVY BANDAGES Roads turn to mud, mud turns to rivers *across the city, through the night* FROM OPEN WOUNDS Snow turns to sleet, sleet turns to rain, turns to sleet again *sudden, oncoming headlights, American, blinding headlights* THE SCENE OF THE CRIME There are ambulances, there are crowds *crawling down the street, on her hands and on her knees* THEY STAND, THEY STARE Former soldiers standing in their white robes and khaki-caps, feral children hanging from the branches of the shrine-trees *raving about poison, asking for help* THEY ARE THE SPECTATORS, WE ARE THE SPECTACLE The Nagasaki Shrine to my right, the Teikoku Bank to my left *the sound of scratching, from under the ground* THE SPECTACLE, THE CRIME I put out my cigarette, I follow the other detectives, up the steps, into the bank *for hell has found us, as hell always finds us* THE SCENE OF THE CRIME Down the narrow passages, through the heavy furniture *dragging it with us, every place we go* IN THE LIDLESS GAZES Between the empty chairs, the rows of desks *on our hands and on our knees* OF THE RECENTLY DEAD The cash on the desks, in piles, the vomit on the floor, in pools *we should tidy, we should clean, straighten the room, wash the cups* I STAND, I STARE In the corridor, on the mats, in the bathroom, on the tiles *you follow a tune, the sound of scratching* I AM THE SPECTATOR, THEY ARE THE SPECTACLE Ten bodies, ten corpses *the sound of whispering, the sound of weeping* THE CRIME, THE SPECTACLE The clock on the wall, its black hands still moving *every place we go, dragging it with us* IN HEAVY WINTER CLOTHES Their hands raised, frozen and petrified, at their throats *on our hands, on our knees* FROM OPEN HUNGRY MOUTHS These men, these women, this child, they died in agony, they died in fear, they died in silence, fallen on

189

each other, lying side by side, faces up and faces down *not speaking, but moaning* THE SPECTACLE OF THE CRIME

3. I stand in the Seibo Catholic Hospital, by the beds of the four survivors *crawling out of hell, on their hands, on their knees* THE CRIME SCENE IN MY MIND Nuns stick hoses down their throats, doctors pump out their stomachs *down the bank's corridors, into the bank's genkan* THE CASH ON THE DESKS, THE VAULT DOORS WIDE OPEN I watch them cough, I watch them wretch, fluid and bile *through the doors, into the street, the snow and the mud* NOTHING OUT OF PLACE, NOTHING BUT THEIR BODIES I wait for them to wake, I wait for them to speak *on their hands, on their knees* THE SOUND OF RUNNING WATER, THE DIRTY CUPS BEING WASHED Beside their beds, beside their lips *it was the drink, it was medicine, a doctor, dysentery* THE CRIME SCENE CONTAMINATED

4. I turn the corner into my street *what fine men, straight as trees* I CAN HEAR HER VOICE, I CAN READ HER THOUGHTS I see my wife, her child strapped to her back, standing with her friend *that one gave you a very friendly eye* HER LASCIVIOUS VOICE, HER WANTON THOUGHTS They are watching the American soldiers passing in their jeeps *look at you, your shining eyes* NOT SPEAKING, BUT MOANING Having fun, I ask *that child is not your child* SKIN UPON SKIN, FLESH INTO FLESH What are you doing here, she asks, shouldn't you be at work *mist rises from under the ground, black smoke from their American ovens* NOT SPEAKING, BUT MOANING I say, I was in the neighbourhood, why *their fog follows me, follows me to work, follows me back home* AMERICAN SKIN UPON JAPANESE SKIN, AMERICAN FLESH INTO JAPANESE FLESH Why nothing, she says, come home, I'll make you something to eat *he thinks too much, his mind wound tight* NOT SPEAKING, BUT MOANING I can't come home, I say, I'm still on duty *it is always so dark, he is always so haunted* HER WORRIED VOICE, HER FRIGHTENED THOUGHTS Is something the matter with you, she asks, you look so distracted *he never even looks at his own child, he will go mad from his own*

thoughts I HEAR HER VOICE, I READ HER THOUGHTS
Nothing is the matter, I say, but I must go *no sunshine, no streetlights, only clouds, only shadows* ALL THEIR VOICES, ALL THEIR THOUGHTS

5. Wake up, Detective N., says Detective Inspector H., shaking my shoulders, kicking my chair *bones aching, chest hurting* IN THE OCCUPIED CITY I sit up, I cough twice *eyes smarting, ears ringing* WHERE IS THE RESISTANCE We've just received a report of a body, sounds like a suicide, at an inn in Shiinamachi, near to the Teikoku Bank *from the smoke, from the tune* THERE IS NO RESISTANCE Take Detective K. and go check it out, says Detective Inspector H., handing me an address on a scrap of paper *from the music-box, the American ovens* THERE IS NO UNDERGROUND We walk down Mejiro-dōri, we cross over Yamate-dōri, then we turn left into the Nagasaki neighbourhood, looking for the Kiraku Inn in Shiinamachi 5-chōme *the smell of burning, the sound of scratching* IN THIS CITY OF COLLABORATORS There is an ambulance outside the inn and a doctor stood with the owner of the inn and his wife *outside the rooms, inside the rooms* IN THIS CITY OF TRAITORS They lead us up a narrow, steep staircase, then down a long, dark corridor to a closed door at the back of the inn *biting, chewing, devouring* EVERY WIDOW IS NOW FOR SALE He's in here, says the owner as he slides opens the thin stained door to a small dim room and a body on a futon, the quilt pulled back, the body clothed *you can always hear their teeth* EVERY WIDOW, EVERY WIFE, EVERY WOMAN It looks to me like a suicide by potassium cyanide, says the doctor, and I read in the newspaper that you believe the killer at the Teikoku Bank may have used potassium cyanide, so I stressed this when I reported the death *for everything decays, decomposes and dies* IN THE MARKET PLACE, IN THE SHOP WINDOW I walk over to the window, I slide back the screen *how many bodies, how many rooms* OLD BODIES, FRESH MEAT The body is dressed in a grey sweater, a khaki coat, and black serge trousers *in rooms that are not yours* TWO-FACES, TURN-COATS A black overcoat hangs by the door, a wallet lies on the floor beside the futon *you open doors, you enter rooms* ON THEIR KNEES, ON THEIR BACKS I pick up

the wallet, I open up the wallet, ¥100 inside the wallet *how many rooms that were not yours, how many bodies that were not yours* MY WIFE, MY MOTHER He gave his name as Yokobe Kunio, says the owner, and his profession as a company official from Komagawa-mura, Iruma-gun, Saitama Prefecture *from room to room, from body to body* IN THE SHOP WINDOW, IN THE MARKET PLACE And he arrived here when, I ask *in the black fog, in the black mist* FOR A NEW MAN, FOR A NEW LIFE About 9:30 p.m. last night, says the owner *in your eyes, in your ears* IN A NEW COUNTRY, IN A NEW CITY How long do you think he's been dead, Detective K. asks the doctor *the sound of whispering, the sound of scratching* THEIR RINGS LOOSE, THEIR LEGS OPEN Not very long, replies the doctor, he's still warm *from the American ovens, from the music-boxes* IN THIS COUNTRY OF NO RESISTANCE He's better off than me then, laughs Detective K. *among the smoke, among the tunes* IN THIS CITY OF NO RESISTANCE How did you discover him so quickly, I ask the owner *you are always so suspicious, you are always so jealous* I HATE THE LOSERS, I HATE THE VICTORS The owner shakes his head, then looks at his wife, and he says, She did *her eyes will wander, her legs will wander* I HATE ALL AMERICANS, I HATE ALL CAUCASIANS I couldn't sleep last night, says the wife, I had such terrible dreams, dreams about the Teikoku Bank, I had a bad feeling, a bad feeling about him *no father for her child, no provider for her needs* THE WHITE STARS ON THEIR JEEPS, THE WHITE TEETH IN THEIR MOUTHS I point at the body, and I ask the wife, A bad feeling about him *you are never here, you are always gone* WHITE SKIN ON YELLOW SKIN, WHITE FLESH IN YELLOW FLESH She nods, About him *what does she see in him* WHERE IS THE RESISTANCE I stare at her, in her *monpe* trousers, in her heavy sweater, and I ask, Why *this woman is much younger than her husband* IN THIS CITY OF COLLABORATORS The wife shakes her head, the wife closes her eyes, then the wife slowly says, Last night, I passed him in the corridor, and he suddenly squeezed my arm, and said he had come to see his friend, but his friend was not here *she could have any man she wants* IN THIS CITY OF TRAITORS He had tears in his eyes, tears on his cheek, she says *a better man than you* I AM THE

DETECTIVE, I AM THE RESISTANCE I cough once, I cough again *an exorcism, an exit* THE ONLY RESISTANCE, IN THIS CITY Is it him, asks the wife, the Teikoku killer *not you, never you* NO RESISTANCE CITY I shake my head, I say, His hair is too long, it can't be him, the Teikoku killer, not him, no *you are no exorcism, you are no exit* NO RESISTANCE

6. I am early, he is late, it doesn't matter *wa-oh-wa-oh* IN THIS FOREIGN CITY, IN THIS ALIEN CITY I enter the dancehall *beat me mama, with that boogie-woogie beat, that Tokyo boogie-woogie, beat me, beat me* ALL THINGS ARE FOREIGN TO ME, ALL PEOPLE ARE ALIEN Jungle music and tom-toms, yellow skin and Negroid hair *the shadows lengthen, in time, the shades advance, in rhythm* NEW DANCES, OLD TUNES The dance among the ruins, the dance of the living dead on the ashes of the really dead *sakura boogie-woogie, jungle boogie-woogie* NO LONGER HUMAN, NO LONGER LIVING Bones on skin, sticks on drums *in borrowed dresses, to stolen songs* DANCING NEW DANCES, HUMMING OLD TUNES In the lights, in the mirrors, everything is reflected *we are always reflected* REFLECTED, FRACTURED, DISFIGURED AND OTHER I see my wife, but is it her *bows and ribbons in her hair* YESTERDAY'S ENEMY IS TODAY'S FRIEND Every woman looks like her, every woman moves like her *in the redness, in the heat* THE BATTLE IS OVER NOW, THE WAR AT AN END I see my Japanese wife dancing with an American soldier *in the smoke, in the fog* WE PRAISE THEIR MARTIAL SKILLS I see them spin upon the floor, fall then roll around *on and on, dancing and dancing, on and on, turning and turning* THEY PRAISE OUR COURAGEOUS HEARTS Why don't the gods blow out the sun, then everyone can roll around fucking and fucking *him, her, hell, hell* WITH FOND FAREWELLS AND SALUTES WE PART No, do it in bright daylight *flesh, filth, man, woman, human, animal* WHEELING TO THE LEFT, THEN TO THE RIGHT Do it like the flies on my hand *in fields and in lewdness, in debauchery and in democracies* IN NEW DANCES TO OLD TUNES The bastard, how he touches her up, how he feels her up, the slut *she curtsies, he bows* NO LONGER LIVING, NO LONGER HUMAN I get up from my chair, I cannot

wait in this dancehall *they clap their hands, their hands are hammers* EVERYTHING FOREIGN HERE, EVERYONE ALIEN NOW I leave *all the things of this world, they are evil things* NOTHING IS SPARED, NO ONE IS SPARED

7. Detective Inspector H. gives me a new file, the Matsui File, and I read the Matsui File, cover to cover *all men have secrets, all men tell lies* BAD MEN, GOOD MEN His was the name-card presented at the Ebara branch of the Yasuda Bank, the name used in the rehearsal for the Shiinamachi branch of the Teikoku Bank *somewhere to someone* IN WARTIME, IN PEACETIME We have already questioned Dr Matsui Shigeru, we have already eliminated Dr Matsui Shigeru; his alibi checks out, his appearance doesn't match *all men are guilty, are guilty of something* WAR CRIMES, PEACE CRIMES But there are things about Dr Matsui that don't check out, there are things in his background that do match *somehow, somewhere* THE CLUES LIE IN THEIR WORDS Dr Matsui works for the Health and Welfare Ministry in Sendai, Dr Matsui served in the Imperial Army as chief of the Public Sanitation and Health Administration Department in Java, Indonesia *crimes never stay secret, secrets never stay secret* IN THEIR WORDS LIES THE EVIDENCE The newspapers printed the story of the rehearsal at the Ebara branch of the Yasuda Bank, the newspapers printed the details of Dr Matsui Shigeru and his name-card, the newspapers printed that Dr Matsui Shigeru was being interviewed by the Tokyo Metropolitan Police Board, the newspapers printed that Dr Matsui Shigeru was employed by the Health and Welfare Ministry, that he had served in the Imperial Army in Indonesia *men always talk, talk to someone* THE EVIDENCE OF THEIR LIES, THE EVIDENCE OF THEIR GUILT Two days after the newspapers printed their stories about Dr Matsui Shigeru, a letter arrived at the Special Team investigating the Teikoku Bank robbery, an anonymous letter, an anonymous letter about Dr Matsui Shigeru, about the things Dr Matsui Shigeru had done in Indonesia, the crimes Dr Matsui Shigeru had committed in Indonesia *in confidence, in betrayal* ALL MEN ARE GUILTY, ALL MEN ARE CULPABLE I keep reading the anonymous letter and I keep remembering this one fact: Dr Matsui's card was the card used, Dr Matsui's name was the name used; so the suspect had his card, so the

194

suspect knew his name; so the suspect knows Dr Matsui Shigeru, so Dr Matsui Shigeru knows the suspect *all men have secrets, all men are guilty* IN WARTIME, IN PEACETIME I put down the letter, I close the Matsui File, I pick up the phone *all men, always* BAD MEN, BAD MEN

Act II

8. Dr Matsui Shigeru has already been questioned about the Teikoku murders, Dr Matsui Shigeru has already been eliminated as a potential suspect, but Dr Matsui Shigeru is still in our custody, still helping us with our inquiries *you seem distracted, Detective* DISPLACED We have drawn up lists, lists of the people to whom Dr Matsui Shigeru gave his name-card, the name-cards exchanged and the name-cards received *is something troubling you, something on your mind* FROM THE PAST, IN THE PRESENT, FOR THE FUTURE We have asked any member of the public who may have exchanged name-cards with Dr Matsui Shigeru to present themselves with the name-card of Dr Matsui Shigeru at their local police station *trouble at home, with the wife* DISLOCATED Now I ask Dr Matsui Shigeru to tell me the names of the people with whom he worked in Java, Indonesia, the names of the people with whom he served in the Imperial Army in the Public Sanitation and Health Administration Department in Java, Indonesia *twenty days straight, no days off, it's not easy, with a wife* UNABLE TO FOCUS, UNABLE TO FORGET My memory is poor, Dr Matsui Shigeru tells me, it must be the effect of that South Asian climate, but I don't remember them well, the people with whom I worked, the people with whom I served *a wife much younger, a pretty little thing, with a young child, both left at home, to fend for themselves* THE FUTURE, THE PRESENT, THE PAST Well one of them, at least, remembers you, and remembers you well, I tell Dr Matsui Shigeru and I pass him the letter, the anonymous letter *naturally it must be a worry, a distraction, always there, at the back of your mind* DISORIENTATED I'll be seeing you again, I tell Dr Matsui Shigeru, so don't be going anywhere now *are you listening, Detective* OUT OF PLACE, OUT OF TIME

9. In the bathhouse *we are letting Dr Matsui Shigeru return to Sendai* IN THE LOOKING-GLASS Men are shaving their faces *as*

you know, Dr Matsui Shigeru suggested we interview his colleague, Mr Hoshi Shōji in Sendai I HAVE MY FINGERS IN MY EARS On their stools *as you know, Detective T. interviewed Mr Hoshi Shōji in Sendai* IN THE LOOKING-GLASS Men are washing each other *as you know, Mr Hoshi Shōji's alibi checks out, Mr Hoshi Shōji's appearance doesn't match* BUT I CANNOT CLOSE MY EYES Buckets of water, over their heads, over their bodies *as you know, Mr Hoshi Shōji suggested we interview Dr Matsui Shigeru's former colleague from Indonesia, ex-medical Sergeant Major Karajima* IN THE LOOKING-GLASS I pick up the soap, I lather the soap *as you know, we issued an APB for ex-medical Sergeant Major Karajima* MY BODY IS NOT MY OWN I wash the shoulders and the back of Detective Inspector H. *as you know, the description of ex-medical Sergeant Major Karajima does not match that given by the survivors* IN THE LOOKING-GLASS You always look so wrought, he says, you always seem so distracted, Detective N. *so we are sending Dr Matsui Shigeru back to Sendai with Detective T., to search through his house, to go through his address book, to collect all his name-cards* ALIEN, FOREIGN Harder, he says, rub harder, Detective *to refresh his memory* IN THE LOOKING-GLASS

10. I turn a corner, blue hope in my pockets, I climb the stairs, my damp hate pulled low, I walk along the corridor, I put out my cigarette, I knock on the door *the city is upside down* HOW MUCH DO YOU LOVE JAPAN Comrade Horie opens the door, Comrade Horie laughs, Oh, no! It's the cops! Hide the books! Hide the pamphlets! Everybody run for your life *the city is inside out* WITH ALL MY HEART But Comrade Horie's one-room apartment is empty, the meeting has already broken up, the party faithful have already left, just stale smoke in the air *the whole country, the whole world* A DWARF WHOSE HEART IS TOO BIG FOR HIS BODY I push past Comrade Horie into the room, the windowless, book-lined room, I squat down on the floor, and I say, Very funny *upside down, inside out* HOW MUCH DO YOU HATE AMERICA Comrade Horie shuts the door, Comrade Horie leans against it, Where have you been, Comrade. We've been very worried about you, worried you'd had a change of heart *back to front* WITH ALL MY HEART Don't you read

the newspapers, I ask *the sun rises with the dusk* A GIANT WHOSE HEART IS TOO SMALL FOR HIS BODY Not the papers you read, no *with the dusk the moon sets* I WANT TO HOPE, I WANT TO BELIEVE But you've heard about what happened at the Teikoku Bank in Shiinamachi, I ask, the mass-poison murder-case *animals on two legs, men on all fours* WITH ALL MY HEART That your case, asks Comrade Horie *a horse rides a man down the Ginza* IN THE POSSIBILITY OF A UTOPIA Not just mine, I laugh, every single detective in Tokyo is on the case, every other investigation suspended *a boy laps rain water from a drain* IF I CANNOT HOPE, IF I CANNOT BELIEVE And do you have a suspect yet *a cow milks a woman's tit* WITH ALL MY HEART Not yet, but it seems there could be a link back to the Americans, I say, at the very least it seems that the killer had access to Occupation information, that he's possibly even employed by them *a woman shits in the street* IN THE POSSIBILITY OF A UTOPIA Comrade Horie sits down opposite me now, the jokes finished, Really. Now that is very interesting, that could be very useful *upside down, inside out* THEN THIS IS PETRIFICATION Useful, I ask him, useful for whom *back to front* THEN THIS IS PARALYSIS The movement, you idiot, he laughs, I should introduce you to Comrade X *a cat kisses a dog in front of a department store* THE PETRIFICATION OF HOPE, THE PARALYSIS OF BELIEF Who is Comrade X, I ask *a man bites the ear off another man in an alley* A NEW ICE AGE He is a correspondent for *Izvestia a hen dances with a pig in a ballroom* IN THE GORGON'S GAZE You're joking, I say, not laughing, no chance *two women fight over a fish in a ditch* ALL WOMEN TURN TO STONE Listen, hisses Comrade Horie, if you're serious about helping us, helping the movement, then you need to start giving us things *I see a rat wearing a suit* ALL MEN TURN TO STONE What kind of things, I ask *a family living in a hole* ALL HEARTS Information *a flea buying a cake* PETRIFIED, PARALYSED And what kind of information do you think I could possibly have, I ask Comrade Horie *a child scratching itself raw* WITH DESPAIR, WITH HATRED About GHQ, about crimes, about conspiracies *lice eating off silver* I LOVE JAPAN, I DESPAIR OF JAPAN About conspiracies, I repeat, what conspiracies *mothers eating their young* I HATE AMERICA, I'M AFRAID OF AMERICA Comrade Horie throws his head back, hands in the air, Oh, wake up! Open your eyes, cop! It's like the war never happened *upside down, inside out* NO POSSIBILITY, NO HOPE Like the war never happened, I say, it's you who should wake up, comrade! You who should open *your* eyes! This city, this country, was destroyed. People are homeless, people are starving. We were defeated! We are occupied *back to front* ONLY PETRIFICATION, ONLY PARALYSIS Exactly, grins Horie now, exactly! But for what. So the same political gangs, the same financial houses, the same military cliques, the same Emperor can stay in power. The more things change, the more they stay the same *on two legs, on all fours* THE DWARF WHOSE HEART IS TOO BIG FOR HIS BODY Tell that to our former prime minister, I say *animals are men, men are animals* THE GIANT WHOSE HEART IS TOO SMALL FOR HIS BODY Old Tojo, laughs Horie, he's not important. He never was. He's just a scapegoat. Maybe a martyr, the way things are going *detectives are suspects, suspects are detectives* ALL HEARTS ARE STONE I shake my head, I light a cigarette, I cough and cough *criminals are judges, judges are criminals* IN THE GORGON'S GAZE Listen, says Comrade Horie, things are changing fast and not for the better. Things are moving backwards. The Americans are scared to death of communism, of what's happening on the mainland. The Americans want things back the way they were before the war. And the Americans are taking steps to ensure that's what'll happen, you watch, they'll be knocking on that door any day now, locking us all back up, throwing away the keys again. Unless we act now, Comrade Detective, we need to wake the Japanese people up! And we need to wake them up before it's too late! Need to do it now! Need to show the people what's happening! And you, Comrade Detective, you can help us show them. Because you can provide us with the proof *the past is bad, the future is good* COLD WARS, ICE AGES Proof of what, I ask him *the present is not what it seems, and seems is not what is present* IN THE GORGON'S GAZE Are you listening, shouts Horie now, proof that the Americans are colluding and conspiring with the old pre-war elites to stifle and extinguish democracy. To destroy and to bury socialism *back to front* THE PETRIFICATION OF HOPE, THE PARALYSIS OF BELIEF

But what exactly is the proof that you think I possess, I ask *upside down, inside out* WITH ALL MY HEART You'll find it, whispers Comrade Horie, I know you will *the moon rises with the dawn* I CANNOT HOPE, I CANNOT BELIEVE I cough once again, I hold my chest, I close my eyes, I see smoke again, animals in the smoke *with the dawn the sun sets* AN ICE AGE IN MY HEART

11. In Kanda, at the Myōjin Shrine, for the Setsubun Festival, I walk with my wife, her child on her back *her child is not your child* AT THE EDGE OF THE WORLD Thank you for bringing me here, she says, I know you should be working *her words are not for you* EVERYTHING SLIPS, EVERYTHING SLIDES Through the crowds, through the bodies *their words are not for you* EVERY LIVING THING PASSES Demons be outside, we shout, fortune be inside *look at her, what a woman* PASSES AND FALLS AWAY All their eyes are on her body *the way she carries herself, the way her ass moves* INTO THE NIGHT, INTO THE FOG The bodies pressed tight together, hands filled with hard soybeans *that's what I call a woman, that's what I call a body* BLACK NIGHT! BLACK FOG! Hands that want to touch her, hands that want to hold her *all that meat to hold, but as wet as a fish* NOT SPEAKING, BUT MOANING Thank you for coming, my wife says again *be like fucking a fish filled with honey* FLESH INTO FLESH You're welcome, I say *that's what I call a woman* AT THE EDGE OF THE WORLD

12. Dr Takase Toyokichi, a senior member of the medical department of the Tōhoku University Hospital in Sendai, walks into Sendai North Police Station *the sound of scratching* MEMORIES Dr Takase Toyokichi reports that at the end of December, or at the beginning of January, a man walked into the pharmacy of the Tōhoku University Hospital in Sendai *scratching under the ground* PRECISE MEMORIES The man was in his fifties, two spots on his left cheek, his hair cut short and grey *we are always talking about you* IMPRECISE MEMORIES The man asked Dr Takase Toyokichi for potassium cyanide, potassium cyanide to kill the fish in his pond *talking about you behind your back* THOUGHTS The man had no prescription but the man had a name

199

we are always whispering about you PRECISE THOUGHTS The man said his name was Dr Matsui Shigeru *whispering about you behind our hands* IMPRECISE THOUGHTS Dr Takase Toyokichi knew this man was not Dr Matsui Shigeru, Dr Takase Toyokichi knows Dr Matsui Shigeru *the sound of scratching* DREAMS Someone else knows Dr Matsui Shigeru, someone who has his name-card, someone who wanted potassium cyanide *scratching under the ground* PRECISE DREAMS Someone who murdered twelve people at the Teikoku Bank on January 26, 1948 *behind your back, behind their hands* IMPRECISE DREAMS

13. I say, I'm sorry about the other night. I tried to call, but you'd already left your office *among the smoke, among the tunes* MY FATHER APPEARS TO ME It doesn't matter, says the journalist, forget about it. You are here now. So what have you got for me, Detective *from the music-box, the American ovens* BY THE RIVER I say, Not something you can probably print, not yet, but it's something you should know *eyes smarting, ears ringing* ON THE SHORE Go on, he says *in the smoke, in the fog* IN HIS UNIFORM What we're not saying in public is the growing feeling that this case is connected with the Tokumu Kikan and Occupied China *on and on, dancing and dancing* WITH HIS MEDALS Very interesting, he says *on and on, turning and turning* WITH HIS SWORD There are rumours of similar cases, cases that occurred back in Shanghai, that the culprit is ex-Tokumu Kikan, with experience handling medicines and civilians, who we should be looking for *him, her, hell, hell* HE POINTS WEST Very, very interesting, says the journalist *flesh, filth, man, woman, human, animal* HE POINTS EAST I say, But what I'm telling you is nothing you can print yet, but there's nothing to stop you looking into the China connection, is there *she curtsies, he bows* EVERYWHERE IS AMERICA Thank you, he says, I will *they clap their hands, their hands are hammers* EVERYWHERE

14. We bring Dr Matsui Shigeru back to Investigation Headquarters, we sit Dr Matsui Shigeru in the interview room *you are always so suspicious, you are always so jealous* IN THE FAMILY ALBUMS, IN THE HISTORY BOOKS I say, Someone used your name to try to buy potassium cyanide from the pharmacy of the

Tōhoku University Hospital *I don't know what you are talking about, I don't know who you are talking about* GÖBBELS ADMITTED DEFEAT, GÖBBELS TOOK RESPONSIBILITY I know, says Dr Matsui Shigeru *what men you mean, what man you mean* HE POISONED HIS CHILDREN I say, Someone also tried to buy potassium cyanide from a pharmacy near Sendai Station on January 20, this year *he was never here, never in this room* HELGA, HILDEGARD, HELMUT, HOLDINE, HEDWIG AND HEIDRUN I know, says Dr Matsui Shigeru *I can't stop them walking past here* HAND IN HAND, WITH HIS WIFE I say, This someone knows your name, they know who you are *I can't stop them looking at me* HE ADMITTED DEFEAT, HE TOOK RESPONSIBILITY AND SHOT HIMSELF, HAND IN HAND I know, says Dr Matsui Shigeru *I can't stop them thinking about me* IN THE FAMILY ALBUMS, IN THE HISTORY BOOKS I say, You must know them, must know their name *I can't make them stay locked in their houses* NOT LIKE OUR EMPEROR, HE TAKES NO RESPONSIBILITY It would seem so, says Dr Matsui Shigeru *I can't make them leave their eyes at home* HE DENIES EVERYTHING, HE DENIES EVERYONE I ask, So tell me who, tell me their name *I can't make them not think what they think* THE FATHERS AND MOTHERS, THE BROTHERS AND SISTERS, THE SONS AND DAUGHTERS I honestly don't know, whispers Dr Matsui Shigeru *I can't stop you being suspicious, you being jealous* HE DENIED US ALL AND HE MARRIED AGAIN I lean forward in my chair, I say, Then you are honestly a liar *put a knife in my belly if you will, but never put your hand on my hand again* IN HIS TOP HAT AND TAILS, AN AMERICAN GENERAL, WITH A PIPE IN HIS MOUTH, HAND IN HAND

Act III

15. In the Police branch of the Public Safety Division of GHQ, they keep me waiting *among the tunes, among the smoke* THE WINNER AND THE LOSER First Miyakawa, the Liaison from the Justice Ministry, keeps me waiting, then Henry Eaton, the man from the PSD, keeps us both waiting *the smell of hospitals, the smell of laboratories* THE OCCUPIER AND THE

OCCUPIED Him in his smart uniform, buttons polished; me in my old suit, buttons lost *white coats and white masks, rubber gloves and rubber shoes* THE MASTER AND HIS DOG I say, I am here on behalf of the Second CID Section of the Tokyo Metropolitan Police Board to ask for the assistance of the Public Safety Division in our investigation of the Teikoku Bank robbery *medicines and drugs, pills and injections* HE SPEAKS, I JUMP I say, I am here to ask for the assistance of the Public Safety Division in locating a Lieutenant Hornet and a Lieutenant Parker *examinations and tests, experiments and trials* I JUMP, HE YELLS I say, We believe that on November 14 last year, the suspect in the Teikoku Bank robbery went to the Ebara branch of the Yasuda Bank in Shinagawa Ward, where he is reported to have told the employees of the bank, 'I came here with Lieutenant Parker in a jeep because a new typhus case has occurred in this area.' The suspect then produced some liquid which he told the employees was a preventative medicine for typhus control and directed them to drink it. They did so, suffering no ill-effects *in rows, in cages* HE YELLS, I COWER I say, On January 26 this year, a man we believe to be the same man appeared at the Shiinamachi branch of the Teikoku Bank in Toshima Ward and stated, 'I came here because there have been many dysentery cases in this vicinity. Lieutenant Hornet will be here very soon. You must take this medicine for prevention.' Sixteen employees drank the liquid simultaneously. Twelve died almost immediately *in rows of cages, in cages of dogs* I COWER, HE BEATS ME I say, We have reason to believe both Lieutenant Hornet and Lieutenant Parker have been associated with typhus disinfecting teams in the Tokyo area; Lieutenant Hornet with the Toshima Team in Ōji Ward and also in Katsushika Ward, Lieutenant Parker with the Ebara Ward Disinfecting Team *dogs barking, dogs snarling* HE BEATS ME, I WHIMPER I say, So I am here to ask for the names and addresses of any individuals either connected with or having any knowledge of the disinfecting work done by either of these two lieutenants, particularly interpreters or individuals who speak English, though we would advise the elimination of individuals below the age of thirty or above the age of sixty *rubber gloves and rubber shoes, white coats and white masks* I WHIMPER, HE PETS ME Henry Eaton yawns like a snarling dog, but I am the only dog here *in the* smoke, *in the fog* HE PETS ME, I WAG MY TAIL Henry Eaton says now, Leave it with me *the dogs are not barking, the dogs all silent now* THE DOG AND HIS MASTER

16. This is Comrade X., says Comrade Horie, in his windowless, book-lined room *you seem distracted, Detective* IN THE LOOKING-GLASS How much do you love Japan, Comrade X. asks me, how much do you hate America *are you listening, Detective* IN HEAVY BANDAGES Let me tell you two stories, says Comrade X., when our correspondents marched into Berlin with the Red Army, we went half-hungry, because all the available food was reserved for the foreign press, mostly Americans. Because the American press were our guests, we wanted them to have the best *people are talking about you, Detective* IN THE LOOKING-GLASS Then when all of us landed in Kyushu, alongside a full Red Army general, the American colonel in command sent his aide to invite us all to dinner *behind your back* FROM OPEN WOUNDS That night, at dinner, we were all seated at the foot of the table, even our Red Army general at the foot of this colonel's table *people are whispering about you, Detective* IN THE LOOKING-GLASS From our seats at the foot of his table, we could see this American colonel well, this American colonel and his other much more important guests: a couple of ill-mannered and noisy girls *behind their hands* IN HEAVY WINTER COATS In the middle of the dinner, one of the girls got up and sang, and all the American officers whistled *you need to see someone, Detective* IN THE LOOKING-GLASS The song she sang was called, 'Will I Sleep Alone Tonight' *are you listening* FROM OPEN HUNGRY MOUTHS They will treat you like dogs, says Comrade X., they will fuck your women and they will lie to you, Detective, they will lie to you *someone who will help you* IN THE LOOKING-GLASS So I ask you again, Detective, how much do you hate America, how much do you love Japan *are you listening to me, Detective, I'm trying to help you* REFLECTED, FRACTURED, DISFIGURED AND OTHER

17. Wake up, Detective N., says Detective Inspector H., kicking my desk, kicking my chair *how much do you love Japan* NOT SPEAKING, BUT MOANING I've just come from a meeting

with Miyakawa from the Justice Ministry, says Detective Inspector H. *a dwarf whose heart is too big for his body* CRAWLING OUT OF HELL, ON MY HANDS, ON MY KNEES Mr Eaton from the Public Safety Division told Miyakawa that no US military personnel are presently employed in typhus epidemic control, and that all involvement by US personnel in such duties ceased sometime in 1946 *how much do you hate America* NOT SPEAKING, BUT MOANING Furthermore, there are no records of any Lieutenants Hornet or Parker ever being involved in such work, says Detective Inspector H., so that would seem to be the end of that *a giant whose heart is too small for his body* DOWN THE BANK'S CORRDIORS, INTO THE BANK'S GENKAN I say, Then I want to go up to Sendai. I want to interview Dr Takase personally. Dr Takase met the man who tried to get potassium cyanide, the man who claimed to be Dr Matsui. Dr Takase met the Cyanide Man *do you hope, do you believe* NOT SPEAKING, BUT MOANING As you know, Inspector K. has already interviewed him, says Detective Inspector H., and I need you in Tokyo *in the possibility of a utopia* THROUGH THE DOORS, INTO THE STREET, THE SNOW AND THE MUD As you know, we have traced sixty of Dr Matsui's name-cards, says Detective Inspector H., and so I need you here to record and collate all the information we are gathering in the field about these sixty name-cards and the ones we are still to find *do you hope, do you believe* NOT SPEAKING, BUT MOANING I say, What about the Matsui name-card we already have. The name-card used at the Ebara branch of the Yasuda Bank. The man who said he was Dr Matsui. The man who said the same thing in Sendai *in an end to petrification, in an end to paralysis* IT WAS THE DRINK, IT WAS MEDICINE, A DOCTOR, DYSENTRY The answer is still no, says Detective Inspector H. again, I need you here and besides, what about your wife, you want to leave her alone in Tokyo while you chase name-cards in Tōhoku *with all your heart* NOT SPEAKING, BUT MOANING

18. I turn the dark corner, I stand outside the door, the door to our room, and I hear her voice *I want to love you like I used to love you* I SMELL THE HOSPITAL, I SMELL THE LABORATORY A long, long time ago, she says, there was a poor little girl who had

no father or mother *I want to love you like I loved you before* THE WHITE COATS AND THE WHITE MASKS Everything was dead and there was no one left in the whole of Japan *I want to love you without suspicion* THE RUBBER GLOVES AND THE RUBBER SHOES And since there was no one left in the whole of Japan, the little girl decided to go up to heaven to where the moon shone down *without jealousy* THEIR MEDICINES AND THEIR DRUGS But when the little girl got to the moon, it was just a lump of rotten wood *I want to love you without the fear of losing you* THEIR PILLS AND THEIR INJECTIONS So then the little girl went to the sun, but when she got there it was just a withered-up sunflower *the fear of hurting you* I SUBMIT TO THEIR EXAMINATIONS And when she got to the stars, they were just little white lice stuck on a piece of dirty old black cloth *like I used to love you* I SUBMIT TO THEIR TESTS So the little girl went back to Japan, but Japan was just an overturned pot of nothing *like I loved you before* I SUBMIT TO THEIR EXPERIMENTS The little girl was completely alone now, and so she sat down and cried *but most of all, I want you to love me* I SUBMIT TO THEIR TRIALS She's sitting there still, all alone, still crying *I want you to love me* IN ROWS, IN CAGES, A DOG

19. I turn another dark corner, I climb another set of stairs, I walk along another corridor, I knock on another door *have you ever seen nature inside-out, have you ever seen nature upside-down, have you ever seen double-nature* I AM NOT DISTRACTED I told you they would lie to you, didn't I, says Comrade X., and here is the proof of my words *when the sun stands high and still at noon, as though the whole world is on fire, how it makes you hold your breath, as though the world was dead* I AM NOT DELIRIOUS Comrade X. hands me a document, a document in English, a document stamped 'CONFIDENTIAL' *then those frightful voices come, they speak to me, when nature is out* I AM NOT POSSESSED As you can see from this, says Comrade X., the Americans have lied to you; a First Lieutenant Paul E. J. Parker, medical officer, was assigned to the Tokyo area between June 1946 and June 1947 to assist in various health-control activities *the world so dark that you have to feel your way around it with your hands* I AM NOT PREOCCUPIED Comrade X. says, This is undoubtedly

the 'Lieutenant Parker' who was assigned to a typhus control team in Ōji Ward in March 1947 *you think it is coming apart, like a spider's web, dissolving and disintegrating in your fingers* I HAVE NO MEMORIES And as you can further see from this, says Comrade X., while there is no record of a 'Lieutenant Hornet', there are records of a Captain J. Hartnett who was similarly engaged in public health work in Tokyo between June 1946 and April 1947 *when something is, and yet isn't, when something is there, yet nothing is there* I HAVE NO VISIONS I say, They lied to me, to us *everything so dark, and yet there's still this redness, this redness from the west, the glow from a distant furnace, a gigantic underground oven* I AM NOT MAD Comrade X. smiles and Comrade X. says, Are you really so surprised, Detective. I told you they would lie. The Americans always lie *it's all in the air, have you noticed the patterns in the air, in the clouds, in the fog, in the mist, and in the smoke* I HAVE EATEN MY CORN, MY AMERICAN CORN, AND I AM NORMAL I say, I don't know what to do *if we could only read those patterns, if one could only read the air, then what things we would know, what truths* I HAVE TAKEN MY PILLS, MY AMERICAN PILLS, AND I AM RATIONAL I will tell you, says Comrade X., I will help you, if you let me *if we could read the air, then we would know the truth* I AM NORMAL, RATIONAL AND SANE

20. I say, I was taking a big risk telling you the things I did, showing you the documents I did. A big risk for nothing! Nothing in your newspaper, nothing about the China connection, nothing about the GHQ connection, nothing about Parker and Hornet. So it looks like I took a big risk just for nothing *your mother's new husband, your never-my-new father* WE'VE SEEN YOU BEFORE Not nothing, says the journalist now, you took a risk, I know, but I paid you *he likes Americans, he entertains Americans* WE'VE SEEN YOU PISSING I say, Not enough, not enough for all the risks I've taken. And now I don't know why I bothered, why I took all those risks, you weren't even listening to me, you didn't even write the story *with your father's money, in your father's house* PISSING IN THE STREET I wrote the story, says the journalist, I gave it to my editor and he read it and he said he liked it, said he liked it very much *on the floors he walked, in the chairs he*

sat PISSING DOWN A WALL I ask, so where is it, this story of yours, this story your editor liked so very much, he liked so very much he didn't publish, so very much they didn't print, where is it then *in the room he lay, in the room they lay* PISSING LIKE A DOG I don't know, says the journalist *your father and your mother* IF YOU CAN'T CONTROL YOUR BLADDER I stand up and I say, Well, you better find out. Or there'll be no more help, no more stories from me *Americans lie, everybody lies* WHAT CHANCE YOUR MIND

21. You are distracted, Detective, says the doctor, you are distracted and you are delirious *you have not been listening, Detective* IN THE FAMILY ALBUMS, IN THE HISTORY BOOKS I ask, What is to be done. What should I do *you have not been following instructions* THE EMPEROR SAYS, I STAND BY MY PEOPLE You are delirious and you are possessed, possessed and preoccupied, possessed by memories and preoccupied with visions *you have not been following orders* I AM EVER READY TO SHARE IN THEIR JOYS AND SORROWS What is to be done. What should I do *you have been making connections, Detective* COURAGEOUS PINE, ENDURING THE SNOW Memories of things that never happened, visions of things that never will *connections where there are no connections to be made* THE TIES BETWEEN ME AND MY PEOPLE HAVE ALWAYS BEEN FORMED BY MUTUAL TRUST AND AFFECTION What is to be done. What should I do *you have been making links, Detective* THEY DO NOT DEPEND UPON MERE LEGENDS OR MYTHS I'm sorry to say, says the doctor now, but in a word, Detective, you are mad *links where there are no links to be made* THAT IS PILING UP, COLOUR UNCHANGING What is to be done. What should I do *you have been imagining things, Detective* NOR ARE THEY PREDICATED ON THE FALSE CONCEPTION THAT THE EMPEROR IS A MANIFEST DEITY I will tell you, says the good doctor, and I will help you, if you will let me *hearing things, seeing things* THAT THE JAPANESE ARE SUPERIOR TO OTHER RACES AND DESTINED TO RULE THE WORLD I ask, What is to be done. What should I do *things that are simply not there* LET THE PEOPLE BE LIKE THIS, SAYS THE EMPEROR Eat more corn, says the doctor,

American corn and take these pills, these American pills *you are suspended from duty, Detective, you are off the case* IN THE HISTORY BOOKS, IN THE FAMILY ALBUMS

Act IV

22. In the Occupied City *in the Occupied City* IN THE OCCUPIED CITY Time passes *time passes* TIME PASSES Seconds pass *minutes pass* HOURS PASS Days pass *weeks pass* MONTHS PASS But the city is still a wound *the city still a wound* STILL A WOUND My father still dead, my mother still remarried *in these half-remembered memories of this half-forgotten detective* MY FAMILY CURSED, MY HOUSE CURSED My wife still unfaithful, my case still unsolved *they will find you guilty and they will hang you* THE GROUND BENEATH STILL HOLLOW GROUND Sharpening pencils, writing reports *until your bladder empties and your neck breaks* UNDER MY CHAIR, UNDER MY DESK Passing time, backward and forward, forward and backward, time passing *in the family albums, in the history books* SOMETHING IS MOVING, MOVING BEHIND ME, MOVING BENEATH ME The city still occupied, the city still wounded *we are all whores* FROM A MUSIC BOX The clock strikes again and the telephone rings *in the ruins of the city, in the eyes of the dead* WHAT IS THAT TUNE, THAT FAMILIAR, SCRATCHED TUNE In the Occupied City, in the Wounded City *through the looking-glass* A LIGHT GLOWING ABOVE THE CITY, A FIRE RAGING ACROSS THE TOWN

23. In the final days of the war, as our Red Army swept over the former Japanese colony of Manchuria, many Japanese soldiers surrendered and were taken prisoner *you've not been eating your corn, your American corn, have you, Detective* ALL MEN HAVE SECRETS Among these prisoners, were men who had served in Detachment 100 and in Detachment 731 of the Japanese Kwantung Army; Detachment 100 and Detachment 731 were bacteriological detachments, both involved in the prosecution of and research into bacteriological and chemical warfare *you've not been taking your pills, your American pills, have you, Detective* ALL

208

MEN TELL LIES In Khabarovsk, in the Primorye Military Area, my comrades from the Academy of Medical Sciences of the USSR have been interrogating these former members of Detachment 100 and Detachment 731 in preparation for their indictment as war criminals on charges of waging bacteriological warfare on China and the Soviet Union, and of conducting bacteriological experiments on Chinese and Soviet prisoners *you've been putting your ear to the ground again, haven't you, Detective* SOMEWHERE TO SOMEONE Of course, we know that not all the criminals responsible for these atrocities are in our custody. We know that these secret bacteriological units of the Japanese army, which were commissioned to prepare for and conduct bacteriological warfare, were formed by the personal command of Emperor Hirohito himself *hearing the sound of scratching from under the ground* ALL MEN ARE GUILTY, ARE GUILTY OF SOMETHING We also know the names of the criminals in the Japanese General Staff and Ministry of War who backed and directed the clandestine work of these secret bacteriological units, who lavishly financed, equipped and staffed them, who sanctioned the research and development of internationally proscribed types of bacteriological warfare, and who planned for the day when they would authorize the launching of bacteriological attacks *tunes from the music boxes* SOMEHOW, SOMEWHERE Yes, we know the names of the contemptible, morally corrupt servitors of Japanese imperialism, generals of the former Japanese army – the bacteriological scientists Ishii, Kitano and Wakamatsu – who were ready to place their special knowledge at the service of the ruling clique of Japan for the purpose of preparing to conduct criminal bacteriological warfare *in the whispering* CRIMES NEVER STAY SECRET, SECRETS NEVER STAY SECRET And we know the names of those wicked misanthropes, the former members of Detachment 100 and Detachment 731, physicians and engineers of the Japanese army – Ōta, Murakami, Ikari, Tanaka, Yoshimura and many others – who mercilessly and in cold blood murdered defenceless people and bred many millions of plague-infected parasites and hundreds of kilograms of lethal microbes for the extermination of mankind *and you've been putting your head in the clouds, haven't you, Detective* MEN ALWAYS TALK, TALK TO SOMEONE We know who they are and we know where they are, outside our borders and outside our jurisdiction, because these miscreants enjoy the protection of those reactionary forces in the imperialist camp who are themselves dreaming of the time when they will be able to hurl upon mankind load upon load of TNT, atomic bombs and lethal bacteria *trying to read the patterns in the air again* IN CONFIDENCE, IN BETRAYAL But you, Comrade Detective, you can help us, help mankind *smoke from the Americans' ovens* ALL MEN HAVE SECRETS For this is a list of the names of men given to my comrades in Khabarovsk by the former members of Detachment 100 and Detachment 731 who are now our prisoners, the names of men who were once their colleagues in Detachment 100 and Detachment 731, men who are now back here, living and working freely in Japan, and I believe among these names, among the names of these men, is the name of the one man, the one man you are looking for, Detective *in the fog* ALL MEN ARE GUILTY Catch this one man, Detective, and expose this one man for the mass-poisonings at the Teikoku Bank, and you will expose all those men for all their crimes, all those Japanese men and all the American men who protect them *in the nut-house, Detective, that's where you'll be* ALL MEN, ALWAYS

24. Another name from the list, another doctor from the list, this one called Yanagi, this one in Chiba *bad men, good men* YOU ARE ALWAYS SO SUSPICIOUS, YOU ARE ALWAYS SO JEALOUS Yanagi had once been a research director in Detachment 731 *in wartime, in peacetime* I DON'T KNOW WHAT YOU ARE TALKING ABOUT, I DON'T KNOW WHO YOU ARE TALKING ABOUT Yanagi had once been in charge of botanical disease experiments *war crimes, peace crimes* WHAT MEN YOU MEAN, WHAT MAN YOU MEAN Now Yanagi is living on a dusty highway between a tobacconist and a butcher *the clues lie in your words* HE WAS NEVER HERE, NEVER IN THIS ROOM Now Yanagi is working in a shabby surgery between a noodle shop and a gas station *in your words lies the evidence* I CAN'T MAKE THEM STAY LOCKED IN THEIR HOUSES For Yanagi is in hiding, for Yanagi is in fear *the evidence of your lies, the evidence of your guilt* I CAN'T MAKE THEM LEAVE THEIR EYES AT HOME He denies and he lies, then he cowers and he whimpers, and now he

confesses to his crimes *all men are guilty, all men are culpable* I CAN'T MAKE THEM NOT THINK WHAT THEY THINK He begs and he pleads, then he betrays and he informs, and now he gives me a name *in wartime, in peacetime* I CAN'T STOP YOU BEING SUSPICIOUS, YOU BEING JEALOUS Another name for my list, another doctor for my list, this one called Sawa, this one in Funabashi *bad men, bad men* PUT A KNIFE IN MY BELLY IF YOU WILL, BUT NEVER PUT YOUR HAND ON MY HAND AGAIN

25. I turn the dark corner, I go up the stairs, I walk along the corridor, I open the metal door, I take off my shoes, I walk through our room, I stand over her body, I lift it up, and I say, Is it still you, are you still here *you are not a bad man, but you are a poor man* I AM THE GOOD DETECTIVE I should be able to see you with my eyes, but I can't see you; I should be able to touch you with my hands, but I can't touch you *nothing but her and this job, this bloody job* NOTHING BUT WORK UNDER THE SUN I should be able to see things, I should be able to touch things *everybody hates the police, nobody talks to the police* THE EARTH HOTTER THAN HELL What a very fine city we live in, what a very fine place it is, even finer with company *the police don't talk to the police, even the police hate the police* I SWEAT EVEN WHEN I SLEEP Did he stand here, this close to you *you'll be giving someone a very nasty cut one day* BUT HELL IS COLD, AND I AM COLD Oh, how I wish I had been him *you go through this world like an open razor* AS COLD AS THE PAUSE BETWEEN A 'YES' AND A 'NO' Your lips are so very beautiful, would you had left them at home today *someone or something waiting, just waiting to be cut* IS THE 'YES' TO BLAME FOR THE 'NO', OR THE 'NO' TO BLAME FOR THE 'YES' Your lips, your mouth, so very, very red; why are there no blisters on your lips, your mouth, I wonder *a good detective takes care of himself and his family* BELOW THIS VERY FINE GREY SKY, ON THIS VERY FINE GREY DAY I can see him now, I can see him standing, him standing here with you *a good detective isn't careless, distracted or foolhardy* I WANT TO HAMMER A PEG, A PEG RIGHT INTO THAT SMOKE Oh, how I wish I had been him *don't cut your nails at night, don't whistle those tunes at night* A PEG TO HANG MYSELF FROM

I see him, I see him, I see him and I see you, I see you, I see you, I see you and I see you with him, I see you with him, I see you with him, I see you with him and I see an abyss, I see an abyss, I see an abyss, an abyss *you have nothing in this world but your wife* UNTIL MY BLADDER EMPTIES If you look inside, every man is an abyss, you get dizzy if you look, if you look down, look inside *you are a poor man, but not a bad man* UNTIL MY NECK BREAKS

26. My colleagues have gone up to Otaru in Hokkaido, gone to arrest a man called Hirasawa Sadamichi *among the tunes, among the smoke* THE SOUND OF SCRATCHING My colleagues believe they have the evidence to prove that Hirasawa Sadamichi committed the Teikoku crime *in the Black Fog, in the Black Mist* SCRATCHING UNDER THE GROUND My colleagues believe Hirasawa Sadamichi has no alibi for the time of the Teikoku crime *we've seen you before* IN MEMORIES, BLOODY MEMORIES My colleagues believe Hirasawa Sadamichi had a strong motive for committing the Teikoku crime *we've seen you pissing* ALWAYS TALKING ABOUT ME My colleagues believe Hirasawa Sadamichi is guilty, my colleagues believe Hirasawa Sadamichi is the killer *pissing in the street* BEHIND MY BACK But I know Hirasawa Sadamichi is not guilty, I know Hirasawa Sadamichi is not the killer *pissing down a wall* OF THOUGHTS, BLOODY THOUGHTS For I know who is guilty, I know who the killer is *pissing like a dog* ALWAYS WHISPERING ABOUT ME I know his name and now I know his address *among the tunes, among the smoke* BEHIND THEIR HANDS And soon, very soon, I will know his face, I will see his face *in the Black Fog, in the Black Mist* THE DREAMS, BLOODY DREAMS, OF THE GOOD DETECTIVE

27. He shouts, I thought you were my man-on-the-inside, my man-in-the-know, but I'm the last-man-to-know, I've been scooped *all things are foreign to you, all people are alien* I CUT MY NAILS, EVERY NIGHT, AT NIGHT Everyone's in the dark, I say, not just me, not just you. They have kept the rest of us chasing suspects with military backgrounds, suspects with medical backgrounds, kept telling us to forget about the name-cards *no longer*

human, no longer living SO I MIGHT SEE AGAIN MY FATHER'S GHOST He shouts, But they told us not to write about the military men, about the medical men, told us to keep it out of our papers and look where that's got us. Duped and scooped *reflected, fractured, disfigured and other* AT NIGHT, EVERY NIGHT, I CUT MY NAILS You think you people, your newspaper, are the only ones who get censored, I laugh, wake up! This country is an Occupied Country, this city is an Occupied City. They can do what they want, when they want, to who they want, how they want. It's an Occupied City and it's a set-up *yesterday's enemy is today's friend* IN THE HOPE YOU'LL COME AGAIN He asks, You're saying this man Hirasawa is innocent then *the battle is over now, the war at an end* THAT YOU MIGHT SPEAK TO ME, THAT YOU MIGHT TALK TO ME Of course he is, I sigh, but they are desperate. They followed the name-cards and this is where it's led them. But there are seventeen name-cards which have still not yet been traced, that are still not yet accounted for. This man Hirasawa is just one of the seventeen and the moment the survivors set eyes on him, that will be that *with fond farewells and salutes you part* THAT YOU MIGHT TELL ME WHAT TO DO He asks, That will be what, what do you mean *wheeling to the left, then to the right* I CUT MY NAILS, EVERY NIGHT, AT NIGHT The end of their case, I laugh, because the survivors won't be able to identify Hirasawa, because it wasn't him, and so then they'll have to let him go again *in new dances to old tunes* THAT YOU WILL TELL ME WHAT TO DO, PLEASE TELL ME WHAT TO DO Now the journalist says, You really think so *no longer living, no longer human* ABOUT MY WORK, PLEASE TELL ME, ABOUT MY HOUSE I really know so, I say, all of us do, all of us except Ikki and his name-card team. It's all circumstantial *everyone alien here, everything foreign now* ABOUT MY MOTHER, PLEASE TELL ME, ABOUT MY WIFE He says, But off-the-record your top men are telling us they are 100 per cent certain about Hirasawa Sadamichi, 100 per cent certain he is guilty. That's why they've gone so public with his arrest *nothing is spared* PLEASE TELL ME, ABOUT MY WIFE, PLEASE And, of course, you believe everything you hear, I laugh, everything they tell you. Well, you just watch *no one is spared* NO MORE NIGHT, NO MORE NAILS

28. You have not been listening, Detective, have you *who else would I be, where else would I go* IN THE FAMILY ALBUMS, IN THE HISTORY BOOKS You have not been following instructions *I am still me, I am still here* HAND IN HAND You have not been following orders *to see things, to touch things* A WOLF IN SHEEP'S CLOTHING You have been making connections, Detective, haven't you *what are you talking about, you must have a fever* A SHEEP IN WOLF'S CLOTHING Connections where there are no connections to be made *you must be delirious, who are you talking about* IN THE HISTORY BOOKS, IN THE FAMILY ALBUMS You have been making links, Detective, haven't you *you give me money, you give me presents, you grab my hand, you grab my crotch* HAND IN HAND Links where there are no links to be made *have you been bitten by a flea, infected with some new form of madness, some new kind of virus or plague* A WOLF ON THE THRONE You have been imagining things, Detective, haven't you *wasps land on my lips, all men are the same* A SHEEP ON THE THRONE Hearing things, seeing things *the days are long and the world is old, lots of people have stood in the same place* IN THE HISTORY BOOKS, IN THE FAMILY ALBUMS Things that have never been, things that are simply not there, things that will never be *a man can see a lot of things with two good eyes on a sunny day* HAND IN HAND You are suspended from duty, Detective, you are off the case *I am still here, I am still me* THE WOLF AND THE SHEEP

Act V

29. In our room, on the floor, on my hands, on my knees, I see it, see it shining, in our room, on the floor, on my hands, on my knees, in the gloom, a golden thing, on the floor, in our room, on my hands, on my knees *among the smoke, among the tunes* UNDER CLOCKS I ask my wife, What is this thing *the winner and the loser* BIG CLOCKS, LITTLE CLOCKS What is what thing, she replies *the occupier and the occupied* WE WAIT FOR DEATH I say, This shining golden thing. Here in my fingers *the master and his dog* ON GREY DAYS, AGAIN AND AGAIN That thing, it's nothing. It's just an earring, she

214

replies *you speak, I jump* A PIECE OF FOOD, IF WE'RE LUCKY I ask, And where did you get this golden earring *I jump, you yell* RATS, IF WE'RE NOT I found it in the street, she says, it's nothing *you yell, I cower* IN ROOMS I say, But I've never found that kind of nothing, that shining golden kind of nothing *I cower, you beat me* ENORMOUS ROOMS, TINY ROOMS My wife says nothing *you beat me, I whimper* WE WAIT FOR DEATH I take a second golden earring, a matching golden earring, out of my pocket, I hold it up to her, I say, I never found that kind of nothing twice *I whimper, you pet me* A KIND WORD, NOW AND AGAIN So what does that make me, she asks, what are you saying *you pet me, I wag my tail* A SMILE, IF WE'RE LUCKY Now I take some money from my pocket, I give it to my wife, I say, I have to go, go back to work *the dog and his master* BLOWS, IF WE'RE NOT I'm a bad person I know, my wife is weeping, I'm bad for you. If I had a sharp knife, I could stab myself. I want to die *the bad dog, the good master* IN ROOMS, UNDER CLOCKS I leave the room, I close the door, I leave the building, I turn another corner, and I'm gone again *among the tunes, among the smoke* WE WAIT FOR DEATH

30. The last name on my list, the last doctor on my list, this one called Sawa Saburo, this one in Funabashi, Chiba Prefecture *across the occupied city, in your borrowed cars* IN OUR HOSPITALS, IN OUR SCHOOLS, AT OUR HOMES, AT OUR JOBS Sawa Saburo had once been a research assistant at the former Japanese Imperial Chemical Laboratory in Tsudanuma, Chiba Prefecture *roads turn to mud, mud turns to rivers* EVERY MINUTE OF EVERY HOUR Sawa Saburo had once been involved in research into the use of prussic acid as a poison *snow turns to sleet, sleet turns to rain, turns to sleet again* A HUNDRED LITTLE COMPROMISES Sawa Saburo was then later promoted to the rank of lieutenant colonel and sent to Pingfan, outside Harbin, in Manchuria *there are ambulances, there are crowds* EVERY HOUR OF EVERY DAY Lieutenant Colonel Sawa Saburo was attached to Detachment 731 *former soldiers standing in their white robes and khaki caps* A HUNDRED LITTLE DEALS Now Sawa Saburo is living on another dusty highway between a clothing shop and a bar *feral children hanging from the branches of*

215

the shrine-trees EVERY DAY OF EVERY WEEK Now
Sawa Saburo is working in a run-down animal hospital between a
bicycle repair shop and a Chinese restaurant *the Nagasaki Shrine to
your right, the Teikoku Bank to your left* A HUNDRED LITTLE
LIES But Sawa Saburo no longer calls himself Sawa Saburo;
Sawa Saburo now calls himself Endo Saiichi *you put out your
cigarette, you follow the other detectives, up the steps, into the bank*
EVERY WEEK OF EVERY MONTH I open the metal gate in
the wooden fence and I step inside the courtyard of the Funabashi
Animal Hospital *down the narrow passages, through the heavy
furniture* THE GUILTY ARE FREE, THE INNOCENT ARE
IMPRISONED The August sun is high in the midday sky and
here in the courtyard there is no shade, only row upon row of cage
upon cage *between the empty chairs, the rows of desks* EVERY
MONTH OF EVERY YEAR In each row there are twelve
cages, on each cage is stacked another two cages, and in each cage is
a dog *the cash on the desks, in piles, the vomit on the floor, in pools*
THESE ARE THE COMPROMISES WE MAKE WITH
OURSELVES The place smells of piss, the place smells of
shit, the place smells of dogs *in the corridor, on the mats, in the
bathroom, on the tiles* MINUTE AFTER MINUTE, HOUR
AFTER HOUR, DAY AFTER DAY But the dogs are not
barking, the dogs are all silent now *ten bodies, ten corpses* THESE
ARE THE DEALS WE SELL TO OURSELVES This place smells
of death *the clock on the wall, its black hands still moving*
WEEK AFTER WEEK, MONTH AFTER MONTH, YEAR AFTER
YEAR A man in a dirty white coat and a dirty white mask, in dirty
rubber gloves and dirty rubber boots, steps out of the office now *their
hands raised, frozen and petrified, at their throats* THESE ARE
THE LIES WE TELL TO OURSELVES The man removes his
dirty white mask and he asks, Can I help you *these men, these
women, this child* A HUNDRED LITTLE COMPROMISES, A
HUNDRED LITTLE DEALS, A HUNDRED LITTLE LIES I
take off my hat, I take out my handkerchief, I wipe my face, and I say,
Dr Sawa *they died in agony, they died in fear, they died in
silence, fallen on each other, lying side by side, faces up and faces
down* A THOUSAND TINY CUTS, A MILLION TINY WOUNDS

31. I wait in our room for her to return, but the child keeps crying *did the world make you sad, or do you make the world sad* HOW MUCH FOR A KNIFE I watch for her from the window, but the child keeps crying *did the world hurt you, or do you hurt the world* TO CUT MY OWN THROAT I pick it up, but the child keeps crying *did the world make you cry, or do you make the world cry* A LOVELY SHARP STRAIGHT KNIFE I hold it in my arms, but the child keeps crying *did the world say yes and you said no, or do you say yes and the world says no* TO CUT MY OWN THROAT I try to sing it a song, sleep angel sleep, but the child keeps crying *did the world make you the person you are, or do you make the world the place it is* A LOVELY SHARP CHEAP KNIFE I walk up and down the room, holding it in my arms, down and up the room, but the child keeps crying *was the world to blame, or are you to blame* TO CUT MY OWN THROAT I pat it and rub its back, but the child keeps crying *was it the world, or is it you* A KNIFE JUST LIKE THAT I try to give it food, but the child keeps crying *this petrification, this paralysis* TO CUT MY OWN THROAT I try to give it water, but the child keeps crying *this despair, this hatred* A CHEAP AND ECONOMICAL DEATH Finally I lay it back down, but the child keeps crying *are these tears for the world, or are these tears for yourself* TO CUT MY OWN THROAT The child keeps crying for its mother *these tears* THE LOOSE CHANGE IN MY POCKET

32. He wipes away the tears from his eyes *no, I think you mean Dr Endo; yes, you are looking for Dr Endo* AMONG THE TUNES, AMONG THE SMOKE He says, It is true that I committed the crime *no, I've not seen Dr Endo for six months* IN THE FOG, IN THE MIST I feel relieved now that everything is over, that a heavy load has been lifted from me *no, Dr Endo has not been here; no, he has not been to work; no, not for the last six months* THE CITY IS UPSIDE DOWN I don't have adequate words to express the regret I have for having committed this horrible crime *yes, you could try his room down the highway; yes, in the building between the men's clothing shop and the bar called Yuki* THE CITY IS INSIDE OUT The police have treated me fairly and properly, man to man, and this treatment allowed me to bring out the

best in my mind *no, Dr Endo said he was going away; no, he didn't say he'd be coming back* THE WHOLE COUNTRY, THE WHOLE WORLD Chief Prosecutor Takagi Hajime has been a gentleman and Prosecutors Sasaki and Umezu have treated me with consideration and fairness *yes, of course I believed Dr Endo; yes, because he said he was dying; yes, because I knew he was dying; because I could see he was dying* UPSIDE DOWN, INSIDE OUT I do not feel like making any statement in my defence at this time, but I can say that part of my motive was due to science *yes, Dr Endo looked like a doctor; yes, he was about fifty years old; yes, he was about 160 centimetres tall* BACK TO FRONT I have been writing poetry and Chief Prosecutor Takagi Hajime has been helping me *yes, his hair was grey; yes, his hair was short; yes, he had two marks; yes, upon his left cheek; yes, he looked like that, he looked like that picture* THE SUN RISES WITH THE DUSK, WITH THE DUSK THE MOON SETS I am a devout follower of Nichiren Buddhism and it is my desire now that my soul might be cleansed and saved by the great mercy of the Buddha *no, you are not the first person to come here; no, you are not the first person to ask about him; no, you are not the first person to suggest he's a killer* THE MOON RISES WITH THE DAWN, WITH THE DAWN THE SUN SETS I want the world to know that I have confessed my guilt of my own free will *no, I don't know where he might have gone; no, I don't think he could still be alive* AMONG THE TUNES FROM THEIR MUSIC-BOXES, AMONG THE SMOKE FROM THEIR OVENS At last I am able to sleep *because the man had his addictions, because the man was dying* IN THE BLACK FOG, IN THE BLACK MIST

33. I say, Come on, it's time, let's go *all men have secrets, all men tell lies* I WANT TO LOVE YOU LIKE I USED TO LOVE YOU Go where, she asks *somewhere to someone* I WANT TO LOVE YOU LIKE I LOVED YOU BEFORE Somewhere, anywhere, what does it matter *all men are guilty, are guilty of something* I WANT TO LOVE YOU WITHOUT SUSPICION It's so dark here, the city's that way *somehow, somewhere* WITHOUT JEALOUSY I won't let you get sore feet again, I promise you that *crimes never stay secret, secrets never stay secret* I WANT TO LOVE YOU WITHOUT THE FEAR OF

LOSING YOU And I've got to get back, the dinner to make, the child to feed *men always talk, talk to someone* THE FEAR OF HURTING YOU But please sit down, please stay a bit *in confidence, in betrayal* LIKE I USED TO LOVE YOU The moon and the stars, she says, they look so very red *all men have secrets, all men are guilty* LIKE I LOVED YOU BEFORE Like the glow from their ovens, like blood on iron *all men, always* BUT MOST OF ALL, I WANT YOU TO LOVE ME So very, very red *always* I WANT YOU TO LOVE ME

34. I career from one man into the next, spilling one man's drink and then the next, until finally I career into one man and his drink and this man turns with all his friends and all the white teeth in all their mouths and he says, If you are looking for a fight Jap, then you've found one *my father appears to me now, for the last time* IN THIS CITY OF NO RESISTANCE The American swings a punch at me, missing me and falling forwards to the laughter of all his friends *by the river, by the shore* I HATE THE LOSERS, I HATE THE VICTORS You little Japanese shit, I'm going to rip that little yellow tongue right out of your dirty yellow mouth and strangle you with it *in his uniform* AMERICAN SKIN UPON JAPANESE SKIN, AMERICAN FLESH INTO JAPANESE FLESH The American throws himself on me, straddling me with his thighs and pinning me to the ground, raining down blows from his fists into my face *with his medals, with his sword* I HATE ALL AMERICANS, I HATE ALL CAUCASIANS You little yellow bastard, I'm going to wipe that stupid smile off your stupid yellow face and knock the shit right out of you *he points west, he points east* WHITE SKIN ON YELLOW SKIN, WHITE FLESH IN YELLOW FLESH The American throws a last punch, standing up and kicking me once in the ribs and once in the gut *everywhere is America* IN THIS OCCUPIED CITY, WHERE IS THE RESISTANCE Had enough already, Jap, he laughs, ready to surrender again, are you *everywhere, he says, everyone* I WILL NOT LIVE ON MY HANDS, I WILL NOT LIVE ON MY KNEES I get to my feet, staggering forward into him, raising my head now, my two black eyes staring into his two blue eyes *there are no more Japanese* I WILL CLOSE MY LEGS AND PULL UP MY PANTS You got something you want to say to me, Jap, an

apology for me, an apology in English, you dumb fucking monkey *no more pure Japanese* I WILL WIPE MY LIPS AND I WILL SCRUB MY FACE I shake my head and I lean back and now I spit in his face and I turn and I walk away through the crowd and through the doors *only mongrel Japanese, only bastard Japanese* FUCK AMERICA, FUCK AMERICA, FUCK AMERICA You dirty yellow bastard, come back here and fight like a man, you dirty yellow monkey, come on, boys, let's get him, get after him *you are the last truly Japanese man alive* IN THIS OCCUPIED CITY, I AM THE RESISTANCE, I AM THE LIBERATION

35. Down by the river, she is still lying where I left her, looking up at the moon and the stars *a poor little girl who had no father or mother* THE SOUND OF SCRATCHING We won't feel the weather now, we are beyond the weather now, not even the damp in the morning *everything dead, no one left in the whole of Japan* SCRATCHING UNDER THE GROUND Perhaps they'll lay us side by side in the morgue and then they'll come with their bags and with their instruments and they'll lift our sheets *so the poor little girl decided to go up to heaven to where the moon shone down* IN MEMORIES, TERRIBLE MEMORIES I kneel down on one knee beside her and pull her up onto me, resting her back on my knee, cradling her like a child, and I whisper in her ear, You are so pale, so very pale now, I say, when you were black, so black with him *but the moon was just a lump of rotten wood* ALWAYS TALKING ABOUT ME They'll press their fingers into our bodies at various points and then they'll sniff their fingers and they'll make their general observations *then the little girl went to the sun* BEHIND MY BACK And your hair is so wild, didn't you brush your hair tonight, I'll tidy you up, don't worry, I'll tidy you up *but the sun was just a withered-up sunflower* THOUGHTS, TERRIBLE THOUGHTS They'll take their largest knives out of their bags and they'll incise our muscle walls *and when she went to the stars* ALWAYS WHISPERING ABOUT ME I lift her up, I stand her upright, the water's just there, there in the river *the stars were just little white lice stuck on a piece of dirty old black cloth* BEHIND THEIR HANDS Then kneeling up on the slabs and taking their saws from their cases, they'll cut briskly through our rib cages *so the little girl went back to Japan* DREAMS,

TERRIBLE DREAMS Come to the river, come to the water, I'll wash everything away, then you'll be clean *but Japan was just an overturned pot of nothing* ALL DREAMS, ALL THOUGHTS, ALL MEMORIES Then they'll lay down their saws and pick up their knives again and incise into us again but more deeply this time *the poor little girl completely alone now* ALL TERRIBLE, ALL BLOODY, ALL IMPRECISE We wade into the river together, up to our knees, then to our chests, now to our necks *she sat down and cried and she's sitting there still* EACH MEMORY, EACH THOUGHT, EACH DREAM Then they'll take out our hearts, and they'll weigh our hearts, on their cold metal scales *sitting there still, all alone, still crying* A WOUND

36. In the Occupied City, I walk away from the riverbank *English words, American voices* CRIME AND POLITICS In this city of no resistance, I walk up to the road *there he is, he's over there* POLITICS AND DISCIPLINE In this city of wounds, I turn another dark corner *back to the car, quickly he's getting away* DISCIPLINE AND PUNISHMENT In my ears, car doors slam *over there, over there* IN THE NEW JAPAN, IN THE NEW WORLD In my heart, the engine revs *quick, put your foot down, quick* THE ENGINE OF AMERICAN CAPITALISM, THE ENGINE OF JAPANESE CAPITALISM In my mind, the wheels turn *over there, quick, over there* THE WHEELS OF THE AMERICAN MILITARY, THE WHEELS OF THE JAPANESE BUREAUCRACY In my eyes, the headlights bright *quick, over there to the left, at the side of the road* THE BRIGHT LIGHTS OF THEIR GREEDY EYES, THE BRIGHT WHITES OF THEIR GREEDY TEETH Bang *did we hit him* THE EYES OF THE PEOPLE OF JAPAN, THE TEETH OF THE PEOPLE OF AMERICA The engine revs again *can you see him* JAPAN WATCHING, AMERICA LAUGHING The wheels turn again *he's there, over there* LAUGHING AT ME, LAUGHING AT YOU Turn and turn again *back up, back up* REVERSE COURSE Bang *that felt like him, like we got him* BANG No more detective *no more mysteries* NO MORE HOPES OF HAPPY ENDINGS Out of the last corner of my eye, I see them coming *half-seen figures, half-heard whispers* IN THE BLACK FOG, IN THE BLACK MIST Paralysis, petrification

on your hands and on your knees REFLECTED, FRACTURED, DISFIGURED AND OTHER Dead. Dead. Dead *is the little Jap bastard dead* IN THE BLACK MIRROR, THROUGH THE BLOOD-STAINED LOOKING GLASS Only truth *only truth* TRUTH Only fragments *fragments* ONLY FRAGMENTS In the darkness *the darkness* IN THE DARKNESS I have left the scene of the crime for the last time *the scene of the crime* THE CRIME, THE SPECTACLE

Beneath the Black Gate, in its upper chamber, in the occult square, in the light of its candles, truth only fragments, fragments only here –

No more mysteries *no more mysteries*

NO MORE MYSTERIES –

No more whodunnit contests, no more cash prizes,

no more solutions sealed in envelopes,

no more puzzles, no more games,

here fragments, only fragments

in the candlelight, in the half-

light, only fragments, fragments here. Here where nothing is rational, nothing is fair, where there are no more happy endings,

no more endings at all; no endings and no beginnings,

no books; no book-to-come –

IN THE OCCUPIED CITY, beneath the Black Gate, among your blank papers, among your dry pens, you are spinning,

spinning and spinning, spinning again,

deaf again to the foot-stair-steps,

to the sirens, to the telephones,

to the familiar whisper of a familiar man, 'I told you before, no more tears. No more tears for him . . .'

that familiar elderly man, that familiar first detective, among his boxes and among his files, dust-webbed and cob-covered,

dragging the dead body of the second detective, dragging it out of the occult circle, away from the light of the candles –

'Where is your mystery, your whodunnit now?' he laughs at you, he barks at you, 'I told you, he did it! He did it!'

'Liar! Liar! Liar-Dog! Dog-Liar! Lie! Lie!' you are shouting again, because you hate detectives, and you hate dogs, and all detectives are dogs, all dogs detectives,

except one; this one,

this one which that familiar elderly man, that familiar first detective is dragging

away,

laughing and barking as he goes, as you try to stand, in the light of the four candles, as you try to stop him, in the occult square, to push him to the ground, to kick him in his gut and kick him in his head again, in his deceits and in his lies again, but he is gone now,

kicking over a candle as he goes, the ninth candle,

gone now with the body of the detective,

the dead body of the second detective,

gone now, now only three candles,

in an occult triangle,

remain. And still this book, this book will not come, still it remains the book-to-come, in the light of these three candles, in this upper chamber, where the shadows, the shadows are shuffling, moving now, advancing step by step towards you,

step by step-step, the shadows and the walls, step by step-step, the walls and the darkness, step by step-step –

For this chamber is shrinking, step by step-step, the walls coming closer, step by step-step, the ceiling coming lower, step

by step-step, one candle behind you, one to your left,

one to your right, closer, step by step-step,

lower, step by step-step, the shadows

and the walls, step by step-step,

the walls and the darkness,

step by step-

step –

In the upper chamber of the Black Gate, in the light of the three remaining candles, now a man is seated on the floor before you,

an old and broken man, his body bones and his hair grey,

his clothes those of a convict, a condemned man,

for this is the man who brought you here –

To the scene of this crime, to the words of this book; this book-to-come, that will not come here –

Here beneath the Black Gate –

The man whose case inspired you, inspired you to write this book, this book-to-come, this old man whose name you had hoped to absolve, exonerate and clear, clear –

Through your words,

through your art, to bring him justice, to give him redemption, to bring you attention,

recognition,

and now this old and broken man raises his head, and your eyes meet as the old man says, 'People have been telling lies about me. I have been telling lies about me. Are you here to tell more lies?'

You shake your head, you smother a sob, and you push a candle towards him, across the tear-splinter-ed floor, and now you say, 'I am here to listen, to listen to the truth, and then to write that truth. For this candle is your candle; your candle, your story . . .'

But the old man sighs, then the old man says, 'I see no candles here, sir. No stories. I see only prisons. Only prisons . . .

The Tenth Candle –

The ~~Protestations, Denials,~~ Confessions of
the ~~Accused, Convicted,~~ Condemned Man in the Cell,
as it really was?

This city is a prison. Its streets and its houses. This room is a prison. Its chair and its bed. This body a prison. My head and my heart.

And they were prisons long before I was convicted of the Teikoku Bank murders, before I was sentenced to death and locked up in this cell in this prison. For I was my own jailer.

My own judge. I was in hell then.

I am in hell now.

Some doctors and my defenders will tell you that I have K-disease, that this disease is the reason I was convicted of murder and sentenced to death, and that this disease has been and remains my first and true prison. And maybe it is true. But I really don't know. I cannot say. For there are so many things I cannot remember. And there are so many lies I have told. But is this because I am a diseased person, or is it simply because I am a bad person –

Not a sick man, but a wicked man?

But I will tell you my story, neither for your pity nor for my own absolution. I will tell you my story for those who mistakenly but unconditionally once had the misfortune to love me –

For my ex-wife and for my children, those on whom I have brought only shame, for them and only for them.

My name, the name I was given, is Hirasawa Sadamichi. I was born, so I have been told and so believe, on 18 February 1892, in the Officers' Residence of the Kempeitai Headquarters in Ōtemachi, Kōjimachi Ward, Tokyo.

Because my father was a member of the Military Police, he was stationed in China during the Sino-Japanese War; however, my mother and I remained in Tokyo. On Japan's victory in the war, my father returned to Tokyo in the autumn of 1904, but was soon transferred to Sapporo in Hokkaido. This time the whole family went with my father and I was enrolled in the local elementary school.

After a short while, my father resigned from the Military Police and took a position in the Sapporo City Office. At this time, my mother began to run a stationery shop from our house.

Soon after I had enrolled in junior high school, my father was again transferred, and my family moved to the city of Otaru, Hokkaido, where many of them still remain to this day.

In elementary school, I had become interested in art and this became my sole interest and one passion in my junior high school, where some of my teachers recognized and encouraged my talent in drawing and in painting. And even at such an early age, I began to show my work in public exhibitions.

My father, though, with his military background and stern traditions, was disappointed in me and my failure to fulfil his expectations for me. He would have preferred that I study *kendō* and not painting, with a view to a military career not an artistic one. This brought great tensions to our household and to our relationship. I believe this pressure and stress caused the neurosis with which I was diagnosed and which in turn led to my two-year absence from school.

However, during my enforced absence from junior high school I was able to continue my studies of art and to further develop my talents. And as a result of my own private studies, and thanks only to the kindness and generosity of my mother, but very much against the wishes of my father, I was able to enrol in the Institute for Watercolour Painting in Tokyo.

At school in Tokyo, I experienced a sense of freedom and fulfilment which I had not felt before. However, I also greatly missed my mother and was always aware of my filial responsibilities. So upon graduation from the Institute for Watercolours, I returned home to Otaru and my parents.

I had now reached the age of twenty-four and it was at this time that I met my wife, who was also living in Otaru. However, and for many reasons, both of our parents were opposed to our marriage and so we were forced to elope to Tokyo. But through my wife's devotion and entreaties, she was able to persuade our parents to accept our marriage and we were then able to return to Otaru. And again, thanks to my wife's devotion and also her sacrifices, we were able to set up our own household from which I tried to make a living, privately teaching drawing and painting.

I now look back upon this period as one of simple happiness and blissful stability, for it was during this time that our first child was born and our life was at its best. At that time, however, I did not appreciate such happiness and stability. My pride and my vanity sought a wider recognition for my talent and my works, as well as bestial cravings for fame and money. So it was that, in November 1931, I moved back to Tokyo again. And so it was that things have turned out the way they have. Would that I had been content with what life had given me in Otaru. Would that I had not returned to Tokyo. But now, of course, it is too late for such regrets.

At first, I lived in my grandmother's house in Koishikawa. But then, soon after, I was able to set up my own house in Nishigahara, where I was later joined by my wife and child. The portents and signs, however, were already visible, had I had the eyes and senses to see and read them; our new residence was soon burgled and I became consumed once again by neurosis and by paranoia. I insisted we move, this time to Komagome, where I also insisted our new house be next to the local *kōban*.

My art, however, blossomed. I achieved success and recognition for my work, the success and the recognition for which I had so long craved. We were able to buy some land and to construct a new house in Itabashi Ward. At first I shunned the company of other artists and I tried to lead a modest life. However, on moving to Itabashi, I now recognize that something changed within me.

I began to invite other artists to our home and I began to affect the airs of a 'genius', of a 'maestro', consumed only by his art, caring only for his talent. And I now see, now it is too late, that, after a short while, these traits were no longer affectations but had infected me and would soon ruin me. And also, more tragically, my family.

Some time before, my wife had been bitten by a stray dog and our entire family given vaccinations against rabies. It was the side-effects of this vaccination that some people believe caused my mental deterioration. As I have said, I am not sure. I cannot say. But things now rapidly began to disintegrate. In 1939 I began an affair with a gallery attendant. And later the very same year, our house in Itabashi Ward caught fire and was completely destroyed. And so we were forced to rent another house close by.

In order to deal with the stresses of my adultery and of the fire, I began to undergo *shiatsu* therapy. And I still believe to this day, that it was this *shiatsu* therapy which saved my life at this time. For it is also true that at this time I frequently contemplated suicide. No doubt for my ex-wife and for my children, given all that has happened since, it would have been better had I taken my own life then.

For things only continued to worsen.

In the early summer of 1940, the rented house in which we had been temporarily living also caught fire, though the damage was not extensive. However, I had had enough of Tokyo and I insisted that we all move back to Hokkaido in order that I might fully recuperate. So it was that we spent the remainder of 1940 in Hokkaido. Of course, this could not last. The lives of my wife and my children were now firmly rooted in Tokyo, not to mention the audience and patrons for my own work.

But on our return to Tokyo I was immediately arrested by the police and taken to Itabashi Police Station. There I was interrogated on suspicion of arson. And I admit, though I was innocent, I almost confessed. However, after one day, I was released.

My troubles in Tokyo, though, were far from over. My mistress had learned of my return to Tokyo and now visited our family home. She had come seeking consolation money. I paid her the money she wanted and the relationship was ended. However, this incident undoubtedly caused great distress to my wife.

But blinded by my own arrogance, by my own insensitivity, I learned no lessons from the pain I caused then and I merely continued in my hurtful and my selfish ways, arrogant and insensitive.

For soon I started another adulterous affair.

At around this time, the war also began.

During the years of the war, my family and I moved many times, sometimes through evacuation orders, sometimes through economic necessity. By the end of the war, my wife and my children were again living in Hokkaido. I had remained in Tokyo, making trips back to Hokkaido to visit my family.

These were hard years for everybody and my family was no exception, though they all survived.

With the end of the war, my family gradually returned to Tokyo. My son came first, and then my wife and my daughters. By 1947 we were all reunited and living in Nakano Ward.

Of course, Tokyo was a very different, very damaged city. However, my life continued much the same as it had done before. I continued to paint and to try to sell my work, supplementing my income with various other activities but often reliant on the money which my children were now able to earn.

My affair also continued.

This brings me now to the winter of 1947–48 and the time of the crimes of which I was accused, convicted and sentenced to die.

Of course, I have been over this period and these events many times with many people. But once again I must state, I give this account now, not in the hope of saving my own life, only in the hope of sparing my family further shame.

As well as the murders, attempted murders and robbery at the Teikoku Bank on 26 January 1948, I was also convicted of forgery and fraud. These crimes of forgery and fraud are the crimes of which I am guilty and of which I want to speak first as they are also crimes which have a bearing on the Teikoku Bank case.

Sometime in the autumn of 1947, I received a cheque for ¥1,000 from a person whose name I can no longer remember. That day, I had little money on my person and so I went to a branch of the Mitsubishi Bank in order to cash the cheque. However, on the way to the bank, I realized I had forgotten my own personal seal. And it was then that I made my first mistake. For rather than return home for my own seal, I went into a shop and had a seal made in the name of the person who had sent me the cheque. I then proceeded to the bank.

Inside the bank, I went to the counter and took a ticket. I then sat down on a bench and waited for the number on my ticket to be called. But beside me on the bench, I noticed another ticket, another number. At that moment, the number on this ticket was called and on instinct, without thinking, I stood up and approached the counter. This was my second mistake. For at the counter, I received ¥10,000 in cash. Of course, this was a huge amount of money and, moreover, it was not mine to receive. But I said nothing, took the money and sat back down to once again wait for my own number to be called. When my number was called, I received my ¥1,000 at the counter and immediately left the bank, still with the ¥10,000 I had received under false pretences, if somewhat by accident or chance.

Of course, I felt most guilty. Then suddenly I had what I believed to be a good idea. I caught a cab to Ueno Park and got out just below the statue of Saigō Takamori. I quickly went into the mouth of the subway station, where over two dozen homeless children

230

were gathered as usual. Here I mumbled some Buddhist mantra as I distributed ¥200 to each of the children until I had finally gotten rid of the ¥10,000. And that, I hoped, was the end of that and I tried to think no more about what I had done.

However, about one week later, while searching through my coat pockets, I came across the bankbook which I had also received when I had taken the ¥10,000. I have no idea where this thought came from, or what on earth possessed me, but I thought I should use the money in this account for the benefit of the Society for Tempera Painters, of which I was a member and from which I had repeatedly been forced to borrow money. In fact, I confess I had embezzled money from the society and I now wished to cover up my crime. So I began to think of a way in which I could take the money out of the account, which was in the name of a Mr Hasegawa.

I visited a seal-maker again, and this time I had a seal made in the name of Hasegawa. I then doctored the bankbook using other seals to show that there was over ¥200,000 in the account. Finally, I visited a moneylender who was living in Ōmori. This first moneylender was obviously suspicious of me and refused my request to borrow money from him on the strength of the money shown in the bankbook. However, he introduced me to a second moneylender who agreed to write me a cheque for ¥200,000 to be cashed at the Ōmori branch of the Dai-Ichi Bank. I do not remember the exact date on which this all occurred but I do remember it was a Saturday afternoon, for I was unable to cash the cheque that day.

Early on the following Monday morning, I went to the Ōmori branch of the Dai-Ichi Bank in order to cash the cheque. However, the moneylender was waiting for me, having changed his mind, and so I was unable to cash the cheque. Two or three days later, though, I again tried to cash the cheque. This time I went into a jewellery shop and told the jeweller I wished to buy a gold ring and a small watch from him, totalling ¥140,000. I asked him if he would accept the cheque for ¥200,000 as payment. My plan, as foolish as ever no doubt, had been to then pawn the ring and the watch for cash and to use the money to repay the amount I had embezzled from the Society for Tempera Painters. However, the jeweller insisted on first telephoning the Ōmori branch of the Dai-Ichi Bank in order to verify the validity of the cheque. I told him I was going out to buy some cigarettes while he telephoned and, of course, I then fled as quickly as I could.

In the course of their investigations into me in relation to the Teikoku Bank case, the police uncovered this case of forgery and fraud. However, these are the only crimes of which I am guilty. I am innocent of all the other crimes for which I was convicted, beginning with the Ebara branch of the Yasuda Bank.

This incident occurred on 14 October 1947. However, I had nothing to do with it and I only confessed to it because I was convinced by the prosecutor that it was the right thing to do. I now regret making such a confession. Also, at that time, the time of my original confession, I had no alibi for the day in question. Now, however, I remember what I was doing on that day.

On the 13th of that week in October 1947, I was visited by my friend Mr Yamaguchi. He asked me to paint pictures of white chrysanthemums on twenty pieces of paper as gifts for guests at a wedding party which would be held that week. I agreed to his request and began to work hard on the paintings. The next day I was still hard at work painting the flowers when I was visited by Mr Watanabe. I remember he praised one of my other paintings and I promised to give him the painting in question. During Mr Watanabe's visit, my wife and daughter Hanako were also present. Mr Watanabe left around 4 p.m. and my other daughter, Shizuko, met him on her way home. I remember this now because Mr Watanabe's visit had interrupted my work on the wedding gifts and so I was still painting them the next day on the 15th, when Mr Yamaguchi came to collect them. So despite my confession, I had in fact been at home all day on 14 October 1947, the day of the so-called rehearsal at the Ebara branch of the Yasuda Bank.

Similarly, on 19 January 1948, the day of the second rehearsal at the Nakai branch of the Mitsubishi Bank, I also now realize that I had an alibi. The day before, I had had lunch at the home of Mr Yamaguchi and his family. I remember we ate *udon* and that we then played mah-jong until the early evening. The next morning I took a walk and I bought some *yokan* sweets. On returning home, I ate the *yokan* with my wife and I remember thinking that I should have taken the *yokan* as a gift the day before when I had visited Mr Yamaguchi and his family. I cannot remember anything else about that day, 19 January, except that I was working on a painting at that time.

As I said during my trial, I do admit to having been to the Nakai branch of the Mitsubishi Bank a few times. However, this was simply because it is near to the market stall of one of my friends, Mr Kazama. That is the only reason I have been to that particular bank and I was certainly not there on the day in question.

And then, of course, we now come to the day of the Teikoku Bank murders itself – 26 January 1948 – a day I had once forgotten but now remember and relive, over and over.

For a long time, from the time of my initial and supposedly routine questioning by the police, to the time of my arrest and official interrogation by the prosecutor, I simply and honestly could not recall what I had done on this day. And then, under questioning, I became confused as to whether certain events happened on that day or, say, happened the week before. For example, I knew that at around that time I had bought some charcoal briquettes from my friend Mr Yamaguchi. However, I was unsure in my own mind whether this had taken place sometime the week before, on 18 January say, or on the day of the actual Teikoku Bank murders. And this, then, was the reason why I later wrote to Mr Yamaguchi asking whether he could remember on which particular day I had purchased the briquettes from him. Not because, as the police and the press have since suggested, I was attempting to concoct a false alibi.

Similarly, I could not remember whether my visit to the exhibition of the Society of Watercolour Painters in the Mitsukoshi Department Store had been on 26 January or on some other day. Initially, I did believe it had been on that particular day. Of course, I now realize I was mistaken. But honestly, and for a while, I was sure I had visited the exhibition with my daughter on that afternoon. Hence, the chaotic and confused nature of some of my statements.

However, I now know that on the afternoon of that day – Monday 26 January 1948 – I went to Mr Yamaguchi's office in Marunouchi. Then, at around 3:30 p.m. – the time of the actual crime – I called at Mr Yamaguchi's house and I returned home at about 5:00 p.m. with the fifty or sixty pieces of charcoal I had bought. I remember that my wife and my daughter were at home when I arrived back with this heavy bag. Also, an American soldier who was friendly with my daughter was also there and we played cards and spoke English well into the evening. That is what I did that day.

The next day, which was 27 January, I do remember reading about the Teikoku case in the newspaper, or maybe hearing about it on the radio, and I also remember discussing it with my wife and my daughters. I distinctly recall asking them, 'What kind of man could do such a cruel and inhuman thing?'

That day, the day after the Teikoku murders, was also my younger sister's birthday and so I remember travelling out to Ichikawa to visit her. And I think it was then that I decided, on the urging of my sister, to go to Hokkaido to see my younger brother. He had been seriously ill for some time with pulmonary tuberculosis and I had been meaning to visit him. And thanks to the money I had recently received from two of my patrons, I now had the cash to visit Hokkaido. So upon leaving my sister's home in Ichikawa, I think I went to a travel agent in Marunouchi to arrange passage from Yokohama to Hokkaido on the *Hikawa Maru*. Or perhaps that was the day after. Anyway, it all occurred around this time.

I am most aware, though, that the initial confused, even contradictory nature of my original statements to the police led them to be suspicious of me and to further investigate me.

However, the original reason that they spoke with me in regard to the Teikoku Bank murders was because of the name-card that I had been given by Dr Matsui.

Of course, when I was questioned, I immediately admitted to meeting Dr Matsui on the ferry from Hokkaido and exchanging name-cards with him the summer before. However, when asked by the police, I was unable to produce his name-card and so they believed that the card Dr Matsui had given me on the ferry was the one which must have been used at the Ebara branch of the Yasuda Bank by the criminal. This might be so, but it would not be because I was the criminal. It would be because Dr Matsui's name-card was in my wallet when it was stolen from me at Mikawashima Station in September 1947.

I had kept the card Dr Matsui had given me, along with a dozen or so other business cards, in my wallet, which, incidentally, was a leather one and of the type that fold in half. And I kept this wallet in the inside pocket of my jacket. That day there was also ¥11,000 in cash inside my wallet. It is embarrassing to say, but I was on my way to visit the parents of a woman I knew in order to repay them ¥10,000 which she had lent me. The train, however, was very crowded and I remember that my bag got caught and that I could not easily get off the train at Mikawashima Station because of all the people and I had to pull the bag hard in order to get off.

It was only when I arrived at the house of the young lady's parents and I reached for my wallet in order to repay them the money that I then realized I had been pickpocketed. And curiously, in the place where my wallet had been, there was now a lady's fan. Of course, I immediately rushed back to the station and reported the crime to the local *kōban*. I also gave the police as evidence the lady's fan which had been placed in my pocket. I believe this was a unique trait of that particular pickpocket, his trademark. The officers at the Mikawashima *kōban* kept the lady's fan. Unfortunately, at that time, I said nothing of this incident to my wife because it would have meant admitting that I had been forced to borrow money from a female acquaintance, which would not only have been embarrassing for me but hurtful for my wife. And so I thought it best to say nothing.

Of course, I now realize that my various deceptions and my many lies to my wife and to my children, not to mention the complicated nature of my finances and many of my relationships, both business and personal, only served to further arouse the suspicions of the police as they continued to investigate and later interrogate me. Now it is a source of intense regret and deep shame to me that I told so many lies, that I created so many deceptions.

In particular, I realize that my financial dealings seemed somewhat irregular and suspicious. In fact, I freely admit now that my financial arrangements were often of a dubious and illegal nature. And I realize now that I should have confessed my financial wrongdoings to the police at the outset.

But as I have already said, this was partly because I had embezzled a sum of money from the Society of Tempera Painters. It was also partly because it involved money I had either borrowed or loaned to my mistress. Finally, there was also cash from some famous and important people who would not want their names mentioning to the police, least of all in connection to such a high-profile case as the Teikoku Bank murders.

To this end, I have kept money in various places. For example, in the sack along with my painting tools. Or in cloth bundles. Even in banks under assumed names such as Hayashi and so on. As a result, I often misplace money or entirely forget that I have even received it in the first place, hard as that may sound to believe. And as I say, most of this money, the money that was in my possession after the Teikoku Bank murders and which the police therefore suspected I had stolen from the bank, this money came from either my embezzlement of the Society for Tempera Painters, to which I did not wish to confess, or from my various patrons, whom I did not wish to involve with the police. Some of these men are of exceedingly high standing.

Anyway, because of the name-card I had exchanged with Dr Matsui, and because of my confused and contradictory alibis, and because of the large amounts of cash in my possession, and because of my sudden trip to Hokkaido that February, and even because of my appearance, I was arrested in August 1948 in Otaru, Hokkaido, and charged with the murders, attempted murders and robbery of the Teikoku Bank in Toshima Ward in Tokyo on 26 January 1948.

At first, the police had come to Otaru 'just in passing' and as a 'matter of routine'; then the police started to come once a month, and again 'just in passing', as a 'matter of routine'; then the police came once a week, not 'just in passing', not as a 'matter of routine'; and then, finally, they came once a day until they never went away, until that August day when they took me away with them.

Now I can recall very little about that journey back to Tokyo, little except for the crowds and the heat, the blanket over my head and the darkness around me and within me. I do remember I was frightened, particularly by the crowds that met our train at Ueno Station. I remember worrying about my wife and my children, about what they must be going through, about what they must be thinking.

Similarly, those first days in police custody in Tokyo are now forgotten and lost to me, forgotten and lost in an accelerating whirlwind of entering rooms and leaving rooms, of sitting down and standing up, a nauseous blur of different voices from different mouths, an ever-more deafening crescendo of questions and accusations–

'You are a bad man, you are a wicked man,' said the voices. 'Is it not possible you are also a murderous man, a killer?'

Some of the voices were aggressive, some of the voices were consoling but, whatever their motivation, whatever their tone, soon I began to feel as though I was being hypnotized.

And in my cell, I now had visions.

Each night, at the window in my cell, a tall man in a black

mask appeared, pointing a foreign gun at me through the iron bars, and the man would whisper, 'Confess. Confess. Confess . . .'

And then the dead, one by one, night after night, the Teikoku Bank Dead came to me and said, 'You are a bad man, you are a wicked man we know. You are our murderer, our killer . . .

'You should be executed, executed by potassium cyanide, to taste the pain we tasted, to suffer as we still suffer . . .'

Then finally, one night in September, as the prison clock struck midnight, the Buddha himself came to my cell and he said, 'Hirasawa, Hirasawa, listen to me carefully. I know you sincerely wish to be cleansed of all your sins and I know you are not the killer, but in order to be truly cleansed of your own sins, you must willingly accept the sins of others. So confess, confess . . .'

I now believed I had only two ways to escape. I could either kill myself or I could confess. So first of all, I tried to kill myself. And three times I tried. First, I cut my left radial artery. Then, I drove my head into a pillar in the interrogation room. Finally, I swallowed five suppositories. But each time I failed to die. And I shed tears –

For I then knew only the other way now remained.

Still, it is hard for me to remember now, and so hard for me to fully explain, what exactly led me to confess to crimes I had not committed. For though I felt hypnotized by the voices, and though I was plagued by the visions, I had not been threatened and I had not been tortured. Nor was I coerced, though I suppose I felt persuaded by the visions, by the voices, that it would be for the best to confess, the best for my wife and for my children, and for my father back in Otaru. And so, one day that September, I confessed –

And not only to the Teikoku Bank murders, but to every bad thing, to every crime I could think of, including to the assassinations of Prime Minister Inukai and Baron Takuma Dan, the president of Mitsui, and every coup d'état I could remember.

And for a time, following my false confessions, the voices ceased and the visions left, and there was a strange silence and benign warmth around me as I learned and repeated the statements they wanted from me, as I copied and re-enacted the crimes they said I had done, in the silence and in the warmth.

I had, in fact, confessed to things I had not done, things of which I was innocent, before. Some doctors and my supporters have stated that such false confessions are a symptom of K-disease, a side-effect of the rabies vaccination. And maybe it is true. But I really don't know. I cannot say. For such behaviour on my part, along with my repeated denials of the things I had done, the things of which I was truly guilty, predates my wife's bite and my rabies vaccination and has, in truth, been a trait of mine since an early age, for as long as I can recall. Now I can only surmise that it was as though my mind was a rope, a rope made from two threads; one thread my true-self, the other my hypnotized-self, until that thread snapped.

For then, one day in November, it was as if I suddenly woke up. I remember I had just been served hot *miso* soup for my breakfast and as I took a sip, I heard a loud *pop*, as though a balloon had burst close-by my brain. And I suddenly recognized what I had done, what I was doing, and I suddenly thought, 'I am incriminating myself, and not only myself, but all the people who love me, my wife and my children, my family and my friends.' And I also thought, 'And I am shaming the victims of the crime. I am protecting the real killer. What if the killer were to strike again, to kill more people?' And I suddenly realized, 'I must recant and apologize to the nation.'

Another way to explain what happened to me that morning would be to describe a stage, a stage where the curtain rises and the stage is bare, but there on the stage is an actor and the actor is naked before his audience. That is what I felt had happened to me now; that the curtain had risen and there I was –

Naked before the world –

Innocent, yet guilty –

And so I remain.

For as everybody knows, despite retracting my confession, I was found guilty and sentenced to death. And so, knowing each day may well be my last, I now live each day in a state of readiness and repentance; readiness for death by hanging and what will follow, repentance for the things I have put my wife and my children through.

My wife has divorced me. My children have disowned me. Rightly, they are ashamed of me and they deny me, deny that I am now or ever was their father. They have changed their name, the name I gave them, my name. They have abandoned and disowned that name, my name. But the blame, the fault, is all mine.

I should not have married. I should not have had children. Not being the person I am. I did not deserve my wife's love. I did not deserve my children's love. Not being the person I am. Not with all the things I have done, not with all the lies I have told.

Now my ex-wife hates me. Now my children hate me. Being the person I am. My wife believes I am guilty. My children believe I am guilty. Being the person I am. And though I am innocent of the crimes my wife and my children believe I committed, I am still guilty. Being the person I am. Guilty of so many other crimes. Guilty of so many other lies. Being the person I am –

A bad and wicked person.

And though I know many kind people do believe I am innocent of the crimes of which I have been convicted, though I know many people work tirelessly to clear my name and to save me from this death sentence, and though I know these same people would be upset, even angry, to read these words, I must confess:

I am resigned to my fate.

For though I am innocent of the Teikoku Bank murders, I am guilty of so many other crimes. Crimes against my wife, crimes against my children, crimes against their hearts. And I truly believe I deserve to die for these bad things I have done, the terrible hurt I have caused them, the lies I have told them. In short, for the life I have led.

The sole reason, therefore, that I allow and I assist in the attempts and the appeals to clear my name and save me, is for the sake of my ex-wife and my children; that their reputations may be restored, and that they may once again live not in fear or in shame.

And that then is the only reason I have told this story, that I have said these words. But these words I have said are not for me. These words are only for those who once loved me, my ex-wife and my children. For I do not seek your pity. And I do not seek the truth. For I do not deserve your pity. I do not deserve the truth.

Beneath the Black Gate, in its upper chamber, between the three candles, the old man now bows his head,

and another candle gutters,

gutters and then

dies –

'No!' you are screaming. 'No, no! Come back! Come back! There's more to say. There must be more. That can't be all. That can't be it. Please, please! Come back! Come back!'

But the flame of the candle is out, its light is gone, and the old man is fading; fading, fading, fading –

'No!' you shout again –

'There's so much more I want to know, much more I need to know. No! No! What about the trials, the appeals? The conspiracies, the experiments, the war? Help me! Please help me to help you!'

But in the dim-light of the last two candles, the old man is shaking his head; fading, fading –

'Wait! Wait! I know you did not murder those people. I know you were never there. I know you were never at the bank. But help me, please! Please help me to help you. For I want to tell your story. I want to prove your innocence, to clear your name . . .'

For now you see, now the old man is fading, going and now gone, now you see and now you know, know what it is,

what it is you want; just the truth –

Not the fiction. Not the lies –

Only the truth –

Tear by drop-drop, foot by step-step, hoping there is still time; still two candles, in this upper chamber, beneath the Black Gate; still two last candles, tear by drop-drop, foot by step-

step, your head now turning, this way,

that way, turning again, and again –

Tear by drop-drop, foot by step-step, for you are not alone, beneath the Black Gate, in this upper chamber,

between these two candles, drop-

drop, step-step, drop-

drop, step-

step –

'We are all in our cages, our cells and our prisons,' says a voice in the shadows. 'Some by the hands of others –

'And some of our own making –

'Of our own design . . .'

This way, that way, left and then right, you turn and you turn again, looking with the candlelight, searching through the shadows,

step-step, right and then left, step-step, that way and this,

step-step, looking, step-step, searching, step-

step, for the author of these words –

'Are you my judge? The man who will accuse me? Accuse and convict me? Sentence and imprison me? Imprison or execute me? Is that you, my dear writer, is that you?'

Beneath the Black Gate, in its upper chamber, in the candlelight, now plague-light; white-light, hospital-white, laboratory-white then grey, an overcast-skin-grey then open-vein-blue, blue and now green, a culture-grown-green then yellow, yellow, thick-caught-spittle-yellow, streaked sticking-string-red, then black;

black-black, drop-drop, black-black,

step-step, in the plague-light,

drop-drop, step-step,

in the plague-

light –

'Would you sit at my table of rotting food?' whispers the voice in the shadows. 'Would you dine with me, drink with me, and then enter a large black cross beside my name? Is that your plan?'

This way and that, you turn and turn and turn, drop-

drop, step-step, you huff and breath-puff –

'Is that what you want, my dear writer? Is that what you seek, here beneath this Black Gate, here among your melting candles?'

You puff and breath-pant, you pant and now-gasp,

for he is coming, step by step-step, whispering and muttering. In your ears, you hear him gaining, step by step-step,

drooling and growling, step by step-step,

A Night Parade of but One Demon . . .

Half-of-monster, half-of-man, you can smell him, you can sense him, but still you cannot see him,

still you can only hear him, whispering and muttering, drooling and growling –

'Every society needs people like you, dear writer, people who will weep at their mother's funeral. But a truly great man will always, already place himself above the events he has caused –

'A man like me. And so behold –
'In this city. In this mirror –
'Here I am . . .

The Eleventh Candle –

The Last Words of the Teikoku Murderer,
or a Personal History of Japanese Iniquity,
Local Suffering & Universal Indifference (1948)

In the fractured, splintered mirror, the child before the man / Before the doctor. Before the killer. Before the dead / The sunlight and the stream, the flowers and the insects / Wings off flies. Legs off frogs. Heads off cats / The skin and the skull, the appearance and the absence / In the fractured, splintered mirror, murder is born

In the Death Factory, at Pingfan, near Harbin, in Manchuria. This place had once been home to villages and farms, to families and fields. The villages had been requisitioned and their inhabitants expelled. Then the Nihon Tokushu Kōgyō Company arrived. The Tokyo-based company hired local Chinese labourers to work day and night for three years to construct the one hundred and fifty buildings which would form the vast complex, the Death Factory.

I can never forget the first time I saw the place. Across a dry moat, beyond the high earth walls and the barbed-wire fences, the square-tiled facades of the central buildings towered, larger than any I had ever seen in Tokyo, reflecting the sunlight and the sky in a brilliant white radiance.

Over the moat, behind the walls and the wires, through the gates and the guards, a whole city, a future city, was waiting for me. There was a runway and a railway, a huge administrative building and an equally large farm, a power house with cooling towers, dormitories for the civilians and barracks for the soldiers, barns and stables, a hospital and a prison and, of course, the laboratories and the furnaces. This was the home of Unit 731, my new home.

The Unit was divided into eight separate divisions; First Division was concerned with bacteriological research; Second Division with warfare research and field experiments; Third Division with water purification; Fourth Division with the mass production and storage of bacteria; the four remaining divisions handled education, supplies, administration and clinical diagnosis.

The Emperor was our owner, Major Ishii was our boss.

On the Black Ship, the Killer sees it stretched out now before him: the Occupied City; its sewers and its streets, its homes and its shops, its schools and its hospitals, its asylums and its prisons. This city is a monstrous place; a Deathtopia of fleas and flies, of rats and men.

On the Black Ship, here in this Deathtopia, no one knows who he is, no one will ever know who he is. Here he will dwell, among the fleas and the flies, among the rats and the men –

The Killer in the Occupied City.

In the twenty-fifth year of the reign of the Emperor Meiji / In a village, in Chiba Prefecture / The fourth son of a rich landowner / In a lavish villa, in a bamboo forest / A tall child, a bright child / In a shaded grotto, before the family graves

In the Death Factory, Major Ishii welcomed the new recruits, his new workers, standing beside an antique vase of white chrysanthemums: 'Our vocation as doctors is to challenge all varieties of disease-causing micro-organisms, to block all roads of intrusion into the human body, to annihilate all foreign matter resident in our bodies and to devise the most expedient treatment possible. However, the research in which you will now be involved is the complete opposite of these principles and will, naturally, initially, cause you some anguish as doctors. Nevertheless, I beseech you to pursue this research based on what I know will become your two overriding desires; firstly, as scientists to give free rein to your instinct and urge to probe for the truth in natural science, to discover and research the unknown world; secondly, as soldiers to use your discoveries and your research to build a powerful military weapon to use against the enemies of our divine Emperor and our beloved homeland –

'This is our mission, this is your work.'

On the Black Ship, among the rubble, in the sunlight, the Killer watches a group of children playing beside a crater. The crater is filled with black water, broken bicycles and the debris of a defeated city. The water smokes, the water bubbles. The children toss pieces of wood into the water and then watch them sink.

244

The Killer remembers a story a colleague once told him in the Death Factory. A unit was sent to the city of Jilin to conduct tests on plague bacteria there. The method involved placing the pathogens into buns and then wrapping the buns in paper. The unit then went into an area of the city where children were playing. The men in the unit began eating buns similar to those in which they had planted the germs. When the local children saw the men eating the buns, they all came running over, asking for the buns. The men then gave the children the infected buns. Three days later, a second unit was sent to the area to record the levels of infection among the children and their families. The area had to be isolated within sheet-metal walls, then everything within the enclosure burnt to the ground.

The Killer looks up from the black water. A man is standing over him, a man he recognizes. A man who has been following him.

The living tend to the graves of the dead / The dead watch over the lives of the living / The lives of the living, divided and dissected / Those whom receive tribute, those that give tribute / Those of substance and those of none, those who matter and those who don't / The child divides, the child dissects

In the Death Factory, my work now began. There were two types of workers; those who were recruited, recruited for their brains, and those who were conscripted, conscripted for their brawn. I was recruited, recruited for my brain; its knowledge of disease, its knowledge of death. Loyal to the Emperor, subservient to the State, deferential yet intelligent, I was the ideal worker; fervent in my devotion to the Emperor, to Japan and to victory; unfailing and unquestioning in my belief in all three. My work was in the field of hygiene.

On the Black Ship, in a coffee-shop, a man is whispering to the Killer, 'I hear many of them have got good jobs now, in the prestigious universities or in the Ministry of Health and Welfare. I heard some of them got payments of one or two million yen. It's unbelievable. Look at us! Look what we've got! Barely the clothes on our backs.

'I think of all I did for them, for Ishii and for the Emperor, and look at me now. I can't get a job and I can't sleep, can't sleep for the memories and for the ghosts.

'I remember one day, towards the end, a truckload of about forty Russians was brought in. But we already had too many logs, more logs than we could use, and so we had no need for this lot. So we told the Russians that there was an epidemic in the region and that they should all get out of the truck so we could inoculate them. And so, one by one, they jumped down from the truck. They stood in line with their sleeves rolled up. Then I went down the line, one by one.

'First I rubbed their arms with alcohol, then I injected them with potassium cyanide. Of course, there was no need to rub their arms with alcohol first. I did it purely to put them at their ease. Then, one by one, they all fell to the ground in silence.

'But I can't forget the way they looked at me as I rubbed their arms and then injected them. They looked at me with trust in their eyes, with relief and even gratitude.'

The Killer picks up the bill from the table. The Killer gets up from the table. The Killer pays the bill and leaves.

Flowers and insects, animals and people / The child collects and the child catalogues / Flowers then insects, animals then people / The child examines and the child experiments / Those with blood and those without, those with this blood and those with that / The child studies and the child learns

In the Death Factory, hygiene was of the utmost importance. Fear of accidents and outbreaks, infections and contaminations, was all-pervasive. Despite the precautions and procedures taken, there were frequent unintended civilian casualties among the staff and technicians of the Unit. Priority was therefore given to hygiene and to research into better methods of hygiene control.

Initially, my work involved only the examination, treatment and prevention of communicable diseases among army personnel and their families. The examination and treatment section in which I worked was separate from the main complex. Our building was known as the South Wing and we also worked closely with the Army Hospital in Harbin.

At first my work was neither particularly demanding nor dangerous and my biggest fear was of becoming infected myself, particularly with the plague. Often we did not know what was wrong with a patient until it was too late. I remember that once a civilian technician from the Unit was brought in with suspected syphilis. However, the man had the plague and soon succumbed and died. When such a patient was brought in, everyone was careful to avoid getting any cuts. Often we did not shave.

My main work was the examination of blood, urine and faeces samples, testing for and measuring changes in haemoglobin. Often this involved visits to the prison building. Whenever I entered the prison, I had to walk through a tray of disinfectant. The samples I received here had been taken from prisoners, who were also known as logs. I believe they were known as logs because the local population had been told that the Death Factory was involved in the manufacture and production of lumber. The samples were needed in order to determine a subject's condition prior to any experiment or trial. Further samples were then taken from logs after they had become infected with various viruses. This was how the data from bacteriological tests was compared. Having received the samples in prepared slides, I would then travel back by truck to the South Wing. Often I would have to make this journey two or three times a day. Often I would also be ordered to bring back and forth research papers and human organs. These were my duties, this was my work.

There was no real research into preventative vaccines in our work at the examination and treatment centre. The nearest we came to any such vaccine was the development of an invigorative solution. The base of this solution was garlic and we would give it to patients in order to speed up their recovery. Often I would inject it myself in order to overcome the depression and the fatigue caused by the isolated location and the long hours. I understood why many of the Chinese and the Manchurians were addicted to heroin. It was a temptation to which many surrendered.

On the Black Ship, the Killer writes a letter, *To Your Excellency Ishii Shirō, Former Lt. Gen. Army Medical Corps* –

Dear Sir,
You must be very surprised to receive this badly scribbled and most rude letter so unexpectedly. But I was one of your subordinates at Pingfan in China and I write this letter, not only on behalf of myself, but on behalf of the many men who dutifully served under you during the war in China.

After the turmoil at the end of the war, we came back to Japan. But the defeated Japan has not been very cordial in welcoming us back. Our homes have been burnt, many of our wives and our children are dead, and the little money we have been given towards our rehabilitation, towards food and shelter, has been consumed by inflation. Because of our hardships, many of us have now been driven to contemplate committing wicked acts in order to simply feed and clothe ourselves.

However, before embarking on such a dark path, I beseeched my former colleagues to wait until I had at least sought the counsel and guidance of you, our thoughtful former commanding officer. Surely, I told my former colleagues, if Lt. Gen. Ishii knew of our plight, he would rescue us, his former loyal subordinates who so faithfully carried out his every order, no matter how gruesome the work, no matter at what cost to our souls.

Of course, because of our current hardships, we all thought of dying as we have retained the means to do so. But then we realized that if you had found the courage to live on, then we certainly should also be able to overcome our present difficulties and accomplish anything with your inspiration and generous assistance.

So please, we beg you, our former commanding officer, that you loan us, the forgotten and unfortunate ones, as funds towards our rehabilitation, the sum of ¥50,000 and which we swear will be returned to you within two months. So please be gracious and kind enough to send the money to the above address.

Of course, we should like to visit you personally but, since we have been so reduced to poverty, we are too embarrassed and so are unable to do so. But please, please help us.

From your former subordinates.

Now the Killer stops writing. The Killer seals the letter in an envelope. The Killer posts the envelope to Mr Ishii Shirō, 77 Wakamastu-chō, Ushigome-ku, Tokyo.

Now the Killer waits.

There are those born with strength and those born with weakness / Those who are healthy and those who are sick / There is order in all matter, there is order in all things / There are structures and there are hierarchies / Those of substance and those of none, those who matter and those that don't / And there is one who matters more than most, the one who matters most of all *

In the Death Factory, in the summer of 1940, I was suddenly sent to Xinjing. An outbreak of plague had been reported in one part of the city. As soon as we arrived, we enclosed the entire affected area inside a sheet-metal wall one metre in height and then burnt everything within the enclosure to the ground. We then conducted examinations of all the Japanese and the Chinese who had been living in the area. Finally, we were ordered to dig up the bodies of people who were suspected of having died from the epidemic, to dissect the corpses, to remove and then preserve the organs. My task was to take small specimens from the lungs, livers and kidneys of the corpses. I then applied each to a Petri dish. Organs that tested positive for the plague were taken directly back to the Unit. The Petri dishes of plague germs which I had gathered were first sent to the Xinjing National Hygiene Laboratory to be cultivated and then on to Pingfan.

It was a high-risk job and one of my colleagues became infected. I do not know how it exactly happened but the man developed a high temperature and suddenly collapsed. He was rushed back to the Air Corps Hospital at Harbin, which was a small hospital and easier to isolate. There he was treated by doctors from the Death Factory. I was told he became well enough to travel and was sent to Port Arthur, then to Hiroshima, and finally to a hospital in Morioka. I was also told he received thirty-six yen a month in compensation, which was then double the salary of a school principal, for example. However, I never personally saw or heard from the man again.

On the Black Ship, the Killer gets a reply to his letter.

Early one morning, an American jeep and a car from the Tokyo Metropolitan Police pull up outside the Killer's address. The police rush up the stairs of the boarding house. The police kick in the door to the Killer's room. The police ransack the room. The police come back down the stairs. The police talk to the Americans who are standing beside their jeep. The Americans and the police get back into their jeep and their car and they leave.

The Killer steps out of the shadows of the ruined building opposite his former boarding house. The Killer has a knapsack on his back and a doctor's bag in his hand. The Killer makes his way to

Tokyo station. The Killer boards a train. The Killer leaves the Occupied City. For now.

He is the brightest boy in his class, he has the sharpest memory / He carries himself with authority / He is the tallest boy in his class, he has a magnetic personality / He hypnotizes everyone he meets / He is abrasive, arrogant and brash, and he is almost blind / He idolizes the Emperor Meiji

In the Death Factory, as the war intensified and the number of soldiers multiplied, most of my daily work increasingly concerned venereal disease. Thousands of our soldiers had become infected, with a debilitating effect upon our military capabilities. Often we were sent to perform VD checks and issue health certificates. The brothels were under civilian management and almost all of the women who worked in them were Korean. There were three classifications for the brothels; Class 1 was for officers, Class 2 for noncommissioned officers, and Class 3 for Japanese civilians and enlisted soldiers. However, due to a shortage of brothels and a surfeit of customers, it became common practice to let different units use the Class 1 brothels on certain days at certain times.

My work involved taking blood samples from the women and conducting health examinations. These examinations were known as *manju* exams. The woman would have to get down on her hands and knees with her buttocks raised. If her sex organ was swollen or discharged any pus it would mean she had been infected with syphilis. On a typical day, I would have to examine over one hundred and fifty women in this manner.

I know that within the Death Factory, research was conducted into venereal diseases with the aim of developing a way to protect soldiers from sexually transmitted diseases. Often I would collect blood samples from women prisoners who had contracted syphilis. These women were usually Chinese prisoners but, on occasion, I collected samples from Russian women. I heard rumours about the ways in which these women had been infected with the disease, that doctors dressed from head to toe in white laboratory clothing, with only their eyes visible, forced male prisoners infected with syphilis to have sex with female prisoners at gunpoint. Also I believe studies were conducted on pregnant prisoners and the effects of syphilis upon the foetus. It was at this time that I took a personal vow of abstinence.

On the Black Ship, the Killer travels across Japan. Day after day, the Killer tries to find a new job. Day after day, the Killer tries to start a new life. But night after night, the Killer goes hungry and cold while night after night, the men the Killer once followed, the men the Killer once served, retire well fed and warm. So night after night, the Killer writes letter after letter; anonymous letters to the Americans, anonymous letters to the Russians; letters listing names, letters detailing crimes. But day after day the letters go unanswered, night after night the guilty go unpunished. And night after night, the Killer's own memories and nightmares return. Night after night, with the smell of bitter almonds.

In the fifth year of the reign of the Emperor Taishō / At Kyoto Imperial University, in the Medical Department / He sits beside his fellow students, his fellow students here to heal / But he is not here to heal, he is not here to cure / With his knowledge of Western medicines, with his knowledge of Oriental traditions / He is only here to study, he is only here to learn / To study disease, to learn of death

In the Death Factory, the Kwantung Army and, in particular, the Kempeitai had always been concerned about the vulnerability of our water supply to poisoning by Chinese saboteurs. However, from early 1942, this concern seemed to become an obsession and began to consume the majority of our time in Hygiene. It was, though, preferable to the interminable VD inspections.

Each day we would be assigned a different village and sent to check each well in the designated area. We were also required to test the local population for outbreaks or symptoms of anthrax, cholera, typhus and the plague in each location. Often we would be away from the Death Factory for weeks on end.

In the beginning the work was monotonous and generally without incident, though there was always the risk of ambush or attack from Chinese bandits. However, the nearer we worked to the front line or the border with the Soviet Union, the more dangerous our work became. The nature of the work itself also began to change.

On the Black Ship, the Killer finds a job. On 15 September 1947,

Typhoon Kathleen strikes the Bōsō Peninsula and the Kantō area. The resulting floods leave over one thousand people dead and hundreds missing and homeless. The affected Ward Offices urgently call for trained staff to assist in the rescue operations and the prevention of disease. The Killer answers their call.

The Killer works tirelessly, day and night, to help prevent the spread of dysentery among the survivors. Finally, here among the dirty flood waters of Saitama and Tochigi, the Killer's memories begin to recede, his addictions begin to retreat.

But then the flood waters also begin to recede, the threat of disease retreats, and the Killer is summoned to the office of the Director for Epidemic Prevention.

The Killer recognizes the Director. The Director recognizes the Killer. The Director is a sympathetic man, but he is also a practical man. The Director knows that SCAP will not allow him to employ the Killer in a full-time capacity. The Director knows that SCAP require him to forward the Killer's name and address to GHQ. But the Director is a sympathetic man and he will ignore that order. Instead, the Director thanks the Killer for all his hard work and he gives the Killer a name, an address and a letter of introduction. The Director wishes the Killer good luck and then bids him goodbye.

His professors recognize his dedication to his studies, the superhuman levels of his energy / There is only science, there is only medicine / His professors recognize the brilliance of his mind, the incredible breadth of his knowledge / Only the laboratory, the next experiment / His professors recognize the importance of his research, the frightening potential of his work / There are no ethics, there are no oaths

In the Death Factory, at the end of 1943, I was summoned to a conference. Many unfamiliar and high-ranking men were present. I was told that the hygiene group of which I was in command had been chosen to participate in a series of experiments and trials involving a new, combined vaccine which had been developed within the Unit to inoculate against typhus, dysentery and tetanus.

A senior doctor explained, 'The procedure for the administration of the vaccine involves the subject ingesting two solutions; first a small dose of the vaccine itself then, after a short interval, the subject should also be given a small amount of water to drink.' It was believed that water helped the vaccine to disseminate more quickly, with greater effect.

We were now ordered to test the new vaccine in any areas where infections were reported. My examination and treatment team would go out into the villages whenever such reports were received. We would treat all the sick in a village and we would also administer the new drug to the rest of the villagers in order to inoculate them against infection. We would then return to the village within ten or fifteen days to check on the spread of the disease, the rate of infection.

The results of our work in these Chinese villages, however, proved largely inconclusive and, therefore, the trials were abandoned.

On the Black Ship, the Killer has a new job. In a hospital, an animal hospital, on a highway, in Chiba Prefecture. Day after day, the Killer goes to work among the cages and the dogs. Day after day, the Killer puts on his dirty white coat and his dirty white mask, his dirty rubber gloves and his dirty rubber boots. Night after night, the Killer returns to his room and his needle. And night after night, the Killer's memories and his nightmares also return. Night after night, the familiar smell of bitter almonds. And night after night, day after day, the Killer knows he is dying, little by little, piece by piece.

Science divides, medicine separates / He collects and he catalogues / The strong from the weak, the healthy from the sick / Those of substance and those without, those who matter and those that don't / He examines and he experiments / There are no patients, there are only candidates

In the Death Factory, in the winter of 1944, I was collected from the examination and treatment centre by a member of the Kempeitai. I was driven to the airfield. I was flown to another airfield. I was driven to an unmarked barracks in an unnamed city. I was taken down a long corridor into a small interrogation room. I was introduced to two other men. These men were not Kempei, these men were Tokumu Kikan. In the room, on the table, was a doctor's bag.

'There has been an outbreak of dysentery in a Chinese neighbourhood in the city,' said one of the men. 'We have located the source of the outbreak and contained it. However, some businesses and their employees in the vicinity still require disinfection and inoculation. You are experienced in the latest inoculation procedures. You will accompany us to the business premises in the area. You will inoculate the employees. And then you will leave. A disinfection team will follow you. Are these orders clear?'

I nodded. I said, 'Yes.'

The other man now opened the black doctor's bag. He took out two bottles, one measuring 200cc and marked ICHI, the other measuring 500cc and marked NI. 'These are the antidotes you will administer using the same procedure you have been using to administer the typhus vaccines. This first drug, however, is of a more refined and thus more potent formula. Be sure to administer only the required dose and be sure to have the subjects swallow the dose straight down, without it touching their gums or teeth. Also be sure to wait exactly the one minute required for digestion of the first drug before administering the second drug. Is that clear?'

I said, 'Yes.'

Finally, the first man said, 'After you have administered the second drug and the inoculation process is complete, please leave the premises as quickly as possible so that the disinfection team can enter and perform their duties.'

I nodded as the second man put the two bottles back in the doctor's bag. He then handed me an armband along with the bag and said, 'Put that on.'

Outside the interrogation room, in the long corridor, I was introduced to my Chinese interpreter. 'This man works for us and has been fully briefed,' said one of the Tokumu men. 'He will explain to the employees what is happening and what they must do. You simply administer the inoculations and then you leave.'

On the Black Ship, in the Occupied City, it is winter again. The Killer knocks on the side door. A young woman opens the door. The Killer presents his name-card. The young woman stares at the card. The Killer asks to see the manager. The young woman asks the Killer to come round to the front door. The Killer goes back outside. The young woman disappears into the back of the bank. The Killer opens the front door. The young woman has a pair of slippers waiting for him. The Killer takes off his boots in the *genkan*. The young woman tells him that the manager has already left, but that the assistant manager will see him. The Killer nods and thanks the young woman. The young woman leads the Killer through the bank. The Killer passes the rows of clerks at their desks. The young woman introduces the Killer to the assistant manager. The Killer bows. The assistant manager offers the Killer a seat. The Killer sits down, his face to the right. The assistant manager stares at the name-card. The Killer tells the assistant manager there has been an outbreak of dysentery in the neighbourhood. The assistant manager now presents his own name-card. The Killer tells Mr Yoshida that the source of the outbreak is the public well in front of the Aida residence in Nagasaki 2-chōme. Mr Yoshida nods and mentions that the bank's manager, Mr Ushiyama, has in fact left early due to severe stomach ache. The Killer tells Mr Yoshida that one of Mr Aida's tenants has been diagnosed with dysentery and that this man made a deposit in this branch today. Mr Yoshida is amazed that the Ministry of Health and Welfare has heard of the case so quickly. The Killer tells Mr Yoshida that the doctor who saw Mr Aida's tenant reported the case promptly. Mr Yoshida nods. The Killer says he has been sent by Lieutenant Parker, who is in charge of the disinfecting team for this area. Mr Yoshida nods again. The Killer has been told to inoculate everyone against dysentery and to disinfect all items that may have become contaminated. Mr Yoshida nods for a third time. All members, all rooms, all cash and all money in this branch, says the Killer. Mr Yoshida stares at the name-card again. The Killer says that no one will be allowed to leave until his work has been completed. Mr Yoshida glances at his watch. Lieutenant Parker and his team will arrive soon to check the job has been done properly, says the Killer. Mr Yoshida nods. The Killer now places his small olive-green bag on Mr Yoshida's desk. Mr Yoshida watches the Killer open the bag. The Killer takes out a small metal box and two different-sized bottles marked in English. Mr Yoshida reads the words FIRST DRUG on the smaller 200cc bottle and SECOND DRUG on the 500cc bottle. The Killer tells Mr Yoshida that this is an extremely potent oral antidote which the Americans have recently developed through experiments with palm tree oil. Mr Yoshida nods. It is so powerful that you will be completely immunized from dysentery, says the Killer. Mr Yoshida nods again. The Killer warns Mr Yoshida that the administration procedure is complicated and unusual. Again, Mr Yoshida glances at the name-card on his desk.

The Killer asks Mr Yoshida to gather his staff. Even the caretaker, his wife and two children? asks Mr Yoshida. The Killer nods. Mr Yoshida rises from his desk. The Killer turns to the young woman and asks her to bring enough teacups for all the members of the branch. The young woman fetches sixteen teacups on a tray. The Killer opens the smaller bottle marked FIRST DRUG. Each member of the branch, including the caretaker, his wife and two children, gathers around Mr Yoshida's table. The Killer asks if everybody is here. The assistant manager counts heads and nods. The Killer holds a pipette in his hand. Each member watches as the Killer drips some clear liquid into each of their cups. The Killer asks each member to pick up their teacup. Each member reaches for their own cup. Now the Killer raises his hand in warning. Each member listens as the Killer tells them of the strength of the serum, the damage it can cause to their gums and tooth enamel if they do not watch his demonstration carefully and follow his instructions precisely. The Killer now takes out a syringe. Each member watches as the Killer dips his syringe into the liquid. The Killer draws up a measure of the liquid into the syringe. Each member sees the Killer open his mouth. The Killer places his tongue over his bottom front teeth and tucks it under his lower lip. Each member watches as the Killer drips the liquid onto his tongue. The Killer now tilts back his head. The youngest of the caretaker's children mimes the Killer's actions. The Killer stares at his wristwatch, his right hand in the air. Each member sees the Killer's hand fall. As the medicine may damage your gums and teeth, you must swallow quickly, says the Killer. Each member nods. Exactly one minute after you have taken the first medicine, says the Killer, I will administer the second medicine. Each member stares at the 500cc bottle marked SECOND DRUG. After you have taken the second medicine, you will be able to drink water or rinse out your mouth. Each member nods again. Now the Killer tells each member to lift up their cup. Each member picks up their teacup. The Killer tells them to drip the liquid onto their tongues. Each member drinks. The Killer tells each member to tilt back their head. Each member tastes the bitter liquid. The Killer stares at his wristwatch. Each member swallows. The Killer tells each member he will administer the second drug in exactly sixty seconds. One member says he does not think he has swallowed any and asks for more. The Killer shakes his head, staring at his wristwatch. One member asks if she can gargle with some water. The Killer shakes his head again, still staring at his wristwatch. Each member waits for the second drug. Now the Killer pours the second drug into each of their teacups. Each member reaches for their cup again. The Killer checks his wristwatch again. Each member waits for the signal. Now the Killer gestures for each member to drink again. Each member drinks. The Killer waits. Each member feels the second liquid in their mouth, then in their throats, now in their stomachs. The Killer tells each member to rinse out their mouth. Each member rushes for the bathroom, the tap, water.

Everyone is dying, everything is dying / The moment of birth is the beginning of decay / Decay then disease, disease then death / Birth manufactures disease, birth manufactures death / The body manufactures disease, the body manufactures death / There is only disease, there is only death

In the Death Factory, I stepped out of the building, back into the street. An ordinary street in Occupied China, with restaurants and shops, women chattering and children playing. I walked down the street, back the way I had come. Then I saw the two men from the Tokumu Kikan walking towards me, but they did not stop, they did not acknowledge me. They pulled down their hats and they pushed straight past me, walking briskly on, up the street towards the bank. I did not look back again. I glanced at my watch and I set off walking down the street again. Then, suddenly, at the first crossroads, a car pulled up. A man jumped out of the front passenger seat and held open the back door. 'Let's go,' he whispered. 'Your work is done here. It's all over now.' And I got into the back seat of their car, always, already a killer.

On the Black Ship, back in Chiba Prefecture, out on the highway, visitors come to the Dog Hospital now. Visitors on foot, then visitors in jeeps. Visitors with brown eyes, then visitors with blue eyes. But the Killer is not at his work, the Killer is not in his room. The Killer has gone.

In the ninth year of the reign of the Emperor Taishō / The student becomes a doctor, the doctor becomes a soldier / In the fractured, splintered mirror, the uniform changes but the work continues /

Collecting and cataloguing, examining and experimenting / In the seventh year of the reign of the Emperor Shōwa / In the fractured, splintered mirror, the Army Surgeon is posted to Pingfan, near Harbin, in Manchuria

In the Death Factory, in June 1945, there were celebrations to mark the anniversary of the founding of Unit 731, but many of us already sensed the end was drawing near. There were many debates among us as to whether or not the Soviets would break the non-aggression pact and attack. Many of us felt that they would and we would be forced to evacuate the complex. Of course, such conversations could only be held in private as they were deemed defeatist and the punishments for such attitudes were harsh. However, we all knew that branch units that had recently been sent to the border had not returned.

Finally, the end came. At morning muster on 9 August 1945, all the members of Unit 731 were told that the Soviet Union had begun their invasion and we were ordered to destroy any personal documentation or evidence on our persons which would identify us as being members of Unit 731. All the men and their families were then issued with potassium cyanide. I was told that one of my responsibilities in the Examination and Treatment Unit would be to 'assist in the deaths of those who were unable to commit suicide themselves'. To this end, our division was given extra quantities of potassium cyanide and also two large bottles of acetone cyanohydrin. It smelt of bitter almonds. I had smelt it before. And I would smell it again. In the end, however, an evacuation order was given. I was then reassigned and detailed to participate in the destruction of the Death Factory. Meanwhile, the upper-ranking officers sent their families, along with all important or sensitive documents, to the airfield to await flights to Tokyo.

Early the next day I was sent into the cells in the prison blocks. All the prisoners, all the logs, were already dead. It appeared to me that they had been gassed. My team carried the bodies to the incinerators. Soon, however, there were too many bodies for the number of incinerators and so we were forced to pile them up outside and to burn them there. It was difficult to keep the corpses burning and it required a lot of fuel oil, which was by now in short supply.

Next, all the rats and fleas had to be destroyed. There were over three hundred thousand rats and countless millions of fleas. All of these were burnt. Also, all the specimens which had been preserved in formalin in the laboratories were either destroyed or dumped into the Songhua River.

Finally, early in the evening on 14 August, the buildings themselves were detonated. In total, it took over three days to destroy the entire complex.

The destruction complete, we were then ordered to evacuate. We all gathered at the railway siding to await nightfall. Suddenly, out of the twilight, Ishii himself appeared carrying a large candle. He said, 'I am sending you all back home. When you get there, if any one of you gives away the secret of Unit 731, I will find you. Even if I have to part the roots of the grasses to do it, I will find you . . .'

We then boarded a long train of about twenty cars. We travelled day and night but, fortunately, there were food supplies and drinking water aboard. On the way we heard many stories of the speed and brutality of the Soviet advance and also of uprisings in Korea. But I was lucky, and within ten days my ship docked in Japan.

On the Black Ship, the Killer lies outstretched on a bed, in a ward, in a sanatorium. A nurse picks up the Killer's wrist and holds it between her fingers to search for a pulse. A doctor then comes and pulls up the Killer's eyelids to shine a light into the Killer's eyes. No dilation, no movement. The doctor lowers the Killer's eyelids. Now the doctor leans across the Killer's heart to listen for a beat. But all he can hear is the sound of the sea.

Beneath the Black Gate, in its upper chamber, in the candle-light of the last two flames, in their plague-light – white, grey, blue, green, yellow, and then red – you are turning, this way,

that way, left and then right,

spinning, that way,

this way, right

and then

left –

Shouting into the shadows, screaming into the silence, 'Is it you? Is it you? Is it really you? Then show yourself!

'Show yourself! And name yourself!'

This way, that way, left and then right, but nothing moves within the candle-light, no one steps into the plague-light,

but still you can sense he is near, for

here, somewhere, somewhere

in the shadows, you know

you are not alone –

And now, at last, there is movement in the candle-light, there is laughter in the plague-light, the shadows

retreating, reflections forming,

reflections in mirrors,

everywhere

mirrors. That laughter now a voice,

that voice reading words –

'You speak, you lie.

'You speak,

'you lie . . .'

'Stop!' you are shouting, 'Stop! Stop! Stop!'

That voice now laughter, that laughter then a voice again, 'Who wrote those fine words, I wonder? Who?

'Who? It was you! You!

'You! You who would accuse me! You who would judge me! Convict and then execute me! Well, writer, your name is vanity!'

And now every shadow is a mirror, every word is an echo, whispering, 'Look! Look at yourself! Listen! Listen to yourself!

'Your every word is a failure, your every word is a lie!

'Failures and lies which murder all meaning!

'That is you and only you, until you die; you are you and only you, until that day; incapable and unwilling, you cannot change –

'Enticed and entranced, deceived and defeated, in-snared and in-prisoned. You remain you, and only you, until you die –

   'Until that day, when you die –

   'Your dog's death . . .'

   Turning that way and this, spinning right and then left,

   there are still only mirrors, mirrors and now smoke,

   smoke and now blossoms, cherry blossoms,

   for you are under a canopy, a ceiling

   of blossoms, each single blossom

   a skull, a human skull, stripped

   of its skin, naked

   to the bone,

   alone, alone in the light of one last candle –

IN THE OCCUPIED CITY, in the upper chamber of the Black Gate, in this place where once there was an occult circle, where once there stood twelve candles, where now there stands only one,

   and where now, before you now, there also stands a single willow branch atop a grass mound, the sound of a drum beating,

   a drum beating and a river flowing,

   flowing through this city,

   this Occupied City,

   the Sumida-

   gawa,

   as feet-step and tears-drop along the banks of the Sumida, the drum beating and the river flowing, feet and tears shuffling,

   a woman's voice crying, 'I am a mother and I am searching for my son. My son who was taken from me in this city . . .'

   And now this woman reaches for you, she takes your hand, and now she says, 'Come, Ferryman . . .

   'Come . . .'

   For this time there is no place for you to simply sit and stare, from where to watch and which to write; this time there is no medium, this time there is no distance; for this time her feet and her tears will carry you, carry you into the words, carry you into the voices –

   'For you are the Ferryman, a writer no more –

   'You are my Ferryman . . .

The Twelfth and Final Candle –

The Lamentations

'This city is a river,' I hear you say. 'Made of blood and made of sweat, made of shit and made of piss, it is the Sumida River.

'And with its blood and with its sweat, with its shit and with its piss, the river is this city, the Occupied City.

'And here in the Occupied City, here on the banks of the Sumida River, here at this crossing, I am its Ferryman. I ferry the people across the river, eastward, and then back again, westward, in and out of this city. And as we cross this river, I tell the people stories to pass the time, I tell them tales, as we go back and forth, in and out of this city. So now in the twilight, here on the riverbank, I stand in the sleet and the wind, among the ruins and the ashes, and I shout, It is sundown! All aboard!'

And now the people whisper, 'We stand in line, bundles on our backs, bundles in our arms, lice in our clothes, lice in our hair, edging forward, step by step, step by step, but turning back, glance by glance, glance by glance, to whisper, lip to ear, lip to ear, about the woman at the rear of our line, the woman with no bundle on her back, no bundle in her arms, the woman who parts the crowd, who stands before us now, a single *sasa* branch in her hand, a mad woman –'

And that woman is me. For it is too true; a poor mother's heart, though not in darkness, may yet wander lost, lost for the love of her child. This I know well as I have roamed astray through this city, along its streets, its riverbanks, among its people, as I seek the place, the place where my son has gone. But how can they know? How can they know . . . ?

And the people whisper, 'See now as the mad woman standing before us, the single *sasa* branch in her hand, begins to dance, an anguished dance, to the sound of a drum, a rotten drum, her feet in the mud and her chant on the wind –'

'Frail is the dew upon the moor,' I sing, 'and I as frail, am I to live on, ever bitter at my lot? I who lived for many years in Saitama, to the North of here, with my only son. Until one day, alas, one January day, disaster fell upon me. For my only son, he left our home for work, work in this city. But he never returned. He vanished from me. And I yearned for him and at last I learned he had been taken from me in the Occupied City. My only son, alas, lost in this city. And this news so distressing, it confused my wits. The one thought left me was go, go find my boy. But now in my quest, I too am lost, so wholly lost . . .'

And now the people whisper, 'A thousand leagues are never far to a fond mother's heart, so they say, when she cannot forget her child. And they say, that bond in life is always so fragile, yet now he is gone, is always so fragile, yet now he is gone –'

'Oh, if only he had stayed for a little while longer, stayed at home with me, a son with his mother. But now we are sundered, a mother from her son . . .'

And the people whisper, 'Just so, long ago, all mothers grieved to see their nestlings fly away –'

'And now this anxious heart can go no further. To the Occupied City, I have come at last. Here where the road ends and the river begins. So to the Sumida River, I have come at last . . .'

And now the people whisper, 'See the woman has ended her dance. Hear the woman has stopped her chant. See the woman now drops to her knees, her face in the cold earth, her hands with the *sasa* branch, outstretched and raised, before the Ferryman –'

'Please, Ferryman,' I ask you, 'let me board your boat. Please Ferryman, I beg of you . . .'

'Where have you come from?' you ask. 'And to where are you going?'

'I have come here from Saitama,' I say, 'and I am searching for someone, wherever that search may lead me . . .'

'You are a woman,' you say. 'But you are mad. And so I cannot let you come aboard.'

'You are a man,' I reply, 'and so too a liar. For if you were truly the Ferryman, the Ferryman on the Sumida River, then you would say, Please board my boat. Instead you mock me and say, You are mad and cannot board. And so I know you are no Ferryman . . .'

'You are but a liar. Not a Ferryman.'

'You are mistaken, woman!' you shout. 'I am the Ferryman!'

'Then, Ferryman,' I say, 'you should know that here at this very crossing, Narihira once sang, *If you are true, then Miyako birds I ask you this; does she live, the one I love, or does she die?*

'Come Ferryman, those birds over there, in the sky up above, those birds are none like I have seen before. So what do you call them, those birds up above? Speak, wise Ferryman, what do you say?'

'They are scavengers,' you say. 'They are crows.'

'Perhaps among the corpses,' I laugh, 'they are carrion. But why don't you answer that here, here on the banks of the Sumida, here those crows are Narihira's own birds . . . ?'

'You are grieving and you are stricken,' I hear you say now. 'I am sorry, I was mistaken.'

'Ferryman,' I ask, 'have you never felt stretched or torn apart? So do not these evening waves now wash us back, wash us both back to times long past, when Narihira asked of those birds up above, *My love, does she live or does she die?*

'So eastward my love goes to the child I seek and, just as Narihira sought his own dear lady, so now I seek my own dear son, asking the same question of those birds up above . . .'

'I know this story well,' you say. 'The story of Prince Narihira. And so I can see, the two stories are one; your own story and his, these two loves now one.'

'So does my child live, or does he die?' I ask. 'For again and again, I question the birds, but no answer comes. No answer ever comes. Oh, Miyako birds, your silence is rude!

'Miyako birds, your silence is cruel!

'So now I stand on this bank and I wait, lost in the depths of the East, I wait for an answer . . .

'So please, Ferryman, your boat may be small, your boat may be full. But, kind Ferryman, make room for a mother and take me aboard, please, Ferryman, please . . .'

'Come aboard, but hurry,' you say. 'This crossing is difficult.'

And now the people whisper, 'See how the woman steps into the boat. See how she stands at the bow of the boat. How she stares out across the waters of the Sumida. How she suddenly points –'

'On the far bank,' I say, 'I see a crowd gathered around a willow. What are they doing?'

'They are holding a Great Invocation,' you say.

'But why?' I ask. 'Why there? Why now?'

'The reason is a sad story,' you say.

'Then please tell me,' I say, 'for you are the Ferryman. To pass the time, please tell me the tale . . .'

'It happened exactly one year ago,' you begin. 'On the twenty-sixth day of the very first month, when the *Ashura* passed by that place, leading a night parade of the recently murdered.

'One among this procession was a youth, more exhausted and feeble than all the rest. Unable to walk a single step more, the youth collapsed on the far bank. But the *Ashura* did not hear him. The *Ashura* walked on and abandoned him there. They left him struggling, they left him weeping.

'But the local people took pity on him. They cared for him as best they could. But no doubt his karma opposed their help, because the youth grew only weaker and weaker, until he was clearly dying a second time. And so the people asked him who he was.

'I am Sawada Yoshio, he said, and I am twenty-two years old. But here I am no longer Sawada Yoshio. Now I am no longer twenty-two years old. Now I am always struggling, here I am only weeping. But it was not always so, not always so. After my father died in the war, he wept, I lived alone with my widowed mother. Then today at my place of work, I was murdered and so taken away. Now I am always struggling, here I am only weeping. That is how I have come to this place. But I worry so much for my mother. And that is the reason I can go no further, that is the reason I cannot follow the others. Now I am always struggling, here I am only weeping. So please build a mound over me, he begged, here on the bank by this river, in the hope that one day my mother might pass, that one day my mother might be near me again.

'These words said, he called out the Holy Name six times, and then it was over. And now we have arrived on the other shore. Now it is time to disembark.'

But the people whisper, 'See how the woman stays standing at the bow of the boat. See the single *sasa* branch in her hand. The single tear upon her cheek –'

'We are here,' you say. 'Please go ashore.'

'Tell me, please, Ferryman,' I ask. 'Please, Ferryman, when did this happen?'

'It happened exactly one year ago,' you say. 'One year ago today, on the twenty-sixth day of the first month.'

'And the youth? How old was he then?'

'Twenty-two years old, I believe.'

'His family name was . . . ?'

'As I told you, his family name was Sawada.'

'And his given name . . . ?'

'His given name was Yoshio, as I told you.'

'And after he died,' I say, 'by this river, a second time, on this bank, no parent ever came looking for him . . . ?'

'No one ever came, I believe.'

'No one ever came?' I ask. 'Not even his mother?'

'Not even his mother.'

'No, of course not!' I shout. 'For he was my boy! The boy this mad woman has been seeking! Oh, can I be dreaming? What plague, what plague is this?'

'I am sorry, so very sorry,' I hear you say. 'I had thought the story I just told, this tale told merely to pass the time, was about someone I myself would never know. But all the time he was your son! What a thing, a terrible thing! But your tears and my regrets are useless now. So in their place, let me take you to his tomb.'

'My eyes shall behold him, or so I believed until this very moment. I travelled far through this Occupied City, down its streets, along its riverbanks, among its people, only to find him gone from this world. The cruelty of it! The horror of it!

'For his own death, he left his home and in this city became but earth, earth by the side of this river. Here he lies buried, lies buried with only the grass to cover him . . .'

But the people whisper, 'Come let us turn this cold earth over one last time, to show a mother her son as he looked in life. Had he lived on, he would have known gladness, but hope was vain. He would have known gladness, but hope was vain –'

'Yes vain; vain as living is to me now, his mother; his mother, whom for a while a lovely figure, he glimmered like all the things in this world and then, like all the things in this world, was gone, like all the things in this world, he glimmered . . .

'And then was gone . . .'

And now the people whisper, 'Such sorrows lurk in the blossoms' glory, just as the moon, through its nights of birth and death, is lost from view, behind clouds of impermanence, just so this sad world's truth is here, so plain to see. This sad world's truth, so plain to see –'

'No lament of yours can help him now,' you say. 'Just call the Name and pray for his happy rebirth in Paradise.'

And the people whisper, 'See how the moon is rising now, and the river breeze sighs as the night wears on, now invocations will surely be heard. So in this spirit all present, urged on by faith, now strike their bells in rhythm –'

'But I his mother, overcome by sorrow, unable even to call the Name, lie here prostrate, dissolved in weeping . . .'

'You must chant the Invocation, too,' I hear you urge. 'For it is his mother's prayers that will bring the deceased the greatest joy. You must take the chanting-bell, too.'

'For my own dear son's sake,' I say, 'I will take up the bell!'

'Cease lamenting,' you say. 'And call with ringing voice.'

'In this bright moonlit night,' I say, 'I will invoke the Name.'

'Then let us both chant together,' you say.

And so together we say, 'Hail, in Thy Western Realm of Bliss! Thirty-six million, million worlds ring with one cry, one Name: Amida!'

And now the people also chant, 'Hail Amida Buddha! Hail Amida Buddha! Hail Amida Buddha! Hail Amida Buddha! Hail Amida Buddha! Hail Amida Buddha!'

In the Occupied City, on the banks of the Sumida, the wind and the waves swell our chorus . . .

'Hail Amida Buddha! Hail Amida Buddha! Hail Amida Buddha! Hail Amida Buddha! Hail Amida Buddha! Hail Amida Buddha!'

'Oh, if you are true to your name,' I call out, 'then Miyako birds, if you are true to your name, add your voices . . .'

'Hail Amida Buddha!' they cry. 'Hail Amida Buddha! Hail Amida Buddha! Hail Amida Buddha! Hail Amida Buddha! Hail Amida Buddha!'

'Stop!' I shout. 'Stop now! Listen! Listen now! That voice, just now calling out the Name; it was my own child's voice! It seemed to come from within the mound, from within his tomb . . .'

'I heard it too,' you say. 'Let everyone stop calling. Let everyone be silent. Let the mother alone now chant the Name!'

'Oh, please,' I beg, 'let me hear that voice again, just one other time! Hail Amida Buddha . . .'

And now the people whisper, 'See here now, atop the mound, a figure stands, stands before her –'

'My dear child, is it you?'

'Dear Mother, is it you?'

And the people whisper, 'See now how the woman goes towards the figure, how the woman reaches out towards the figure, how the woman touches its shoulder, and how the figure slips away, slips back into the mound –'

'My child!'

And the people whisper, 'See again how the figure appears upon the mound, and see again how she reaches towards the figure, taking hold of its hand –'

'Mother!'

And the people whisper, 'But again the figure's shape fades and is gone, her fond longing waxing as in a mirror, as again the figure slips, slips back into the mound –'

'My child!'

And the people whisper, 'Remembered form and present illusion fuse, now seen, now hidden once more, as light streaks the sky and dawn breaks the day, his shape, his shape vanished for evermore, as waking breaks into dream –'

'My child!'

And the people whisper, 'What once seemed a lost child now found is but wild grasses on a lonely tomb, their dull blades nodding in sign over the wastes of this river, the wastes of this city, in sorrow, nothing else remains. Only sorrow, nothing else remains –'

'In this city, the Occupied City,' I hear you say. 'Beside this river, the Sumida River, in this dawn, before this mound, I hear feet-step and tears-drop, so many feet, so many tears –

'Shuffling, still shuffling.'

And now the people whisper, 'This burial mound, though covered in wild grasses, is not made of earth. This burial mound is made of masks, a pile of clay masks. See now how the woman picks up the masks. See now how she tries on mask after mask –'

'I am a mother,' I say, 'and I am a sister. And I am a lover. And I am a wife. And I am a daughter . . .

'I am a sister and I am searching for my brother. My brother who was taken from me in this city . . .

'I am a lover and I am searching for my man. My man who was taken from me in this city . . .

'I am a wife and I am searching for my husband. My husband who was taken from me in this city . . .

'I am a daughter and I am searching for my father. My father who was taken from me in this city . . .

'Through earthquake and through war, we have walked these streets, the banks of this river, and we have survived. Survived . . .

'Now you say – he says, they say, all men say – the city has changed, the world has changed. But my city, my world has not changed. The shade of your skin, maybe, the style of your uniform, perhaps. But your collars are still dirty, your fingers still stained.

'Post-war, après-guerre you say – he says, they say, all men say – but it's always been post-war, already après-guerre.

'Conquered from birth, colonized for life, I have always, already been defeated. Always, already been occupied –

'Occupied by you –

'Born of me, the death of me. Blood of you, the death of me. Come in me, the death of me. Rob my name, the death of me. Born of you, the death of me –

'In the snow. In the mud. Beneath the branches. Before the shrine. In the *genkan*. In the bank. On a street in China. In a wardrobe in Tokyo. With your poison. With your pen.

'It is you. And only you.'

The Black Gate is gone, its upper chamber is gone, the occult circle and all of its candles now, now you are in darkness –

The candles out and the medium gone,

the story-telling game is over.

Come and they came, stand and they stood, sit and they sat, strip and they stripped, take this medicine and they did,

though it's poison, still they did,

die and they died, for you,

and only you, in agony,

in fear, in silence –

In white paper, their bodies prone, their faces contorted. In black ink, their heads shaved, their mouths stitched, they are yours,

and only yours, in their costumes and in their masks, all your actors and all your characters, for you are the writer,

you are their wound, you are their plague,

wrapped in paper, wrapped in ink, they are raised, frozen and petrified by the sorrow you brought them,

the suffering you left them –

IN THE OCCUPIED CITY, this city is a coffin. This city is a notebook. This city is a purgatory. This city is a plague. This city is a curse. This city is a story. This city is a market. This city is a wilderness. This city is a wound. This city is a prison. This city is a mirror. This city is a river. And this city is a woman –

'In sorrow,' she whispers. 'Nothing else remains. Only sorrow. Nothing else remains. Only sorrow . . .'

In tears and in truth, pouring down upon you now, this heavy rain, this water-fall, flooding down upon you now,

drowning you in water and in salt,

in her tears and in her truth,

her tears, her truth –

'Remains . . .'

And she has tied you to a chair, tied you to a desk, a pen nailed to your palms, bound to your fingers,

life leaking, death dripping,

but not in ink, in tears,

in tears and in truth,

at last, at last,

no more costumes and no more masks, no more actors and no more characters, no more stories and no more lies,

the book always, already written,
written and abandoned,
in-caesura.

Author's Note

Hirasawa Sadamichi was convicted of the Teikoku Bank murders,
attempted murders and robbery on 24 July 1950,
and sentenced to death.
Despite the dedication and efforts of the Society to Save Hirasawa,
Hirasawa died in Hachiōji Prison on 10 May 1987.
Hirasawa was ninety-five years old.
The appeals and the campaign to clear Hirasawa's name,
posthumously, continue to this day.
At the time of writing, the nineteenth request for a retrial,
which was filed on 10 May 1989,
is still being examined by the Tokyo High Court.

David Peace, Tokyo, 2008
The Year of the Rat

Sources

The structure of this book was suggested by *Rashōmon* and *In a Grove*, two short stories by Akutagawa Ryūnosuke (1892–1927), both of which have been translated into English many times, most recently by Jay Rubin in *Rashōmon and Seventeen Other Stories* (Penguin Classics, 2006). Kurosawa Akira's 1950 film *Rashōmon* was also influential, as was the Rutgers University Press book *Rashōmon* (1987), edited by Donald Richie.

The murders at the Teikoku Bank in Tokyo in January 1948 have been written about in English in *Flowering of the Bamboo* by William Triplett (Woodbine House, 1985) and in *Shocking Crimes of Postwar Japan* by Mark Schreiber (Yenbooks, 1996). In fiction, the case was also the subject of *Averse d'automne* by Romain Slocombe (Gallimard, 2003).

The following were also used:

731 by Aoki Fukiko (Shinchosha, 2005)
731-Butai Saikin-sen Shiryō Shusei CD-ROM edited by Kondō Shōji
   (Kashiwa Shobō, 2003)
Akuma no Hōshoku by Morimura Seiichi (Kadokawa Shoten, 1983)
Asahi Shimbun newspaper for 1947–8
Civilization & Monsters by Gerald Figal (Duke University Press,
   1999)
Curlew River by Benjamin Britten, to a libretto by William Plomer;
   particularly Olivier Py's production at the Royal Lyceum
   Theatre, Edinburgh, in August 2005
The Diary of a Madman by Nikolai Gogol (1835)
Discourses of the Vanishing by Marilyn Ivy (University of Chicago
   Press, 1995)
Factories of Death by Sheldon H. Harris (Routledge, 1994)

Japanese Ghosts and Demons: Art of the Supernatural edited by Stephen Addiss (George Braziller, 1985)

Keiji Ichidai: Hiratsuka Hachibei no Shōwa Jiken-shi by Sasaki Yoshinobu (Sankei Shimbunsha; Nisshin-Hōdō Shuppanbu, 1980)

Materials on the Trial of Former Servicemen of the Japanese Army (Foreign Languages Publishing House (Moscow), 1950)

Nippon no Kuroi Kiri by Matsumoto Seicho (Bungei Shunju Shinsha, 1960)

Nippon no Seishin Kantei edited by Fukushima Akira, Nakata Osamu, Ogi Sadataka, Uchimura Yushi and Yoshimasu Shufu (Misuzu Shobo, 1973)

Nippon Times and *Mainichi* newspapers for 1948

A Plague Upon Humanity by Daniel Barenblatt (HarperCollins, 2005)

Shōsetsu Teigin Jiken by Matsumoto Seicho (Bungei Shunju Shinsha, 1959)

Sumida-gawa by Motomasa Jūrō (*c.* 1400–32), translated by Royall Tyler in *Japanese Nō Dramas* (Penguin Classics, 1992)

Teigin Jiken by Morikawa Tetsurō (Sanichi Shobō, 1980)

The films and diaries of Andrei Tarkovsky

The plays and texts of Heiner Müller; particularly Elio De Capitani's production of *Waterfront Wasteland Medea Material Landscape with Argonauts* at the Teatro dell'Elfo, Milan, in 2006

The poems and prose of Paul Celan

Unit 731 by Peter Williams and David Wallace (The Free Press, 1989)

Unit 731 Testimony by Hal Gold (Yenbooks, 1996)

A Universal History of Iniquity by Jorge Luis Borges, translated by Andrew Hurley, in *Collected Fictions* (Penguin, 1999)

Ware, Shisu-tomo Meimoku-sezu: Hirasawa Sadamichi Gokuchu-ki edited by Hirasawa Takehiko (Mainichi Shimbunsha, 1988)

Woyzeck by Georg Büchner, translated by John Mackendrick, in *The Complete Plays* edited by Michael Patterson (Methuen, 1987)

Acknowledgements

I would like to thank the following people for all their help:

Nagashima Shunichiro, who once again provided and translated important documents from the Japanese; Mark Schreiber and Romain Slocombe, who both discussed the case with me and generously shared their own research; Stephen Page, Angus Cargill, Anna Pallai, Anne Owen, Sarah Savitt, Tanya Andrews, Trevor Horwood and all the staff of Faber and Faber in London; Sonny Mehta, Diana Coglianese, Sarah Robinson and Zach Wagman in New York. Once again, Sawa Junzo, Hamish Macaskill, Peter Thompson and all the staff of the English Agency Japan. Also in Tokyo, Simon Bartz, Steve Finbow, Mike and Mayu Handford, Kaetsu Kazuko, Cathy Layne, Jeremy Sutton-Hibbert and Steve Taylor. In England, my parents, Andrew Eaton, Tony Grisoni and Jon Riley. I would also like to particularly thank Lee Brackstone for both his patience and his belief in this book. Finally, and most of all, to William Miller, my agent, without whom this book would have been abandoned a lot, lot sooner.